STEALING
MIDNIGHT

Also by Tracy MacNish

VEILED PASSIONS

VEILED DESIRES

VEILED PROMISES

Published by Kensington Publishing Corporation

STEALING MIDNIGHT

TRACY MACNISH

ZEBRA BOOKS
Kensington Publishing Corp.
http://www.kensingtonbooks.com

ZEBRA BOOKS are published by

Kensington Publishing Corp.
119 West 40th Street
New York, NY 10018

All Kensington titles, imprints, and distributed lines are available at special quantity discounts for bulk purchases for sales promotion, premiums, fund-raising, educational, or institutional use.

Special book excerpts or customized printings can also be created to fit specific needs. For details, write or phone the office of the Kensington Special Sales Manager: Attn.: Special Sales Department. Kensington Publishing Corp., 119 West 40th Street, New York, NY 10018. Phone: 1-800-221-2647.

Zebra and the Z logo Reg. U.S. Pat. & TM Off.

ISBN-13: 978-1-4201-0170-6
ISBN-10: 1-4201-0170-6

First Printing: October 2009

10 9 8 7 6 5 4 3 2 1

Printed in the United States of America

For my mother, Trish,

for endless help,

bottomless belief,

boundless enthusiasm,

and unconditional love.

Thanks, Mom.

Acknowledgments

The author's sincerest thanks and best wishes to my editor, Audrey LaFehr, for artistic freedom and enthusiasm, and to my agent, Mary Sue Seymour, who can always be counted on for gracious support.

Most of all, to my best friend, Katrina Campbell, for pulling me out of the deep, dark pit and helping me find my way—without you I don't know what I would have done. Every girl should have a friend like you.

Chapter One

Chester, England, 1806

The night air fell damp and misty around the graveyard, and a filmy, chilled fog crept across mounded graves and silent crypts.

The night watchman took his bribe and left. Twenty minutes, he warned. No longer.

They would need every second, and so moved quickly—dirty fingers feeling around a freshly sealed tomb, seeking a crevice in which to insert a pry bar. The rusty metal bar groaned between the stone walls and iron door as chunks of crumbling lead came raining down from the broken seals. The lock gave way with a metallic crunch.

The men pulled hard, and beneath their efforts the door gave way. It slid open slowly, releasing a waft of stagnant, fetid air redolent of fresh rot and putrid remains.

A rasp of flint, a spark of light. A tiny, flickering flame revealed two male bodies, one a few days dead, bloated, stiff, and gray, the other lain on a slab of stone only that morning, unearthly pale and still.

The snatchers stripped the bodies before they bagged them in burlap sacks, grunting with their efforts, oblivious to the stench. Well into the stages of decomposition, the older corpse would only bring half the price, but at three months their regular salary, was still well worth the risks. The fresh one, however, would pay double, and was the one for who they'd come.

The specimen was grand: a young male aged approximately thirty years, his body well-muscled and devoid of wounds.

A muffled bell tolled twice in warning. The snatchers tossed the bagged bodies over their shoulders and put out their light. Disappearing into the darkness, they hurried down the rolling hills to where their cart sat hidden in a dark grove of pine trees.

With rags bound to their horses' feet to muffle their sound, they drove their macabre bounty across the countryside, leaving the walled city of Chester behind them as they made their way to the River Dee.

Amidst whistles and tugs they urged the horses to pull the wagon onto the small barge, and once aboard, they set about securing the wheels with thick ropes. With a small splash and the lapping of water against a battered hull, they rowed west across the river and crossed the boundary into Wales.

Once on the other side, they drove the wagon on a narrow trail that led through the valley of two craggy mountains. Small dots of yellow lights could be seen in the distance: the village of *Penarlâg*.

They kept going, past dark, misty sheep fields and lichen-coated stone walls. Just on the northern outskirts of the sleeping village rose the crumbling estate owned by Rhys Gawain.

Carrying the bodies around back, the snatchers dumped them at the doorstep. One reached for the dangling cord and rang the bell. They waited a long while before ringing again.

For the bounty the corpses would bring, they would wait all night.

The door finally opened, revealing a sleep-tousled young woman. In the yellow light of the tallow lanterns, her gray eyes were translucent, her black hair an ebony cloud streaked with lightning. The villagers had long ago named her a witch, attributing her odd appearance to a pact made with Satan himself.

Olwyn Gawain raised a brow as she looked down on the heap, a fiercely mocking look that had the men taking a step back. "Two?"

"Aye," one of the snatchers confirmed, kicking at one of the corpses with his booted toe. "The big 'un is fresh. Just put in this marnin'."

"I'll fetch your pay." She left for only a moment, returning with a small leather sack. Handing it over, she said, "Come back in a fortnight if you can find a female."

As the snatchers departed, they heard a noise that sounded like a laughing sob, fading like mist into the foggy, cold night. They looked at each other in the darkness, and without a word, hurried away.

The rotting dead was not nearly so frightening as a living witch.

Olwyn belted her wrapper tighter around her waist, the damp chill of the wee hours making her wish for a peat fire and hot spiced tea. But with the two bodies lying on the back step, she had no time for such luxuries. Rushing through the crumbling stone corridors and up the enclosed spiral stairs to the master's chambers, Olwyn mentally prepared herself for what would come. She rapped soundly on her father's oaken door.

And then, with her breath coming in quick, shallow gasps, she forced herself to calm, waiting with trepidation to discover which incarnation of her father would greet her.

A few moments passed before Rhys opened his door. Olwyn immediately noted he wore a relatively clean night-shirt, buttoned to his chin. His black, hawkish eyes shone clear and sharp beneath his bushy, dark brows. Relief swept through her apprehension.

She didn't apologize for waking him; he would have been furious if she hadn't. "We have a delivery. Two this time."

"Two? Well then, we'll be busy, won't we, girl? Good, good," Rhys said, and he rubbed his hands together against the cold. "Wake Drystan. I'll get into my work clothes and meet you down there."

Olwyn didn't demur, even though her heart fell into the pit of her guts. She did as she was told, fetching Drystan by pounding on his door. As he was usually drunk on the nights he didn't work, it took some doing to rouse him. When he answered, the stink of unwashed skin, greasy bed linens, and sulfurous belches hung in the air around him. At her word, he grunted, scratching at his crotch as he headed down the long corridor. As part of his duties, he would pull the bodies inside, strip them of their burlap sacks, and lay them out.

After he'd gone, Olwyn moved like a wraith through the ancient keep. The stone walls held the chill and dampness, her footsteps a hollow echo reaching into the dark corners untouched by tallow lanterns.

Reaching a small, curving staircase so narrow it only al-lowed for one person's passage, Olwyn ascended to the tiny landing that led to her chambers. She withdrew her key from a cord around her neck, and unlocked and opened the door.

A grouping of three small rooms warmed by a central fireplace comprised Olwyn's sanctuary. There were only three windows, tall, thin, and arched, their stained glass as ancient as memory. Those she left uncovered, leaving the red-gold light to spill in from dawn to dusk.

The room smelled of strong incense: amber and Tamil mint, sage and sandalwood, cardamom and ginger. She burned a tiny bit nightly, her one indulgence, necessary to chase away the nightmares. The scented smoke clung to the drapes and rugs, her hair and her clothes.

Olwyn closed and locked the door behind her, a matter of constant practice since Drystan began watching her with increased interest.

Alone in her chambers, she breathed a sigh of resignation. The task before her loomed with gristly promise. But someday, she promised herself, she would escape. She needed to believe that, or else succumb to insanity.

Over her door, the brass bell jangled. The bell had a long, thin cord that ran down to the lower levels, so that she was able to be summoned. The few servants they'd had before had long ago been dismissed, so it was Olwyn who was called to duty.

With a fleeting, impotent glare at the hated bell, Olwyn quickly dressed. For the task ahead she wore a simple, muslin sheath that was easily laundered, and topped it with two thick, woolen robes that had been washed so often they were soft and fringed with threads. To keep her hair from her eyes, she braided it into a thick twist that hung heavily down her back. She left on her knit stockings and pulled on thick boots made of lamb's wool that laced to her knees. The dungeon floor held a chill that would quickly leech the warmth of the living.

Those who believed hell to be hot had never stepped into her father's frigid nightmare.

Olwyn grabbed her throwing dagger and slid it into her belt, took her pistol, checked its priming, and tucked it in her waistband at the small of her back.

The bell rang again, this time five rapid tolls that smacked of irritation and manic obsession. And Olwyn had nothing further to delay her. The time to return to hell had come again.

"You take too long, girl," Rhys muttered as Olwyn entered. He never looked up from the naked corpse in front of him, but waved his hand at the other. "Get started on that one. This one needs to be opened immediately. He's only got another day or two left in him."

Drystan had dragged the bodies down to what had once been a dungeon, located in the oldest part of the keep. It was now Rhys's workroom, for the permeating coldness helped to keep the corpses fresher.

It still bore the feel and look of its original purpose, however. The stone walls and floor were dark with the perpetual seeping wetness of the underground. Torches and lanterns hung from iron spikes, their smoke a thick wreath against the ceiling, the smell of which did not disguise the stench of rancid blood and rotting flesh.

Iron bars separated a few tiny cells which were now filled with crude shelves that housed her father's collection of organs and brains preserved in brine, the abnormal ones beside the normal, each showing various stages of depredation.

And high above them, an old iron cage was suspended from the ceiling. It had been used in years past for madmen, when the former lord of the land saw fit to restrain them.

It had also been used for Olwyn, one dark night when her escape had been thwarted. After the dogs had attacked her on the property border, her father had dragged her back and put her in the cage. A lesson, he'd said, for a girl who'd dare to abandon the last member of her family.

She tried to avoid looking at it. It held memories of the worst night of her life, wounded, afraid, and alone in the dark dungeon, with the rats.

Scuttling rodents kept to the shadows, fat, bold, and rapacious from feasting on the scattered bits of flesh that regularly fell to the floor.

Olwyn's hand rode lightly on the hilt of her dagger. She could shoot a rat in the head at fifty paces, could hit it with her dagger at half that. The rats seemed to know it, too, skittering to the corners when she entered.

Lord, but she hated them. They plagued her nightmares, their long, naked tails dragging behind their slick, dark bodies as they wallowed in the chest cavities of the corpses.

She peered into the shadows where they waited. She could see their eyes glittering in the torchlight. A shiver took her and she stamped on the floor as she walked, hoping to frighten them further away. The effort remained futile, though. The rats were as brash as they were ugly.

Olwyn moved to the stone slab that held the other corpse, just as her father instructed. Tuning out the meaty sounds of Rhys's work, she got to her own.

The body was male, aged between twenty-five to thirty years of age. He was well formed and well fed, healthily muscled, and looked as though he had been in vigorous, perfect health at the time of his demise. Her eyes swept over his naked body, taking in his details. A scar on his arm, a birthmark on his thigh, a thick thatch of dark bronze hair surrounding his long, flaccid penis.

If she ever found a man who did not fear her a witch or sorceress, at least she could go to his bed not fearing his nakedness. Rhys did not cover the sexual organs of the dead to preserve Olwyn's innocence. His determination to figure out why the human body aged, succumbed to illness, and ultimately died consumed him. Everything else that concerned the living had become an extraneous detail to which he gave no notice.

The sound of grinding bones beneath a saw mingled with the grunts of her father's labor.

Olwyn inwardly cringed and kept her eyes on the body before her. He had not been dead long, she thought. He'd not yet flattened on the bottom, and he had no signs of stiffness.

Sadness touched her heart, as it often did when the specimen had been cut down in their prime. Did a young widow weep for him at night, her bed empty and cold without him? Was his father holding his mother in comfort, even as he shed tears for his son? Did a small child sleep, dreaming of a father he would spend a lifetime trying to remember?

Olwyn's gaze slid up and down the naked man's body. Even in death he was handsome, with dark gold hair gleaming in a thick halo around a visage that when alive, must have been quite a sight to behold. He wore joy on his face, in smile brackets around his lips, and in thin lines stretching from the corners of his closed eyes.

And taking up her papers and charcoal, she was full of regret that she could not sketch him as such, a virile, vibrant man full of life and laughter.

Instead, she drew his body as it was, long and lean, a study in symmetry and masculine beauty. She worked fast, and as she did, she tuned out the noise behind her and focused on the man whose life had been cut so short.

Olwyn drew his hands, his sinewy arms, the bulge of muscle and elegant shape of his shoulders. She tried to capture his face, so still and beautiful in death, and a lump thickened her throat once again. Did he have sisters who mourned him? Brothers who longed for just one more day?

"Olwyn, look at this," Rhys said, his voice brimming with excitement.

Obediently, Olwyn laid down her work and moved to the side of the partially dissected cadaver. Rhys had made a long incision down the center of the torso and across the chest and gut, allowing him to pull back thick flaps of flesh, fat, and muscle. The sawing she'd heard had been the removal of the front of the ribcage, leaving the organs exposed.

"Look, girl. See the liver. Look at his nose, bulbous, thick with veins. I've seen this correlation before. I'm onto something here." Rhys lifted his head and his black eyes were lit with an urgent fervor that too closely resembled madness. "I need the liver of the other man for comparison. Drystan! Get my scales." He sank his hand gently into the chest and palpated the heart, pausing to look back up to Olwyn as if he'd forgotten why she was there. "Are you finished your sketch?"

"Nearly. It will take about ten more minutes, Papa." She'd learned to move quickly, but he expected the impossible.

"Fine. Wait. No. The other one can wait a moment. Come sketch the way the liver looks now, before I remove it, so I can refer to it later." He rushed her by waving at her stack of blank paper. "Don't you stand there, girl. Move, move. This carcass rots as you breathe."

Olwyn snatched up a nub of charcoal and a fresh sheet of paper, and leaning it on a flat plank of wood, drew in detail the distended liver. As soon as she finished, her father grabbed it away from her and furiously added notes about the color and smell, the shape and thickened texture.

Rhys threw the paper at Olwyn and dug his hands into the corpse's torso. Olwyn heard a sucking sound as her father pulled the liver out, and she swallowed hard against the rising bile in her throat. No amount of assisting her father numbed her to the revulsion.

As the liver was weighed, measured, and examined, Olwyn returned to drawing the other man.

She drew him lovingly, the plane of his flat, lightly furred belly, the rise of his muscled abdomen from his narrow hips. Soon enough his torso would be split wide, his organs pulled and placed into glass jars, his entrails dumped in a bucket. Olwyn shivered with disgust and regret combined. How sad his family would be to know their son's body had been so violated.

Her cheeks burned as she drew his genitals. As her charcoal scratched against the paper, she envisioned his penis slit open and examined beneath a magnifying glass. She pushed the thought away and instead imagined him alive.

She saw him on horseback, racing over a rolling green field. Wind filled his dark gold hair and his eyes sparkled with pleasure.

Olwyn set aside her charcoal for just a second and brushed her fingertips over his cold face, tracing his closed eyes. His eyelashes were long and lay dark against his pale cheek. What color had shone from his soul? she wondered. She touched the square line of his jaw, the stiff brush of his stubbly beard feeling lifelike over his frigid skin.

A sudden urge to protect the man came over her. She wanted to cover his nakedness, defend him against her father's knives and saws, and see him properly returned to rest. He did not deserve such a ghastly end.

But even as the thought occurred to her, Rhys came behind her, his wickedly sharp scalpel winking in the yellow lantern light.

There was nothing Olwyn could do to stop him; Rhys spent all their money on corpses. He would never consider not performing an exam on one, just because Olwyn didn't want him violated in such way. Her needs and wants and desires had ceased to matter the day her brother had died. On that day, Rhys became a man obsessed in his search for the key to life, and the reason for death.

Servants had been dismissed, food was rationed, luxuries were denied. And her mother, Talfryn, had run away. She'd never come back, and not a trace of her was ever found.

Olwyn had been left with her father, trapped like a rat.

Rhys stepped up to the side of the body and looked over it carefully. He lifted the head, the hands, and the feet, examined every inch of the skin.

"Not a mark on him," Rhys muttered. Without being told, Olwyn wrote down his words. "No visible wasting from sickness, no bruises or sign of injury. No physical mark indicating cause of death."

Rhys glanced quickly at the timepiece. His stomach growled and he snapped his head around to Drystan. "Tea and eggs. A heel of bread, too." And then he trained his black, shining eyes on the broad, muscular chest of the dead man before him. "Let's get started, eh?"

Rhys palpated the chest and abdomen before taking his knife into his hand. Olwyn held her breath and silently said a prayer for the man's family, that they would never know what became of their handsome son and his perfect body. She moved to the other side of the slab, and not caring if her father noticed, took the dead man's hand in hers. It was solid and square and as cold as the crypt from which he'd been taken.

Could it be that she had been alone and desperate for so long that she was falling in love with a corpse?

In that moment, Olwyn knew she'd reached the lowest depth of despair, so pathetic that she'd come to crave the company of a dead man.

Tears burned the back of her eyes as Rhys slid the tip of his blade into the center of the chest.

And then they both gasped and froze in place as blood welled from the incision.

Corpses don't bleed. Only a pumping, beating heart moves blood through a body.

Olwyn held her breath and looked at Rhys with huge, round eyes. "He's alive," she whispered.

Rhys pulled the knife back and watched the blood slowly leak scarlet across the dead man's chest, visceral proof of life. He seemed to be in a trance, and when he brought his black eyes up to Olwyn's, they glittered like obsidian.

"I need his liver," Rhys said. He spoke with such flat determination that Olwyn's blood ran cold. Her father pointed to the passage that led out of the dungeon with the dripping edge of his scalpel. "Go to your room, Olwyn."

Chapter Two

"No," Olwyn breathed in horror. "'Tis murder."

Rhys didn't move, but his voice grew harder, merciless. "This is necessary work I'm doing here, girl. Now hie yourself out of here and leave me to it."

"I cannot. I will not." Olwyn laid her hands over the bleeding wound. The man's chest was cold, so cold, and no heartbeat could be felt. But he lived. The blood was proof of it. "If you murder this man, I will reveal it."

"No one would believe you," Rhys said with certainty. His eyes, so dark they were fathomless, glittered like hard round gems. "They all think you a witch, whilst I am a respected anatomist."

"They think you a ghoul," Olwyn stated flatly. "They fear you look at them with a longing to cut out their innards."

"I do." Rhys grinned, a ghoulish expression that matched Olwyn's assertion. "We're all meat on feet, girl. Someday I shall find the secret part that makes it all work. The essence of our humanity. It must be in there." He looked down on the man whose body clung to the barest bit of life. "Here is a man on the precipice. What part of his body controls the sway?"

"Perhaps 'tis God, and you have no right to interfere."

Rhys dipped his finger in the blood, rubbed it as if to feel the texture, held it to his nose, and sniffed. "He is nearly dead. Feel how cold, how lifeless his skin. Even his blood is cool. It won't be long for him. But think of the opportunity here. To dig in and see if I can find the link between spirit and flesh. 'Tis my life's work, girl. This is the moment I've been waiting on."

Olwyn leaned her body forward, protectively shrouding the man. She met her father's eyes and dared to threaten him. "Cause him harm, and I swear it, I will expose you first, and then I will take my own life. I will not live in the house of a murderer, nor will I live with it on my own conscience. I'd sooner die."

Drystan entered the dungeon with a clatter of thick earthen mugs and plates on a tray. He set his burden down on a small worktable before coming over to the side of the bleeding man. His bushy eyebrows betrayed his surprise. "Not dead yet?"

Olwyn ignored him. She kept her eyes on Rhys, studying him intently. She knew not to show fear. She knew not to show weakness. She did not, however, know how much she mattered to Rhys, so consumed as he was with his quest.

Hoping that her father's mind was not completely beyond reason, she gestured to the partially dissected cadaver behind them. "That corpse was days dead, father. There's not much time left in him before his stench drives us to put him in the ground. Give this living man to me. I'll tend him for a few days. If he dies, he is yours, and no murder or suicide will stain your conscience."

Rhys tightened his hand on his scalpel. It was poised over the belly of the man between them. Suddenly Olwyn hated her body, so slim and slight. She simply could not cover the dying man with her form, and her arms, slender and feminine, were no match to Drystan's strength and her father's madness. If Rhys chose to plunge it deep into the naked gut stretched out before him, there was nothing Olwyn could do to stop him.

"I do not care to be dragooned by my own child," Rhys said, his tone dangerously calm. "How dare you."

Olwyn changed her tactic. "Father, I beseech you. If I mean anything to you, anything at all, grant me this man's life. Please. I am begging."

In the yellowish, dingy light of the tallow lanterns, Olwyn saw Rhys's eyes change. He still looked at her with his penetrative stare, but something changed. She thought he looked hurt, and maybe just a bit embarrassed. As he spoke, her heart broke just a little. "You have never had more of the look of your mother than you do just now, Olwyn."

"I am not like her," she whispered.

"You think I am a monster." He sounded distant, but his grip on the scalpel was firm and still poised above the man's belly. "If you could have gone with her, Olwyn, would you have left me, too? Tell me the truth."

Olwyn remembered the day Talfryn had left the keep.

The morning had dawned as it always did, but something had been wrong. Fires were lit and breakfast was served, but no mistress presided over the table, and her father had sat with his head bowed. He had turned to Olwyn, who was only three and ten, and said, "You're the woman of the house now."

And now her father dared to ask the question that hung between them all these years. Would she have left with her mother if she'd been asked to go?

The sting of Talfryn's abandonment never faded. Nor did the longing for her mother's touch, scent, and laughter.

"Of course not, Father," Olwyn lied. Instead of the truth, she said exactly what she knew Rhys wanted to hear. "My loyalty is to you. I am Olwyn Gawain, the proud daughter of Rhys Gawain."

She watched as Rhys's chest expanded a bit with pride, his chin rising with her words.

And then he changed again, his mercurial moods dangerous. "You tried to leave."

"I told you before, Papa, that I was only hoping to find Mother and bring her home." The lies burned in her mouth, along with the sting of her own submission to her fate. She'd wanted to escape, had dreamed of it, had planned for it for so long that it had become the only thing that kept her sanity. But after the night when the dogs had attacked her, she'd lacked the courage to try again. "Haven't I been a good girl? Haven't I done everything you've ever asked of me?"

Silence filled the space between father and daughter, the only sounds that of dripping water and scurrying rats. They faced each other in the watery, yellow light, with a naked, nearly dead man between them. Drystan turned away, busying himself with tidying up the burlap sacks that the bodies had been brought in. As he folded them, a musical clinking sounded on the stone floor.

Olwyn did not dare to look to see what made the noise, but kept her eyes on her father's. Out of the corner of her eye, she saw Drystan drop to the floor in search of what had fallen.

In the flickering light, she saw Rhys's decision. Olwyn pulled her pistol and took aim. "Drop it. To the floor."

Rhys froze; he knew she wouldn't miss. He let go of the scalpel, and she heard its metallic clank on the stone floor. When she didn't lower her weapon, Rhys grew angry. "You can't be serious."

"A daughter doesn't hold a gun on her father if she's anything but," Olwyn said flatly. "Take a step back."

Rhys twitched, as if he'd been slapped. "You wouldn't."

"If there will be a murder in this dungeon, it won't be of this defenseless man."

Olwyn thought quickly, plans forming fast. No more witch in a crumbling keep, she would take this man and leave Wales, once and for all. Just like her mother before her, she would escape and never be seen again.

All her nights spent dreaming of running away would finally serve her purpose. She had everything she needed— stolen money and maps given to her by the kindly trader who was the only man who'd ever shown her sympathy.

She steeled herself, letting every bit of her desire to escape fuel what must be done.

"Drystan. Grab her," Rhys commanded.

"Try it, Drystan," Olwyn invited with a smile. She spoke to her father then, and truth rang in her voice. "I've wanted to shoot him for years, for his perverted perusal of my body, and his disgusting advances when he's drunk. Go on and risk the life of the only man who has stuck by you since you began your ghoulish obsession. I'll put a shot between his eyes, and it will not trouble me to do so."

Caught as they were in the moment, neither of them noticed that the man lying between them opened his eyes.

Drystan saw, however, and began whispering a prayer, begging for God's mercy even as he concealed what he'd found on the floor.

Rhys's voice sounded more like a growl, a prelude to violence. "Olwyn, you are playing a dangerous game. Put the pistol down now, and I'll not punish you overmuch."

"Step away from this man," she countered, her voice ringing off the wet stones of the dungeon walls.

With every word, Rhys grew louder and louder, until he was shouting, "And then what? Will we go on with our lives, with me pretending my daughter did not pull her traitorous weapon on me, and threaten my life?"

"No," Olwyn answered calmly. "We won't."

She gestured to Drystan, snapped her fingers. "Drystan, take my father, by force or willing, I care not."

Drystan's eyes flicked from the man between them to Rhys, and then again to Olwyn. He seemed to be weighing the course of least danger.

"That's right, Drystan. I will kill you if you don't obey me," Olwyn said with a certain amount of cheer. She withdrew her dagger. The hilt fit perfectly in her small hand. "Take him and put him in the cell."

"This is madness!"

"Now, Drystan, or I'll plant my blade in your gut and still have a shot to finish you."

Both men knew Olwyn capable. And she suspected that Drystan heard the ring of sincerity in her words, for he moved to Rhys. Rhys scrabbled away and put up a fight, but Drystan was younger, faster, and much stronger. He grabbed him by the arm and pulled him to the nearest cell, pushed him inside, and slammed the door shut.

"Turn the lock and bring me the key."

"I'll beat you senseless, girl! I'll whip the skin off your back," Rhys raged, his fists tight around the iron bars.

Olwyn ignored him. "Carry the man up, wrap him in furs and blankets."

"He's awake," Drystan whispered.

Olwyn glanced down and saw that the man had indeed awakened. He stared at her intently. She'd wondered what color his eyes would be.

Blue.

Deep, dark Prussian blue, like fathomless lakes and sapphire skies.

He flicked his eyes over to where her father was screaming for release. And he raised a single brow slightly, quizzical.

"You'll live," she told him, and when he didn't seem to register her words, she realized he probably didn't speak Welsh. She spoke to him again, repeating the words in English. "You'll live."

And she allowed herself to touch him, a slide of the backs of her fingers against his arm. He was still as cold as death, but was most certainly fighting for his life.

So would she, for his and hers alike.

No more prisoner to her fears of leaving, or her father's control. Today would be the day that Olwyn would seize her freedom, for she'd sealed her fate the moment she pulled the gun and held it on her father. There would be no going back.

But she needed Drystan's cooperation, and there seemed to be precious little of that with him frozen in place, staring at the man who'd opened his eyes.

"Dispense with your superstitions, Drystan. Surely a live man is less frightening to you than a dead one, and Lord knows you've carried your share of those. Pick him up and carry him out of here."

"He's come back to life," Drystan said, still whispering as if he feared waking the other corpse behind him. "Do you think he's possessed?"

"Don't be absurd," she snapped, her impatience growing with each second. "More like he's woken from a coma, is all. Do you not know how common it is for a man to be thought dead and yet still have life in him? 'Tis why there are wakes, after all."

Behind them there was the smashing of glass against the stone floor, and a brain rolled from the fluids in which it had been suspended. Rhys had thrown it across the room, to momentarily stop the rats from feasting on the eviscerated corpse. "You're interfering with my work!" he screamed, and whether he meant Olwyn or the rats, she knew not.

Rats fled the area, scuttling back into the shadows as Rhys railed and raged at his daughter, calling her vile names and questioning her parentage.

Drystan glanced back to Rhys, and then to Olwyn, his face a mask of fear.

"He'll forgive you," Olwyn told him. "It's me he'll hate forever."

Drystan gave one more cautious glance to the man before him, and reached out to poke his muscular flank. When the man did not react, Drystan grabbed him by the arms and lifted him, put him over his shoulder, and began carrying him up the long flight of stone steps that had been carved from the earth more than six hundred years before.

And Olwyn pulled her gaze away from the long, well formed body draped over her father's servant. She turned and faced her father, who stopped his ranting. For once, it seemed he would listen to what she had to say. She hoped he would remember, for his mood swings caused lapses in his memory.

"I know you want me to stay with you, and help with your work, but I cannot do it any longer. I'm miserable," she confessed softly, "and so lonesome that I have begun to long for death. Only the image of you carving me up to see my insides has stayed my hand on many an occasion, and for that, I hope you are ashamed."

Olwyn's gaze slid over her father, and she struggled to remember him as he used to be, before her brother took sick and died. Olwyn often thought that her father's sanity died that day, too.

"I will never come back here. I will never see you again. Do you have anything you want to say to me before I go?"

"Curse you, Olwyn. Curse you to hell." Rhys's hands tightened on the iron bars until they were white. "You may leave me here with these rats, but you'll never find a better life. Never. No one will want you, ugly and marked as you are. Everywhere you go, people will revile you. You are a hideous, piebald beast of a woman, and your heart is as ugly as your face."

"Farewell, Father," Olwyn said softly. Her lips shook and turned down at the corners, but she did not weep. If she were to have a coin for every time her father had called her ugly, she would need a wagon to cart them. "I will arrange for your release in a day's time. The rats should be busy enough with the corpse until then."

And she turned and left him behind, trying to not hear him scream that she would never, ever find a man who would love her. That no man, not even a half-dead one pulled from a crypt, would ever be able to see past her unsightly face.

The final taunt reached her as she neared the top of the stairs, and she knew that it would ring in her ears for the rest of her life.

"Saving him won't make him love you."

Olwyn closed the door to the dungeon and locked it. Gripping both keys in her hands, she leaned against the door and took a few steadying breaths.

She told herself all the right things: that she hadn't gone to such extreme measures because he was so beautiful she couldn't bear to see him cut apart. And that certainly she did not expect he would wake, like some reverse tale of *Sleeping Beauty,* and sweep her off her feet to his castle, fall in love with her, and make her his wife.

Those sorts of things were for fanciful girls.

Beautiful girls.

Olwyn Gawain was neither.

And knowing all that, Olwyn couldn't help but wonder why her father's words had cut so deeply.

She could hear Rhys's screams, like an enraged animal, deep, long bellows that echoed off the stones.

Olwyn walked away as fast as her feet could carry her. She found that Drystan had laid the man in front of the fire and was covering him with blankets and furs, just as she'd instructed.

The tall arched windows in the great hall showed the early streaks of dawn lighting the sky, and Lord be praised, it was cloudless. For a woman who rarely felt in fortune's favor, Olwyn felt it was a good sign that she was not making the biggest mistake of her life.

She didn't need to hold the pistol on Drystan. He seemed ready enough for her to leave and take the awakened man with her.

But she held it to him, just the same, even as she stooped down to check on her charge. He'd closed his eyes again, but he looked far less pale, and when she touched him, he felt warmer.

Her fingers played over his forehead, brushing his thick, slashing brows, and swept lightly over his closed eyelids. She noticed the tips of his lashes were darker, the fringe of them thick, their covetous length a sweetly boyish curve against his cheek. His lips looked soft, the bottom slightly fuller than the top, and had Olwyn wondering what it would be like to be kissed by such a man.

Her fingers moved again to his hair, burying into the thick softness of it as if of their own volition.

Drystan coughed, clearly subduing laughter. Yes, she supposed she made quite a sight, holding a pistol in one hand while stroking the sleeping man with the other.

Olwyn could not dismiss Drystan to do her bidding, couldn't risk him unleashing the dogs.

"To the stables, then," she directed crisply. "I'll be needing the horse and wagon."

The small stables were about five hundred years newer than the keep, a humble structure that smelled of hay and manure, leather and horses. The early morning sunlight filtered through the high, grimy windows, casting dusty streams of light down into the dimness. In the corner there were a few wagons in various stages of disrepair, too necessary to be sold, as they were used for carting various necessities from the village.

The dogs were in their pens, and they bumped the gates with their noses, baring their teeth as they barked. They didn't even seem to register Drystan's presence, but aimed their aggression at her. "Quiet! Lie down!" she commanded, but if she could hear her own shrill fear, surely they could smell it.

The big black one smiled as he growled, a hungry sound that made her flesh crawl. She wondered if he remembered what she tasted like, for ever since the attack he went wild when he saw her, bumping the gate of his pen as if he hungered for more of her blood.

Olwyn dug into the bin of scraps her father kept for the dogs, and pulled out two old soup bones. She threw them into the pens, as far against the wall as she could get them.

The dogs launched themselves hungrily on their quarry, and as their teeth ground against the bones, Olwyn imagined the long sharp teeth sinking into her arms.

No time for fear.

Olwyn grabbed her tack and rushed to the horse's pen, while Drystan readied the wagon. The mare, Nixie, nickered and nuzzled her arm as Olwyn buckled her straps. She was old and far too placid to prance with excitement, but still she tossed her head and swished her tail in anticipation.

Leading her out, Drystan hitched Nixie to the smallest wagon they owned; the bigger ones, she reasoned, would be heavier and more likely to tire Nixie. While the wagon was secured, Olwyn quickly packed up a few horse blankets and a feed bag, and had Drystan lift the fullest sack of grain into the wagon. She also took two oiled tarps and a coiled length of rope, and threw them on top.

With that completed, she and Drystan drove it back to the keep, and though she kept her pistol at the ready, he made no efforts to stop her. He was far too compliant, following each of her instructions without demur, and once or twice she thought she spied a smug grin on his face.

And she wondered if he had a plan. He most certainly was up to something.

"Stop here, Drystan," she instructed. Olwyn nibbled at her lip for a second. "Get the man, put him in the back. Layer a few wrapped hot bricks beside him."

And instead of readying herself, she waited, holding the pistol.

When he was finished, she directed him into a small windowless room that had once been a butler's lodging. It had a small bed and a chamber pot.

"What are you going to do to me?" Drystan asked, eyeing her suspiciously.

Olwyn didn't hide her smile. "You'll see."

She locked him in there for the time being, and spared a glance at the timepiece in the great room as she ran through it. Up to her rooms she ran, and with the excitement of a woman who had longed to escape for years, she gathered up her belongings.

A few sacks of clothing were already packed; she put those by the door, along with another bag she kept ready to go. It contained her pouch of stolen money, both her bottles of whiskey, the book of poetry that had been her brother's favorite, and her pouch of incense.

She stripped her bed of the bed linens and blankets, rolled them into a bundle. She took tinder and flint, candles and a lantern, her thick, warm boots, and an extra pair of shoes.

It took two trips to carry it all down and pack it into the wagon, and then Olwyn made a quick stop in her father's room, stealing an old, ratty cloak, a long, threadbare nightshirt, and two pairs of thick woolen stockings. Rhys didn't have much in the way of clothing; it was all she could find. But naked as the unconscious man currently was, these clothes would be better than nothing.

A trip to the kitchens yielded a loaf of bara brith she'd baked the day before, a wheel of cheese, some dried figs, and two sacks of nuts. She took the jar of honey and the tea, a rasher of bacon and a jug of water. Once she had everything loaded into the sides of the wagon, Olwyn covered her provisions with the tarps.

"Are you awake?" she whispered in English. "Can you talk?"

He slit his eyes for the briefest second, and she swore she saw fear in those blue depths.

Did looking upon her spark horror in him? Was she truly so hideous?

The keep didn't have a looking glass, and Olwyn hadn't seen her own reflection in anything more than a distorted glimmer in a bucket of water.

The villagers reviled her, but she'd hoped it was

because they feared her a witch, not because she was truly deformed.

Well, be that as it may, she told herself. It mattered not. This beautiful man with the face of a prince and the form of a warrior was not in the wagon now because she hoped for his love. Doing the right thing would be its own reward.

Sparing a final pat on the bundled man who lay on a pallet between all the rations and supplies, she said, "Well, whatever may come, it'll be better than your fate in the dungeon."

Olwyn left him there once more, and went inside to deal with Drystan.

After making her preparations, she opened the door and found him on the cot. He had his back against the wall, his legs outstretched and casually crossed at the ankles. A smirk twisted his lips, and his watery eyes had an unusual sparkle in them.

"What are you up to, Drystan?"

"Not a thing, girl. Not a thing, and why should you be asking when it's you holding a pistol at my head and me doing your bidding?"

Olwyn didn't answer him, but instead handed over a bottle of Drystan's beloved whiskey with a cup overturned on its neck. "Drink up."

Drystan looked askance at her offering, trying for suspicion despite his own longing. He licked his lips like a man who'd just crossed the desert. "It's not payday."

"This'll work better than tying you with ropes, Drystan, and will surely be more enjoyable for you. Go on. Drink up, and come tomorrow when you're sober enough to pick open the lock, you'll find a note on the kitchen table. Take it down to the dungeon and my father will read it for you. It tells the location of the key to my father's cell."

Drystan ran his tongue out again over lips that were

already shining with saliva. "Well, if you're forcing me, I've no choice at all."

He reached out and took the bottle, filled the cup, and began to drink.

With Drystan's drunken songs echoing through the keep, Olwyn left her home behind. Hoping she hadn't forgotten anything vital, Olwyn jumped onto the driver's board, lifted the reins, and gave Nixie's back a hearty slap.

The wagon lurched into motion. She urged the horse to a quick clip.

Olwyn's heart raced, her blood sang, and her spirits soared. She did not think of the risks involved. Those worries were for another day, another time, and she thought recklessly, another woman.

Right now, she was seizing her freedom, an emancipation from her father's madness and a life that would never improve.

She wondered if her mother had felt that way, the night she left them all behind.

And creeping into her happiness and hopes was the question that her heart never stopped asking, and would never be answered: why had Talfryn abandoned her?

Sadness threatened to steal her optimism. There are, Olwyn reasoned, always ways to justify doing the right thing for oneself, to ignore the needs of others, and to find a way to make putting oneself first seem like the only rational thing to do.

But there was always a price to that, Olwyn knew.

Olwyn turned back and looked down on the tarp-covered wagon. She spoke aloud to the man who slumbered beneath it. "Whatever happens, know that I did my best."

She faced front and urged the horse to pick up its pace. And refusing to let Talfryn's abandonment ruin her excited anticipation for the future, Olwyn consulted her maps, looked to the horizon, drove the wagon south, and thought about freedom.

Chapter Three

Warwick, England

Mira Kimball watched discreetly out her parlor window, impatiently tapping her foot. She tried to focus on something besides her boredom, even toyed with the idea of painting a picture of the landscape.

The sky shone smooth and silver with clouds, the sun a watery gold smear behind tangled, bare trees. Warwick was lovely, stark and beautiful in the way only England can be on a cold winter's morning.

She envisioned Padraig Mullen finding her seated prettily before an easel, painting the countryside. Would he then report of her talent to his brother, Aidan? If he did, would Aidan be cheered that his betrothed possessed an artistic bent?

When she saw the team of horses and the shiny black carriage bearing the Mullen crest coming up their long drive, her heart picked up its pace and her boredom could be put temporarily aside.

She rushed from the parlor and found her father in his study, pouring over the latest issue of *The Herald,* the paper he owned and highly prized. Mira did not trouble herself to politely interrupt, but burst out, "Papa, he is here."

Andrew Kimball, the Earl of Falconbergh, set down the smudged copy and leaned back in his chair, regarding his daughter over the rims of his spectacles. "Who?"

Mira blew out her breath in annoyance, and whirled from the room. Her father, indulgent and doting though he was, did not spare a single moment for her flirtations. It seemed to Mira that he did not realize that she was betrothed to the most lucrative fish in London's sparsely populated male sea. Other than a few widowers with a few of their own brats, court was littered with impoverished men of good title, and its fair share of unappealing, and dare she say ugly, men of lower birth.

Mira Kimball had set her sights on the Mullen twins, for they were rakishly handsome, incredibly wealthy, and one would be duke.

And after a few glasses of champagne, coupled with just a bit of added insurance, she'd succeeded in securing Aidan Mullen as her own. The cost of her virginity had been a paltry price to pay, and he was now honor-bound to do the proper thing.

It had been perfect. Mira had wept tears of remorse, and Aidan had proposed.

As Mira had planned, she would get exactly what she wanted—a handsome husband whose marital bed would not be burdensome, along with the wealth that she was accustomed to and deserved.

She rushed to the anteroom outside the ballroom, where the accoutrements of a lady's beauty were laid out. Standing in front of the oversized, gilt-framed looking glass, Mira dusted her nose with powder, pressed a few drops of scented oil behind her ears, and patted her perfect coiffure. Mira, satisfied with her appearance, turned and walked sedately toward the foyer where her betrothed's brother was most likely being greeted by their butler.

Her hands trembled with anticipation, and so to cover,

she folded them demurely across the narrow column of her high-waisted gown. She'd worn one of her finest morning dresses, made of the palest, shimmery pink silk; it flattered her skin and was so fine and delicate, it begged to be touched. And her décolletage, daringly low and dangerously sheer, begged the same as well.

Mira paused in the corridor that led to the massive, two-storied grand foyer. She could see him, Padraig Mullen, her betrothed's twin.

He was as tall as Aidan, as muscled, and their faces both bore the hint of a Celtic fable, testimony to their Irish heritage. While Padraig was dark of hair and green of eyes like his father, Aidan bore the look of his mother, golden as an Adonis, with blatant sensuality and eyes the color of sapphires.

But as to which of the twins would be duke, the secret had been guarded all their lives by their parents, who had wanted them raised without rivalry.

That may have been true in their youth, but Mira suspected the secret was maintained to keep greedy young women slightly at bay.

And the thought made her so self-satisfied, she wanted to squeal and clap her hands, for she'd managed to snag herself one of them, and was the envy of every girl at court.

Padraig caught sight of Mira, turned in her direction, showed a fine leg, and swept into a formal bow. "My lady, 'tis good to see you."

Sweet soft laughter tinkled down the hall. Mira laughed as she entered the foyer, and held out her tiny hand. He bowed over it, pressed a kiss upon her glove, and breathed in her feminine scent. Straightening, he took in her petite blond beauty, as softly fragile and adorable as a kitten.

While he could clearly appreciate her charms, he still couldn't quite understand why his brother had proposed to her. They were an odd match, he thought, and she was not the sort of woman he'd have thought his brother would have wanted to marry.

"You've gotten even prettier since we saw you last," Padraig said.

Mira tapped him on the chest with her folded fan. "Such gammon, my lord. I look exactly as I always do."

"If you were this beautiful six months ago, how did Aidan let you leave London?" he asked, saying the right things, but not thinking them. In truth, he'd been glad to see her go.

"Winter in London is dreadful. All that wet soot and those dirty puddles." Mira pursed her rosebud lips and lightly shuddered. "At home here in Warwick, I love it when the gardens slumber beneath a blanket of snow, and I am tucked up beside a warm fire with my sewing. 'Tis a fact that I don't require much to make me happy. I'm quite satisfied with simplicity, really."

If Mira thought the great stately mansion in Warwick simple, Padraig would not disabuse her of that notion. True, she was spoilt and indulged, but that was only part and parcel to the rearing of a proper lady. For that he could forgive her.

Padraig wondered how his brother thought he could marry a girl such as Mira. She was like a little porcelain doll, with her flaxen hair and her fine, fair skin. Her lips were always pink and pouting, and her wide cornflower eyes, so innocent and adoring, were the very picture of ladylike perfection.

He couldn't imagine bedding her; she looked breakable. And, he couldn't help but think, she looked highly proper as well. Too proper, most likely, to enjoy the earthy, sensual delights he hoped to find in his marriage bed.

Padraig steered his thoughts in a more gentlemanly direction. It wasn't appropriate to be envisioning the woman his brother would wed in such a way, and Aidan certainly wouldn't appreciate it. His brother had such an overreaching sense of honor where women were concerned. Come to that, his brother had an overreaching sense of honor, period. Aidan was a man who always did the right thing.

"Have you heard from my brother?" Padraig asked.

"Yes, I received a letter sent the day before he was set to leave Ireland," she answered sweetly, and her eyes sparkled. "Have you?"

"Aye, a letter reached me as well, written the same day. He mentioned that he looked forward to us all reuniting in Chester."

"I miss him so," Mira sighed.

If that were true, Padraig thought, perhaps she could have worn a less revealing gown. The bodice, so sheer and clingy, was not the sort of thing he thought a proper lady ought to be wearing, especially in front of her fiancé's brother. He could scarcely stop looking down.

"Last I saw you, you mentioned you had a special project you were working on," Padraig said, hoping for a distraction from her nipples. "I'm sure Aidan won't mind if you showed me."

"Never mind my silly project. I must see to your refreshment." Mira gestured to the parlor but Padraig shrugged off her offer.

"I've no needs. Why don't you show me what has so absorbed you. I'm intrigued."

"Very well, if you insist," Mira answered, and she lowered her eyes modestly, as if uncomfortable having such attention lavished on her and her project. "It really isn't much. Certainly nothing in comparison to the ships your company builds. Isn't it true that you're one of the largest shipbuilders in the world?"

"'Tis a bit of an exaggeration," Padraig demurred smoothly. If Aidan's venture in Ireland went as they'd planned, however, Mira might indeed be correct. Padraig could scarcely wait to get to Chester to meet up with his brother and hear how things turned out.

Mira led the way to a set of closed double doors, and placing both her hands on the knobs, tossed a questioning look over her shoulder. "You're certain? 'Tis not my wish to bore you with my trivialities."

Padraig thought he saw something in her clear blue eyes for just a second, a shine of pure pride. Or was it something else?

Was there more to her than she usually showed? Padraig wondered. He hoped so. Both his mother and his grandmother were formidable women, complex and dynamic. It would be good for Aidan to find that Mira possessed qualities beyond the normal simpering flirtations of the spoiled and wealthy daughters of the peerage.

Mira opened the doors and they entered. The grand, richly appointed room smelled strongly of varnished wood and fresh paint, a smaller version of a very fine museum. The walls were lined with glass-fronted cabinets; the floor space filled with tables that had been built so that glass lay in the top, showcasing shallow recessed cases. The marble floors shone without a speck of dust, and the tall windows were draped with gold velvet hangings.

"What do you keep in here?" he asked.

Mira cast her eyes to her folded hands, and her sweet voice drifted through the cavernous room and off the high, coffered ceiling. "When I was a girl, I used to love to play in our attics. You see, they span nearly the entire manse, and are filled with hundreds of years worth of my family's belongings. About two years ago, it occurred to me that a hobby was what I needed. Something to do that was more useful than painting tiny boxes and such. And so, my lord, I have been cataloging and displaying the Kimball artifacts that tell the story of our history."

Padraig moved to one of the glass cabinets. Behind it was a battle-scarred medieval shield, its flaky paint displaying the Kimball coat of arms. It had a brass plaque beneath it, engraved with a small paragraph about Lord Randolff Kimball, the first Duke of Somerset, whose valiant service to the king was greatly rewarded.

All around the room were various such treasures: ancient swords and tapestries, journals and Bibles, chain mail and armor, and an entire case filled with ancestral jewels and jewelry.

"You did all of this yourself?" Padraig asked, greatly impressed.

"Yes. Papa allowed me to hire contractors to build the cabinets and such, and of course, he has indulged me with many trips to various towns so I could gather information. In fact, 'tis part of the reason I journey to Chester on the morrow. I am in search of any information about a Marquis in our family line, who apparently was quite the hero. I have his journals and a riveting log he kept during the War of Spanish Succession. He kept a home in Chester, and I've been in correspondence with the current owners, who have agreed to allow me access to their attics."

Mira brushed her fingertips lovingly over one of the highly polished tables. "There is much, much more for me to do. I have only begun to sort through the many treasures in our attics. But I am taking my time with it, and enjoying the process. 'Tis been quite absorbing and rewarding."

"What you're doing here is wonderful."

Mira blushed and fluttered her lashes. "I'm merely expressing my familial pride. Someday I shall do this same thing for my future husband's family, should he approve of it, of course."

Padraig fought the grin that wanted to break across his face. Mira Kimball did not waste time on subtlety. But her veiled promises aside, he couldn't help but wonder if he or his brother would ever find the rarest sort of a woman: one who spoke her mind and heart.

Mira turned her eyes up to his, and laid a hand on his arm. Her touch was light and fleeting, as if a tiny songbird had landed on his jacket. "My lord, may I show something remarkable?"

"Certainly."

Mira led him to the center case and pointed down at a slip of paper that was pinned to a soft cushion of velvet. The letter had tattered edges and a rich velvety texture that made the scrolling words bleed into the parchment. Though it had been carefully smoothed out, it still bore the lines that told tale of once being crumpled down the center, as if by an angry fist.

An odd weight settled in Padraig's gut, though he knew not why.

Mira, oblivious to his reaction, said, "Look, my lord. Here is a letter summoning my great-uncle, Bret Kimball, to your family's property in Southampton, then called Beauport. 'Tis dated 1742, and appears to be written by the hand of your great-grandmother, Amelia Bradburn, the Duchess of Eton." Mira turned her lovely face toward him, obviously quite proud of her discovery. "Isn't it wondrous? It seems our families have known each other for more than sixty years."

Padraig leaned forward and inspected the letter with more interest. "Her handwriting looks like my grandmother Camille's."

"Yes, well, that may be. There is more, however, my lord." Mira's eyes were shining, and her enthusiasm was evident. She fairly vibrated with it. "I have found journals from my great-uncle, as well. Bret Kimball was a man who understood history, I think, for he left several diaries that are filled with his writings. I've yet to read them, but the discovery spurred me to send a request to your mother, asking if I might tour the attics of the home in Southampton. Who knows what other links I might find between our families?"

"You did?" The girl was certainly tenacious. The property in Southampton was where Aidan had made his home, far away from London and court, where he could pursue his own interests. Mira could have waited a matter of weeks for Aidan to return, and asked him if she could join him there.

"I just couldn't wait. Aidan is always so busy with his animals and his ships and his whiskey nonsense." Mira wrinkled her nose prettily. "Your mother was just lovely about it. Not only did Her Grace send permission for me to spend as much time as I needed at Beauport, she sent a letter to the staff there, letting them know I am welcome anytime."

Padraig smiled, thinking of the appropriateness of his mother's formal address, Her Grace. Yes. If there was one thing Emeline Mullen had in spades, it was that.

Mira continued, burbling on, seeming nearly manic in her enthusiasm. "I am very passionate about my family's venerable and prestigious history, and now to find such a link between the Kimballs and the Bradburns has just exceeded my wildest expectations."

Mira drew in a deep breath, a sigh of pure happiness and excitement. "As soon as I am finished in Chester, I am going to travel to Southampton, to Beauport. I cannot wait to see what fantastic discoveries that will yield."

And Padraig couldn't help but notice that Mira hadn't

acted nearly so excited at the prospect of seeing Aidan again as she was to go digging in their attics.

Nor had she indicated that she thought of Beauport as more than a place to discover historical facts. When Mira and Aidan married, it would be her home.

Chapter Four

The sound of the night was broken by the creaking, rattling wagon and the wheezing of a horse that'd been pushed beyond its limits. Olwyn Gawain knew it was time to stop running, if only for a few hours.

She reined Nixie in to a stop in a small thicket, where hopefully, no one would be around to ambush her when she, too, stole a moment's rest.

Fatigue was a crushing weight on her shoulders, and her back ached from sitting on the bare plank of wood that comprised the wagon's seat. Her belly grumbled, unsatisfied by the few bits of bread she'd managed to swallow every time she stopped the wagon to climb into the back to coax water and honey down her charge's throat.

But he looked better, she thought with satisfaction. As she unhitched her horse, tethered her, and strapped on the feed bag, Olwyn allowed herself to be proud of her accomplishment. She'd saved a man's life, after all, and her own with it.

No more wasting her life away, desperate and alone. She was seizing the possibility of something more.

The wet from the grass seeped into her homemade boots

and touched her feet with chilly fingers, making her shiver as she finished the last of her tasks. With Nixie tended to, Olwyn let the mantle of her weariness slide over her, no longer fighting it.

The wagon creaked as it took her weight, and Olwyn slid into the narrow space in the center, wiggling beneath the covers and furs to lie beside the man who slept there. She shifted the blankets so they covered them both, and as she did, she felt his skin.

It occurred to her she was about to bed down for the night with a man who was completely naked.

Olwyn dismissed the indecency of it. Sharing their warmth was only practical, she told herself.

So why then could she do nothing but think about dark gold hair framing a Prince Charming face, a long, smooth, muscled body, and large square hands?

And there in the dark, in the cold, and completely alone, Olwyn blushed hot and red as she envisioned his most private parts.

He moved in his sleep, and her body molded to his as if made to fit against him. The nest she'd made for him was surprisingly warm, and heat seeped into her skin, relaxing her.

It did not escape her awareness that she had not touched another live human being since the day her mother left.

It felt so good to have his skin near hers, to hold him as she liked, and to give the simplest of affection: a hug. So she let her arm drape over his broad chest, and she held him to her.

Olwyn mentally named him her prince. And laughing at the fanciful nature of her imaginings, she let her mind wander down a path that was dangerous for all its allure.

She envisioned him waking, and added that it began with her kiss. Why not? It was her fantasy. She would have it as she liked.

And so she kissed her prince awake, and he fell in love with her from the start. He whisked her off to his castle, wooed her gently, and welcomed her into his life, his embrace. And of course, she added, they lived happily ever after.

It was a dream as nebulous as a bubble, easily popped with reality's prick.

She well recalled the fear in his eyes when he'd looked at her.

Her prince stirred in his sleep, and a low sound of contented comfort came from his throat. It stirred her in a curious way.

"Do you like my body against yours, as much as I like yours against mine?" she asked him, emboldened by the knowledge that he could not hear her.

Testing the waters, she ran her hand over his chest, touched the small nub of his nipple, feeling the springy hairs there.

He sighed and shifted toward her.

She propped herself on her elbow so she could look down on his face, his handsome sleeping face. "If I kissed you, would you wake?" she whispered.

Smiling at her own fancy, she leaned down and kissed his lips. She'd meant it to be a quick peck, but his breath exhaled against her mouth, and so she lingered, inhaling his essence. His lips tasted of the honeyed water she'd given him, and they felt soft and alive.

She pulled back and touched his face with her fingertips, skimming over his features with a butterfly caress.

He made a sound in his throat, distinctly of pleasure. And so she kept stroking him, over his ears and down his neck. "You are alive," she told him. "And soon, when you're healed enough, you'll wake."

Olwyn stroked down his chest and over the narrow plane of his belly, felt the firm tautness of it, and growing bolder, ran her hand down his flank. She couldn't help but admire him; he was beautifully made, like a sculpture, an Adonis of a man.

Her prince turned his head toward her, still sleeping, his breath warm on her face. And he sighed with another sound of pleasure.

"Come alive," she urged him, and beneath her hand she felt the warm curve of his large thigh muscle as it ran down into his knee. "Wake and find your life again."

He moved once more, curling against her warmth.

"Who are you?" she asked him in another whisper. "Are you my prince? Will you save me the day you come alive?"

She leaned down and kissed him again, a slow, gentle pass of her lips over his. All the while she stroked him like a cat, long, slow petting over his smooth, soft skin, admiring the taut, tensile strength beneath it, and the masculine shape of him.

And knowing it was so very, very wrong, Olwyn let her hand drift to where it ought not be unless she were his wife. It was the briefest touch, but she felt his warmth there before pulling her hand away, her face flaming.

He moved again, closer still.

"I am sorry," she told him, her voice hushed with shame and hesitant with curiosity. "I should not have done that."

She lay back down beside him, wrapped her arm across his chest and cradled him to her in an embrace that was less than chaste, but the best she could manage.

Hours passed before she found sleep.

Olwyn spent the next day like the first, following the map the trader had given her.

And by the time night fell, she began to feel safer.

Surely she was now beyond Rhys's grasp; she'd taken

their only horse. On foot, he had no chance of catching up to her.

Olwyn lit a lantern and pulled back the blankets to look at him. Still unconscious, the man's color had faded once again.

The night was still and quiet around her, the sky thankfully clear, but lacking in much light as there was only the thinnest sliver of a moon.

She needed to get her charge by a fire.

Olwyn consulted her map again. According to the trader, there should be a small stone hut up ahead.

As she drove by, she passed tall standing stones. They were her markers, proof that she was on the correct path. Shivers traveled over her skin, prickling awareness of the ancients who'd erected the stones. They loomed like sentinels guarding the secrets of the past, of the Druids who'd peeled bark from trees, worshipped the sun for the life it gave, and left the timeless stones behind when their mortal bodies returned to dust.

Up ahead a dark shadow on the horizon suggested she neared a pile of stones, perhaps a cairn, or perhaps the shelter she sought.

Nearing it, her heart began to thud in nervous expectation, for she could see it was in fact a small, round dwelling, built into the side of a hill in the manner of medieval construction. There were literally hundreds of such stone huts dotting the English, Scottish, and Welsh countryside, a few occupied by humans, most inhabited by small animals.

She approached the structure in relative quiet. No lights came from within it, and as she drew even closer, intense relief slid over her like a warm blanket.

It was still abandoned.

She reined Nixie to a stop and, taking her lantern, hopped down to investigate.

Its hewn door listed to the side, and two tiny windows were on either side of it, as darkly blank as vacant eyes. The oiled skins that had once covered them hung in tatters, their torn, wispy remains moving gently in the night breeze. The part of the dwelling that protruded from the hillside was thatched, its floor merely dirt, but Olwyn would not find fault. It would provide them shelter.

She silently thanked the kind trader. He had not failed her.

Olwyn set the lantern inside the structure, and quickly got to work. Delighted to see that it had a fire pit hollowed into the hillside, she rushed to pull kindling and squares of peat from the wagon and immediately began building a fire.

Years of living without servants had taught Olwyn well; in a few minutes she had a fire burning in the pit, and was busy laying a pallet in front of it. When a makeshift bed had been laid, she grabbed two blankets, doubled them, and tacked them into place, using the iron pins that had once held the oiled skins taut. Hopefully that would hold in some heat and keep out the winds.

And then, taking a deep sigh of resignation, she turned her attention to the task of moving the man by herself.

She backed the wagon up to the door, and pulling, tugging, swearing, and hauling at the wraps around him, she managed to slide him from the wagon bed down to the ground. Rolling him, she heaved and pushed until he was finally settled on the pallet in front of the fire.

Completely exhausted, Olwyn leaned against his bulk, waiting for her breathing to return to normal. Her belly clenched with hunger, and she needed to get up, get to the wagon, unhitch, feed, and water Nixie, bring food, water, and more firewood into the shelter. But her body would not obey her, and despite her best efforts to stay awake, warmed by the fire and her relief, she fell fast asleep.

* * *

Aidan Mullen became aware of pain before anything
else. His body felt as if it had been badly beaten. Every
single inch of him ached and burned.

Too weak to even open his eyes, smells wove their way
into his senses: fire smoke and earth, tanned furs and
boiled wool, musky incense and sage.

The last thing Aidan recalled was dying. It came back
to him in sickening detailed snippets of memory. The
heaving, rocking ship. The throat that felt as if it were full
of hot, broken glass. The burning fever. The spasms of
wrenching, wracking convulsions. And the gradually
encroaching black shroud of death, numbing him until
there was nothing left.

His body remembered the pain, and he shuddered as the
memories rolled through him.

Aidan slowly began to come more awake. He realized
he was completely naked, his skin prickling with awareness against scratchy wool and silky furs.

His fingers twitched. His foot moved.

And beside him, a person shifted and sat up.

Aidan's heart, already weak, nearly stopped. Where was
he, and who lay beside him?

Aidan held perfectly still, eyes kept closed, feigning
deep sleep. Fingers gently touched his neck, feeling for his
pulse. Hair fell over his face like silk rain, scented with
exotic incense. A cheek pressed against his, soft and most
definitely female.

She whispered in his ear, a quiet, fluid stream of language he did not know, a lilting melody that sounded like
a song. Her voice was sweet and slightly husky, and when
she finished speaking, she sat beside him silently, stroking
his cheek.

Aidan stayed motionless, but inside, his mind spun.

Who was this woman? What had happened after he'd slipped away on the ship? He searched his memory, but there was nothing there but a huge gaping black hole.

It seemed as if he'd died and awoken in another life.

There he lay, nude and covered in furs, before a fire and atop what felt like cold, hard earth. The woman beside him spoke a strange tongue, and touched him all too familiarly.

Before he could muse upon it further, she rose, patting the covers snugly around him before tending to the fire. Aidan slit his eyes, trying to see her through the fringe of his lashes, not wanting her to know he had awakened.

He could only make out her silhouette, limned by firelight. The light stung his sensitive eyes and he quickly shut them, but not before he had noticed her slim form, clothed in garments more suited to the Middle Ages than 1806.

He fought to stay awake, but his fatigue swept over him and he faded again, dreaming of standing stones, ancient fables, and tales told over bonfires of travelers that came from different times.

Chapter Five

Chester, England

Padraig stood in the magistrate's office and tried very hard to listen to the words that were being spoken to him, but he felt as if he were trapped in a nightmare. The men seemed far away, their voices muffled, the meaning obscure. The room was paneled with dark wood, and the walls pressed in on him, suffocating, smothering.

Like a grave.

The words were getting through, however, and Padraig's blood had turned to ice, his skin hot and sweaty.

An outbreak of morbid croup, the man was saying, more than sixty passengers and crew struck, and Aidan amongst them.

Padraig could barely hear the man. Recrimination had his mind spinning.

"In truth, my lord, 'twas such great respect for your brother's station that prevented him being thrown overboard, along with the others who sickened," the magistrate said in a low tone that was obviously meant to be soothing. But Padraig wanted to grab him by the throat and rip out his words before he could speak any more.

The magistrate swallowed heavily before continuing, obviously reluctant to deliver such dire news. "Your brother's remains were handled with the greatest consideration, I assure you, and were kept in his stateroom until the ship docked, at which time he was afforded a space in our city's crypt. We dispatched a notice to your family, but were forced to inter him immediately. Fear of contagion, I'm sure you understand."

Padraig understood nothing, except that the man before him who stank of garlic and body odor was telling him that his twin, his brother, his best friend in the entire world, had perished.

Padraig's hands curled into fists, and though he wanted to battle for his brother's life, there was no one to fight. His heart insisted that Aidan was not dead. He hung onto that thought, the only one that made sense in a world that had suddenly turned to quicksand.

"It can't be true," Padraig whispered, more to himself than to the others in the room. "I would have felt it."

"My lord, I am so sorry," Mira said softly, standing at

his side. She laid a tiny hand on the sleeve of his coat, and Padraig had to restrain himself from swatting her away.

"Leave me," Padraig said harshly. He turned away from them so they could not see the mask of horror that he knew must contort his face.

"*A deartháir, a leathchúpla, a anam,*" he whispered aloud, like an entreaty, a prayer. My brother, my twin, my soul.

There was no life Padraig could envision that did not have Aidan in it. No laughter, no joy, no future.

The magistrate cleared his throat awkwardly. "The letter was sent by messenger just yesterday, my lord. If it arrives on schedule, His and Her Grace ought to receive the missive by Monday."

And Padraig's grief spread through his body like a malignant cancer, eating him alive, slowly killing him. He could see his parents' faces as clearly as if they stood in front of him, and Padraig knew that this was their worst nightmare. It was Padraig's, too.

Questions arose in his mind like smoke from fire: did he suffer? Did he call out for his family? Did he die alone and afraid?

As if reading Padraig's mind, the magistrate reached into his vest and pulled out a letter. "He wrote this before . . ."

Padraig whirled around. The man held out a rolled sheet of paper. With shaking hands, Padraig took it.

Mira wept softly as she stood there beside him, dabbing at her eyes with a lacey handkerchief. Why should the young woman's tears be so enraging? She was Aidan's betrothed, after all, and was entitled to her own grief.

Padraig reached deep for a semblance of manners. He bowed, keeping his gaze averted. "Excuse me. I need to be alone."

Gripping the paper that bore Aidan's last words, he left the office and went outside. The frigid air bit at his face, but he took no note. He wandered a bit, not quite knowing what to do. The parchment was crinkled and dry, and a few days before it had been beneath Aidan's hand. Padraig wanted to read it, but he was afraid. If he read it, Aidan's death would be real.

All around him the city of Chester bustled with afternoon activity. The world seemed normal enough, the streets were ringing with the rattle of carriages and the clopping of horses' hooves on cobblestones. Shopkeepers conducted business, women bought assorted sundries, children played around the legs of their mothers, and somewhere in the distance a dog barked.

Padraig glanced up and down, north to south, east to west. The normalcy of the sunlight seemed an insult. Aidan was dead. The sun should not shine, the birds should not sing, the sky should not be such a beautiful, clear blue. Padraig wanted darkness and rain, whipping winds and pounding, howling storms.

His driver called to him, and Padraig saw that he held the door to the carriage open in invitation for him to take refuge, take comfort.

But there was no such thing in a world without Aidan.

There on the sidewalk, Padraig unfurled the paper. The handwriting was unmistakably Aidan's, and looked like it had been written with a trembling hand. Huge blotches of ink told tale of long pauses.

Tears splintered Padraig's vision as he read.

Father, Mother, Brother,
   It pains me to write this letter, but I fear I am at the end. So many have died already, and I must consider that might be my fate. I want to live, and I'm fighting, but I write this for fear of not saying a few final words to each of you.

This illness has been short and difficult, and as I am weak, so too will this letter be.

Da, I am ever grateful for the father you have been. My respect for you is only exceeded by my love. Forgive me, but I'll ask one more thing of you. At my wake, raise a glass of whiskey and remember the good times. There were so many. I will miss you, Da.

Mum, I'm sorry for your tears. A mother shouldn't have to bury her son, and I'm sorry for it. Always know that I tried to be a good son, to make you happy and proud. You were a wonderful mother, the best in the world. I wish I could kiss you good-bye. I love you, always.

Padraig paused and wiped his face, scrubbing his hand over his streaming eyes. Every word was a dagger stabbing him all over, leaving a million tiny wounds. He forced himself to read the rest, the part intended for him.

The first word made him suck in his breath, as if a heavy blow had just landed against his back. *Dorchadas*. Gaelic for darkness. Aidan was the light, *Lóchrann*. Their father, Rogan, had called them by those names when they were boys, two twins, one with hair as black as night, the other golden, kissed by sunlight.

And it now seemed prescient, for Padraig felt as if a great light had truly gone out.

Dorchadas, I do not know what to say to you, brother. What are words between us, when you and I share our own language? Do you feel this, Pad? Do you feel my suffering now? Will feel me go? I hope not. I hope you are spared that, at least.

Padraig wanted to scream in frustration, because he hadn't felt it, and he knew he should have.

> *If there's one blessing for me in all this, it's that I won't have to live without you. You're going to carry the burden of it, and I'm sorry.*
> *There is no I, nor you. Only us. Death cannot take that.*
> *Live your life well. Live it for us both.*
>
> > *My love to you all,*
> > *Aidan*

Padraig clutched the letter to his chest, and not caring who saw, dropped to his knees in the street, rocking back and forth, sobbing for his brother.

Mira Kimball stood just inside the magistrate's office, watching Padraig through the window. She sighed heavily and dashed away a tear. She touched her ring, a large sapphire surrounded by diamonds, given to her the day Aidan proposed.

Her father glanced down to her, clucked his tongue, and shook his head. "I am sorry, dove."

"Yes," Mira said on another sigh. She shrugged and looked back out the window. Padraig, grief-stricken, keened in the street without a thought to his dignity. As dramatic a scene as it was, Mira did wish he would display a modicum of control.

"My dress," she whimpered, unable to conceal the disappointment that she would never get to wear it. It had been made to her specifications, a sparkling, lacy confection that had been sure to be all the *on dit*.

"You'll find a new beau, and we'll design an even prettier gown. Do not fret, my darling girl."

"'Twill be an eternity," she whined. "I'll have to mourn the appropriate time."

"Right, right," Andrew murmured. He looked over his daughter's shoulder to Padraig. "He really ought to take his grief indoors, wouldn't you say? 'Tis frightfully undignified of him to carry on so."

Aidan's visage swam in Mira's memory, dark blue eyes, burnished gold hair, his face sensual and painfully handsome. She'd wanted him because he was a good match, true, and also because he had a half chance at being the heir to the dukedom. She'd also wanted him because all the other girls that she knew wanted him, too. It had been so delicious, being the first to snag one of the Mullen twins, and call him her own.

But all those selfish reasons aside, she'd enjoyed his company. Aidan had been quick-witted, generous, and his kisses had been scandalously exciting.

"Oh, Papa, he really did die too young."

"He did, he did. Sad. Now let's see if we can't put a smile on your face, darling. What say you to a new bonnet?"

Mira dabbed away the last of her tears and smiled up to her father. He truly was the very best man in the entire world, and Mira knew that no matter what husband she chose, no one would ever be half the man her father was to her. "Yes, that sounds good."

"Come, my dove." Andrew took her hand, settled it in the crook of his elbow, and gave her a series of comforting pats. "You've had a wretched day."

"I have," she agreed, pursing her lips in a pout. Mira looked up to her father's loving eyes. Inclining her head toward the window and Padraig, she perked up marginally. "'Tis sad, indeed, but also somewhat fortuitous. My betrothed is lost to me, but perhaps his brother and I will seek mutual comfort." She lowered her voice as she leaned in, whispering to her father what she knew everyone would be thinking, "At least now we know for certain who is the heir."

The Earl smiled indulgently down on his daughter. He very gently tweaked her nose, and Mira caught the scent of pipe smoke lingering on his glove. "You are a precocious child," he said with a laugh.

"Precocious?" Mira lightly shrugged her shoulders and cast her gaze outdoors once again. Padraig hadn't moved, and even from a distance, she could see his shoulder shaking as he wept.

Mira gave a moment's thought to how she would handle the situation and turn it to her advantage. Her mourning Aidan's loss would give her something in common with Padraig, a bond to tie them together.

And what would all the other girls think, if she'd managed to catch the other twin after her betrothed died? Mira couldn't resist thinking of their jealousy, and she smiled. "I am tenacious, Papa."

Aidan woke again, and to his dismay, his reality hadn't changed. He still lay nude by a fire, the pelts over him smelling faintly of tanning, peat, and incense.

He moved his hand to his side; the woman was not there.

Opening his eyes, he looked around, seeing that he was in a tiny, round structure made of stone and thatch. Blankets covered the windows, and diffused sunlight filtered its way through the fibers, casting the humble room in shadows. The fire threw off some light, and Aidan noticed that a stack of provisions was neatly set along one curved wall.

He pushed himself to his elbows, weak but determined to find out where he was and what had happened to him.

From his elbows he managed to roll to the side, and get up to a seated position.

The fire warmed his naked back as the furs slid from him. And before he could make it to his feet, the door opened and a woman walked in.

She gasped and dropped the kindling she held in her arms. She spoke to him again, a whisper of that strange, fluid tongue. She wore odd garments, a clingy underdress that had wide sleeves belling over her hands, covered with a sleeveless mantle that she had belted around her slim waist. He saw the hilt of a dagger peeking from her wide leather belt, and he had the inkling that the woman knew how to use it.

"Who are you?" Aidan tried to ask, but his voice wouldn't work. What came out was a thin croak of a sound.

The woman rushed inside, hefted a jug, poured him a cup of water, and pressed it into his hand. Aidan drank greedily, water running down his chin as he gulped it in big swallows.

She knelt before him. Her gaze was bold as she looked at him, devoid of coy flirtation or feminine wiles. "I knew you would wake," she said, her voice accented with the lilting melody of the Welsh language.

Aidan lowered his cup, his eyes fixed on her. She was unearthly beautiful, like a medieval Druid from the distant past. Her face was ancient Briton, her chin a tiny point, her eyes wide, heavily fringed with black lashes, and as gray as a storm cloud. She had prominent cheekbones, high and touched with the faintest blush, over milk-white skin. Her mouth, small and expressive, possessed a slight, secretive curve.

And her hair. Aidan had never seen hair quite so black, and streaked with a mark of pure white that ran through the long, wavy spill of it, like lightning slicing across a midnight sky.

"Who are you?" he asked again, and this time his voice did not fail him.

"Olwyn Gawain," she answered. "And you?"

So he was a stranger to her, Aidan realized, or at least she would claim him as such.

And because he felt as if he'd been stripped, literally and figuratively, of everything he knew, he did not give her his real name.

"Lóchrann," he told her, thinking of his brother. Did Padraig have any idea what had become of him? Aidan could only wonder what series of events had landed him in this woman's care. "Have you been caring for me?"

Her eyes dipped down to his bare chest before darting away. He followed her gaze and saw he had a wound, a straight, deep slice over his breastbone.

Looking back up to her, Aidan noticed her blush had deepened. "Who cut me?" he asked.

Olwyn glanced to the fire, and rose to tend to it. "You need to stay warm," she said as she added a square of peat to the blaze. "Are you hungry?"

"Aye, very," Aidan answered, and he was, ravenously so.

He spied a tray with a cup, dropper, and medicines. It also bore tea, honey, and a cup of water. So she'd been caring for him like a babe. Bemused, he touched the cut on his chest. It was coated in a thick medicinal salve.

Olwyn put together a plate of dense speckled bread and poured a puddle of amber honey beside it. She handed it to him, instructing, "Dip the bread in the honey. For strength."

He met her eyes, and this time she blushed and looked away. Aidan was suddenly aware of his nudity.

"I'll make you fresh tea," she murmured, moving to the fire.

He started for a second as he felt the soft, silky fur drape over his shoulders and back. Looking up to the beautiful stranger, he saw that she had her gaze averted as she covered his skin.

"You need to stay warm," she whispered in explanation. "You've been very ill."

The gesture was wifely, her words were caring. And Aidan felt a shameful punch of guilt and lust combined. He tried to ignore it. Turning his attention to the food, he ate everything she'd given him.

She watched, her face reflecting relief and satisfaction, wariness and fear.

His hunger momentarily sated and his curiosity stirred afresh, he asked, "Where am I, and how did I get here?"

Olwyn didn't answer him for a long while, as if she did not know the answer, or chose to not reveal it.

Once again, Aidan had the feeling that he'd traveled through time. There was nothing familiar, save the earth beneath him, fire burning in the hearth, water in his cup, and food on his plate. And like a touchstone, the timeless attraction to a beautiful woman.

"Tell me," he pressed, hoping she would understand how completely unsettling it was to not know what had happened and how he'd gotten there. "I can only recall dying."

Olwyn stopped her tea preparations and sighed. She did not turn to face him, however, and Aidan began to wonder what she was hiding.

"I fear the truth would upset you," Olwyn finally said. "You do not have your strength back."

Aidan felt his temper begin to build. "I've a right to know what's become of me, aye? You'll tell me the truth. Now."

He watched her stiffen, as if he'd slapped her with his words.

Olwyn swung around, her gray eyes piercing even in the dimness of the tiny stone hut. She smiled, a witchy curve of mouth that turned her into a Druid priestess about to cut his heart straight from his chest. "That's a fancy notion, of your having rights, as you sit here naked, defenseless, and weak as a lamb. Settle back, stranger. I'll make you tea, I'll feed you, and when you're well I'll set you free, but in the meantime, I'll not take orders from you."

Chapter Six

Olwyn's hands trembled, but she held them flat against her thighs lest he see and know her nervousness.

"What do you mean, you'll set me free? Am I your prisoner, Olwyn?" Lóchrann asked. He used her given name with a mocking familiarity, as if he tried to bait a further outburst from her.

"My meaning is quite clear. Yes, I saved your life, and when you're well enough you'll be on your way, and I'll be on mine," Olwyn replied with what she hoped sounded like a flat decree. In reality, she was completely shaken to her core. She turned back to preparing his tea, unable to continue looking at him.

Lord, he was magnificent, she thought, a tawny male animal alive with sexuality. The firelight illuminated his hair in shades of gold and amber. Unbound, it hung around his face in soft waves that were streaked with the sun. Its tousled, touchable softness contrasted the hard angles of his face, which had lost every vestige of what she'd perceived as boyish charm whilst he slept. He bore the stubble of several days' growth on his cheeks, and as she'd spoken to him, he'd rubbed a big hand across his stubbly jaw.

No boy, he. And no prince, either, if that meant a man accustomed to being cosseted. This was a man, virile, tall, tightly muscled, and self-possessed.

As for his eyes, she'd seen their color briefly in the dungeon, but he clearly had not been fully awake. She had not noticed then the sensuality found in the dark fringed beauty of Prussian blue so deep and dark they could only be likened to a fathomless lake.

Olwyn had never been alone with a man, but Rhys had spoken often enough of their animal nature. Hadn't she spent the past years locking her door against Drystan's drunken lust?

Now she'd gone and made herself completely alone with a stranger, and a large one, at that. And though he was physically weak, the look in his eyes was anything but.

When Lóchrann got strength back, he would be formidable. He could ravish her. Kill her, even, leave her for dead where no one would ever know where to look for her. She had no idea who he was or where he'd come from, and she berated herself for her foolishness, a mix of maternal instinct for a helpless person, coupled with silly notions of love and affection for a handsome sleeping man.

The water boiled. Her hands trembled as she poured.

Suddenly being closeted in the dim, stony shelter seemed unwise. Olwyn set the tea down beside him without meeting his eyes. "I need something. I'll be back."

She hurried to her feet, lifted her skirts, and all but ran outside. Nixie raised her head and looked placidly at her crazed owner, blinking as if curious to her mood.

Olwyn leaned her back against the wagon, breathing heavily, looking to the sky as if for answers.

What had she done?

There wasn't time to gather her composure. Lóchrann appeared in the tiny doorway, nearly filling it with his broad shoulders and tall frame. He leaned against the doorframe, obviously weak, but just as obviously determined to get an answer from her. Still nude, he clutched a fur around his hips.

And Olwyn's eyes widened at the sight.

His legs were long and muscled, his belly narrow and tapered. The chest that her father had nearly cut open was wide, and looked hard and unyielding. Her eyes traveled up his neck, masculine in its width. And then to his face.

His lips were curled as if in a half smile, his eyes questioning.

"Surely you've seen all God gave me, Olwyn. Why the modest blushes?"

"I played nursemaid, not slut," she snapped. And recalling the touches she'd stolen, felt ashamed.

"I'm not diminishing your care. I live, and I'm grateful for your tending."

Olwyn ducked her head from the disconcerting sight of all that male flesh. He was right—she'd seen his skin. And stroked it. But when he'd been unconscious, she'd not found him so overwhelming. Now, however, she couldn't help but envision every last inch of that body, and the memories made her cheeks burn. "Cover yourself."

"Gladly. Where are my garments?" Lóchrann touched his chest once again, to the cut that her father had made. "And I wore a pendant, also."

Olwyn rummaged in the back of the wagon and withdrew the long, tattered nightshirt, stockings, and cloak she'd stolen from her father. She handed them to Lóchrann without meeting his eyes.

"These are not mine," he said.

"You were nude when I found you," she told him, knowing this would prompt more questions from him, but not knowing how else to explain his lack of possessions. "I saw no pendant."

Lóchrann let out a little laugh, but he didn't sound happy. He held the garments up for inspection, clearly noting that they were made for a man shorter and plumper than himself.

Olwyn stole a glimpse at his face, saw the frustration evident in his expression. He seemed to struggle for a moment to gain his composure, before biting out, "Where, pray tell, did you happen to find me, Olwyn?"

Olwyn opened her mouth to answer, but words failed her. The truth was horrifying. He'd been pulled from a crypt and dumped on her doorstep. Her father was a ghoul and Lóchrann's corpse had been lain out in their dungeon, ready for dissection.

He didn't seem to remember waking in the dungeon.

She could lie to him, and maybe when they parted ways he would remember her as the woman who saved his life, and not the scion of a fiend who'd perched at his side, prepared to sketch his liver.

Lóchrann's mouth flattened. Those dark blue eyes bored into hers, transfixing her. The hand that gripped her father's garments tightened into a fist. "Olwyn. Some truth, please."

He was so handsome. The truth was so ugly.

If she told him, he would be repulsed by her. Just like all the men in her village.

"You were brought to our keep, stripped and presumed dead," she whispered. Lies were for cowards.

"Your keep," he repeated, stressing the latter word with what sounded like disbelief. "Who brought me there?"

Olwyn closed her eyes, took a deep breath, and said, "The resurrection men."

* * *

Aidan fought back a wave of dizziness that swept through his brain, and his legs were so weak they trembled with the effort of standing.

Resurrection men. Yes, he knew who they were and what they did. They were gravediggers who pulled bodies from crypts and graves so they could sell the corpses.

His gaze traveled around the landscape. The rolling hills were stark and lifeless, the trees black and naked against the steely silver-white sky. Above them a hawk glided on a cushion of air, and in the distance he heard its screaming call, a hunter's warning to its prey.

Aidan brought his attention back to the strange woman before him. In the full light of day he saw her beauty, her strangeness. Her eyes were as gray as the sky behind her, like hammered metal. The garments she wore clung to her form in fey, draping swirls and belled sleeves, their smoky shade of plum contrasting her fair skin and black hair. That white streak drew his eye, and seeing his train of vision, she touched it self-consciously.

"Where are we?" he asked.

"Somewhere in England," she replied. He watched as Olwyn's lips trembled. She glanced at the wagon, and then back to him. "Cheltenham, Gloucester, perhaps. I am not certain. But for now, you really ought to go lie down. 'Tis too cold for you to be outside."

"You are traveling?"

"I am."

"Where do you go?"

"South," she replied, as if that were answer enough.

Aidan didn't have much strength left. Soon he would need to go lie down again. And yes, the warmth of the fire beckoned.

Looking at Olwyn, however, he found himself rooted there, caught up in the sensation of being in another time. It felt like he and she were removed from civilization as he'd known it, reduced to stone huts and fire pits carved from the earth.

And Aidan realized he rather liked it, the notion of being in this woman's care, pulled from the grave into a different time and a new life.

For years he'd felt buried, suffocated. His life never felt quite like his own, and the map of his future had been kept from him. Yet Aidan had always felt honor-bound, a slave to it, never free to be his own man, make his own way, and live his own life.

He toyed with the notion of not asking more questions, but just going off with this odd, witchy woman into an unmapped future. He envisioned what that could be like, simple, sensual, stripped to basics.

Everything about Olwyn was mysterious and different, from her clothing to her hair, the way she spoke with such forthright self-possession, and the way she smelled of a hauntingly unfamiliar smoky perfume. Looking at her lips, he realized he wanted to touch them, kiss them. He wanted to ease that pointed chin down and plumb her mouth with his tongue.

Aidan reveled for a moment in the fantasy of burning his past and becoming someone different. No one would know who he was, his titles or his heritage. No one would look at him with that all too familiar glitter of curiosity: which twin is the heir? Which twin will be duke? Questions to which even he did not know the answers.

He could just be Lóchrann.

Olwyn and Lóchrann, two names as ancient as the soil they stood upon, as the humble building behind them, and as the standing stones he saw in the distance.

He imagined what that future could hold: a journey, discovery, primitive attraction. And if Olwyn found herself enamored with him and he her, Aidan would not fight it. He would follow his impulses. He would handfast with her, a ritual nearly lost in an age of published banns and licenses to wed.

Such strange thoughts ran through his mind, driven by a single curiosity: what did her body look like beneath that unusual gown?

Aidan pulled back from his own thoughts in disgust, mentally scolding himself. Where was his loyalty to Padraig, his parents, and his betrothed? Why had he so easily forgotten Mira's gentle sweetness and sunny smiles, spellbound as he was by this raven-haired enchantress?

It seemed impossible. Aidan did not think himself the sort of man whose romantic attentions were easily diverted. He was loyal. Steadfast.

And yet . . .

"Are you some sort of witch, Olwyn?"

She hesitated only the barest second.

"People stopped burning witches a hundred years ago," she answered, her tone brittle. "Surely you don't believe in such nonsense."

"That's not an answer, is it?"

She raised one of her slashing brows. It formed a peak above her eye. "The streak of white in my hair is a birthmark. My mother had it, and her mother before her. 'Tis a family trait, not a mark of Satan."

He suddenly felt foolish, addled by sickness and disorientation. He was behaving as indecorous as his surroundings, primitive and without any veneer of civility. "I apologize. I meant no disrespect."

"I cannot imagine how I took offense," she replied dryly. "After all, you only inquired as to whom I render my worship, the Lord or the Devil. I assure you, sir, the only spirits I consort with are of the distilled variety, though 'tis rare, and always in secret."

Aidan nearly laughed, and though it came in response to his speaking so out of turn, he appreciated her ready wit.

"Truly, I am sorry," he said, and shrugged his shoulders. "Forgive me, but I have awoken in a most unusual circumstance, naked, wounded, weak, and without an idea where I am and how I got here. To be told 'twas the work of gravediggers isn't exactly easing to the mind, aye? I cannot help but wonder why men are bringing you corpses, and why you brought me here."

Aidan watched those fair cheeks of hers turn pink, her gray eyes flinty, and knew that he was touching on a subject as tender as a bruise. He avoided asking all but the most pointed question plaguing him, for his legs were sapped of strength and his heart pounded with the exertion of being upright. "Please, Olwyn, forgive all my many impertinences and tell me this: what year is it?"

Her soft mouth turned up slightly on one side. The witch faded, and in her place stood a young woman, tender with concern. "Have you lost memory, Lóchrann?"

"Aye. No. Not exactly, I don't think." Aidan scrubbed his face with his hand and shrugged his shoulders again. The wintry air made him shiver, but it cleared his head.

He liked the way she called him by his name, and not by formal address. It was unpretentious, uncomplicated. Intimate.

Olwyn approached him. She reached out, as if she would touch him, as if touching him had become natural to her, but then seemed to think better of it. She dropped her hand. "You are cold."

"I am."

"You should go inside, lie down in front of the fire."

"Tell me first."

A slight crease formed between her brows. "'Tis 1806. Now, please, go lie down and get warm."

Regret and relief swamped him in strange emotions.

Yes, he would see his family again, and no, he was not lost in a different world where he knew no one. He was still betrothed to Mira, would wed, and give his parents grand-children.

But the regrets were just as strong. He was Aidan Mullen, and not Lóchrann. He was not going to disappear into a new life with this woman. He would go home and resume his business, his courtship, and see to his future.

Why, he wondered, should that seem disappointing?

"Is that not what you expected?" she asked, studying his expression intently. "What year did you think it to be?"

"Your garb. This shelter. I thought perhaps . . ." he trailed off, unwilling to admit to something so impossibly absurd.

"My garb?" Her cheeks flushed.

"I have not seen its like, is all. I meant no offense. Per-haps 'tis the fashion in Wales?" he said lamely, hating him-self for sounding so insipid. He added, "You look lovely in it. It suits you."

Olwyn ran her hands over her gown, and her face re-flected her emotions, shame, sadness, and weary dignity. "I make my own garments. I am not a skilled enough seamstress to manage anything more intricate than these. I copied their lines from old gowns found in the back of my mother's wardrobe, and altered the gowns that were still serviceable to fit my frame." She lifted her chin in an age-old expression of defiance. "I am far too poor to con-cern myself with what is fashionable, and I've done my best to outfit myself with what meager talents and fabrics I possess."

An awkward silence filled the space between them.

"If you are so much a fool that you do not know better than to take shelter from the cold, I can see how you're so easily confused by outmoded garments," she said finally, her tone betraying her wounded feminine pride.

Olwyn brushed past him and went indoors. She busied herself with tending the fire, leaving Aidan to stand there in the doorway.

He *was* a fool. The cold had him shivering, his skin pebbled with gooseflesh. He ignored the physical discomfort, immersed as he was in a welter of confounding feelings. He realized he was fascinated and uncomfortable and intrigued. Out of his element, out of his depth.

Following that notion, he discovered that for all the odd circumstance, unanswered questions, and his own physical weakness, he'd never felt more alive.

Chapter Seven

Chester, England

A slow, soft rain fell over the people who huddled before a stone crypt, pattering on the slate roof and dribbling down into little gullies that formed tiny muddy moats amid tussocks of grass. The earth smelled fertile and freshly turned, and the gray sky felt closely oppressive. Above them, perched on the bare, knotted arm of a tree, was a huge black buzzard, its volant wings extended in the manner of a raptor mantling its kill. The great bird watched the group as if waiting for them to open the door and reveal the bounty of carrion within.

Padraig Mullen stood without an umbrella or hat, ignoring the wetness. "Open it."

The officials who'd accompanied him hunched underneath their umbrellas, and the one who bore the key to the crypt put up one final fight. "My lord, it is like to be ghastly by now. He's many days dead, and will not bear the look of himself. I warn you once more—this is a sight best unseen by loved ones, and the stench is likely to make you lose your belly."

"I'm likely to lose my temper." Padraig turned a hard stare on the man. "I'll see my brother, and if 'tis him, I'll take him home for a proper burial."

The man fumbled for the key, and as he inserted it and turned the lock, he muttered, "Seal's been broken again, John."

He pulled the heavy, creaking iron door open, and out rolled a wave of musty, putrid smells, mold and dust and rotted skin all together. A few of the men coughed.

Padraig stepped inside. Small motes of dusty light fell over two empty slabs, and a pile of garments were piled haphazardly between them. Bending to inspect the clothes, he saw they were torn in places. As he lifted a shirt that was finely crafted enough to have been Aidan's, a few buttons fell to the slate floor, and a thin gold chain slithered from the bottom, landing on Padraig's shoe.

He picked it up, turned, and faced the men who sheepishly stood in the doorway. Violence seethed in Padraig's blood, and he wished for a sword in his hand, a pistol in the other. But holding to the control that had been as ingrained in them as their honor, Padraig remained calm. He held the gleaming gold chain up for their inspection. "I wear the match to this. 'Twas a gift from our parents."

"The resurrection men," one of the officials spluttered. "They are a scourge! A blight!"

Padraig noticed that the night watchman hung back, his eyes turned away from the accusingly empty slabs.

He tightened his hand on the shirt, wringing it the way

he wanted to wring the necks of the men who goggled at him.

"You there," Padraig said to the watchman, hearing the snarl in his own voice. He didn't care. "You have three seconds to tell me who took my brother's body."

The watchman made a sound in his throat that burbled like a croaking groan. His eyes darted wildly. "I didna see nothing! I was ill that night, shittin' in the privy!"

"Two seconds left."

The man's gaze slid up and down Padraig's form, and he seemed to suddenly notice that the officials had stepped away from him, leaving him to his own defenses. He held up his hands. "I've got a family, me lord."

"One." Padraig's lips flattened and he closed the gap between them. Looking down on the watchman, he could smell the stingingly sharp scent of his sweat. The man's pupils dilated, and his breath left him with an odorous whoosh.

Padraig grabbed the man by the throat and squeezed. Letting go just the barest bit, he whispered, "I could rip your heart out, and no one would stop me."

Then the truth came out in a rush, of the body snatchers and the crazed Welsh anatomist who paid for fresh bodies.

After he was convinced that he had gotten every bit of information the watchman possessed, Padraig strode out of the crypt and back to his waiting mount. He vaulted onto his horse's back. The saddle, slick with cold rain, soaked wetly into his breeches, but Padraig scarcely noticed.

He lifted Aidan's shirt to his face and held it against his eyes, as if it could block the image of his brother's body being desecrated, piece by piece. He breathed deeply, hoping to catch a whiff of Aidan in the cool, soft linen. He could only smell dust and mildew.

A dark, killing rage became a boil in his blood, snaking

through the slippery chambers of his convulsing heart, filling it with a lust for vengeance.

No one disturbed his brother's eternal rest and hacked his body apart as if he were some common criminal. Padraig touched his chest where his medallion seemed to burn against his skin.

This Welshman had begun something that Padraig would be certain to finish.

England

Aidan Mullen took another peek at the leaden sky. He was uncertain how he'd get home, how he'd manage to send word to his family. Not only was he stripped of his garments, but also of any coin, as well. But those were problems for tomorrow. Today he could only focus on how grateful he was to be alive.

The sickness on his ship had killed scores of people, and likely there were those who like Aidan, had succumbed to a coma and were thought dead. Those sad souls had been tossed to the sea to prevent contagion; Aidan, because of his family's titles and power, had left to lie in his berth, stored in a crypt when his body reached his destination.

Aidan felt the pain and shivering of the remnants of sickness and cold. He reveled in those sensations; they were the stuff of life, and he was happy to feel the sting of survival.

He lifted his face to the sky and breathed deeply. A frigid rain began to fall softly, scenting the air with the clean scents of damp, mossy earth and pine trees.

How strange life is, he thought. His life, hanging by the barest thread, had been saved by the most incongruous means—gravediggers.

It brought to mind the letter he'd penned when death seemed certain.

In his mind, he thought hard about his brother, their way of communicating that neither of them quite understood. But always, as babies, as boys, and as men, they'd spoken a certain language that could not be defined or contained. It was as if energy passed between them, unaffected by time or distance. Thinking of this now, he sent a mental message, as strong as he could make it: *I am well, Padraig. Do not worry, Dorchadas. I am alive.*

Turning, he ducked into the tiny stone shelter that had become the makeshift home for him and his strange nurse-maid.

There she was, this woman who called herself Olwyn, tending the fire. The orangey, yellow light made her fine skin glow, and turned her hair into a lustrous black lacquer framing her delicate features. That striking white streak shone like ivory set into an ebony sculpture, and Aidan wanted to touch it, to make it feel real beneath his fingers.

Instead, he dropped his fur, donned the odd garments she'd given him, and reclined by the fire. He pulled a few furs over his legs, lifted his tea, and drank deeply, draining the sweet herbal taste of it.

"'Tis raining," he told Olwyn.

She cast a sidelong glance to the window, and he saw worry shape her features. What a face she had. It hid nothing, each of her emotions as plainly read as the written word. "I've no place for my mare. She's too old to be out in the weather."

"'Tis too small an opening to bring her in here," Aidan said, looking at the narrow doorway and low ceiling. "Can we rig a makeshift shelter for her?"

Olwyn bit her bottom lip and gave it thought. "I've tarps in my wagon. I could maybe drape them over a tree branch, and tether her beneath. With her blankets on, she might be warm enough."

"Aye, that would work." Aidan pushed himself back to his feet. "I'll help you."

She frowned and shook her head. "You're weakened and undernourished. You'll catch your death."

"I've already caught my death, aye?" He grinned at her, and when the ghost of a smile touched her face in return, he winked. "And I lived to tell the tale."

Olwyn looked away from him, and her cheeks flushed lightly.

Aidan felt her discomfort, a palpable thing. "Am I doing something to unsettle you, Olwyn? I assure you, you have nothing to fear from me."

She shrugged slightly, the barest perceptible movement of her shoulders. "I am unaccustomed to the company of men."

"Oh?" Aidan couldn't keep the grin from tugging at his lips again. He was alive, after all. Alive. He swore he would never take such a miracle for granted again. "Have you been locked in a tower, then? For certainly if there were a man within twenty paces of you, he must have wanted a chance to pay court."

Slowly, so slowly, she turned back to meet his eyes. In the dimness of the small stone structure, he could see confusion take over her face, followed by fearful anger. She thought he was mocking her.

"Do you not know you're beautiful?" he asked softly.

"You are far too forward." There was a warning in her voice, but something else in her clear gray eyes. Was it hope?

"You've saved my life. Shall I pay you back with compliments?"

"No," Olwyn whispered. She pulled her cloak over her shoulders, lifted the deep hood, and pulled it up until she disappeared in the cowl. "I need no repayment, and I've no patience for lies."

She hurried from the hut and went out into the rain without seeming to notice it. Aidan followed her, and soon they were working together, lashing the tarps over a tree branch, tethering the old woebegone mare beneath it. Olwyn gathered large rocks and piled them along either sides of the makeshift tent, anchoring the oiled material to the ground. Aidan helped her, but she avoided making eye contact with him. When they finished, she spread thick horse blankets across Nixie's bowed back, and gave her a ration of feed and a bucket of water.

The old mare nuzzled Aidan's arm, and he returned her affection with a few strokes between her eyes and down her long face to the small velvety patch just behind her nose.

"She likes you," Olwyn said, sounding surprised. "She's usually very shy."

"I've a way with animals." Aidan gave the horse a final pat before looking up to assess the sky once more.

Turning to Olwyn, he read the worry on her face.

"We may be here a while," he told her, his breath a cold frost in the air. "Perhaps we should set out traps. We could maybe catch a rabbit."

"And be arrested if we're caught with so much as the hide? Are you some sort of highborn lord that you think you can poach game without recrimination?" She looked at him as if he had sprouted ten heads. When he didn't answer her, she seemed to take that as reply enough. "I've enough food that we'll not starve anytime soon. And we'll leave tomorrow, no matter what the weather," she said flatly, and she turned and walked away.

Chester, England

Padraig stormed into the inn where he'd taken a room. He changed his clothes, strapped on his sword belt and his pistol belt, tossed his cloak over his shoulders. He stopped for a moment, and had the strangest sensation of having his brother's thoughts in his own mind.

The feeling was familiar, and it made him want to weep. If he were going to still have those senses of his brother, Padraig could hardly bear to imagine his future, filled with a million tiny funerals every time something reminded him of Aidan.

Still, Padraig couldn't help but fancy the notion, fleeting though it was, that Aidan was alive and able to send him that peculiar awareness.

Padraig, however, was not the sort of man to engage in wishful thinking. Instead, he sought out the sort of reality he could see, touch, and measure. He wanted answers, not feelings.

Heading through the dining hall of the inn, he nearly mowed down Mira Kimball, who stood in the entranceway.

Mira's mouth formed an O, her pretty blue eyes wide. "My lord, where are you off to?"

Padraig used every ounce of his self-control to keep from pushing her out of his way. "I've got business to attend to, my lady. Please step aside."

"But, my lord, I have incredible news."

"Not now," Padraig bit out. He couldn't help but noticing how lovely she looked in her pale, silky gray gown, trimmed with black lace. He noticed a decided lack of tearstains, and of swollen eyes. Did she care nothing for his brother? Another thought dawned, and he narrowed his eyes. What was the girl up to? "Did you come alone? Where's your maid?"

"Right there," she answered, and her tone suggested

offense that he would think her improper. She gestured to the simply-garbed woman who stood at a discreet distance.

Holding up a yellowed leather-bound book, Mira said, "Do you recall the letter I showed you in Warwick? Well, I had found a few of these old journals in some crates in our attic, and I brought them on my travels so I would have something to read at night."

Padraig stared at her, slightly agog that she would continue pattering away about her family history in the light of all that had occurred. Did it matter nothing to her that Aidan was dead?

Mira continued on, her face glowing with satisfaction, "'Tis incredible, my lord. You see, I brought a carton of papers and journals from Warwick, so I'd have something to occupy me in the evenings, and it has yielded the most interesting findings!"

She held out the old, tattered book as if she were presenting it to a king. "This is the journal of Bret Kimball, the same one who your great-grandmother, Amelia Bradburn, summoned to your family's home in Southampton. And even more intriguing is that my great-uncle was apparently promised to wed your grandmother, Camille Bradburn."

"That's nice," he said tightly. Padraig moved past her.

She reached out and touched his cloak. "Are you not interested at all?"

Padraig swung back around, and the bloodlust that sang through his body must have shown on his face, because Mira gasped and took three steps back.

"My brother is gone, and my thoughts are consumed with my grief. I can't seem to summon an inkling of interest in your petty dabbling into the past, and your insipid nattering about a marriage that quite obviously never occurred." Padraig bowed slightly, and trying to hang onto the barest vestige of control, said, "Do not speak of this nonsense to me again. My brother, *your betrothed,* is dead, and as such we will not be family after all. So forgive me for saying so, but I cannot fathom what he ever saw in you in the first place."

Mira's face reflected her shock, but it quickly faded and her eyes took on that same glitter as the day she'd shown him her museum. It was the look of a woman who showed far less than she felt, and for that alone Padraig felt a stab of pity for her.

"Well, my lord, you've certainly made your true feelings known, haven't you?" she said softly, and that shine in her eyes took on a nasty light. However, her tone was as sweet as always when she said, "'Tis my turn to beg forgiveness. Perhaps you and I grieve differently. 'Twas only a wish to distract myself from the pain of losing Aidan that had me reaching for the diversion of my hobby. I am sorry I bothered you."

The meekness of her words did nothing to soften that light, nor did it detract from the brackets that formed at the corners of her lips. Mira Kimball was quite obviously not accustomed to being spoken to in such a manner.

Padraig mentally apologized to Aidan. This was certainly not how his brother would have wanted him to treat the woman he was going to marry.

"My lady," he began lamely. "My own grief is making me act like a madman. Your pardon, please, for my brutish words. My brother would have called me out had he heard me speak so unjustly to his beloved."

Mira's expression softened; the glitter in her eyes did not. "'Twas rude of me to come to you with such triviality."

"No, you'd had the right of it, thinking to give me a diversion from my grief." Padraig didn't think he'd ever lied so boldly. He gestured to several men who'd gathered out on the street, thick thuggish men in seamen's garb. "Excuse me, my lady, but I've my own form of distraction to see to. Good day."

"Make it up to me," Mira said softly.

"Pardon?"

"You could join me for dinner." Mira smiled invitingly. She held the journal in her hands in such a way that Padraig caught the glint of the ring Aidan had given her, worn over her lacy glove.

"My lady," he began, but she cut him off.

"Not tonight, of course." Her smile deepened, and she reached out to pull an invisible piece of lint from his cloak. "You'll just owe me, my lord."

Padraig managed to extract himself from her presence, wondering once again what Aidan had ever seen in the girl. There was something about her demeanor that discomfited him, an edge to her smiles, and that glitter in her eyes. Mira Kimball struck him as a woman whose beauty veiled a dark ugliness inside.

Dismissing the girl from his thoughts, Padraig headed outside and joined the men he'd asked to accompany him to the Welshman's keep. There were three of them, well muscled, well armed, and well paid. Together they would see to it that the anatomist gave up his secrets.

Penarlâg, Wales

Smoke hung like a fat angry cloud over the ancient, crumbling keep, darker than the gray stormy skies. The winds blew hard, freezing, wet, and gusty, carrying whiffs of the burning bonfire to Padraig and his men.

Padraig recognized the stench; it hit him in the gut, turned his stomach, and made him instantly enraged. He kicked his mount into a thundering gallop, urging the beast on as he pulled his pistol.

The winds blew hotter as he drew closer, throwing bits of ash and bright red cinders high into the air, swirling, whipping eddies that reeked of burning human hair and flesh.

And Padraig knew with a terrible certainty that if his brother were in that bonfire, he'd slaughter the Welshman and throw his body in alongside Aidan's. Justice would be served in their own private Gehenna.

Padraig reined in the stallion as they reached the gates to the property, but the animal had seemed to sense his bloodlust. It pranced and snorted, reared up on its hind legs, and scraped at the sky.

As if summoned by hell's own messenger, an old man came flying from the keep. He wore ragged outer garments, outmoded breeches, and shoes made of animal skins. His hair was long and wild and silver, his black bushy eyebrows drawn into a deep scowl. He had the look of a crazed eremite, waving his arms in the motion of pushing them back.

"Begone," he screamed. "Get off my land! Begone, begone!"

Padraig waited for someone else to come, someone to be drawn to the ruckus the man made. But there was silence behind him.

The blackstone building must have been a thousand years old, and bore the signs of years of neglect. What had once been huge ramparts were now rutted and pitted, the fallen stones returned to the earth to be slowly reabsorbed. A huge portcullis listed against one tall wall, once a daunting fortification barring entrance to an intimidating dwelling, but now nothing more than a trellis for climbing vines.

Padraig leveled his pistol at the man, cocked it, and

hoped the fool was not so addled as to no longer understand mortal danger. "I know everything the night watchman in Chester's kirkyard knew," he warned him. "You bought my brother's corpse. I'm here to reclaim his body."

"Gone! She's gone, and he with her! Where is Olwyn? My Olwyn, my girl." The man hopped and danced like a puppet on strings, his madness causing him to tear at his hair. He suddenly stopped, frozen in mid-motion. His black eyes widened, and he looked as if he were going to drop over dead of apoplexy.

"Are you well, man?" Padraig demanded. "Do you hear me? I'm here for my brother's body."

"Gone," the man whispered. "Gone, gone, gone. Everyone's gone."

He dropped to his knees, and rocked back and forth. His gnarled fingers slid back into his hair, slowly twisting, pulling. A long, low moan came from his throat, a strange singsong chant in his lilting Welsh tongue.

Another man emerged from the keep. He was disheveled, dirty, and had the thick nose and watery eyes of a drunk. He must have been tending the bonfire, for his sleeves were singed and his shirt bore sooty smears.

"Your brother isn't dead," the man said. "His body was brought here, intended for autopsy, but he was alive. The woman of the house, this man's daughter, took him and fled."

Padraig lowered his pistol. "My brother lives," he said softly. He remembered the sense he'd had, the feel of Aidan, and relief had his heart thudding hard against his breast. "Of course," he said to himself. "Aidan lives."

"I don't know where she took him," the man said simply. "She has only one horse, an ancient nag that won't take them far. She has your brother in a wagon, and took provisions." Inclining his head to the wildly muttering madman, he added, "Mercy for him, please, my lord."

"Forget it. I care only about finding my brother."
Padraig scanned the horizon. There was a storm coming,
but it would not stop him. He'd send word to his parents and
gather trackers. Wherever Aidan had been taken, Padraig
would find him.

Chapter Eight

England

Night drew in around the hut, a thick shroud of black
without so much as a single star to break its absoluteness.

Olwyn's teeth chattered as she tried to keep her back
from touching the stone wall. She huddled beneath a fur
and a woolen blanket, but they felt thin and inadequate
against the damp, frigid wind that blew easily through the
cracks.

The fire burned low; they did not want to risk too much
of their provisions. Lóchrann sat in front of it, the flickering light sending licks of shadows and burnished gold
across his face in equal measure. She saw his frown, the
narrow look he sent her way.

"Olwyn, I'm finished with asking you to come share
this meager warmth. You'll come sit beside me, or by God
I'll drag you over by your hair."

"Try it."

"You'll dare me?"

"Aye," Olwyn said, trying to keep her teeth from rattling together like a child's toy.

"I wish you wouldn't. I've no wish for things to grow unpleasant between us."

"I'm fine here," she managed to say between clenched teeth. "Don't think to manhandle me or you'll test my blade."

Lóchrann changed tactics. He cocked his head to the side, and Olwyn wondered if he knew how handsome he looked with the firelight shifting through his dark, gold hair. "What is wrong with you?"

"Nothing."

"You're behaving very strangely."

"We aren't acquainted well enough for you to make that claim."

Lóchrann shifted and turned the full weight of his regard to the fire. He poked it with a thin stick, stirring up glowing embers and causing the flames to flare up. Olwyn watched as he clumsily laid another square of dried peat on the top. It smoldered then, banked for the moment in a way that could cause it to burn out.

"You did it wrong," she said, and she heard the incredulousness in her tone. What sort of man could not lay a proper fire? "You must allow some air to circulate."

Lóchrann moved to the side, gesturing to the pit. "I've never burned peat before. Show me how, Olwyn."

Unwilling to risk what little warmth they had, she scooted forward and knelt in front of the fire. The warmth touched her like sunshine, like life, and she knew she was daft to stay away from the heat that she needed.

But he was large and male, and his presence unnerved her. She'd seen him naked. She'd nursed his body, fed him drops of honeyed water like an infant. She'd cradled his head in her lap, stroked his hair, and confessed her darkest secrets and fears.

She had not, however, been prepared for him to wake and be so virile, so alive.

"Like this." Using two long sticks, she adjusted the dried pungent square so that it would not smother the embers beneath it. "Are you so rich, then, that you burn nothing but wood?"

Lóchrann laughed a bit. "Well, I got you by the fire, anyway."

So he'd played her as a fool. Before she could react, his hand grasped her upper arm and held it in a grip from which she knew she could not break free. So much for sickness. She turned her head away, staring into the darkness so he could not see the effect he had on her.

"Stay by the fire," he commanded softly. "I will not have you freeze in the corner rather than sit beside me. Look at me," Lóchrann urged her. "In my eyes. Look at me."

He shook her a bit, gently enough, but with an urgency that she felt in her bones. Olwyn dragged her gaze to his face, and yes, she met his eyes.

In the dim light, they glistened dark and limpid. The slant of them was compelling, fringed by long lashes beneath slashing brows. He had a sensual languor in his eyes, belied by the strength and insistence of his hand on her arm.

"I see I unsettle you."

Olwyn hadn't had a friend since her brother died, hadn't had a kind heart to trust in since her mother left, hadn't had a single soul in the world to view her as something other than evil since the villagers found out what went on in her father's keep. Neither had she had a suitor. Ever.

And so she said nothing, her silence her only protection. If she were to speak, the truth might come pouring out.

Unsettled? How about undone, uncertain, and unnerved? He was attractive to her in a way she feared, and she had a painful longing for him to think well of her, to maybe respect her in a way, and yes, perhaps to even grow to like her.

"We're strangers of a sort, true," Lóchrann continued. "You have no reason to trust me. But I give you my word, you will not come to harm. I owe you my life, and I'll repay that debt in full, of that you can be certain. I'd lay mine down before I let anything happen to you."

His word shouldn't mean anything to her. It was true. They were strangers. Olwyn had no cause to think him honorable, no reason to trust him. But she saw no threat in those dark blue eyes, felt no violence in the warm, strong hand that held her arm.

In fact, she felt only his heat and vitality.

"Let go of me," she whispered. He did, with a sudden release. Her arm grew colder again. She glanced back to her chilly, dark corner. Returning to it was insanity. "I suppose it only makes sense that we share the heat."

Lóchrann lifted the corner of the furs that he had draped over his legs. "Share all of it, Olwyn. Let's see if we can keep from freezing to death, aye?"

Capitulation didn't come easily to Olwyn, but neither did stupidity. Giving in, she slid beside him and let him tuck the blankets and furs around them.

"I've questions for you, Olwyn."

The words inspired dread in her. He must have felt her stiffen, because he sighed heavily and decided to relent. "Very well, never mind for tonight. I've no wish to chase you back into the corner. Stay here, and I'll leave the subject alone."

She relaxed marginally, grateful for the reprieve. With the combined heat of the fire and the furs and the man beside her, she began to slowly thaw. Her feet, once frozen numb, began to prickle with a thousand stings of returning blood flow.

Lóchrann leaned into her a bit, shoulder to shoulder, arm to arm, hip to hip. Warmth that had nothing to do with the fire touched her skin.

"Are you tired?" she asked.

"I've slept enough, aye? An eternity."

"I suppose," she answered, all too aware of the size of him beside her. He felt so big, so present. It seemed as if the hut was full of him. Lóchrann's form was so tall and brawny, a man with a handsome face and a tough body. How had she ever managed to move him? she wondered, even as a strange pride filled her. The arm touching hers was hard with muscle, making her very aware of her own thin build and lack of defenses.

She'd saved this man's life.

He swore she was safe with him because of it. Olwyn relaxed further. Yes, she believed him.

Olwyn cast a sidelong glance his way. Spotting it, he met her eyes for a brief moment before looking away.

"I suppose we could get to know each other a bit," Lóchrann offered. "I know nothing of you but your name."

He shifted his blankets and she felt the press of his thigh against her own. She thought of when he'd been unconscious, and how she'd lain with him to warm his body with her own. It had been practical then. Now, however, practicality was the furthest thing from her mind.

"There's not much to tell, I'm afraid," Olwyn said, and felt a kick of pride at how calm she sounded, as if she had nothing at all to be embarrassed about, and as if touching a man were the most natural thing in the world. "Why don't you tell me about yourself?"

The question was more than just a polite invitation for him to make conversation. Lord, she wanted to know everything, she realized. She wanted to know who he was,

where he lived, what sort of life he'd made for himself.
Was he married, did he have children? What had he been
like as a child? Favorite foods, favorite colors, favorite
books. She wanted every bit of it, and more.

Mentally she taunted herself. *So needy, Olwyn. How
desperate. How pathetic.*

She had, quite obviously, been lonesome for far too long
a time.

There came a long pause. He seemed to be weighing his
response.

"Same here. Nothing to tell, really." Lóchrann laughed
a bit, a rueful sound. "Surely we both can't be this unin-
teresting."

He's hiding something, she thought. Well, wasn't everyone in some way or another?

"How about you tell me where you're traveling to,"
Lóchrann said.

The rain found tiny slips to filter through, dripping to
the floor to form tiny puddles. A small drop plopped on
her shoulder, and she scooted slightly over, closer to the
fire.

Olwyn deflected Lóchrann's suggestion with one of her
own. "We should choose a neutral topic. Aren't they usually about the weather and road conditions?" He turned
again to meet her eyes. This time, he held her gaze, lambent flames reflected in his lambent eyes, a mesmerizing
sight if she'd ever seen one.

"I despise chatter," he replied mildly.

She laughed nervously. "Well, now I know something
about you."

"Aye, you do. If the conversation's to be such drivel, let's
just not have it."

"I have a better idea," she whispered before she could
change her mind. Caught in the thrall of his beautiful eyes
and his demand for her to choose between truth or silence,

she said, "Plain talk, no secrets, no lies, and no equivocation. And when we go our separate ways, we'll both remember that for the space of a few days, we spoke our
minds and we hid nothing. How many people do you think
ever really do that? We'll tell the truth, no matter how ugly,
painful, or humiliating."

He smiled, a long, slow, heart-stopping spread across
his face. His face was like a fairy-tale hero of yore,
strongly featured, golden, and sensual. He was masculine
and yet beautiful, putting her in mind of an animal that can
exude power, and yet invite a soft touch, all at once.

And the idea that she might be privy to the thoughts
behind those eyes stole her breath. If all she had to do was
bare her own truths in return, it would be worth the cost.

"That's quite a suggestion, Olwyn."

"Yes, isn't it?" Heat stung her cheeks, regardless of the
frigid temperature. A ludicrous thought ran through her
mind: humiliation, the cure for freezing to death. But she
would not show her embarrassment. She would behave as
boldly as the words she had spoken. Mimicking the way he
smiled at her, she curved her own lips in what she hoped
resembled a dare. "Too forward for your taste, Lóchrann?
Perhaps chatter is looking better?"

"So much for the girl who cowered in the corner," he
said with a laugh.

Such a resonant voice he had, pleasing to hear, deep,
rich, smooth. His laugh filled the hut, and warmed her to
the tips of her ears.

"Who will start?" he asked.

"Because it was my idea, I'll go first." She took a
deep breath and plunged right into the truth as if it were
a bottomless, fathomless pool. "I have not been able to
forget that you called me beautiful."

The look in his eyes shifted, turned thoughtful. "Did
you like me saying it?"

"I did." She feigned only her bravery. Everything else was pure truth, in its rawest form. "But it frightened me, too."

"Why did it?"

"I am not sure," she whispered. "Perhaps because I wanted it to be true, but also I feared that you said it only to manipulate me."

"In truth, I find it hard to keep from staring."

Olwyn dropped her eyes to her lap where her hands were tightly clasped. Lóchrann touched her chin with his forefinger and thumb, gently tilted her face back up.

"Don't hide."

"I think it is your turn," she whispered.

"Very well, I'll tell you something real. I thought I'd awoken in another time. 'Tis why I asked you the year." Lóchrann's expression changed, turned pensive for the barest second. His voice grew very quiet, and never breaking his gaze, he said, "I wasn't sure what answer I wanted to hear more."

"Do you not like your life as it is?"

He shrugged, lifted his hand, and then dropped it. "A new life has a certain appeal."

"So if it had been true, and you'd awoken in another time, what sort of man would you recreate yourself as?"

"A swordsman—I'm good with a blade. Perhaps a soldier, then." He thought about it further. "No. Not that. Maybe what I'd really want is to live on a mountain somewhere, far from civilization. Build a cottage, have dogs and horses, hunt with hawks. Grow a garden, live simply. Most of all, be free. Completely and totally free." He smiled at his own fancy, and added, "Of course, I'd have to try to lure a woman into thinking it romantic so she'd stay with me. I'd want to live simply, but not as a monk."

"You aren't married, now?"

"No. Not yet. I'm engaged to be. We are set to be married this June."

"Oh." Why should that surprise her? she wondered. She tried not to show her disappointment. After all, she mocked herself, did she really think a man like Lóchrann would be unattached? Women must throw themselves at him.

Indeed, there was much to recommend him that he had found a woman with whom to settle down. A man such as he could easily have descended into decadence, pursuing only pleasures as they appealed to him.

The woman who'd captured his heart must be someone quite special, Olwyn thought. So why should that make her feel so sad, so lonesome, and so bitterly let down?

"Do you love her very much?" she whispered.

He frowned and shrugged. "'Tis a difficult thing, that."

"What could be difficult about love?" Olwyn allowed herself to sound every bit as wistful as she felt. "Someday I hope to have it for myself."

"'Tis complicated."

"How so?"

Lóchrann blew out a little breath. "Honesty, aye?"

Olwyn lifted the corner of her mouth and shrugged. "Unless 'tis too much for you."

Aidan grinned at her dare, warming to Olwyn's game of honest talk. There were not many people with whom Aidan spoke so truthfully. Even Padraig had become distant of late, perplexed and annoyed with his engagement to Mira Kimball.

"I am nearly thirty years old, about time for a man to marry, aye? Time to find a suitable wife, settle down, have children. I met Mira, and she is . . ." Aidan shrugged and finished lamely, "suitable."

"That's it? No passion, no love?" Olwyn's brow raised again, formed the sharp, witchy peak that was becoming familiar to him. "That's pathetic."

"There are other things to look for in a mate. She is kind and sweet and gentle. She loves her own family the way I love mine, with pride and boundless affection, and she does not ask me . . ." Aidan stopped.

"Doesn't ask you what?"

"Doesn't ask me for anything," he finished, and reviled himself for not living up to the demand for complete honesty.

But he was so tired of the question of who would be the duke, and yes, he was tired of not knowing the answer himself.

He did not know who was firstborn, he or Padraig. He did not know which of them was their father's true heir.

And yes, he admitted to himself, he resented his parents for keeping it secret from them.

"Is she beautiful?"

"She is pretty," Aidan said, and picturing Mira, continued, "As fair as a princess, with golden hair and blue eyes. She is delicate, feminine, and reminds me of a tiny doll that could break with the slightest misuse."

"Oh." Olwyn dropped her gaze to her lap again.

"You don't like that answer?"

"Is it true?"

"Aye."

"Then how can I find fault with it?"

Aidan touched Olwyn's hands, tightly clasped on her lap. Had he offended her feminine pride? His uncle Matteo had told him long ago that when speaking to a woman, a man must treat her as if she were the only woman in the room, the only woman in the world. Feeling clumsy, he asked, "You wanted honesty, aye?"

The fire burned low and filled the small, damp room

with its fragrant smoke. Icy rain pelted the thatch and stone, and cold wind seeped though every crack. It should have been an uncomfortable and unpleasant way to spend a night, but strangely, it wasn't.

He heard Olwyn sigh, long and deep. She lifted her head and raised her hands up, displaying them for Aidan's inspection.

"These hands know real toil. They slaughter chickens, they scrub floors, they haul water, they wash clothing, and they hoe fields. I am more work mule than pretty doll, and I cannot fathom a man fearing he might break me. I am far too hardy, I suppose, to be likened to a princess." Olwyn smiled, a sad curve of her lips that trembled as if she held back great emotion. She opened her mouth to speak several times before she could manage to get the words out. "That's not to say that I wouldn't fancy such a thing."

Aidan tried to picture Mira doing anything more taxing than reading a book, and he had to suppress a laugh. "Well, I have to say, Olwyn, that if given the choice of whose hands I'd have wanted to place my life in, I'm glad I fell into yours."

"I am a fool," she whispered. "I have run away from my home, and I have nowhere to go."

"I'll help you. You've saved my life, and so I'm in debt to you, aye?"

"You owe me nothing. I did it for my own conscience."

"Well, that may be, but I'm not a man to neglect my obligations. I'll do whatever I must to see to it that you're compensated and well taken care of." And mentally he jeered at himself. Isn't that what he always did? The right thing.

Olwyn sighed again. She glanced from the fire to the draft blowing past the oiled tarp over the window, to the dark corner where she'd huddled to keep herself from him. Her voice was small and low as she said, "'Tis a night for spirits, no?"

Before he could say anything, she rose from the nest of blankets and rummaged through the provisions. She returned with a bottle and a cup made of thick earthenware. "As long as we're being honest, I consort with this spirit far more often than you'd think. It warms me on cold, damp nights such as this. We'll have to share the cup. I only have one."

He watched as she uncorked the bottle and poured a healthy draught. The smell rose to fill his sinuses, the woody, malted scent of Scotch whiskey. Olwyn handed it to him, and he gave it a swirl, a sniff, and a full sip.

"Ahhh," Aidan said, deep in his throat. It was good; balanced, sweet with cherrywood and oak, a touch of peat deep in the finish. "I could kiss you for this."

Olwyn blushed a little, betraying her uneasiness, and reached to take the cup from him. "Not necessary."

She, too, sipped long and deep, and Aidan smiled. He couldn't ever recall seeing a woman drink hard liquor with such easy delight, as if it were watered wine or sugared tea.

"Where did you get this?" Aidan asked. He had a passion for whiskey, and had been making his own for more than ten years. This particular batch was smooth and even, well blended and well aged. "'Tis quite good."

She cast a narrow look at him. "You're making judgments against me, aren't you? Too poor for firewood or fashionable gowns, but in possession of fine whiskey."

"Were you me, wouldn't you be curious?"

She pursed her lips as if annoyed. "I didn't steal it."

"Did you hear an accusation in my question?"

"I make good trades with a man who comes to our keep," Olwyn relented without answering his question, a sign of stubbornness and reason combined. It made Aidan smile, reminded him of himself and his brother.

"The man is a traveling trader, and has a large wagon filled with textiles, peat, iron pots, bags of spices, medicines, and the like. Whatever makes for a good trade. And yes, of course, he always has a few bottles of whiskey. He usually comes once each season, and I am ready for him with cheese, baked goods, and chickens."

Olwyn's mouth curved up on one side, and he saw she was regretful. "He is a nice man. I will miss him."

"You'll never go home again?"

She met his eyes over the rim of the cup as she sipped. She handed him the whiskey and then raised a brow. "Not if I can help it. But if my father finds me, I imagine I'll be beaten and dragged back."

"I told you I would protect you."

"He's my father. You'd have no right to interfere."

"I'd make it my concern," Aidan said flatly. "If things were troublesome enough that you'd run away in winter, carting a half-dead man along with you, I don't guess you're making much ado about nothing, aye?"

She shrugged and glanced at the whiskey in his hand. Aidan obliged her, taking his sip and handing it back.

"Will you tell me why you ran away?"

Olwyn drank again before she set the cup down to their side. She fiddled with the fur wrap that covered her, petting it as if it were a live animal.

He watched her long fingers, slim, graceful, buried in the fur, and a pang of lust hit him below his navel, a tight, hot arousal that reminded him that he was very alone with a beautiful woman, and also very engaged to another.

"Is our time for honesty over?" he pressed.

She ceased her petting, met his eyes. She spoke so softly that her voice seemed like nothing more than a sigh, a thin wisp of a confession. "I could tell you of the horrors—there were more than a few. But beneath it all, I left because I was lonely."

Chapter Nine

"Tell me why," Lóchrann invited.

His voice, so seductively deep and reassuring, entreated her to give voice to her burden, to lay it down. He promised to help her, to protect her. Looking at him now, so big and undeniably, vigorously male, she believed he could, believed he would.

Olwyn lifted her cup and drank again, from the place where his lips had touched. The whiskey was warming her, limbering her muscles, lightening her mood, loosening her tongue.

So she would tell him the truth. What did it matter? Soon enough they would part ways. She would never see him again.

"Until I was twelve years old, my life was unremarkable. Father, mother, brother. We were normal enough, if perhaps not a little eccentric. My mother saw to our education, my brother and me, and she was a great lover of books. She instilled that in us. The keep was a happy place, and we owned the surrounding land, had many renters, enough to provide us with a good life."

Olwyn spun the cup in her hands. Aidan gestured to it, and she handed it to him, watched as he drank. He lowered the cup then, and she saw the whiskey glisten on his lips.

She wondered what that might taste like, the man and

the whiskey combined. She licked her own lips, an involuntary motion.

Best not to dwell on such things. He was promised to be married.

She swallowed heavily and continued. "And then my brother took ill and died, and my father was never the same. He couldn't save him, you see. Couldn't do anything but watch as his life faded."

"And then things changed?"

"An understatement, if ever there were one," Olwyn said on a breath. "My father became a man obsessed, driven to find the reason people age and die, determined to find the link between life and death."

Flashes of memory came unbidden, vividly colored images of eviscerated corpses, buckets filled with innards, brains suspended in fluids. The dungeon's stink filled her nose, death and rot and filth. She shivered uncontrollably, recalling in unwanted detail rats the size of cats, and roaches as long as her hand, huge from feasting on human remains.

She summed up things for Lóchrann the best she could. "Our lands were sold off, the help dismissed. My mother, disgusted, frustrated, and unhappy, abandoned us. I was trapped there, and out of necessity became a cook and a servant, a seamstress and a gardener. Every last bit of our money was spent on corpses, bodies stolen from graves and crypts so he could take them apart, bit by bit, in the nightmarish pursuit of the most impossible quarry. The soul."

Lóchrann's expression was one of incredulity. "This is why I was brought there? To be examined in this way?"

Olwyn nodded, lifted the whiskey, and drank. Lóchrann took the cup from her and drained it. Olwyn poured more, this time nearly filling it. It was a good night for it, and they both drank more, sharing it until the cup was empty again.

"You don't remember?" she asked. "You woke."

"Maybe." He frowned, searching his memory. "How awful for you," he managed to say, clearly trying to regain his composure. He ran a hand through his hair, then across his face. Looking down, he touched the wound on his chest.

Olwyn laughed then, a wry, sad sound. She was becoming drunk, she knew, but she didn't care. Instead she courted the numb warmth by pouring yet more whiskey. She was speaking of things that were vile and humiliating, but she barely felt the familiar shame. It came out so easily when whiskey paved the path. "That was far from the worst of it."

"What was the worst?"

"The villagers found out, and word spread quickly. Suspicion, fear, and superstition had their way, and rumors were started. I was said to be a witch." Olwyn watched Lóchrann's face, wishing she could read his mind. But now that she was talking about that which she'd only ever felt, she could not find it in her to stop.

It poured out, all her fears and loneliness and hurt. "The children I grew up with would not even look at me. They crossed the street when I approached. They threw things at me, garlic and stones. Women pleaded aloud to God to spare the village from me, and the men said I was Satan's whore."

"Such ignorance and cruelty," Lóchrann whispered.

"Are you so different? You took a look at me and thought me a witch," Olwyn reminded him. "I ran away because I thought that perhaps I could make a new life elsewhere, and that maybe without the stigma of my father's obsession, I might find a place to call my own. But when you thought it of me, without even knowing the truth of who I am, I realized that I am a fool to think anything will be different."

Strangers would still think her odd and suspicious. She would never, it seemed, be free of it.

Olwyn raised a hand to her hair. "I am marked."

"You are beautiful," Aidan told her, and he meant it. She had the northern Celtic structure in her face, pure and finely boned.

But as lovely as her face and form were to look upon, they were galvanized by her manner and her demeanor. She spoke with such elegant straightforwardness, as if it did not occur to her to equivocate.

And while she told him of why she'd run away, Aidan could only imagine how she'd managed to take his unconscious body with her. He must outweigh her by double. Though she was fairly tall, she was slight of build and very thin, her bones in her face and shoulders clearly delineated.

Olwyn Gawain was, quite obviously, a woman of incredible determination.

He could scarcely imagine the life Olwyn had led, and how lonely and frightening it must have been. Aidan had been raised with his mother's gentleness and his father's firm guidance. He'd never known anything but love and acceptance.

And as the son of a powerful, wealthy duke, he'd been welcomed wherever he'd gone, had always had whatever he needed, and had never had to worry for a single moment about his future and his place in it.

Compassion and admiration for the young woman before him took seed and grew. Olwyn was fierce and gentle, and altogether strong.

Perhaps it was the whiskey, or maybe it was gratitude and respect for her, Aidan didn't know. But he wanted badly to kiss her, to taste those small, perfect lips, to watch her gray eyes go soft and close in sensation.

Olwyn seemed to sense it, because she leaned forward, closer to him. "I am cold," she said softly, as if in explanation.

"We should share our warmth. It will only get colder through the night." Aidan moved closer and pulled the blankets tighter around them. He put his arm around her, and she snuggled up to him. He realized she had drunk too much, for her head lolled against his chest.

"I think I ought to lie down," she said.

"Yes," he agreed. "The hour feels late."

Aidan made adjustments to their nest of blankets and furs, laid another square of peat on the fire, and settled in beside her.

Olwyn immediately fit herself against him, and Aidan had a shadow of a memory, as if his body knew the woman better than he did. The whiskey had definitely had its way with her. Gone was the shy, uncertain woman who'd hidden in the dark, cold corner to avoid him. He heard the change of her breathing. She slept.

She molded against him without reservation. He wondered if she had shared her body heat with him when he was unconscious, just as she did now. The thought stirred a curious sensation in his chest. More tenderness for this woman. He tightened his arms around her and held her closer still.

Against him, her body felt taut and lithe, vastly different from the soft, pampered women he'd held. Women like Mira, who had never known labor.

Mira. Her image came into his mind. Golden, fair, refined, always smelling so sweetly of flowers and powder. She was delicate and kittenish, fragile and helpless.

As long as he was admitting truths to himself, he acknowledged that he didn't quite believe Mira wasn't cunning enough to recognize that marrying Aidan was a gamble with fifty-fifty odds.

Aidan lowered his face to Olwyn's hair, inhaled the scent of incense, peat smoke, and whiskey. She smelled elemental, earthy, and real. And as he held the length of her to his body, he couldn't help but notice that she felt supple, tensile, and tempting.

She stirred, made a quiet sound of contentment in her throat. His testicles tightened as if she had touched him there. Yes, his body knew her.

Eyes closed, Olwyn tipped her head back and smiled up at him, every muscle in her body as malleable as potter's clay. "Lóchrann," she murmured.

"Go back to sleep, Olwyn."

"I have been alone so long."

"You're not alone now."

"I will be," she whispered. She sounded sad, resigned. She shook her head, eyes still closed, a stubborn shake. "I am not a witch."

"I know you're not."

"If I were, I would cast a spell on you." She laughed softly, shifted her body, and lay full against him. "You would stay with me."

Aidan stroked her hair, and soon she fell silent again, her breathing slowing. Her hair was silky and fragrant. He touched the streak that shone brightly, like argent set into onyx.

Surely there must be a man he knew who would take her to wife, and give this resourceful, unusual woman the sort of life she deserved.

Aidan mentally ran through his male acquaintances. Perhaps he could find someone who'd see in Olwyn the same beauty and strength that he did, and who would find her just as compelling.

Perhaps even Padraig.

He promised himself he would try to find someone for her, even as he inwardly mocked himself. Playing matchmaker, like some doddering, interfering old woman.

The hour must be late, he mused, and he knew he should try to sleep. The thought made him smile. Try, indeed. For years he'd suffered from horrible insomnia, unable to rest, prowling his home and property at nights in search of a distraction from his wakefulness.

It struck him as funny that he'd slipped into the dark sleep of a coma so deep he'd been thought dead. Maybe he'd just needed his rest.

And it hadn't been too bad. It had, after all, landed him in the earthy, compelling company of Olwyn Gawain.

After years of feeling buried by his familial obligations and the constrictions of the aristocracy, he felt alive, unburdened, and for the time being, free.

Aidan held Olwyn closer, telling himself it was just for warmth, necessary for survival.

After all, he was betrothed to a woman who wore his ring and planned their wedding day. Aidan Mullen was a man of honor.

But his body knew Olwyn. It responded like the ungovernable beast it was.

The night might have been frigid and wet, but inside the hut, beneath the furs and blankets, there was nothing but heat and reluctant restraint.

And to Aidan's surprise, he found himself falling asleep, curled around Olwyn as if their bodies had been made to fit together.

When Aidan woke, the first thing he noticed was that Olwyn was gone. He sat up, looked around, and saw that though the fire burned and tea and bread had been set out for him, the rest of the provisions were also missing.

He jumped to his feet and went outside. The blue sky pierced his eyes with its brightness, and the cold, thin air stabbed his lungs after the night spent breathing peat smoke.

Olwyn was outside. He saw she had the provisions neatly lining the wagon, the horse tacked up and ready to go, the tarps cleared off and folded, and the seat of the wagon covered with a thick fur.

Aidan made a mental note to never underestimate Olwyn Gawain.

She glanced over to Aidan. "We're mostly packed up, but for the remaining things in the hut. Did you eat?"

"Not yet," he answered. "How are you?"

A quizzical frown touched her brows. "Fine."

"You drank a lot of whiskey, aye?"

"Not really. Go eat and then gather the rest of the furs and blankets. You can ride in the wagon beneath them since you don't have adequate garments."

"I'm not a churl to ride in comfort while a woman drives me."

"Not a churl, indeed. But are you an idiot, Lóchrann?"

Aidan laughed. "Only when it comes to women."

"Well, be that as it may, I didn't save your life so you could squander it on pride."

"Why did you, then?"

That frown between her eyes grew deeper. She turned her attention back to readying the wagon. "'Tis a long story, and we've got a lengthy journey ahead of us."

"Long stories are good for lengthy journeys," Aidan said before going back inside to get ready to leave. He didn't hang around to hear her argument. He'd have the rest of the truth, and he'd get it riding by her side. Olwyn wasn't the only one of them who suffered from a streak of stubbornness.

Soon enough they were on their way, Aidan beside

Olwyn on the seat, blankets and furs wrapped around them both. They had heated bricks at their feet, and Aidan held the reins, though he'd nearly had to wrestle Olwyn for them.

He'd had to assure her he felt well, and indeed he did. After the food, tea, and rest, he felt hale and fit, ready for whatever came.

As the sun rose, so did the temperature. Tiny droplets of rain wobbled and fell from tree branches, and birds darted to and fro, twittering as if they were grateful for morning. Despite the cold air, the sun was warm and there were no winds.

And again, Aidan relished his life, rejoicing in the simple act of breathing and taking in the beauty of the world around him.

The old wagon rattled and lurched, bumping along the narrow path they rode upon. The mare clomped through the muddy wetness without too much trouble.

Olwyn cast a final glance behind them, taking in the hut and the signs of their camp. She unfolded her maps.

"So where do we go, Olwyn?"

"South," she murmured. "There is a port in Southampton. I've money to book passage on a ship."

"Oh, aye?" Aidan ran five of his own vessels from that port, as Southampton was where he lived, in his family's estate called Beauport. It was where his grandmother, Camille, had been raised, and no place on earth felt more like home to Aidan.

He loved the smell of the sea air there, the rocky stretches of beach just beyond the woods, and the tiny cottage he'd found in a little meadow. Behind that little cottage there was a well that gave up the sweetest water he'd ever tasted, and it made for some fine whiskey when he got the proof just right. He had his dog there, whose company Aidan sorely missed, and a mews full of hawks that he flew for hunting.

It was, he mused, ironic that Olwyn would want to board a ship there. He could easily send her anywhere she wanted to go aboard one of his vessels, and could see to her protection. So why, he asked himself, did he not tell her so?

Instead of thinking about that, he asked, "Where are you off to when you board your ship?"

"I'm headed to the Americas," Olwyn told him.

"That's a long way to go. Why so far, and what do you think will become of you there, alone in a new country with no man to protect you?"

"The trader who sold me these maps told me that there are fifty men to one woman there. I'm a hard worker, and can likely produce children, so this should make me more attractive as a potential mate," she answered him, her tone rather defensive. She seemed to reflect on her words, and added, "It's not a bad plan, really. I can read and write, so would make for a governess if I needed work, and should I find a man to marry me, he would probably be grateful that his children wouldn't be ignorant. The trader assured me that since there are so few women, the men are far less concerned with a woman's appearance, and that I shouldn't have troubles finding a mate."

Aidan nearly laughed at the absurdity of her final comment. "Was the trader blind, Olwyn?"

She turned to him, quizzical. She obviously missed his meaning, because she answered as if he were dimwitted. "No. How else could he find his way around, if not for his eyes, Lóchrann?"

Aidan just shook his head and kept driving south. He took her maps and looked them over. At the pace the single horse set, having to stop frequently to clear her hooves, warm her, and let her rest, a journey of several days could take weeks.

And she'd planned on going it alone, dragging a comatose man with her. The enormity of her foolishness stunned Aidan. Hadn't the trader seen fit to warn her of the dangers, or was he, too, caught up in the romantic notion of a benevolent world that would welcome and shelter a runaway girl?

Clearly Olwyn thought that booking passage on a ship was enough protection for her, if she could have made it that far. Little did she know that she would have been fortunate to not be grabbed up by a man who would steal her money, rape her, and sell her into bondage.

"What were you thinking?" he asked her. "Running off by yourself with this sort of trip ahead of you. Don't you know 'tis not safe for a woman to travel alone?"

"Or I could have withered away at home," she said calmly. "I've a pistol, a rifle, and a dagger, and I'm good with them."

He snorted. "That only gives you three shots, Olwyn."

"I wouldn't miss."

"And if there was more than three men?"

"I've a dagger."

"Right. Three shots and a single throw. I stand corrected. You had the right of it. I'm sure you'd have been as safe as a babe in its mother's arms."

"Don't mock me."

"What? Mock you? How could I, when clearly your plan was without a single flaw. I'm not so daft that I'd go poking fun at such brilliance."

Olwyn glanced over to him, her brows drawn in a scowl, her lips pursed with annoyance.

Aidan winked at her and grinned, and she could not maintain her anger. She laughed then, a sound that fit the cold winter morning as nothing else, high, sweet, and clear, like a songbird heralding the promise of spring.

"Perhaps it wasn't brilliant," she conceded, the laughter still warming her voice, "but there was nothing else to be done. It was run and hope to live, or stay and wish for death."

"As bad as all that, then?"

"Aye," she said slowly. "It was."

"Tell me about it, Olwyn."

And so, as the wagon lurched and bumped along, she told him of her life as her father's assistant and servant. Aidan listened without interruption, and when she finished he remained silent a long while.

He envisioned her life—a slave to a madman, forced to become a servant in her own home, and a pariah in her village. How long until her father's man found a door unlocked and forced himself on her? How long until she sickened from one of the corpses? And none of those concerns touched on the basic human needs for love, for meaning, for hope. She was correct in one thing, he knew. Had she stayed, her life would have never improved.

"I could see myself many years on," she said softly, interrupting his thoughts. "I'd be haggard from misery, deeply resentful of my lot in life, bitter and a bit mad after a life of isolation. I'd probably be razor thin from too much work and not enough food, and every time I ventured into the village to get food, people would run from me. Babies would cry. Children would laugh."

Olwyn lifted her face to the sky, and he heard her inhale deeply as if she pulled freedom into her lungs. "I should rather die than live that life," she said. "Call me fool if you must, but I see it another way. I would have been a fool to stay."

"I admire you," he said softly, and he meant it. How many times had he fantasized about his own freedom? Too many times to count, he thought, and he had a fortune at his disposal and a family who loved him at his back. And still, he let himself do everything he was supposed to do, was expected to do.

They fell silent in companionable agreement. Aidan noticed the way her shoulder bumped his arm as they rode, her body swaying in time to the motion of the wagon. Holding the reins in one hand, he reached around her and pulled her closer. She turned her face up, so close to him now that he could kiss her.

"I'm cold," he lied. The truth was, she felt good against him.

Olwyn nodded, looked away. He obviously still made her uncomfortable, despite the night spent safely in his arms.

"You've yet to tell me about yourself, Lóchrann," she whispered.

Aidan knew he owed her some truth. She'd revealed herself to him in so many ways, and he'd yet to tell her anything about who he really was, and that even the name she called him was not his true name.

Before he could form an answer he saw her turn her head, even as he heard what called her attention. Rhythmic hoofbeats, like distant thunder. Aidan listened closely. More than four, he thought, and they were coming up behind them, fast.

"You've got that rifle?" Aidan asked.

Olwyn reached beneath the seat, pulled it up, and checked its priming with a precision that would equal any soldier's. "Ready."

Aidan put his hand out. "And the dagger?"

Olwyn reached into her belt, pulled it out, and handed it to him hilt first. "It's not balanced. Aim two feet higher than the target."

"Fine. Give me the pistol, then."

The drumming of the horses grew closer. Aidan ran a hand across his bristly chin and glanced around. The field rolled and stretched, dotted periodically with tall, thin, bare trees and low, scrubby clumps of bushes. With the tracks they were leaving in the mud, hiding was impossible.

They could only wait and see, prepared to hold their ground with a rifle, a pistol, and a single dagger. Aidan held to the hope that whoever rode along the unpopulated open fields had no mayhem in mind. There was nothing else to be done. Just like life itself, he mused, they could only prepare as best they could, wait, and hope.

Aidan corrected himself. There was one more thing to do—seize the moment. He turned to Olwyn, and beneath the furs that covered them, he felt her body, already tensed with fear, turn supple in expectation. Her body knew his, and like before, responded.

Without hesitation, he put his hand beneath the soft waves of her black hair, curved his fingers around the shape of her skull, and pulled her to him. Those gray eyes widened, but she did not fight his advances.

Aidan lowered his mouth to take hers and then faltered. He held back, unable to take what had not been given, unwilling to press her if she did not want the same thing.

Olwyn answered his unvoiced question. She leaned up and pressed her lips to his.

Olwyn shook as his lips moved against hers. She'd imagined what it would feel like to be kissed by him. She had not even come close.

He tasted of salt and honey, and something she could not name. She licked at his lips to taster deeper, and Lóchrann made a noise in his throat that sent a deep throb of warmth to her groin. A slippery dampness, shameful in its heat, had her pressing her thighs together.

He slanted his head and opened his lips, and as his

tongue touched hers, she tasted him deeply. Everything was texture, soft lips and wet tongue, teeth as he nipped her bottom lip, his stubble an erotic brush on her skin that was purely male. Her body responded in ways she could not fathom, as if her flesh and blood and bones understood the kiss, and knew the secrets of what passed between men and women.

She was hot and liquid, and she would melt into a puddle beside him. Nothing else was remotely as real, not the riders coming up fast, not the crumbling keep she'd left behind, not the ship she hoped to find freedom aboard. Lóchrann's mouth became a primitive shelter she could hide inside forever.

The hand that gripped the back of her head grew harder, more insistent. He pulled at her as if he wanted to climb inside her. That noise sounded again in his throat, urgent and deep, like pain and pleasure combined. And when he pulled her bottom lip into his mouth and lightly sucked it, she heard the same sound come from her throat, driven by a force she could not control.

The sound of the riders grew closer still, the galloping of the horses like the rapid racing of her heart.

And then he released her.

He leaned his forehead against hers for a moment, and whispered, "You taste as good as you smell."

Olwyn did not respond, for she had no words for the feelings that rippled beneath her skin, all nervous desire and curious wonder.

Aidan turned his head toward the horizon. He waited, listening. And then he rapped out orders as if nothing had just passed between them. "Get down, Olwyn, and take some cover behind the wagon. Pull your hood down further over your face, and hold your rifle so they cannot see it. We don't need to announce that we're the least bit worried. We'll just go casually about our business here, and hope they ride right on past."

Olwyn did as she was told, balancing the rifle so it was hidden behind the bed of the wagon. She watched as Aidan hopped down and hid the dagger in his sleeve, the pistol inside his cloak. He bent over a wheel so it looked as if they were making a small repair, rather than trapped in an open field like two frightened rabbits.

The riders appeared high on the hill. Olwyn counted them, dread forming in her gut as she did. "Seven," she said.

"Aye. We'll do, Olwyn. Don't worry."

"About the kiss, Lóchrann. Thank you for it."

"Thanks, is it? Well, I have to say that's the first time I've been thanked for kissing a woman." She saw his slow grin, and he lifted his eyes to hers for a brief moment. "I ought to thank you."

She cleared her throat and shifted her weight. The rifle in her hands gave her an odd feeling of security, enough that she asked, "Was it good?"

His sapphire eyes grew far more serious. He licked his bottom lip as if the taste of her lingered. "Better than good."

Her courage, scarce as it had just been, faded before the sensuality of his gaze. She still felt the throbbing slickness of her own arousal, and her face grew hot.

"Mind your hood," he said. "They're within spotting distance if they've an eyeglass."

She dropped her face so that she stared at the ground, grateful for the hood that fell forward, obscuring her from view. Looking down at the rifle, half-sick with nervousness, she listened, hearing the drumming of hoofbeats growing closer and closer.

Chapter Ten

The riders slowed as they approached, calling out to the two people by the wagon with a "Ho, there!"

Lóchrann lifted his head and turned with a casual ease that Olwyn envied. Her hands sweated on the rifle.

The men approached at a canter, the ground vibrating. They were armed, every one of them, and were draped in thick cloaks to protect them against the wet. Olwyn noticed damp patches on their garments. So they'd been riding through the night's weather, she thought with growing dismay. Highwaymen, no doubt, and she and Lóchrann pathetically outnumbered.

She widened her stance. If she had to use the rifle, she'd need her feet planted beneath her.

The horses were foaming and blowing steam, great white plumes of it coming from their flared nostrils. Olwyn took a peek at Lóchrann. He was leaning against the wagon's wheel, his arms folded across his chest as if he hadn't a care in the world.

And then she watched in utter amazement as Lóchrann let out a yell, and went running directly at the riders, calling out in Gaelic as he did. He made quite a sight, his dark gold hair riding the wind, the ratty old cloak he wore flying behind him.

One of the riders reined his horse in hard. The beast reared up, hooves clawing the air, before crashing down. The man threw himself from the saddle and ran to Lóchrann. They embraced hard, slapping each other and laughing.

The man clutching Lóchrann was the same height, similar in build and breadth, but his hair was black as a raven's wing. He wept as he held tight to Lóchrann's shoulders.

Olwyn heard him, then, his deep voice sounding just like Lóchrann's in tone and accent. "My brother, you are alive."

They pulled apart, and began talking in low voices. She saw Lóchrann turn slightly, gesturing to the wagon and Olwyn. His brother looked her over with interest, from her face to her clothes to the ancient mare and rickety wagon.

Olwyn lifted her chin and met his stare with her own. He wore expensive garments, she noticed, fine wools lined with fur, tall leather boots, and a hat that must have cost a hefty sum.

And she realized that Lóchrann had never actually told her anything about himself.

Lóchrann's brother went to his steed, unbuckled saddlebags, and handed them to him. "I saw you left the crypt in your skin."

"Aye, and thanks for thinking of it. I'm freezing," Lóchrann replied. He opened the bags and withdrew a bundle of clothing and boots, and as he did, Olwyn noticed the leather was embossed with a family crest. "How did you find me?"

"You left a trail the sightless could follow."

"Well, I wasn't trying to stay missing, aye?"

Right there in the middle of the barren landscape, Lóchrann began to dress, shucking the shabby, oft-mended garments she'd given him, and pulling on the ones his brother had brought. Olwyn averted her eyes, a hot blush burning her cheeks.

His brother sounded serious, his voice dropping lower, and slowing as he said, "You frightened me but good, Aidan."

Aidan? She listened intently, trying to get a gauge on this unexpected turn of events.

"Oh, aye? Well, good then, because frightening you is just what I had in mind when I played dead and let them bury me alive. 'Tis nothing so satisfying as when a solid plan succeeds."

The other man laughed easily, and he sounded just like Lóchrann. Or was it Aidan? Olwyn began to feel like a fool, with all her talk of stolen moments of honesty. He'd not shared a single thing that she could think of. And she'd babbled on and on about herself, giving away pieces of her private heart that she'd never shared with anyone.

Olwyn glanced up, her gaze drawn inexorably back to this man who again felt like a stranger. A stranger who'd kissed her with passionate urgency.

The man before her had transformed into someone else. He had garbed himself in buckskin breeches and black boots laced to his knee, a linen shirt, black jacket, and a fur-lined black cloak. With a dark leather strap, he pulled his hair back into a club, making his face, as sensual as it was, appear leaner and more chiseled. He looked like a wildly handsome, disreputable lord, rich and dangerous, sensual and remote.

Olwyn didn't think she'd ever felt more embarrassed of her dress and appearance. She curled her toes in her home-made boots. They were nothing more than lashed leather and fur. The shoes of a peasant. Her hand went to her ragged hair. It hung in limp snarls and likely made her seem more a witch than ever before.

Deep within her came the pride that had sustained her when the villagers mocked her and cast aspersions on her family.

She knew it was dangerous to continue her journey on her own, but she'd told Lóchrann that he owed her nothing, and she'd meant it.

Olwyn hefted the rifle and slid it beneath the driver's

board before hopping up onto the bench. The old wagon creaked beneath her as she picked up Nixie's reins.

She called out, her voice strong and sure in the clear, wintry air. "I see you're safe now, Lóchrann, and returned to your people. Godspeed you home to your beloved and your family. If you'll only return my weapons, I'll bid you farewell."

He strode over to her, his long legs eating up the space between them. Standing before her in his wealthy garb, he looked up at her as she sat high on the wagon's seat, and his eyes lied to her, such as they appeared straightforward and honest.

"I owe you an explanation, and after that, an apology," he said simply.

"I don't even know your name," Olwyn replied softly. And she let a little of her hurt show when she said, "You took a piece of me last night. I did not deserve to be treated with contempt, for I've been nothing but truthful with you."

His sapphire eyes bore into hers, holding her rooted there. She was painfully aware of the men who looked on, watching them. He opened his mouth to speak, but she cut him off before he could utter a single word.

"My pistol and my knife," she demanded tightly.

"Listen to me a moment."

"To hear more lies, Lóchrann? Thanks to you, but no."

"I am Aidan Patrick Mullen, the son to a powerful duke."

Not a prince, after all, but close enough to make Olwyn feel completely at odds. She'd never spoken to a member of the aristocracy, and knew nothing of the world they lived in, save it was nothing like her own.

Looking down on him now, impossibly handsome in his clean, beautifully made clothes, she didn't think it feasible that she could feel any dirtier or unkempt than she had before, and yet, she did.

"I didn't tell you because I have grown so tired of never knowing if one's interest is truly in me, or if 'tis in my titles and my wealth," he confessed softly. "What we shared last night was more real than any other exchange I've ever had with someone who was not my immediate family, and I was loathe to risk ruining the moment. However, I promised you honesty, and I'm sorry I didn't deliver it."

Olwyn raised her brow and gave him a half-hearted smile. "Forgive me if I cannot muster too much sympathy for you, *my lord*. But you see, I have spent my entire life being reviled for who I actually am, and yet, I told you no lies."

"You are right to be angry. Go on and hate me for as long as you need to." Aidan leaped up easily into the wagon's seat and removed his cloak, settled it around her shoulders, and with nimble fingers, fastened it.

Olwyn gasped at his rudeness and slapped at his hands, but he ignored her. Aidan turned to his brother and his men. "Unhitch this mare and hitch the wagon to a stronger horse. The poor old thing will do much better as we travel if she doesn't have to pull the wagon."

"Aye, my lord," one of the men said, and he swung out of his saddle and set to do Aidan's bidding.

Olwyn ignored that the cloak was warm and comforting and smelled of clean wool and rich leather from the bag it had been transported in. She would not snuggle into its soft confines and let this man begin ordering her about, as if she were nothing more than a subject easily bent to his will.

"I have no interest in continuing on with you, my lord."

"Well, 'tis a coincidence that I reside in Southampton and will be heading that way. You could travel there alone and vulnerable, or in relative comfort with me and my men. I have several ships docked there, and can easily see to it that you are sent safely on your way to the Americas. So what will it be, Olwyn, practicality or pride?"

Beneath the cloak, Olwyn twisted her hands in her lap. But outwardly, where Aidan watched her every expression, she raised her chin and focused on a far treetop. She kept her voice cool and unaffected, unwilling to show in the slightest that he unsettled her.

"To behave as though I have a choice in the matter insults us both, my lord. So why don't you just do as you damn well please, and drop the pretense of caring a whit for my preference?"

Aidan grinned, and she saw it in her peripheral line of vision. So she amused him, did she?

"I have never met a woman so honest," he said, admiration heavy in his voice, along with suppressed laughter.

"Likewise, my lord. I, too, have yet to meet a man as truthful as I."

Her remark hit its target, for his grin faded. "I did say I was sorry."

"Aye, you did." Olwyn turned her head to meet his eyes then. "But I do not forgive the slight."

"I promise I'll make it up to you."

"I don't want anything from you."

Aidan was silent for a moment, the only sound the metallic scrape of brass buckles and the rattle of rigging as the horses were exchanged.

"I think you are making more of this than it is," he said finally. "I did not do anything to hurt you."

"You took the warmth of my body, my whiskey, my truth, and my first kiss. You let me show you my heart, and you gave nothing in return. Must you now diminish your actions?"

Another long pause filled the space between them, and the man who finished with the horses spared them a quick, quizzical glance before leading Nixie away. He tethered Nixie behind the wagon, and two of the men doubled up on a stronger, younger horse.

Aidan didn't spare them notice. He said to Olwyn, "I am sorry I hurt you."

"Will you tell your betrothed of your indiscretion?"

His eyes darkened and his brows came down in a scowl. He turned his face away, and she saw a muscle in his cheek flex. "So I should hurt another woman? No matter what I do, I am forced to play the cad."

"There is a simple remedy, and you might want to keep it in mind for future reference. You could, next time, choose to not touch what does not belong to you," she said. And though she knew that it was her embarrassment talking, she did not keep herself from saying, "Or has your life of privilege left you with a sense of entitlement?"

Even as she insulted him, Olwyn could not keep from noticing the square shape of his hands that held her reins. Everything about him looked good, even his hands. Especially his hands. She could scarcely stop looking at them—smooth skin, wide palms, and long, blunt-tipped fingers. They looked like the man himself: strong yet elegant, capable yet sensual.

Olwyn hated the way that his handsomeness made it difficult for her to stay angry with him. Her own appearance caused the opposite reaction in others, made them instantly dislike her. Didn't she want people to see beneath her face to the woman within? And what did it say about Olwyn that she, too, was shallow, wanting to forgive him because looking at his handsome face faded her anger?

Perhaps it stemmed from her life of isolation and the surety of her own ugly face, she mused, that she could not quite dismiss that for a few moments, he'd made her feel desirable. Even pretty.

Hadn't Rhys even said that a man would call any woman beautiful if it got him between her legs?

The memory of her shameful arousal haunted her. A few more kisses and a few more compliments, and she'd have stripped her skin bare, right along with her soul. Lóchrann. Aidan. My lord. It didn't matter what she called him; she craved the desire he'd shown her when it had been just the two of them alone.

Her weakness sickened her.

Aidan would return to his beloved, a woman he'd described as fragile and pretty, like a princess. Olwyn thought it perfect—a fair princess and her handsome prince, a fairy-tale existence.

Perhaps he didn't regret their stolen kiss, but she did. Olwyn knew that as long as she lived, she would never forgive him for stirring her emotions to such turmoil. She had never felt as ugly as she did now—a beast of a woman beside a beautiful man.

Padraig called out to his brother, "We'll head to the nearest town and get fresh horses and a carriage. I've already sent word to Mira. She was overjoyed to hear that her beloved lives, and has plans to go to Beauport and reunite with you there."

The men on horseback kicked their mounts into motion. Without looking at Olwyn again, Aidan lifted the reins and slapped the back of the flashy, magnificent stallion that now pulled her rickety, weather-beaten wagon.

And Olwyn wished, rather fervently, that she had not said any of the things that had formed the uncomfortable silence that now hung between them.

Mira Kimball swayed in time to the carriage as it bore her south through England's countryside. The roads were muddy and pitted, but the conveyance had the very best springs, and the interior boasted the finest appointments: plush velvet seats, cushioned pillows, hanging lanterns, a warming pan that gave off the soft essence of vanilla, and thick robes to keep her warm. And so she and her father traveled in relative comfort, pleasant enough as they each read to pass the time in companionable silence.

Mira found herself absolutely riveted by Bret Kimball's journals.

The pages were yellowed and brittle, the penmanship ofttimes scrawled as though written in a mad rush.

But the story it told was nothing less than galvanizing.

She carefully turned the page and dove back into the past, when her great-uncle had been betrothed to Aidan's grandmother, Camille Bradburn.

London, 6 January, 1744
   I am unmanned, unmasked, and undone. I am for-saken, forbidden, and for my great sins, forever un-forgiven. Oh, that I could kill her, that hag of a harridan who owns my soul, I would, for I am already damned. But in her power I am trapped, and by her power I am pricked.

Mira knew from her previous readings that he spoke of Camille's mother, Amelia, when he referred to the harri-dan. Amelia had been the Duchess of Eton, and by all Bret's accounts, knew secrets that could have ruined the Kimball family name. Amelia had apparently wielded these secrets like a whip, keeping Bret in her control.

   Today marks my greatest sin. A pathetic word, sin. 'Tis a word too soft and pale for the deed I commit-ted. A word too small for the pain I inflicted.
   That whore of a duchess is my taskmaster. She moves my hands, blinks my eyes, forms my thoughts,

until I am merely a puppet on her strings, dangling, twisting, and acting on her whims.

Would that I had the strength, I would take my own life.

I look forward to a future that is charted for me, and my one consolation, my beautiful rose, Camille. I know, however, that her heart belongs to another. She will never look upon me as she did him, never want me, never love me.

Mira pulled her gaze away from the journal and recalled the day she'd met Aidan's grandmother, Camille.

There had been the faintest interest in Camille's vivid green eyes, and Mira could remember her reaction to Aidan's announcement. Camille had raised her brows, turned to her husband, Patrick, and said, "And so we have come full circle."

Mira had wondered what in the world she'd meant. Now she could only muse upon the Kimball-Bradburn connection. Why, she asked herself for the hundredth time, had Camille Bradburn Mullen not seen fit to tell Aidan that she had known Mira's great-uncle well enough to agree to become his wife? Why had Camille kept that secret? And what sin had Amelia Bradburn forced Bret Kimball to commit?

Mira returned to the journal, hoping that Bret would reveal the answers in his own way.

If only I could go back and change everything, I would never have sold my soul.

If I were not such a coward, I would confess my sins here in the sanctity of my private journal. But there will be no absolution for me, and were someone to see the words, only condemnation and the hangman's noose.

Camille, Camille, Camille. Her name resounds through my mind, consuming me with obsession, with regret, with sorrow. How can one so sweetly innocent be the offspring of one so wretched and bitter?

I do not know precisely the day I became snarled in this trap, but I am caught in it now and will never be free. The guilt is haunting me, plaguing me. 'Tis my daily wish that I will succumb to an illness that will take my life, and end my guilty misery.

"Are you unwell, my pet?" Andrew asked of his daughter, peering at her over the top of his reading spectacles.

"Why do you ask, Papa?"

"You are pale, and clenching at the cushion beside you as if for your very life."

"'Tis only this journal." Mira brought her gaze up to her father's. "There was something very dark between my uncle and Aidan's grandmother."

"Ancient history," her father declared, dismissing its importance with a wave of his hand. "Why fret over something that happened so long ago?"

Mira held the musty journal to her breast, deeply offended to have her passion for her family's history so disregarded. "Why, indeed. I shall tell you why. Amelia Bradburn was able to manipulate Bret Kimball because she knew his secrets. My great-uncle lost his life at the hands of that woman as a direct result, and I mean to find out what she made him do, and what she held over his head."

"To what end, darling? Perhaps when you are as old as I, you will value the wisdom of letting sleeping dogs lie."

"I do not wish to be disagreeable, but I wholeheartedly differ. When I marry Aidan Mullen and join our families, I will not suffer to sit in his grandmother's presence knowing that she knows secrets about *my* family that I do not."

Mira settled back in her seat, and readjusted her robes and pillows so she was once more cushioned against the jostling of the carriage. She arranged the journal on her lap once more, and laid her hand open upon its yellowed pages, splayed wide as if she guarded the truths and mysteries contained in Bret Kimball's words.

"Full circle, indeed, Papa." She narrowed her eyes as she thought of the clues Bret had left, the guilt and remorse, his obsessions and sins. "I will find out what happened, and I will protect our family's interest in the process."

Andrew clucked at his daughter, a tender little *tsk-tsk* at her obstinate nature, her fierce familial pride. And then he gave in and smiled benevolently. "Of course, Mira, pet. You shall have whatever you wish, my darling girl. Whatever you wish."

Chapter Eleven

Olwyn and the men arrived at an inn late in the night. Stone weary and nearly delirious with fatigue, Olwyn allowed herself to be steered to a room, Aidan's firm grip on her arm. He put her before a big tester bed, thick with quilts and plump pillows.

She noticed that the fireplace burned fragrant logs and not peat, that the candles were wax and not tallow, and that the room was clean and appointed with luxury. On a small table stood a tea service, linen napkins, and a plate heaped with cakes and scones and biscuits. Even the chamber pot was elegant, painted with cheery flowers and set behind a wooden screen. Such was wealth, she thought.

"We'll leave first thing in the morning," Aidan said. He set two of her sacks on the floor. They looked as she must, out of place in the graceful surroundings, dirty, tattered, and shabby.

Olwyn didn't respond, but stood swaying on her feet, wondering if she had the strength to wash before falling onto the bed.

Aidan moved to stand in front of her. He seemed awkward, unsure. He took her hand. "In the hut, Olwyn," he began, clearing his throat. He used her given name again, and it irritated her that he did not think her worthy of polite formality. "In the hut when you were so honest . . ."

"Leave me alone." She tried to pull her hand away.

"The first words you've spoken since your parting insult in the meadow, and you sound just as angry. I would have thought so many hours on the wagon seat would have dimmed your anger, or at least, exhausted it a bit."

Olwyn wouldn't dignify his words with an explanation. "I don't care to have this conversation with you. I'm weary, and I just want to go to sleep."

"Aye, and you will." He bent down to his knee and began removing her muddy boots as if he were a prince helping her with a fancy slipper.

She looked down at the expanse of his shoulders and the crown of his head. His dark gold hair gleamed like burnished bronze in the light of the fire and the candles. He set her boots before the fire so they would dry, a thoughtful gesture.

The boots sat sadly on the marble hearth, slumped and filthy.

Aidan turned to her and met her eyes for a split second, and in the flickering light she thought she saw desire. She struggled to remember that she was angry with him for lying to her, and for letting her reveal herself to him while giving nothing in return. She reminded herself he was engaged to be married.

Aidan took his cloak from her shoulders, and draped it over the back of a chair before following with his coat and his shirt.

He shucked his boots, removed his stockings. He moved to the washstand, and began to wash.

And as he stood there in his breeches, his wide chest naked and gleaming in the firelight, iridescent soap bubbles clinging to his wet skin, Olwyn realized he meant to spend the night with her.

"Get out." It was a snarl, a vicious snap.

Aidan half-turned, cast a glance to the door. "No."

"I'll not bed down with you."

"You will," he replied calmly.

"I am poor, I am defenseless, and I am not of noble blood, but that does not put me under your rule, and it most certainly does not make me your whore."

"The last thing you are is defenseless," Aidan said as he rinsed the soap from his skin.

He toweled off, and Olwyn had to avert her eyes from the sight of all that male flesh and muscle.

Aidan poured himself a cup of tea and bit into a small cake. He swallowed it down and let out a satisfied sigh. "These are good. You should eat."

"You're not my lord and master."

He met her eyes, dark sapphire blue against flinty, stormy gray.

"No. I'm not."

"I demand to be left alone."

"No," Aidan answered easily. "I know you're furious with me, aye? And I know you've got as much pride in your blood as I do. 'Tis likely you'd decide to try to leave, because if I were in your position, hopping angry and feeling out of place, it's what I'd do. So see, Olwyn, I'm treating you as an equal. A woman to be reckoned with.

"Do you understand? This is a sign of my esteem for you, that your pride would forbid you to take the comfort my coins have bought, and that you'd strike out on your own, not taking anything from me. I ken how you feel, and I respect it. But frankly, I'm tired, Olwyn. I don't have the energy to chase you down into the night, and as a man, I'd have to do it anyway, you see. I've got some pride of my own, aye? So to keep things simple, I'll keep you here by my side, and we'll both get some rest. Perhaps in the morning, you'll have a bit more perspective."

Olwyn lowered her eyes to the floor. Her feet were cold, as were her hands, and her heart. "There is nothing simple about our situation."

"No, maybe not. But we're stuck with each other for a bit. Let's make the best of it."

She inclined her head to the bed. "For my best, or yours, my lord?"

"I'm not a rapist, nor am I a cad, if that's what you're implying."

She stared at him, wordless. Perhaps her silence would win out where her words did not.

Aidan moved a little closer to her, and she could smell the soap on his skin. It made her feel dirtier. His chest seemed to fill the room, wide, expansive, compelling. She knew the feel of it, the warmth of it. Must he stand so close?

"Do you have any idea why you're this angry, Olwyn?" he asked her softly. "Do you not think you're overreacting a bit?"

Olwyn did not answer his questions, for she knew he had the right of it.

All she knew for certain was when she'd pulled this man

from the dungeon, he'd been half-dead and in need of her help. She'd been prepared to save him, fight for him, and nurse him to health.

She'd not expected that he'd wake and be so hale, so strong. She'd not expected to feel so unnecessary and uncomfortable.

Her father's words haunted her. *Saving him won't make him love you.*

But she'd not try to explain any of that to Aidan. The time for Olwyn to open up and be honest with him was over. She'd not go out on that limb again. Not when he'd shown that he could, and would, take it and give nothing in return.

And so she changed the subject, switched tactics.

"If you had any regard for me, you would allow me to have the privacy that as a woman, I deserve." Olwyn said the words with stiff pride, but it was all lies.

The truth was, she knew she had no choice but to do as he said. He'd taken her pistol and her dagger, and he had seven men at his disposal.

If she ran, he'd catch her. If she hid, he'd find her. She was outmatched and outmanned.

And so it meant that she had no recourse but to lie with him in that great big soft bed. The thought of it weakened her legs, warmed her ears, turned her belly.

"All right," he replied softly. "Take a few minutes to gather yourself together."

He went to the room's only window and looked down. "Four floors up and nothing to hold onto to climb down. You'll not risk your neck, will you?"

"No," she answered quietly. The last of her pride was gone, decimated beneath the grinding heel of her own surrender. She knew she wanted to feel the weight and warmth of him beside her in that bed, to feel for one more night that she was not completely alone.

"Very well. I'll be back in a bit."

Aidan pulled on his shirt and coat, went to the door and paused, turning to her again. "What I wanted to say, Olwyn, was that if I could go back and do it again, I'd not change a thing. For you see, having you angry with me now is a small price to pay for what you gave me. I'd never before enjoyed the regard and company of a woman whose eyes didn't glitter with interest that had nothing to do with me, the man."

Olwyn couldn't help herself. She asked, "Your betrothed, my lord? Do her eyes glitter?"

Aidan sighed and rubbed a hand through his hair. He seemed to think a long time about the question, as if he himself had puzzled over it long before Olwyn spoke the words. He shrugged and opened the door, stepped out of the room, closed and locked it from the outside.

Alone, finally, Olwyn raised trembling hands to her hot cheeks, pressing them against the bones beneath the flesh. She didn't linger like that for long, however, knowing that Aidan would return soon enough. Rummaging through her bags, she found what she needed and began preparing for bed.

Aidan went down to the inn's common room. He found Padraig sprawled in a chair by the fire, a tankard of ale before him on the table reflected in the smooth polish of the varnish. The room smelled of food and wine, leather and fire smoke. In the corner, a lone guitarist strummed out a melody as if playing only for himself, a sweet, lonely tune that tugged at Aidan's heart.

"Is the witch sleeping?" his brother asked.

"She's not a witch." Aidan dropped into the chair across from his twin, Padraig's face as familiar as his own.

"She's the look of one."

"And you've the look of an Irish bastard, aye?"

"Aye," Padraig answered with a laugh. "Do you want an ale, brother?"

"I'll have a whiskey, if they've a good one."

Padraig raised his hand and a server rushed to the table, took the order, and returned swiftly a glass filled with pale amber. She bobbed deep in front of Aidan as she proffered the drink, and Aidan took it with thanks and took a deep sip.

"'Tis good," he said with satisfaction. He lifted it to the light, swirled it, inhaled its aroma, and sipped again. "Almost as good as my own."

"High praise."

"I'm feeling generous. Coming back from the dead will do that to a man."

"Speaking of that, fill me in on what happened."

And so Aidan told his brother what he could remember, from the sickness to the black void he'd slipped into, and finally, waking in a hut beside a stranger, a woman.

"There's something about her that's different. Strange," Padraig mused, obviously speaking of Olwyn. "I've never seen a woman so unusual."

"You don't even know her, have never even spoken a word with her," Aidan said quickly, rising to her defense with a heat in his gut he didn't quite understand.

Padraig regarded him over the rim of his glass for a long moment, and Aidan knew that his twin could see things in him that even Aidan did not recognize. It was a blessing and a curse combined, this knowing they had of each other. It made for a tight bond, but sometimes, that bond became a tether.

"You're to be married, Aidan," Padraig said slowly, and Aidan knew that when his brother used his given name, it meant he was deadly serious. "Are you looking to change that, I hope?"

"I came down here for a moment's peace, not a lecture regarding decisions made long ago. Decisions you're too afraid to make yourself, aye?"

"I'm not afraid of marriage. But I'm not going to rush off into it to prove a point, either."

"I've got nothing to prove."

"Liar," Padraig said quietly. He took the last draught of his ale, and set the tankard down with a soft thump. Leaning forward to add emphasis to his words, he said, "Don't think I don't know what you're doing with Mira Kimball. She's a good match from a good family, and she's pretty enough. But marrying a girl like Mira is your own life sentence, and if you can't see that with your own eyes, you're a fool. She'll never be enough for you."

Aidan stood. "So much for a peaceful fireside chat, brother."

"Well, it takes a friend to tell you the truth, and last I checked, I was your best. So I'm sorry, Lóchrann, if the truth stings you."

Aidan's hand tightened around his glass of whiskey. To hear his brother speak his darkest feelings aloud made anger brew in his body, poisoning his blood. With Padraig there was no privacy, not even in his heart.

A vision of Mira flashed in his mind, of her smiling face and pretty blue eyes. Surely marriage to such a woman would not be without its pleasures, and didn't Aidan once think himself a relatively lucky man? So why, then, did he feel so dissatisfied and restless? Why had he wished that he'd woken in another time, to a future full of the promise of freedom?

And that future had included a woman with strange gray eyes as clear as a crystal, and a lightning streak of argent in her ebony hair.

Aidan pushed that thought out of his mind. What Padraig didn't know was that there was more to his marrying Mira. He'd taken her virginity, and owed it to her to make it right.

He remembered the night it had happened, and the powerful lust that had pumped through his body, making stopping impossible. Surely if he could feel that way for her once, he would again, and his marriage bed would at least have passion, if it did not have love.

"I will wed Mira Kimball come June, and when she is my wife, you'll afford her the proper respect."

"Aye, I will. But until that day comes and the vows are spoken, I'll speak the truth."

"Good night, brother," Aidan said, cutting him off. He turned to leave.

But before he could escape his brother's presence, he heard him ask casually, as if speaking to himself, "I wonder if you will tell Miss Mira Kimball about the witch you've insisted on keeping in your bed?"

Aidan kept going, through the dark hallway toward the pool of lantern light puddling around the base of the stairs. He took them two at a time, the whiskey sloshing in his glass. He reached the door and hesitated.

This woman, this strange witchy woman, had cast a spell over him. He could find no other explanation for the confusion that muddled his mind. All he could think of since the moment they'd arrived was having her beside him in the bed, her body formed to his as if she were made specifically for him.

And so Padraig's reminder of Mira set his temper on edge.

Reaching for calm, he promised himself that nothing would come of it, that he kept Olwyn near him only to assure himself she would not run off, and that when they reached Southampton, he would repay her properly and let her go.

He opened the door and entered, locking it behind him.

A smoky rich scent hit him with a lusty punch to the groin, burning incense that filled the room with exotic fragrance: amber and Tamil mint, sage and sandalwood, cardamom and ginger.

It was the scent of her hair and her clothes and her skin. It made him think of gyrating hips in a sultan's tent, a seductive gypsy's dance surrounded in swaying smoke.

His reaction to the fragrance was immediate, physical, primordial. It aroused in him a fierce hunger that had nothing to do with food.

Coming from the shadows, Olwyn emerged into the firelight. She wore a long, flowing dressing gown, and as she passed in front of the fireplace, the light illuminated her slim form moving beneath the shroud of white muslin. He saw the shadowy shape of her legs, buttocks, and waist, and his mouth went dry.

Olwyn approached him. The light was to her back and he couldn't see her face or read her expression. She'd washed, however, for he could smell her soap on her skin, the same fragrance as the incense. Her hair hung down her back, reaching to her waist, freshly brushed waves of black against the white of her gown.

And as he stood there, the cheeky witch reached out and took the glass of whiskey from his hand. She drank from it, deeply, before handing it back as if it were the most natural thing in the world, to share his glass.

"Olwyn," he said, trying to sound normal. "What are you burning?"

"Incense. I burn it every night before bed. It helps me sleep, and protects me from the nightmares."

"What nightmares?"

"Rats," she answered shyly, as if embarrassed of her fear. "I hate rats."

He could smell the whiskey on her breath, and he

wanted her to drink it again, hold the liquid in her mouth, and let him sip it from her lips.

He recalled how she'd snuggled against him when she'd drank whiskey before, and he wished he'd brought up the bottle from downstairs.

"Does it bother you?" she asked.

"Rats?"

Olwyn laughed softly. "No, my lord. The incense. Does the incense bother you?"

"It makes me dizzy, I think." *Or is it your beauty, your scent, your smile?*

"No, my lord. It is the whiskey that does that."

"I haven't had much," he said, even as he wondered at her game. The woman he'd left had been angry, defiant. And now she was mellow and yielding, smelling of sun-dried muslin and exotic spices. "You've put aside your anger?"

"I am a practical woman, my lord. I do not hang onto emotions that do not serve me." She shrugged and spread her hands. "I simply wanted what I believed about you to be true. But it is not, and after contemplating the matter, I've decided that it is useless to be disappointed."

Olwyn glanced at his glass again, and this time Aidan automatically proffered it to her. He watched as she drank, her lips wet with the whiskey. His gut tightened as her tongue slid along those lips, savoring every drop.

He would think she was trying to seduce him, if he didn't know that she was completely unaware of her own beauty.

"What did you believe?"

"I thought you were honorable," she said gently, as if she did not want to hurt him, but could not keep from speaking the truth.

Aidan turned away from Olwyn, struggling to remember why he'd closeted himself alone with her in the first place. Letting her leave seemed infinitely safer than spending the night with her. He busied himself with readying for bed, once again shucking his coat, shirt, and boots.

He heard her moving around behind him, the rustling of the sheets and covers as she slid into the big bed. He turned and saw she was huddled all the way to one side, and had placed a few pillows down the center to form a soft, plump battle line.

She watched him from the shadows, her eyes wide, the reflection of the fire moving through the hammered gray depths. The bed engulfed her, made her look fragile and small as she huddled on the far edge.

Aidan banked the fire and slid into the bed, wordless, for he did not trust his voice. It felt so strange to lie with her in civilized comfort, when they'd taken the warmth of each other's bodies upon frozen, packed earth.

"You don't need the bloody pillows lined up like that. I won't touch you," he finally snapped, reaching for annoyance to cover his desire. "But if I were going to, a barrier of feathers would hardly stop me."

"You said you were not a cad."

"And you said I was not honorable."

"You are engaged to be married, but you kissed me. Does that action speak of honor?"

"A moment of weakness. Am I not entitled to a few of those by virtue of my humanity?"

"I suppose," she said quietly, her voice lost in the dimness and the roaming shadows cast by the banked fire.

Silence fell over them, awkward and uncomfortable. Aidan lay still, his body hard and hot with awareness of her beside him. The incense seemed to fill his brain with fog. Nothing made sense. He reached for sanity, for the honor he'd been raised to demand of himself.

But in truth, it seemed a beast inhabited his body, a

roguish scoundrel that cared nothing for nobility. His blood thrummed with the pulse of his desire just from being beside Olwyn. Holding and kissing Mira had never inspired such unadulterated lust.

It seemed as if his honor had died when his body did not. It had succumbed to the sickness, lost in the black coma that had landed him in Olwyn's company.

How could he marry Mira Kimball when he felt such a dark craving for another woman?

'Tis cold feet, he told himself, a normal reaction for a bachelor about to take a woman to wife. He would ship Olwyn off to the Americas, as she wanted, and the unsettling feelings would fade.

"Will you have one more lapse, my lord?"

He hesitated. Surely she did not mean what thought. "What are you asking?"

Another long pause filled the darkness. Her voice broke it again, this time tentative and very quiet. "Will you hold me?"

Chapter Twelve

"What is this? Some sort of test?"

In the dark, Olwyn flinched at the sound of Aidan's voice, ragged and angry. Her own boldness shocked her. It seemed she had no boundaries where he was concerned.

All she could think of was that they would arrive in Southampton, and she would board a ship and never see him again. All her protestations and accusations were meaningless, sounds in the air that had no real heat or depth.

The truth was she wanted his arms around her. She wanted to be held tightly against that long, big body, cupped in those large square hands. And yes, she wanted another of those dizzyingly delirious kisses.

"We are alone in this room," she whispered, afraid of his rejection, terrified of her own longing.

He rolled to his side and raised himself up on his elbow, peering down on her in the scarce light. "You are unbelievable."

Shame flamed her face. And she felt instantly like an ugly hag who'd propositioned a handsome prince. His incredulousness cut deep. Olwyn raised her hand to her hair, to the mark that drew other's eyes. "I am sorry, my lord."

"You call me on my lack of honor, and then ask for the very thing you deride me for."

"I am sorry. Truly. Forgive me," she said, and tried to roll so that her back was to him.

But his hand on her shoulder stopped her, a hard grip. He let go for an instant, and in the darkness she saw the flash of white pillows being thrown to the floor.

"Why?" he asked, a harsh one-word demand for her truth once again.

"I told you once before of how lonely I've been," she answered softly. "If you wouldn't mind, perhaps you'd see it as a favor I'm asking . . . just put your arms around me. We are both here, lying in the darkness. Just hold me, and let's see if we can just forget the world for a few hours."

Aidan hesitated. She could feel the coil of his tension and frustration radiating from him. "I am only human, Olwyn. To have you here beside me and not touch you is difficult enough, aye? But when you invite it . . ." His voice trailed off and she felt him move, a slight shrug of his shoulders, the twitch of his arm as if his muscles flexed with the exertion of holding himself back.

And the feelings she felt were overwhelming, feminine

power and desirability. Perhaps others found her to be ugly, but for some reason, this man responded to her. He wanted her.

It was a private wanting, something dark and visceral trapped between shadows and the soul, an inexplicable and undeniable draw that Olwyn now knew they both felt. It was not a typical attraction to a beautiful thing, but rather something mysterious and harder to define.

It was lust, she realized. Absolute, unadulterated, monstrous lust.

Alone in the dark with him, surrounded by the hypnotic smoke of her incense and the vital vibration of him beside her in the big soft bed, Olwyn gave in to the wanting of his warm skin pressed to hers.

"Lóchrann," she whispered. "Touch me, Lóchrann. No one need ever know."

He, too, gave up the battle.

Aidan grabbed her again, and this time he pulled her to him, a fiercely tight embrace that was everything she'd craved from the moment she'd surrendered to his demand to keep her with him.

His hands slid into her hair, cradled her head, and pulled her face up to his. Olwyn expected his kiss, but instead she felt his mouth against her ear, his breath hot, his words incendiary.

"You deserve better than to be held in secret," he whispered to her.

"I don't care." And she didn't. If this was all of him she'd ever have, Olwyn would take it and be grateful.

His body was so hard and yet so inviting, all wide planes and warm bulges, his strength like a shelter. She wanted to slide against him like a cat, slithering over his skin with her own until she no longer knew where she ended and he began.

"Don't do that. Don't move like that." His voice was a harsh, whispered command in the dark.

"I can't help it."

"Hold still, *acushla*. I'll just hold you, as you asked."

"Lóchrann," Olwyn sighed the name he'd called himself when it had been just the two of them, alone in a stone hut. Her body fit against him the way honey melts on a heated spoon, fluid, her flesh against his. She ran her fingers across his back, over his shoulder, down his arm, delighting in the soft skin over taut muscle. "You are so warm."

"Be still, please," he said on a breath. "Don't wiggle like that."

"This is like a dream I had long ago," Olwyn confessed. "Of a man who would hold me just like this. Only you are far more real than anything I could have imagined."

Aidan held her from him a bit, and said distinctly, "If you wish to leave this room a maiden, you had better lie still."

That snapped Olwyn from her reverie. She stopped moving.

"That's better," he said softly. "Just let me hold you, and nothing more need come of it."

But inside the privacy of her own heart and mind, Olwyn couldn't help but wonder what it would feel like to lie beneath Aidan Mullen and let nature take its course.

Arousal heated her between her legs, a damp, hot awareness.

Aidan stroked her hair, his fingers weaving in and out of the long tresses, and it sent tingles through her legs, reaching her toes. He skimmed her cheek with the backs of his fingers, a caress that felt authentic in its caring, even though she knew he loved another woman.

"Your skin is so soft, so fine," he said quietly, and Olwyn thought how the darkness amplified his deep voice, reminding her of whiskey, smooth, complex, full of subtleties.

Olwyn wondered if he'd ever held Mira Kimball that way, with such tenderness. She didn't ask, however, wouldn't do anything that might break the spell of his affection, no matter how temporary it might be.

She knew she played a dangerous game, asking him to hold her in secret. But her heart, her silly, romantic, vulnerable heart knew nothing of restraint, cared nothing for risk.

Aidan Mullen was here, now, all masculine flesh and gentle touches, his body a temple of her worship.

The room they shared was quiet, nothing breaking the silence but the crackling of the fire. It made for a magical feeling, as if they were set apart from the rest of the world, suspended in their own cocoon of fire-warmed comfort, in a place all their own.

Olwyn mentally laughed at herself. Such dreamy, unrealistic thoughts for a woman who called herself practical.

But it seemed he, too, was caught in a similar spirit, for he put his lips to her forehead and pressed them there, an extended kiss that felt like a benediction and a beseeching for forgiveness combined.

"I am sorry I took your truth and held myself from you," he whispered against her flesh. He laughed a little, a rueful sound. "I usually regard myself as a man of high principle."

His tone spoke volumes, for he held a woman who was not his betrothed. His actions spoke volumes, too, for he did not let her go.

"Don't worry, my lord. It is over, and I am no longer angry."

"My brother is my twin," he continued, as if she had not spoken. "We are very alike, but also very different. 'Tis why I told you I was Lóchrann. 'Twas not a lie; my father calls me that. It means light in Irish, and my brother is Dorchadas, which is dark, he being black of hair, and me being fair like our mother."

"Your father is an English duke. How is it that he speaks the Irish?"

"He's half Irish from my grandfather, who is common, a former sea merchant. My father is duke because of primogeniture, the only male heir left in the family. But he was not born to such power, his aristocratic blood comes through his mother, my grandmother, Camille, who was born a Bradburn."

Aidan hesitated before continuing. "You see, my brother and I were born minutes apart, and my parents decided to keep secret who was firstborn, who is my father's heir. And so, all my life, I have lived with that hanging over my head. Never knowing who I am, what my life will be, and if I will have to assume the mantle of my father's responsibilities."

"They must have their reasons," Olwyn said, her eyes closed, her forehead still against his mouth. His breath was warm and humid, his lips soft, his arms strong. She could have stayed like that for eternity and not felt a moment had been wasted.

"They wanted us raised fairly, with equality. They said they felt no difference in preference or love for either of us, and they wanted us to be treated equally by our peers, so that we could both grow up as individuals not defined by a title and rank. My father was raised simply, with honor, loyalty, and love. He wanted nothing more than that for us, lest we slip into decadence.

"So we were raised with a work ethic and pride in our heritage, common and aristocratic alike. We learned the language of our ancestors, and also learned our father's business and what it means to be an English lord."

"This troubles you? I should think you would be grateful to have been raised with such wisdom."

"In a way. And I love my da, aye? I love him completely. He is as wise, strong, bighearted, and hard minded as any man I know. But I am nearly thirty years old," Aidan said, and his voice, still quiet, was sheathed with an anger so old it had become resentment. "A man full grown, and deserving to know my life path. Perhaps 'twas wise when we were children, but we are men."

Olwyn thought a long while at what Aidan had told her, looking at it from both sides as best she could, parent and child. He'd resumed stroking her hair, long sweeps of his hand that were as gentle a touch as had ever been bestowed upon her.

"Do you long for it, Lóchrann? Do you want to be duke someday?"

"No," he replied without hesitation. "I do not. There is not a day that goes by that I pray it isn't me who was firstborn."

"What do you want?"

He laughed against her skin, the warmth of it sending shivers of delight through her. "You're the very first person to ever ask me that, Olwyn."

"I suppose they don't ask because if it's to be you, you have no choice in the matter."

"Aye," Aidan said slowly, his tone giving way to dismay.

"But still, you are only human. You can't help but have your own hopes and dreams, no matter what realities of fate may or may not befall you."

"You know, Olwyn, you are a rare woman to think of it that way." His arms tightened around her. "Most other women would place far more value in a dukedom than in hopes and dreams."

Olwyn shrugged off his praise. "I have lived an entire life with nothing to sustain me but possibility, and without it, I would have surely perished." She paused, thinking of what she'd just said, and offered a correction. "Well, not my body, but my soul. It certainly would have died. So, to say there is anything more worthwhile than what we aspire to is to minimize the power of imagination, and I don't think there is a single more redemptive thing that a human can do but to hope and dream."

Olwyn tilted her head up, trying to see him in the dim light. "You've already died, Lóchrann, in body but not spirit. So ask yourself, who will you be now that you are reborn?"

She could make out his shadowy features. Everything about his face spoke of sensuality, a hidden promise in his mouth, thoughts unspoken in his eyes. The urge to bury her fingers in the rich wealth of dark gold hair possessed her, but she controlled it.

"That's been decided," he said finally, and he sounded distant, regretful. "You should sleep, Olwyn. We have a long day ahead of us."

"I do not long for sunrise," she whispered. "Here in the dark, I am happy."

"But it will come," Aidan warned her, and the meaning in his words were clear. Dawn would come, and with it, reality.

In reality, Olwyn had no place in his arms.

When morning slanted the faintest glimmers of light through the windows, Aidan rose and unwillingly left the tangled, warm nest of the bed and dressed to meet the day.

He glanced behind him where Olwyn slept, her black hair strewn across the pillow and her face, long tangles of waves across pearly, ivory skin. She had one long slim arm slung over the pillow he'd just vacated, and he noticed that her dressing gown was clumsily sewn, the seam that fell over her wrist crooked, the stitches looped and uneven. A handmade garment by a woman who must have taught herself to sew.

It tugged at his heart for a reason he couldn't quite name.

She stirred in her sleep, and her long slim fingers stroked the empty pillow as if seeking his skin as she rolled to her side.

Her hair slid from her face, revealing its perfection in the pinkish light of dawn. Her brows formed two slashes over her closed eyes, her lashes dark and long against her high cheekbones. Aidan stared at her mouth, his eyes tracing the shape of her lips.

Olwyn Gawain might have the look of a witch when she opened her eyes and stared at a man with an expression so forthright it went straight on through. Those gray eyes were piercing, unusual, searing for all their cool, striking beauty.

But in repose she appeared defenseless and small, her face nearly feline in its shape, wide across the eyes, small and pointed at the chin.

She is beautiful, he thought, inside and out.

Holding her as he had in the night had amounted to one of the most meaningful exchanges he'd ever had with another human.

That was all it was, Aidan counseled himself. He'd never spoken to anyone the way he'd spoken to Olwyn.

Aidan made a resolution then and there: he would try to speak as honestly to Mira. Perhaps he could find a similar connection there. Yes, he decided. It was his own fault for never having looked deeper.

Olwyn sighed in her sleep, a hushed, intimate noise that went right to his groin.

And Aidan struggled to remember Mira's prettiness, her fine features, her elegant bearing. Most of all he struggled to reconcile himself to his future marriage.

He did, after all, owe it to Mira to make good on a mistake that he'd forever regret. Flashes returned to him of twined limbs, murmured protests, drunken cajoling, and ultimately, the loss of Mira's virginity.

Aidan was not the sort of man who would ruin a young lady and send her merrily on her way. He'd taken her innocence, and for that, he would pay full price.

Mira came from a good family, understood the English aristocracy, its pressures and commitments, its unspoken rules and nonsensical whims. She would make a fine duchess, if it came to pass that Aidan was Rogan's heir. She was, as Aidan had told Olwyn, suitable.

And hadn't he held Mira's small body to his and found a surprising amount of passion in her kisses?

Aidan rubbed his hand over his face, turning away from the mysterious Druid who lay sleeping in the bed. Certainly marriage would bring many temptations, he told himself. He would have to learn how to subjugate his baser desires and impulses, to turn away from the temptation of a beautiful woman who was not his wife.

Such was life. He couldn't expect not to be attracted to other women. But neither could he indulge every inclination he felt to surrender to that attraction.

He knew, deep in the secret places of his heart, that if he could resist Olwyn Gawain, he could resist any woman. She pulled at his heart and his soul like no one else.

And he'd slept peaceful as a babe beside her. How many nights had he roamed his halls, unable to do what others found so simple, to just lie down and sleep? But curled beside her, his body fitted to hers, he'd found the dark serenity of slumber.

Behind him he heard the rustling of sheets. He turned and saw she'd awoken, and was sitting up in the bed, her hair in swirling disarray around her.

"Good morning," she said shyly, as a blush touched her cheeks the way the dawn lit the sky. She clutched the covers, held them up so they covered her body. The gesture annoyed him, at odds with the woman who'd wriggled against him in the dark.

It annoyed him equally that he longed for the incense-scented darkness, the feel of her against him, and secrets spoken in stolen moments.

"Is it time to go?" she asked.

"Aye. Get dressed and meet me downstairs in the common room for breakfast. We don't have time to dally. My brother tells me that my betrothed is also journeying to Southampton, and I am eager to be reunited with her." Aidan heard his own abruptness, and saw the hurt reflection of it in her face, and a wary betrayal replaced her sleepy contentment. "Dress warmly."

"Of course, my lord."

"Hurry," he commanded her, and he left the room.

When the group of travelers emerged outside, no wagon stood with the stamping horses, nor was her mare, Nixie hitched up and ready to go. The horses belonging to the Mullen brothers and their men were packed and ready, their saddlebags bursting with provisions, tents and pallets rolled and ready, lashed behind their saddles.

Aidan gave her a curt explanation when he saw her looking around for the faintest familiarity.

"Your mare is old, and your wagon older. They will only slow us down. I've made arrangements for them to be driven to Southampton. 'Twill be easier for everyone, including your poor mare." He approached her and handed over her dagger and her pistol. His sapphire eyes were hard and guarded. "I had no right keeping them. They're yours."

"Thank you, my lord," she said, and she knew then and there that whatever passed between them in the darkness did not exist in the light.

She slid her dagger back into her belt, and attempted to

feel as she once had, self-sufficient and strong, before Aidan Mullen had been dragged to her door like a mouse caught by a roaming cat.

He regarded her for a moment, the seconds crawling by as he stood before her. "About last night. I am engaged to be married, and I was wrong to lie with you, no matter how chastely."

"I should not have asked," she whispered.

The look in his eyes changed, grew unfathomable. "'Tis up to me to maintain my own honor."

Aidan turned and walked away from her, and after everyone was mounted, they set out into the cold, damp morning.

The day passed slowly, each moment crawling by as Olwyn rode behind one of Aidan's men. The stranger was youngish, thickly built, square of head, and quiet. He seemed uncomfortable, stiff, and he did not speak a word to her.

Loneliness returned to mantle her with stifling gloom.

They rode through the countryside, passing tiny farms and the small outcroppings of villages, little clusters of civilization that dotted the rolling, frozen hills.

They stopped periodically to relieve their needs, share a small bite of sustenance and a nip of whiskey for warmth. And then, with Aidan avoiding even the most casual look her way, they rode again.

Olwyn tried, and failed, to not care.

She could not help but steal glimpses of him, tall and handsome in the saddle as he rode alongside his brother. He wore all black once again, making for a dashing, dangerous figure on horseback. Watching him furtively, an ache bloomed in her chest and would not dissipate.

Her Lóchrann of the darkness was not the same man who rode nearby. No, that was Aidan Mullen, the man who might be duke, and who would most certainly be married.

Nighttime had fallen by the time they made their camp, erecting small tents around a fire as there was not a town nearby.

Olwyn didn't stay by the fire with the men, but shut herself inside her tiny tent. She bundled warmly, lit her incense, and placed it beside her pallet. The tiny lump flared with flame briefly before she blew it out to let it smolder, and as the fragrant smoke filled her sinuses, she lay down to pass the night in isolation.

But the smoke no longer offered the comfort it once had. It now smelled of stolen embraces, and a man who would never love her.

She woke hours later with a start, scrabbling to reach for a weapon as a scream rose in her throat.

"'Tis me," Aidan said gruffly, and she relaxed her guard.

He smelled of whiskey and fire smoke, horses and leather. He stood there, silent, hunched beneath the low slope of the tent wall. He radiated indecision in his posture—should he stay or go? And he swayed on his feet as if he'd drank more than he ought to.

"The hour nears dawn," he slurred. "And I cannot sleep."

Olwyn shifted and peered up at him, unable to see his face. And then, knowing that it would only hurt more later, Olwyn lifted the corner of her pallet in invitation. Apparently that decided it for him, for Aidan slid down beside her in the pile of covers and furs and took her in his arms.

"Lóchrann," she whispered. He still wore his boots and cloak, but the latter hung open, revealing the expanse of chest that had become more than familiar. It had become home.

"You have cast a spell on me," he breathed thickly. He sounded frustrated, a little angry, and very drunk. "What else explains how I cannot get you out of my mind?"

"Were I a witch, Lóchrann, you would not leave me in

the daytime," Olwyn answered him, and she reached up so she could slide her fingers into his thick, soft hair.

"I am a churl to take this from you."

"You are. And I am fool to let you."

His lips found hers in the darkness, and he kissed her with unveiled desire. His lips clung to hers, tasting of scotch and passion. Olwyn slid her hands from his hair to his face, cupping the perfection of it, her fingers traveling over the chiseled landscape of cheekbones, soft skin, and the bristle of his beard on his jaw.

She felt the taut tension of his body straining against hers, felt the hot thickness of his manhood, now rigid against her belly.

Olwyn wanted to grip it, to explore every inch of his flesh, for it wanted her, responded to her. Her own sex was hot as well, wet with arousal.

And the ground was spinning, spinning, or was it her head?

He pulled back suddenly, and Olwyn tried to hold him from leaving her mouth, tried to pull him back down into the abyss of their stolen kiss.

Aidan resisted her, peering down in the scented darkness. He pulled her against him. The whiskey was heavy on his breath as he whispered harshly against her ear, "I am sorry for this."

Olwyn knew she was weak, but she couldn't find it in her to care that he came to her only in the night to take from her what he tried to resist wanting. She couldn't care that he ignored her by daylight. And she acknowledged to herself that she was just needy and greedy enough to take whatever he gave her.

She snuggled against his wide, warm chest and said, "I'm not."

Chapter Thirteen

Beauport
Southampton, England

A dog barked as it raced down a long, winding driveway to greet the riders who approached their property. Oaks lined the drive, long knotty branches forming a canopy that in spring and summer would shade the entirety in cool green light.

Olwyn pulled her legs up as high as she could when she heard the barking, and when the dog came bounding into sight, she stifled a scream of pure terror.

It was a huge English mastiff, only a few hands shy of being as tall as the horse Olwyn rode upon. Its head was enormous, powerful, with jaws that could tear a human in two.

Aidan let out a sharp, high whistle, and the barking ceased instantly as the dog stopped in its tracks, dropped to a seated position, and with its eyes on Aidan, waited for his command.

As the procession of mounted riders rode up the driveway, Aidan whistled again. The dog fell into step alongside the horses, trotting at the same pace, easily broad and tall and strong enough to be saddled and ridden.

At the sight of its obedience, Olwyn relaxed marginally, but kept her hand on her dagger's hilt.

Dark clouds rolled in the distance, blowing closer. Olwyn looked up to the sky, and saw that they had arrived in good time. It would rain soon, the sort of fast, windy storms that blew in quickly from the coast. As if summoned by her thoughts, thunder rumbled like the faraway sound of a drum.

The scent of the sea hung in the air, a briny reminder that a few miles away, the ocean rolled in against rocky shores. And anticipation brewed in Olwyn's chest, for she'd heard tales from the trader about the magnificence of the sea, and had once even touched and smelled a seashell that the trader had brought.

Olwyn could see woods far off in the distance, beckoning her with its untamed tangle of trees and bushes, a part of the land left to be wild and free.

But not so of the manicured grounds they crossed. The slumbering fields did not even have a stray leaf or stick upon their well trimmed grass. Everywhere she looked there were signs of a gardener's hand, and she knew that come spring, the property would be in full bloom, lavishly verdant.

Olwyn suppressed a gasp as the mansion came into view. It stood massive against the horizon, a three-storied mammoth structure comprised of red bricks and white stately columns. The many mullioned windows glittered, and formal gardens slumbered around the property, their fountains tossing thin sparkling streams of water high in the air.

Servants rushed from behind the manse to greet them, and stable hands readied to take the reins of the weary horses. Olwyn slid from the horse, sore and tired from four days of riding, and looked to Aidan, watching as he dismounted. He seemed limber and fit, so vital and handsome Olwyn could scarcely believe that not that long ago he'd lain naked on her father's slab, prepared for dissection.

Olwyn also kept a wary eye on the giant dog. It seemed docile enough, more interested in greeting its master than attacking her. Aidan grinned broadly at his dog, bent down and laid his cheek against the huge head, whispering in his ear as he petted him lovingly.

And Olwyn felt a pang of jealousy. *Jealous of a dog,* she mocked herself. *Pathetic.*

A slim petite woman opened the front doors and emerged. She had silver hair, and though of a certain age, her face held its beauty, her emerald eyes vibrant and shining as she came down the wide front step.

"Aidan, thank the Lord. You are alive," she called out, her voice ringing with happiness. She turned her attention to Padraig, smiling at him, her green eyes the mirror image of his. "And thanks to you, Padraig, for bringing your brother home safely."

"Grandmum!" Aidan's voice boomed the word, and he grasped her in a huge hug, lifting her from the ground. "How are you? Are you well? And Grandda, where is he, and is he doing well?"

Aidan's grandmother laughed like a girl as her grandson swung her back down to her feet, and she pressed a hand to her immaculately coiffed hair. "We're all doing fine. Patrick's been handling the distillery, and loving the work. Only the dog has suffered your absence, howling at night for his master."

"I've missed him, too," Aidan said with a grin, and he rubbed the dog between the ears.

Padraig embraced his grandmother, kissed her fondly on the cheek, and as Padraig began seeing to the needs of his men, she turned her attention back to Aidan.

Those green eyes missed nothing, it seemed. She appraised her grandson for the briefest moment before saying, "Your beloved is here, as well, Aidan. She and her father arrived late last night."

Aidan's face barely had time to register any emotion before his grandmother turned to Olwyn. She put out her hand, a friendly gesture, and Olwyn noticed that though her manner was genial, her eyes reflected curiosity. "I am Camille."

"My lady," Olwyn said, and she took the proffered hand and dipped into a low curtsey as she pressed a kiss to her glove. It smelled of lavender, the white silk as soft as a breath.

Camille laughed and withdrew her hand. "I am not a queen, nor do I bear any titles. Please, rise and be at ease. Such formalities make me uncomfortable." She glanced at her grandson, he of the gleaming dark gold hair and suddenly awkward demeanor. "Who is this delightful girl?"

"This is Olwyn Gawain of Wales. She saved my life," he answered softly, and for the first time that day, he met Olwyn's eyes.

Heat curled through her, for in that instant he had the look of Lóchrann, the man who had sought her out every night since he'd come to her in the tent. He came drunk, reeking of whiskey, drawn, it seemed, by a temptation he could not dull with scotch. He'd held her to his body, wordless, surrounded by incense smoke and a million unspoken truths. He would kiss her and then curl around her. Wrapped together, they slept.

And Olwyn, like a needy fool, had reveled in the feel of his arms around her and his kisses, and had not asked questions.

"Oh?" Camille murmured. Her emerald eyes appraised Olwyn with a look that went straight to the soul. "I shall have to hear all about that."

"Olwyn will be staying with us until spring comes. She's headed to the Americas, and I'm going to see to it she gets there safely aboard one of my ships."

"Spring?" Olwyn turned up her eyes to Aidan's, feeling trapped and tricked. Aidan had promised he'd help her leave England. He hadn't said it wouldn't be until spring. "Why so long?"

"'Tis too dangerous. The North Atlantic in winter is thick with icebergs and ice storms, sickness strikes ships, and twenty foot swells batter them. I'll send you in the spring, when you'll be much safer."

His reply was reasonable enough, but there was something more, a truth he didn't speak. Olwyn did not dare to think that Aidan was keeping her in England for any other reason. He was, after all, a wealthy English lord who was about to be wed.

Olwyn was adrift, unsure of what to do. The prospect of spending months near Aidan and his betrothed was an acid burning in her belly.

She already had more feelings for Aidan than she ought. Such proximity to him would not help matters, for Olwyn could not look at him without wanting his arms around her, his mouth on hers, his breath in her lungs, and yes, she wanted his hands on her naked skin.

Watching him plan his wedding with his bride-to-be would be torture.

And yet, all of that did not even compare to the fear that her father would somehow find her. She shivered at the thought of Rhys's anger, and cold dread turned in her stomach at the prospect of returning to the keep.

Olwyn spoke to herself with reason. Rhys had no idea who Aidan was, she'd taken their only horse and wagon, and Rhys was far too focused on his obsession with anatomy to abandon the keep and go looking for Olwyn like the proverbial needle in a haystack.

And yet, a chill had seeped into Olwyn's blood. Staying until spring smacked of spitting into the eye of danger.

"My lord, my darling." The voice came from the open doors to the manse, and Olwyn knew before she even looked that it would be the woman who Aidan would take to wife.

There stood Mira Kimball, her small, delicate form

gowned in a pale pink morning dress that gleamed like the inside of the seashell Olwyn had once held. Her golden hair was dressed high atop her head, and little ringlets fell from it in artful disarray, resting on her shoulders.

And if Olwyn had ever seen a more beautiful feminine face, she could not recall it. Mira had the cool beauty of the truly well-bred: fine, perfect skin, clear blue eyes, regal features. But when she smiled she looked anything but cool, for her smile radiated sweetness and sunlight.

Like a princess, Aidan had said. A porcelain, fragile, tiny doll of a princess.

Lifting the hem of her gown, Mira rushed down the stairs to greet Aidan, her face beaming with pleasure. "My darling, you are returned to me."

Aidan embraced her, and Olwyn noted with a small amount of satisfaction that it was a formal embrace, cheek to cheek, their bodies held at a distance.

It was nothing like when Lóchrann held her, their mutual warmth mingling into heat, the smell of his skin surrounding her. When Lóchrann came to her in the night, it might be in secret, but at least it was primitive and real.

Mira linked her arm through Aidan's, ready to steer him toward the house, but her gaze snagged on Olwyn. Her crystal blue eyes crinkled at the edges. "Who is this?"

"Olwyn Gawain, of Wales," Aidan repeated for Mira's benefit. He politely said to Olwyn, "This is my betrothed, Lady Mira Kimball."

"And how is it you're traveling with Miss Gawain?" Mira asked.

"'Tis a long story, but basic of it is that Olwyn saved my life."

Mira held her head to the side, considering this bit of information. She swept her attention over Padraig and his men, and then back to Olwyn. Her eyes roamed up and down over Olwyn's appearance, raking her from head to heels.

Olwyn held her breath, unsure what this young woman saw. Surely she was ragged in appearance, with snarled hair and wrinkled, dirty garments.

A pang of envy assaulted Olwyn, but it was not for the expensive garments or jewelry that Mira had, but simply that Mira was seeing something that Olwyn hadn't seen since she was a small girl too young to remember—her appearance.

Mira's face registered the faintest repulsion before she turned away. She tilted her head back so she could look up to Aidan, who seemed uncomfortable, his hands jammed in his pockets, his eyes on the darkening horizon. "You all must be famished, and 'tis going to storm. Let's go indoors, where we can see to your comforts and you can tell us all about your adventure."

The group began to head inside at Mira's suggestion, and as they walked, Olwyn heard Mira's cultured voice remarking to Aidan, "Where did you say you found her? Wales?" Mira laughed lightly, the sound like the tinkling of a bell. "Or perhaps 'twas the eleventh century? Darling, she is positively *medieval*."

Olwyn didn't hear Aidan's response, for a cold fury filled her ears with a buzzing sound. Olwyn's hand moved of its own volition to the hilt of her dagger.

Medieval, was it? She longed to show this Mira just how true her words were, for she could have thrown her dagger and sliced a gleaming ringlet from Mira's artful coiffure at twenty paces.

She felt a hand on her shoulder, turned and saw it was Padraig who touched her. "Wait here a moment with me." He glanced at her dagger, and raised a brow. "Before you do something you might regret, aye?"

His face was so like Aidan's, a rugged Celtic beauty that

galvanized her attention. She sought to separate their differences from their similarities: emerald eyes and not sapphire, black hair and not dark gold. They were both handsome, rough, and tall, built with wide shoulders and muscular forms. How strange that Padraig's presence did not have the same effect on Olwyn, that she did not feel that mysterious lust, that mindless pull of attraction and desire.

He waited until the others had entered the manse.

"Ignore Mira," Padraig said simply. "She is insecure in her place in my brother's life, and well she should be. I know he is finding his attention"—he cleared his throat and finished—"diverted."

Olwyn cared not one whit for the pampered princess's tender feelings, but to be polite she said to Padraig, "If my presence bothers her, I am happy to leave now."

"You're our guest, and she's far too focused on securing her place here to give you too much trouble. Mira will comport herself, at least outwardly."

Olwyn wasn't certain that she understood Padraig's meaning. She strove to make herself clear.

"I am out of place here," Olwyn said bluntly. Padraig's eyes were sympathetic for all their intensity, and so she was able to find it within her to say, "To find that my presence is unwelcome makes it worse. I want to leave. Please, my lord, allow me to go with my dignity intact."

Padraig hesitated, and then sighed. He let go of Olwyn's arm and rubbed his hand over his face, a tired gesture. "I know my brother went to you every night as we traveled here."

Her face flushed. "Nothing happened."

"I know," Padraig said slowly. "He's my brother, my twin. I'd feel his shame if he'd dishonored the woman he's to marry and ruined the woman who'd saved his life, all in one fell swoop."

"So what's your point, then? I assume you have one, and if you want me to understand, I suggest you speak it clearly."

"My point?" Padraig laughed. "Aye, I'll get right to it. If having you here causes my brother to not marry that woman, you're a fool if you think I'd help you leave."

Olwyn glared up into Padraig's green eyes with a building anger in her own. "What are you saying, my lord? That you want your brother to humiliate his betrothed, even if it costs me my virtue, because you don't want him wed to her?"

Padraig laughed again, this time deeply. "Aye. If it needs come to that."

"I'm not bait, my lord," Olwyn bit out.

"Maybe not." Padraig shrugged affably, but the expression in his eyes was anything but. He studied her for a long moment, and Olwyn grew more and more uncomfortable beneath his regard.

What did he see?

Confirming her deepest insecurities, Padraig asked, "Why do you think he comes to you?"

The question had insults buried within it, and Olwyn couldn't help but take offense. "I have not cast a hex on him, if that's what you're implying."

Padraig seemed about to reply, but was interrupted by his grandmother.

"Miss Gawain, won't you come in? We've arranged for tea and a light repast. After days of travel, perhaps you'd also like to lie down," Camille said. Her tone was gracious, her manner kind, as if she took no notice at all of Olwyn's poverty.

Olwyn turned away from Padraig and slowly mounted the steps to greet the small woman whose goodness was a palpable thing. Olwyn felt instantly drawn to Camille, and knew why she felt it. She'd long been a motherless girl desperate for an older woman's wisdom, and yes, perhaps a gentle touch.

From the exterior, the manse had intimidated Olwyn with its size and grandeur. Inside, it completely disconcerted her with its opulence, a veritable assault on her senses. The marble floor bore an inlaid family crest, stunning in its detail. On either side of the foyer, dark mahogany tables held large floral arrangements of Tudor roses.

The sweet scent of the blooms filled the air, perplexing Olwyn. How was it they had flowers in late winter?

Prisms of light roamed around the room, drawing Olwyn's gaze upward to a huge crystal chandelier. It sparkled in the light of the many windows, blazing with the fire of a thousand diamonds.

No, she most certainly did not belong here, she thought. It was another world, one in which she had no place.

She must look like an urchin in comparison to the surroundings, a ragamuffin beggar. It seemed she'd stepped into a painting, and was a dirty blemish against its perfection.

"I'll have a room prepared for you," Camille said. "You must be exhausted."

"Thank you, but no need, my lady. I'm feeling fine," Olwyn said. But in truth, she felt hollow, as if her spirit had abandoned her body, and she was only going through the motions of being present.

Just off the foyer was a parlor, and in there Mira, seated on a silk settee, heard Olwyn's comment.

"Her stock is bred for hardship," Mira said with what sounded like admiration. "Why, she could probably bear a child and be out mucking the stables the next hour. I've heard of the fortitude of common women, and I say, 'tis most impressive."

"My lady," Aidan said from across the room. Olwyn

could not see him, but she could hear the warning in his voice. "Stop."

"She saved your life, darling. I certainly mean no disrespect. Quite the opposite, actually."

Olwyn turned her attention to Camille, a blush staining her cheeks. In Camille's eyes she saw compassion and understanding, and something else she could not quite name.

"I do not belong here," Olwyn whispered, and she hoped to find a kindred soul, or at the very least, an indulgent one. "Please, is there an inn where I could take a room? I have money of my own, and I would be indebted to you if you'd please have your carriage take me into town. I'd see to it myself, but your grandson made arrangements for my wagon and horse to be left behind."

"You'll be fine here, I assure you. You are our welcomed guest."

This was Aidan's home, Olwyn thought. He was born to this sort of wealth.

He was meant to be with a woman like Mira.

It underscored the plain truth: Aidan Mullen had no business lying in the dark with Olwyn, not for any reason. It occurred to her that perhaps his attraction to her was something vile, a dirty thrill for a handsome English lord, slumming with an ugly peasant when he had a lovely woman to make his wife.

"No," Olwyn breathed, desperation edging her voice. She couldn't remain in the mansion, surrounded by such affluence it staggered her mind. She couldn't sit at an elegant table and eat fancy foods, all the while wearing her ragged handmade garments that were not even designed after fashions of the current century.

Most of all, she couldn't bear another of Mira's repulsed expressions, as if being in her presence offended her high-born sensibilities.

It was worse than any of the people of her village calling

her a witch. It was so far worse that Olwyn longed for
Penarlâg. At least there, she was reviled for something
she was not. Here in Beauport, she felt the sting of being
precisely what they thought of her—common, ugly, unkempt, and poor.

She tried to keep her manners intact, to keep the horror
from her voice as she said, "I appreciate your offer, and I
mean no rudeness, but I won't stay here."

A light frown touched Camille's brow. Finally she
reached out and took Olwyn's hand in her own, twining
them with her slim, silk-covered fingers, a maternal gesture.

"I know something about feeling out of place," Camille
said quietly enough so that no one else could hear, preserv-
ing what little dignity Olwyn had left. For that alone,
Olwyn could have kissed her feet. "I'll help you, Miss
Gawain, but going to town is not the answer. 'Tis a seaport,
and the inns are filled mostly with travelers and sailors.
You wouldn't be safe there, and my conscience wouldn't
permit me to leave you to your own defenses. Wait here a
moment whilst I speak privately with my grandson. I'm
certain we can find a place for you where you'll feel more
comfortable."

Olwyn nodded, unable to speak. Relief filled her throat
with a lump of tears.

She watched as Camille called Aidan to her, and they
strolled down the hallway away from listening ears.
Though she couldn't make out what was being said,
Olwyn could hear Camille's voice, gentle and quiet, and
Aidan's deep whiskey-smooth tone answering her.

Olwyn turned away so that she could not see Mira. She
stood in the center of the foyer, her hands clasped together,
struggling to remain calm.

And there, far on a wall in what looked like a music
room, she caught the silver glimmer of a mirror hanging
above a fireplace.

Olwyn was drawn to it as if by a magnet's pull. She walked to it inexorably, uncertain of what she would see, afraid of how ugly she might actually be.

Her father's words screamed in her mind: *No one will want you, ugly and marked as you are . . . a hideous, piebald beast of a woman.*

Curiosity and terror ran in tandem through her as she moved toward the looking glass. Her hand touched her face, roamed over the familiar planes of it. How many times had she tried to discern her appearance through her fingertips?

Olwyn made it as far as the clavichord when she heard Camille's voice behind her. Feeling as if she'd been caught trespassing, Olwyn sheepishly turned away from the mirror to the older woman. "My lady?"

"Aidan will see to your comforts. I hope this new arrangement suits you, and if it does not, please let me know. You did, after all, save Aidan's life. No request is too great or too small. Please know that."

"I thank you, my lady."

Aidan entered the room behind his grandmother, standing more than head and shoulders over her. He hesitated for a moment before meeting Olwyn's eyes across the room.

She knew hers flashed with anger and betrayal, for she felt the flare of those emotions the moment he looked at her.

How dare he hold her so tenderly in his arms in the darkness, and pretend she was a stranger in the day?

"I'm sorry you are uncomfortable here. If you will come with me, I'll get you settled elsewhere."

Though his smooth, deep voice was mild, the look in his eyes was anything but. His was an inscrutable look, burning with internal mutiny. It occurred to Olwyn that Aidan Mullen might not be so happy to be home and reunited with his betrothed. But that was not her problem. She squelched her sympathies for the plight of the incredibly wealthy and handsome lord.

"I'd prefer someone else take me, my lord."

"If you want to leave my home and have me make alternate arrangements for your hospitality, you'll come with me."

He turned on his heel and left, leaving her no choice but to follow in his wake. Aidan hefted Olwyn's knapsacks, recently deposited on the floor by a servant, and tossed them over his shoulder. As they walked through the foyer, Mira leapt to her feet and rushed to Aidan's side. "I'll come with you, my lord. 'Tis a beautiful day for a ride."

"No, thanks. I'll see to her arrangements, and then I'll be in the distillery and the mews."

"Must you put your precious hawks and whiskey above my importance? I have barely had a moment with you."

"You'll have a lifetime of moments with me, aye? Right now I have to check on things."

"But what of Miss Gawain? Surely 'tis inappropriate for her to accompany you alone." Mira clucked her tongue as if thinking, and then added, "Do commoners hold to propriety?"

Olwyn reached her breaking point.

She faced Mira Kimball head-on and interjected before Aidan could answer. "I do realize that your betrothed's business is yours, but *mine* is not, so don't mind it for me. For now, I'll wait outdoors while you decide how long a tether he requires. Let me know if that process will take some time, for if so, I'll be sure to find a stall to muck in order to properly pass the time."

Olwyn brushed past both of them and stepped outside. And then, standing on the landing of the grand entrance, she smiled to herself, feeling better than she had in days.

It wasn't long before Mira and Aidan emerged. Aidan's

slashing brows were drawn in a scowl as he proceeded down the steps.

Mira's eyes narrowed ever so slightly, but she did not spare Olwyn a glance. Instead she smiled, a radiant, sweet curve of lips and dazzling teeth. "I'm sure you are correct about everything, darling, and I have plenty of reading to keep me occupied. I will see you at dinner."

Aidan nodded curtly and kept going. He cut a dark, imposing figure, tall, broad, clothed in all black, contrasting the burnished gleam of his dark gold hair. His wide shoulders tapered down to a narrow waist, and Olwyn warmed to the memory of his nude body, as exquisite as a sculpture.

Mira spoke behind Olwyn as she followed Aidan, a hushed warning carried on the barest breath, spoken just as she passed through the mansion doors.

"Watch yourself, peasant."

Penarlâg, Wales

Rhys Gawain woke on his bedroom floor. He hadn't quite made it to his bed. He also hadn't quite made it to the chamber pot; vomit was splashed on its sides and formed a puddle that had trickled onto the hearth of the fireplace.

Beside Rhys lay the empty bottle of rum he'd drunk the night before. He rolled to his side, his entire body aching, his belly sick, his tongue swollen and dry.

He lifted the bottle, peered into it and saw not a drop remained. How had he let himself get so drunk?

It was Drystan's fault, he answered himself. Always coming back to the keep with fresh bottles of the swill, and Rhys, overcome with his anger and outrage at Olwyn's treachery, would invariably drink until he no longer cared.

The madness had to stop.

Rhys staggered to his feet and managed to make his way

to the nightstand, poured himself a cup of water with hands that shook, and greedily downed it. He dragged his sleeve across his face as he walked unsteadily from his room, padding in his bare feet across the stone floor.

He'd find Drystan and tell him—no more.

Coming down the steps, he noticed the filth and disarray, testimony to the fact that Olwyn hadn't been there to clean up after the two men. Plates were on the tables, hardened food dried upon them, and cups littered every surface, liquid moldering in the bottoms. The rooms stank, fetid with spoiled food and stale air.

Olwyn had made a habit of keeping the place swept and clean. She'd taken out the garbage, washed the dishes, cooked the meals, and tended the fires.

He looked down at his dirty dressing gown, torn and splattered with food, drink, and vomit. His hair was greasy, his skin unwashed, and he had a sudden surge of anger, stronger than his hangover, more powerful than his nausea.

If Olwyn were there, she would have seen to it that he'd bathed. She would have washed his gown and sewn up the holes.

Unable to locate Drystan in the keep, Rhys went out to the barn, passing the frozen gardens that Olwyn had cultivated in the warm months, and the chicken coop that had kept them fed with eggs, meat, and goods that Olwyn traded.

All Rhys saw was disloyalty.

He hadn't forgiven her for holding a gun to his face. And he would never, ever forgive her for her seditious heart.

She was just like her mother, running at the first opportunity. Probably spreading her thighs for some man to pay her way, too.

It made him sick to think he'd fathered such a girl.

Rhys entered through the open door of the barn and heard an odd sound, metal on metal, and a man's frustrated grunts. What was Drystan up to? he wondered.

He crept around the corner, saw Drystan's back was to him. Drystan was hunched over a worktable, so immersed in his task that he did not notice that Rhys advanced.

And there in the dim, dusty light, Rhys saw the unmistakable glitter and gleam of gold and gems, riches beyond their imagining.

Drystan was trying to pry a sapphire from its setting.

"Liar," Rhys screamed.

Drystan jumped upright, one hand clutching a small, metal instrument, the other the gold disk. He glanced at the incriminating evidence and offered his only defense. "I didn't steal it."

"Give it to me."

As Rhys took the jewel-encrusted medallion from Drystan, he saw one of the gems was missing, obviously pried free and sold for booze. And Rhys's anger grew to epic proportions, for he'd fallen for Drystan's explanation of his sudden coin and believed that he'd been winning at cards in the village.

"Where did you get this?"

"I found it," Drystan answered weakly. He licked his lips, his eyes fixed on his treasure, for it would pay for years of drinking himself into oblivion. "Give it back. It's mine. I found it."

"Where?" Rhys advanced on Drystan, ready to grab his throat and wring the information from him. How dare he have such a thing in his possession, and hide it? They could have bought a horse to replace the one Olwyn stole, and been well on their way to finding the treacherous little bitch.

"The man, the one who woke. It fell from his sack, and I found it."

Rhys looked at the medallion with new interest. It was carved with a family crest, crusted with jewels.

Suddenly he knew that he'd find his daughter. The medallion would be their guide, for the man who'd owned it was the man Olwyn had taken from his dungeon. Rhys felt an exhilaration like never before. Here was a new purpose set before him—find Olwyn, bring her home, and teach her what loyalty meant.

Rhys inspected the medallion closer for clues as to its owner, turned it over, and saw it was engraved with script. Taking it to the window, he held it up to the meager light.

Quod incepimus conficiemus.

Long before life had let Rhys down, he'd been a scholar. He mentally translated the Latin, and as the full meaning dawned, the words sent a shiver down his spine, a premonition of things to come.

Quod incepimus conficiemus.

"What we have begun, we will finish."

Chapter Fourteen

Beauport
Southampton, England

Olwyn hesitated on the last step. Aidan was walking away from her, but she could not force her legs to move. She called after him, "Where is the dog?"

"Patrolling the property borders, I assume. He has free reign," he answered over his shoulder. He kept going. "Hurry, Olwyn. The storm comes."

"It is enormous," she said, and heard the quaver in her own voice. She still could not move, glued to the safety of house behind her.

Aidan heard it, too. He stopped and turned to face her. "His breed is bred for guarding, but they are not mean dogs for all their size. Mine is called Chase. He's been with me since he was a pup, and he's as far from vicious as a dog can be. Just by seeing you with me, he knows you are welcomed here. Don't worry. He won't hurt you."

"Dogs don't like me." Her hand drifted to her left arm, where the thin white scars were evidence to just how much they did not. Aidan raised a brow, his lips curled in amusement. Before he could say anything, Olwyn interjected, "And no, they do not sense I am a witch."

He laughed, and the easy sound of it pulled a smile from Olwyn. It made her feel good that he responded to her wit.

"'Tis likely they sense your fear of them, and respond to that. But don't fret about him, Olwyn. Chase is far too well trained to act on impulse, no matter what. I trained him myself, and can promise you that you're safe with him. He's not bitten anyone, ever, and I'd trust him with a child."

Thunder rolled through the storm clouds with an ominous warning, and Olwyn saw the staccato flash of lightning.

"Hurry, Olwyn. If we'll get you settled elsewhere, we must be going."

Olwyn braced herself with a deep breath, lifted her skirts, and rushed forward before she could change her mind. Aidan walked to the stables with long strides that had Olwyn running to keep up with him.

And Olwyn put aside her annoyance with Aidan, unable to sustain the feelings in the face of her excitement to be alone with him, and to see where he was taking her.

They reached the stables, and after they'd entered, Olwyn could only look around in wonder, for the horses at Beauport lived better than most humans. The wide-planked floors were immaculate, the stalls were clean, and everything spoke of order and attention to detail. Even the windows did not bear a speck of dust.

And the horses; there were so many of them. Beauty after glossy well-bred beauty in the labyrinth of stalls. Some ducked out their heads in curiosity, and Olwyn saw a white horse put her head out to see them. It looked at Olwyn with big, dark, long-lashed eyes, and had a long mane of gleaming, pale hair.

Thunder rumbled again, and the white horse snorted as if annoyed by the noise.

"Its name?" Olwyn asked softly as she approached the magnificent animal, drawn to touch the soft patch of gleaming, velvety flaxen fur just beneath the ear. It had the ethereal look of an enchanted steed upon which a beautiful woman would ride through a watercolor dream.

"Her name is Angel, and she's very sweet. Do you want to ride her?"

Olwyn stepped back, unable to keep from mentally picturing herself upon Angel's back, an ugly, uncombed witch riding a horse stolen from a mystical dreamscape of castles and fairy-filled forests. "No. A more serviceable mount will do just fine."

Aidan seemed perplexed, and instructed the stable lad to saddle Angel, and a mount for himself, as well. Olwyn looked at him, annoyed he'd ignored her request, and embarrassed, knowing he would soon see the incongruity of an ugly beast mounted upon a beautiful one.

"Why not ride her for the pleasure of it?" he asked softly.

And once more he was Lóchrann, his voice deep and whiskey-smooth, the sound of shadows and incense and heat. How did he manage to arouse her with a change of tone? she wondered. Her body responded to him in ways that were beyond her knowing and outside her control.

Lóchrann of the darkness—he wanted her. She well recalled the heat and hardness of his arousal when he held her. And so it lessened her trepidation somewhat. She might not be pretty like a princess, but despite her appearance, his body knew hers, and he desired her.

After the horses had been saddled and Olwyn's belongings were secured, Olwyn accepted Aidan's help and swung up and into the saddle. It was luxurious, with its soft, supple leather, made for a woman's size and shape. She eased her knee around the pommel, and took the reins in her gloveless hands.

Olwyn didn't care how she looked anymore, was unable to muster the vanity. The horse was beautiful, just gloriously beautiful, and she rode her out into the gusty, salty air, absorbed for the moment with exactly that. The moment.

Aidan watched Olwyn ride, her black hair caught free in the wind, her smoky plum gown draped over the horse's flank like a medieval banner.

She was earthy, natural, and sincere, a woman not bound by conventions or society or position. Olwyn was just herself, unaware of her beauty, oblivious to her allure. Her sensuality was like the woods they rode toward, untamed, uncultivated, and elemental.

It drew Aidan to her, for he had never before met a beautiful woman who did not use her appearance to gain a man's favor. Indeed, he was more accustomed to women like Mira, who knew the power a woman had over a man, and wielded it.

A grin tugged at his lips as he recalled Olwyn's cool retort to Mira, her glib words made into a challenge by the witchy peak of a raised brow over the silvery flint of her regard. The look on Mira's face had been priceless, evidence that no one had ever dared speak to her so impertinently.

Aidan urged his mount forward, regretful he could no longer observe Olwyn, but needing to take the lead into the woods.

He took the familiar path that led into the thicket of brambly undergrowth and rotted logs. The naked limbs of the trees spiraled up into the sky, creaking as the winds whistled through their branches. The horses picked their hooves high, stepping lightly through the tamped-down tangle of ferns and vines and bare bushes.

And Aidan felt the peace of the place settle over him, the ancient trees and timeless rocks soothing him as they always did. It made him feel intensely alive, aware that he was a part of life itself, living, breathing, reproducing, dying. He could not enter the woods without it inspiring in him a surge of humble gratitude that he was part of the cycle.

He glanced behind him to check Olwyn's progress, and was struck by the look of pure wonder on her face. It tugged at his heart, for she wore the expression of the very emotions he felt—wonder, tranquility, and the happiness that comes from appreciating the simple things that make a moment perfect.

She met his gaze, her piercing gray eyes lit from within, the exact color of the stormy, steely clouds that raced in from the ocean.

"I love it here," she whispered, as if she did not want to disturb the silent splendor of the woods. Her hair was tossed with wind, her cheeks pinked with cold, and Aidan did not think he had ever seen a woman more artlessly lovely. She looked like a medieval portrait come to life, an ancient Druid riding upon a white horse through winter-stripped woods.

A lump formed in his throat and he turned back to the trail. If he would ever be free of the spell she had cast over him, he would need to stop such poetic waxing.

He spoke without looking at her. "Aye. 'Tis a special place."

"Even with the winds and the storm coming, it remains quiet here with a certain stillness I cannot name. It is unlike any place I've ever been."

His belly tightened at the sound of her tone, her hushed reverence, as if she were on sacred soil.

Aidan remembered the day he'd brought Mira there, and the confusion on her face as to why he looked at her expectantly.

Mira had not felt what Aidan felt.

Olwyn did.

He tried to tell himself that it didn't matter. He assured himself that there was no deeper meaning. One woman responded to the place and another did not. It was hardly a sign that he would not have a successful marriage.

And he failed to believe his own lies.

The trees thinned into a meadow, and in the center stood a cottage made of sparkling stone and a thick thatched roof. It had a sturdy oak door, and a few windows with mullioned, wavy glass. All around it were studded, sleeping rose bushes, the bare climbing vines still clinging to the stone walls.

Olwyn reined her horse to a stop and looked upon the cottage, transfixed. A strange feeling ached in her chest, and she turned her eyes up to Aidan. He did not look at her.

"Is this where I will stay?" she dared to ask, her voice a hushed whisper.

"Aye, if it suits you," he answered. "Dismount, Olwyn, and I'll see to the horses."

She slid down from the saddle, and still without meeting her eyes, Aidan took the reins and led the horses to a run-in barn that was behind the cottage, nestled in the shelter of the trees.

Olwyn stood rooted there, caught in time it seemed, unable to move. If it suited her, he'd said. Yes, it suited just fine, she thought. The little cottage in the meadow, surrounded by a ring of trees, was, in her estimation, far more welcoming than the stately mansion they'd just left behind. The cottage, humble as it was, lured her to touch its stone walls, to peek through the wavy windows, and to open that thick oak door and enter to find comfort.

The prospect of staying in such a magical place until spring suddenly seemed worth the risk that her father might find her. Olwyn let out a wistful sigh as she wondered if she would get to see the roses in bloom before she left.

The first fat raindrops began to fall, and the wind picked up as Olwyn hurried to the door. Aidan came up behind her and reached across with a key, and as he unlocked it, Olwyn leaned into the sanctuary of his body, drawn by his heat and scent.

He pushed the door open and pulled away from her, his face averted as he entered and put down Olwyn's bags. The rain began to fall in earnest, and to chase the chilly, dim gloom, Aidan lit a few candles and made a fire.

Olwyn glanced around, taking in the rustic perfection of the interior. A cavernous fireplace boasted a thick hewn mantel where bottles of scotch were lined up, some full, some only half so. Two comfortable chairs sat in front of the fireplace, a table between them. Across the room a tester bed was beneath the single window, thick with quilts and plump pillows. There was a table and chairs, and shelves above them with glasses and mugs, tins and plates, and beside a fat-bellied stove Olwyn saw there were pots and a kettle.

"I stay here sometimes. I sleep better here than most places," Aidan said.

Olwyn didn't know what he meant, for he'd slept like a babe beside her.

He gestured to a small armoire by the bed. "I'll remove my things to make room for yours, but I'll leave the books. You enjoy reading, aye?"

"I do." Her mother had seen to it, and Olwyn had spent more than half her life with her nose in a book, happily lost in the story, removed from her reality. She'd read every book she owned more than ten times each. The thought of having new stories to dive into made Olwyn so happy she could not quite speak.

"Good, well, you'll be busy then. I've got quite a few of them in the bottom drawer there. Shakespeare, Milton, Marlowe." He glanced at the fireplace, and she thought she saw the rise of a blush on his cheeks. "I have a distillery just down the path, if you follow it through the woods by the run-in barn. 'Tis comfortable, I think, and a nice quiet place to be alone."

Olwyn watched him as he pulled out a cloak, a coat, and a thick sweater, and rolled them together. He was ready to leave, she sensed, chased away by his desire for her.

Aidan kept talking as he walked toward the door, his things under his arm. "There's firewood in the bin, and more in the run-in. I keep the candles in the box under the table. There's a well around back, so you'll have water, and I'll pull you up some before I go. In the tins you'll find some tea, and please do enjoy the whiskey if you'd like some.

"I'll have the staff bring your meals, if you don't want to join us at the main house, and I'll also have them stock the cupboard with fruit, cheese, and biscuits. I'll assign a servant to you, who'll come several times daily to see to needs as you might have them.

"But know that you're welcome, anytime, to come and sup with us and enjoy some company. We're a genial bunch, and not too difficult to get on with. The exception of one, of course, but I'll deal with that."

And as he put his hand on the door, his back to her, his face turned away, he said, "If you change your mind, you're free to come to the main house to stay. Please remember, we only want you to be comfortable. You're not banished here."

"I couldn't be happier with the arrangement, my lord," she said softly. "'Tis a magical place, and I am deeply grateful that you're seeing to my comfort in such a way."

He hesitated, and Olwyn noticed the tension in his body, the flexing muscle in his jaw. Why wouldn't he look at her?

"Is there something more, my lord?"

"I'm sorry about Mira. She had no right to treat you with such derision, and I want to assure you that I will take her to task for her behavior."

"Her opinions are meaningless to me." Olwyn tried to sound offhand, but really, she appreciated that he cared for how she'd felt about it. "Your betrothed is quite beautiful, and obviously privileged. Perhaps she is unaccustomed to people of my . . . lack of station."

"Nothing excuses her actions, Olwyn, and I found it very unbecoming of her. I wanted you to know that, and to know that she will not get away with it."

Olwyn laughed lightly. "What will you do, my lord? Climb into her heart and create compassion there the way you just built a fire?"

"I'll make it clear that no wife of mine would ever treat

someone in such an untoward manner, and that she'll comport herself or find she is one groom short come June."

And he still didn't look at her. Olwyn pressed further, hoping to get him to turn around. "Such a threat, my lord. I wouldn't think a few snide comments would disintegrate the foundation of a relationship. Doesn't love forgive, endure, and abide?"

Aidan cleared his throat, and she saw that his hands were fists. "Aye. It does."

He seemed to notice it as well, for he uncurled his hands and rested his right on the doorknob. He was going to leave. Knowing that, Olwyn said what she really thought, afraid that it might be her last moment alone with him.

"These woods, this meadow, and this cottage—it is Lóchrann's place, isn't it?" she asked softly. "This is where you feel the most like yourself, where you feel your own essence."

Aidan slowly turned and faced her, wordless. His eyes met hers across the small space, electrifying the air between them.

A thousand unspoken words were in his expression, and in the lines of his face she could see his restraint and his desire. He swallowed, and Olwyn watched the movement of his throat with the attention of a woman who wished to press her lips against it.

He took two steps toward her. Her belly clenched with anticipation. Aidan stopped, glanced from the bed to the floor and then back to Olwyn.

"You understand me in ways I cannot explain," he said roughly, his voice angry, his eyes hard. "But what good is that knowing? What are you after?"

The rain slapped against the windows and a flash of lightning lit the dim room for a second, bathing him for the briefest moment in otherworldly light, a silvery statue, an Adonis. Thunder rolled above them, and

Olwyn felt the answering vibration of it beneath her feet. And inside herself, she felt the quaking of her own brewing storm.

"I told you once before, I want nothing from you," she said.

"That's not entirely true, is it?"

And she saw the desire in his eyes. Indeed, she felt it, too, a palpable burning.

His demand for the entire truth made a thrill of lust curl through Olwyn's body, so powerful it shocked and ashamed her. She did want something from him—his body. And he knew it, and he wanted hers in return. Olwyn's voice came husky and quiet as she answered him, "Not entirely, my lord."

Lord, but he was beautiful, she thought. Tall and strongly muscled with a face from a Celtic fable, his dark blue eyes full of sensual promise, and a mouth full of mysteries she longed to solve. And his hair, thick, dark, burnished gold, an alchemist's fantasy.

But it was not just his appearance that drew her. It was something indefinable, a current that moved between them, unexplainable, indescribable. As he stood there before her, she could feel him the way she'd felt the vibration of the thunder, tension, sexuality, and aching desire that pulsed in the air.

And Olwyn couldn't help but wonder what it would be like to make love to him, nearly frightened of the idea of surrendering to the passion that she felt for him. The fire that burned inside her might be fanned into a conflagration that would consume her soul, leaving nothing in its wake but cinders.

"This wanting between us is dangerous," Aidan said, as if reading her mind. "It cannot continue."

Annoyance rose like her passions. How dare he make it sound as if she controlled the wanting? "If you'll recall,

I tried to stay away from you. It is you who kept coming to my tent, and you who keeps me here, in England, when I planned to leave straightaway. And now, keeping me in your cottage. In the bed you've slept in." Olwyn's hands shook, and she longed to touch him. She twisted them together. "I wanted to stay in an inn."

"'Tis not safe."

"Neither is this," she pointed out. "I will stay here in this cottage, but it's up to you to keep away from me."

He held her gaze, silent for a long moment. "Do not play the woman wronged. You begged me to hold you."

"Only once did I do that. And when morning came, you pretended you did not know me."

"I am engaged to be married, Olwyn."

"To a sharp-tongued woman with a superior air. I wish you good fortune, my lord."

"You're not so sweet-tempered yourself, aye?"

"My temperament, my lord, is hardly your concern, as I am neither your betrothed, nor your lover."

Thunder rumbled again, farther away this time, and the rain that had pelted the cottage slowed to a gentle patter. But the storm inside the cottage was not even close to spent.

Aidan's eyes narrowed, and his hands curled into fists once more. His eyes were two hard, hot sapphires, and his slashing brows drew down into a dark scowl. A muscle twitched in his lean cheek, and he bit out, "I'll stay away from you."

The anger that had risen inside her swirled and blew, not even close to passing, and for Olwyn, was easier to manage than her appalling lust. "Try to remember that when you're in your cups, Lóchrann."

"Aye, I drank to drown the wanting," he admitted. The look in his eyes was inscrutable, and his tongue passed over his bottom lip as if in memory. "But the whiskey tasted of you."

"Stop saying such things," Olwyn whispered, at once further aroused and angered by his words. How dare he plant such things in her mind? Olwyn would never recover. For the rest of her life, she would remember the incendiary things he'd said and would long for him.

And still tormenting her, he continued talking as if he needed to say it all before he turned and left. "It is like some spell has been cast over me, and I cannot understand it. I didn't want it, and I don't know how to break it. I have spent my entire life trying to do the right thing, but with you, honor is the last thing on my mind."

Her breath came fast and shallow. If he did not leave soon, she would launch herself on him, drag him down to the floor, and ravage his mouth with her own. Olwyn clung to the sanity of her anger.

"You are only curious about that which you cannot have, my lord. The proverbial forbidden fruit." But really, she was speaking about herself, her only hope that the intensity of the longing was the age-old attraction to something that could never be had. That perhaps, once away from him entirely, the fascination would dissipate.

"Aye, maybe 'tis curiosity," Aidan agreed softly. "The sort that kills cats."

"Get out then, if you truly want to be free of me. If you want to kill the wanting, you need to smother it, bury it."

Aidan dropped his things and strode toward her, closing the gap between them in an instant. He grabbed her around her waist and pulled her to him, holding her against the full length of his body.

Olwyn struggled against him for a second, hating him for making it so difficult, hating herself for the heat that leaped in her blood as if she'd been touched by lightning.

And just as quickly, she surrendered. Held to his body,

her defenses crumpled. Her head fell back, and she knew that no matter what surrounded their circumstances, her desire for him overwhelmed all else. Her arms slid around his neck, her fingers sank into his thick hair, curving around the shape of his skull.

"Witch," he muttered, and he pulled her up so that her feet only skimmed the floor, her body against the long length of his.

His mouth came down to claim hers, his kiss fierce, savage, all take and no give. He held her tight, his arms like iron bands around her, binding her to him. It hurt, but it was also a pain that felt good, for it was the intensity of his passion that she felt, frustration and longing and unwilling capitulation.

And Olwyn burned for him, in her heart, her soul, and deep in her body, a hot, wet, visceral wanting that didn't respond to reason.

He carried her to the bed and he leaned her down upon its softness, laying on top of her with the full length of his body pressed into hers. She could feel his manhood full and hard against her, a hot throbbing that her own body answered in turn.

"Lóchrann," she said aloud, but in her heart she cried out for him, words she dared not release. *Love me, want me, never leave me.*

A knock sounded on the door.

Aidan looked down on Olwyn for a brief second before he whispered, "Kiss me good-bye."

She did, a quick, soft press of her lips to his, her tongue touching his in a mating that was as old as time. He tasted of urgency and desire, and when he pulled back, his eyes looked sad. He brushed his fingertips over her cheek. "I'm sorry, Olwyn."

And then he stood, adjusted his garments, and crossed the room to open the door. Olwyn leaped up, smoothed the bedcovers, and put her hands through her tangled hair, raking the worst of the snarls.

"I saw the horses and thought it was you," the man at the door said, and he grabbed Aidan in a hard hug, slapping his back. "Good to see you, lad. You gave us the hell of a scare."

"Grandda, I've missed you," Aidan replied, and as he pulled back from the embrace, he gestured to Olwyn. "Let me introduce the woman who saved my life. This is Olwyn Gawain of Wales. Miss Gawain, this is my grandfather, Patrick Mullen."

Olwyn noticed Patrick's height—he was as tall as Aidan, and was without a doubt the sire of the brood. He had auburn hair streaked with silver, and his face, though craggy with age, was handsome and purely Celtic, and his stormy blue eyes were kind.

"My lord," she said, dipping deep into a curtsey. "It is a pleasure to make your acquaintance."

"Stand, Miss Gawain, I beg you. I'm not a lord, but am as common as the Irish soil on which I was born."

Olwyn remembered that Aidan had told her that his grandfather was an Irish sea merchant, and then realized that Camille had abandoned wealth and the aristocracy to be with this man.

The thought caused insidious hopes to bloom deep inside Olwyn's heart, hidden flowers that needed to be trampled beneath crushing reality.

She glanced over to Aidan, and then to the floor. In her mind she laughed at herself for even daring for one second to imagine that Aidan would ever consider taking a common woman to wife.

Aidan might be duke some day. He would need a wife who would understand what that meant, who would pass noble blood to their children. And even if he were not duke, he was still an aristocrat.

She reminded herself, rather sternly, that she'd not stepped into a fairy tale. Men of Aidan's stature might dally with common women, but they did not marry them.

And then she thought of the mammoth brick mansion she'd begged to leave, and realized that it was all for the best. She could never feel at home in a place so rich.

"Olwyn will be staying in the cottage until spring," Aidan told his grandfather.

Patrick grinned and glanced around at the small interior, his eyes resting briefly on the floor in front of the fireplace. "I hope you enjoy it here, Miss Gawain. 'Tis a very special place."

Olwyn regarded Patrick Mullen, curious, for she sensed there was much more meaning in his words. "Do you have memories of your own here, Mister Mullen?"

"Aye," Patrick replied slowly. He seemed to consider whether or not to say more, but finally chose to speak. "I married my Camille on a rocky stretch of beach about a mile down the way, and we spent our wedding night here."

"You did?" Aidan said, surprise heavy in his voice. "I never knew that. Why did you never tell me that?"

"You never asked," Patrick replied simply, and he met Olwyn's eyes with a conspiratorial wink. "This cottage is older than all of us, aye? I'm sure it holds more memories than mine, though I treasure my own as nothing else."

Though Aidan looked stunned, a smiled played in the corners of his mouth. "Why is it I suspect there's much you've never told me?"

Patrick laughed easily, a sound similar to Aidan's smooth chuckle. "How I managed to steal Camille away is a long, long tale, and best told late at night with plenty of whiskey. But the best of it is the life we've made, and the happiness we found. Aye. 'Tis the very best story."

"Late tonight, then, Grandda. I'll bring a bottle."

Patrick grinned and readied himself to depart. "The rain

stopped, and I promised Camille we'd go into town later today. 'Tis good to see you, lad, and I couldn't be happier that you're safe and well." Patrick bowed to Olwyn and gave Aidan another fast, hard hug. "See you tonight."

After Patrick left, Aidan stood in the open doorway. He leaned out and gave a series of three high-pitched whistles that trilled like a falcon's scream. He turned back to Olwyn, leaned on the doorframe, and regarded her with a strange expression. Fresh air blew into the cottage, scented with the salt tang of the sea and rain-soaked earth.

"You see things in people," he said. "All these years, I never knew that this cottage meant something to my grandparents. I just took it over, made it my own."

Olwyn didn't answer him, for a lump had formed in her throat. He stood in the doorway. This was good-bye.

"I'll stay away, Olwyn. Nothing good can come of me being around you. You've the right of it. If we're to let this . . . infatuation . . . between us die, we need to keep apart."

"*Hwyl am rwan*," she whispered. Good-bye for now, she told him in her own tongue. She couldn't bring herself to say forever.

She studied him intently, taking in every detail, committing it to memory. The broad shape of his body, the lean, chiseled features of his face, the sensual slash of his lips, the dark sapphire of his eyes. She remembered the feel of his skin, the thick softness of his hair, the weight of his body on top of hers, warm and hard and inviting.

"I'm sorry for any trouble I've caused," she said softly.

"You did nothing wrong. All the faults are mine."

"I wish you well," she added. "I wish you the very, very best."

He gave her one final deep, penetrative stare before turning to leave. As he stepped from the cottage Chase came bounding through the woods and into the meadow, summoned, no doubt, by Aidan's series of whistles. He came to attention, eyes on his master.

Aidan gestured to Olwyn in the cottage. "Watch," he bade him sharply. "Guard."

Dark, brooding eyes turned to Olwyn and took in the sight of her in the cottage interior. Chase barked, a single, deep *woof* that rumbled the ground and made Olwyn's entire body quake with fear. Aidan patted his giant head before turning once more to Olwyn.

"He'll keep you safe," he said simply, before raising his hand to dismiss the dog. Chase lumbered off, ambling it seemed, though Olwyn suspected he was far more alert than his easy posture suggested.

Aidan looked at her one final time. In his blue eyes she saw unvoiced apologies and unspoken longings, but she did not ask him to release them.

He bowed to her, a deep, regal, formal sweep, as if he were a prince and she a princess. And with that, he left.

Olwyn watched him ride away until she could no longer see him, and then she listened until the muffled thudding of his horses' hooves faded. Finally there were no more sounds except the hushed rustle of wind through the evergreens and naked treetops, and the far off keening of a hawk.

She turned and entered the cottage, closed the door behind her, and turned the lock. She put a log on the fire and sat before it, alone and lonely. Because there would be no denying them, Olwyn let the tears come.

Chapter Fifteen

Olwyn started as the knock came at the cottage door. Aidan had left more than a few hours ago. Had he come back? she wondered with a little frown. She put aside the stockings she'd been washing and rushed to the door before pausing awkwardly. The knock sounded again, and Olwyn opened it, afraid of how deeply she wanted to see him again.

Two sweet-faced young women bobbed a quick curtsey before entering. One bore a basket filled with food, enough for three people it seemed, the mouthwatering scents filling the cottage as she set it on the table. The other had a bundle of blankets, linens, and a beautifully made dressing gown, all tightly rolled and stuffed in a large wooden bucket. The girl unpacked them and laid the nightdress on the bed.

One of the girls had nut brown hair beneath her cap, coiled in a neat knot against her nape. Her blue eyes were bright and she smiled as she bobbed in another curtsey. "I'm Alice, miss, and this here's Molly. We'll be seeing to your needs while you're staying on as a guest."

"The lady of the house said as you might want a bath after all the traveling you've been doing," the one called Molly said, and Olwyn knew she spoke of Camille as the lady of the house. Molly's face was round and her smile was friendly. "There's a large tub around back, plenty big enough for you to sit in, and we'd be happy to attend you."

"That's not necessary," Olwyn quickly answered. "I can draw it myself later."

"You are a guest of the family," Molly replied as if that were obvious. "Tending to your needs is our duty."

Alice smiled as she took up the pile of dirty clothes that Olwyn had been planning on washing and hanging by the fire to dry, and stuffed them into a sack. "I'll return these tomorrow, miss. For now, perhaps you'd like to enjoy your meal while we heat the water for your bath?"

Olwyn held her breath, unable to respond or react. She'd never in her entire life had someone wait on her, much less two people who were there for the sole purpose of seeing to her comfort. What little servants they'd once had were for the larger duties, not ones of pure luxury. Accepting their help made her feel strange, like an imposter or a thief. Finally she drew a breath in deep and said, "I am content to see to my own needs. I am used to doing so. But thank you."

"May I ask a question?" Molly asked politely.

Olwyn noticed that the girls wore gowns of sturdy gray muslin, with crisp, clean white aprons, and that their black shoes were shined and finely made, the articles far nicer than anything Olwyn possessed. She remembered the roses clustered in large fragrant arrangements in the grand foyer of the mansion, impossible flowers blooming in winter, and realized that she was completely out of her depth.

"Of course," Olwyn managed to say.

"We have been given our assignment, and we're happy to do it," Molly said, and her eyes traveled over Olwyn. "You've never had a maid attend you?"

"No," Olwyn whispered, and she wished to be left alone, free of the humiliation of being looked at in such a way. She rubbed her hands down her coarse, dirty gown self-consciously.

Alice drew near to Olwyn and touched her hair with a gentle hand. She did not seem repulsed or even afraid to touch her. "You are only in need of a little sprucing. Come miss, let us take care of you. It is our responsibility, but it will also be our pleasure."

Molly took Olwyn by the elbow and steered her to the table. "Go on, miss, and enjoy the food while it's hot. Never you mind what's new and strange, what with us being here."

Olwyn let her tug her gently to the chair, and gratefully sat. There seemed nothing more to do than to submit to their ministrations, for Camille had set them to a task, and it was not Olwyn's place to countermand the lady of the house. It also occurred to Olwyn that she'd put the family to considerable trouble, as her staying in the cottage meant servants would be dispatched to tend to her several times a day. Not wanting to seem difficult more than she already had in requesting an alternate place to stay, Olwyn sat quietly as Alice set down a plate, napkin, and utensils.

A generous portion of food was laid before her: roasted quail and savory stuffing, a fluffy biscuit and a generous portion of pudding, along with a tin of dried fruits and a fragrant heel of cheese.

Olwyn ate as the girls pulled water from the well and heated it on the stove. Together they wrestled the tub from behind the cottage and carried it inside, setting it before the fireplace. Soon the air was filled with the steam of scented waters being poured into the tub, and when Olwyn had finished eating, she sat and waited until they'd finished their task. Alice built the fire up high so Olwyn would not be chilled, and only when they'd gotten everything just so did they motion for Olwyn to come.

Standing before the water that Olwyn had not had to heat and lug and pour for herself was another brand new experience, but more so was when the girls began to unbuckle her belt. She blushed as they unlaced her and took off her clothes. She'd never been nude in front of anyone, but she endured their ministrations and let them assist her into the bath as if she were a highborn lady.

The water was soothing after so much travel, and Olwyn sent a mental thanks to Camille for seeing to such a luxury. It eased the muscles that ached from days on horseback, and relaxed her more than she could have imagined. The fire warmed her, touching her naked skin.

"Lean forward, miss, and I'll wet your hair."

Olwyn felt the water rushing over her entire body, not too warm and not too cool, a completely new sensation for a woman accustomed to dipping her head in a pail of tepid water. The girls lathered her hair and rinsed it clean, rubbed it with scented oils and piled it on her head before taking up flannels and scrubbing her clean. They rinsed the oil from her hair and Olwyn stood, the water sluicing from her in rivulets, her skin rosy from the bath and the fire's heat.

They wrapped her in thick towels and Olwyn sat on the chair and let them comb out her long hair. They were gentle, Alice and Molly, and patient as they untangled the snarls. Soon her hair lay in smooth waves that hung down past the arms of the chair. They patted it and combed it again, the blazing fire helping her hair to dry, and they took their time as if they had not another care in the world.

It was a sensation unlike any other Olwyn had ever felt, to be so pampered and tended to. The brush of the comb against her scalp, and the feeling of their hands on her hair sent waves of relaxation through her, easing away every tension.

The dressing gown they'd brought was soft and white and beautiful, and feeling completely relaxed, Olwyn lifted her arms and let them drop the lovely garment over her. Olwyn had never worn something so exceptional—lace trimming the wrist and hem, the sewing of its seams so fine they were almost invisible, and a row of tiny, pearlescent buttons that ran from the neckline to the naval.

It felt good to be clean, to have her hair smell fresh, and to wear a crisp dressing gown. It was a simple luxury for which Olwyn was extremely grateful.

The girls cleaned up the messes that had been made with brisk efficiency, and soon the cottage was restored to normal. They left the dried fruit and the cheese, pulled fresh water and filled her pitcher, turned down the bed, and placed the hair comb on the washstand.

Molly bobbed into a quick curtsey. "Do you have any other requests before we go, miss?"

"You've both done so much for me, I dare not ask anything else," Olwyn answered. "Thank you, both of you, for being kind to me. It is not something familiar to me, and I'm grateful for it."

Molly held Olwyn's bundled clothes in her arms, and her round face was bright with exertion, little wisps of her pale hair sticking out from the water's steam. She laughed, a free and easy sound. "You're a delight, miss. Think nothing of it. We'll see you in the morning."

Both girls' arms were laden with their burdens, and Olwyn did not want to keep them from finishing their tasks. "Good night."

They left, and Olwyn stood in the center of the cottage feeling quite at a loss. She had bathed with water she hadn't heated or drawn, her hunger had been sated by delicious food she hadn't prepared, and she was wearing a gown she hadn't sewn.

In the distance she heard the deep *woof* of the giant dog, and felt a strange sense of protection. The animal looked after her, was Aidan's dog, and she somehow trusted that. Everything was different and new, and yet, felt good. Safe and good.

Later that night, Olwyn set aside her book and snuffed the candles. She lit her incense and sank into the bed, surrounded by the familiar smoke and the unfamiliar luxury, the scent of Aidan on her pillow and the taste of his whiskey in her mouth. Though she knew it was futile, she wished fervently that he would come to her, hold her, and make the night truly perfect.

Long after dinner had been enjoyed, brandy had been consumed, the tale of Aidan's journey back to the living had been recounted several times, and the household had retired for the evening, Aidan Mullen stood in the open doorway of his balcony and let the frigid air wash over him.

Sleeping would be impossible.

He looked up to the moon, watching the thin, wispy clouds drift across it like silvery apparitions.

A brandy sat on a tabletop nearby, untouched. Aidan craved a splash of whiskey, but knew that the peaty, smooth, earthy taste of it would unleash other desires.

No good could come from staring across the property, his thoughts consumed with a witchy woman who slept in his favorite place.

He knew what he needed to do.

Turning away from the stark, solitary beauty of the moon as it presided high and fat over the tangle of woods in the distance, Aidan reentered his sleeping chamber and closed the French doors. He removed his jacket, cravat, and waistcoat, and tossed them over the back of a chair. He unfastened the top buttons of his shirt before grabbing a bottle of whiskey from his armoire, along with two water glasses.

And then he abandoned his rooms, prowling through the darkened corridors of the stately manse that he'd made his home.

He stopped outside of Mira's room and knocked on the closed door. The hour was late, but he saw a thin sliver of light reflected on the hardwood floor. He waited a few moments, then knocked again.

Finally he heard her voice on the other side. "Who calls?"

"Your betrothed, my lady."

He heard her soft gasp, and it made him smile. Mira Kimball could benefit from the occasional breach in etiquette, he thought.

"I will see you in the morning, my lord. At breakfast, if you wish."

"Mira, let me in."

"My lord, are you ailing? What cause brings you here, this late? I am set for bed, and my maid has long been dismissed."

"Mira," he said again, this time striving to maintain what little patience he had left. "Open the door."

A long pause was followed by another protest. "Please, my lord. 'Tis a most inappropriate request."

"I've a matter to discuss that won't wait. Open it, Mira, or I'll open it myself."

He heard her sigh in resignation before she unlocked the door and opened it. Aidan brushed past her before she had a chance to change her mind.

The room smelled of Mira's rose-scented powders and lotions. A fire burned merrily in the hearth, and her bed had been turned down. Candles lit the space, making it warm and inviting, and he saw that she had a reading lamp on a table by a chaise. A fluffy blanket was spread out there, alongside several leather-bound journals that looked quite old. On a piece of paper, Mira had made notes in her even, precise handwriting.

"Working?" he asked. He saw a few lines she'd written: *The ring is a* Kimball *heirloom—what has become of it?*

Mira rushed to tidy up her mess, and she tucked her notes into a journal, stacked them and set them aside. She lowered the wick to her reading lamp. "Family journals," she answered softly, her eyes lowered. "You know my passion for revering history, especially as it pertains to the Kimballs."

"Aye, and I admire that," Aidan said. "'Tis one of the things about you that I most respect."

"Thank you, my lord." Mira seemed uncomfortable. She moved to stand behind the chaise, putting it between them. "What did you want to discuss that could not wait until a more opportune time?"

Aidan looked at his betrothed. She wore a flouncy, pleated, embroidered nightdress, complete with silky bows and ruffles of lace, topped with a festooned wrapper. With her flaxen hair combed out into silky waves, and her fragile, porcelain beauty, she looked every inch the virginal, wellborn young girl that she was.

Well, he amended, not so virginal. And wasn't that why he was marrying her? He had no one to blame but himself.

Aidan tried to find her appealing, made an effort to be aroused by her delicate prettiness, her fineness. And he forced himself to not think about smoky scented darkness, and a woman who muddled his mind until he no longer knew who he was.

"There is no time like the present," Aidan said lamely. He held up his whiskey. "Care for a dram?"

"Of spirits?" Mira spoke so incredulously that it could have been that Aidan had just asked her to drink horse piss. "What has gotten into you?"

"Have a drink with me, Mira. Come, let's sit by the fire. 'Tis been months since I've seen you, and I was hoping to find a private moment alone with my betrothed." Aidan strode across the floor and hunkered down onto the thick rug in front of the fireplace. He set the two glasses down and poured them each a nip.

"You want me to sit on the floor?"

"Why not?"

Mira put the tip of her tongue between her teeth before heaving a sigh. "Very well." She sat before him as if at a picnic. "But I shall not imbibe. Honestly, my lord, I don't know what you must think of me that I would drink liquor with a man in my rooms at night, unchaperoned and underdressed."

"But I am not 'a man.' I will be your husband. Do you not want to spend some time with me before you take that vow? I mean, the real me, Mira. Not Aidan Mullen, but me, the man."

"The real you?" She let out a little exasperated breath. "Who have been, then, if not the 'real you?'"

"Isn't there a secret person inside you? Don't you have thoughts and feelings you feel you can never express to anyone?"

"Not really," Mira replied, but Aidan thought he saw something there, the glimmer of what he was looking for.

"What do you want from life? If you could choose anything, what would it be?"

"I want what every woman wants: a husband who will treat me well, and a few children when the Lord sees fit."

"What of titles. Are you hoping to be duchess one day?"

They had never spoken of Aidan's future, and he watched her, saw her weighing her words with care. He'd hoped for raw honesty, but it seemed he would get a cautiously worded response.

"I will be content as your wife, regardless, though I will not be upset if it came to pass that the dukedom was yours," she said, her voice as sweet as the rose-scented powder she wore.

"Do you marry the man, or do you marry the status? What if I were a farmer or a fisherman? Would you still want me, Mira?"

"That's a silly question, my lord. Were you either, I

would never have made your acquaintance. And why are
you using my given name as such? I would be far more
comfortable if you used the proper form of address."

"Is that the way it'll always be, even after we're wed?
My lord, my lady, Master and Mistress?" he asked, and
deep in his heart he knew he wanted something different.
Something more meaningful.

"'Tis how things are done."

"Call me Aidan," he urged her, but his thoughts whispered, *no, call me Lóchrann, and say it in the darkness.
Something for just the two of us.*

But he didn't want that from Mira.

"Pardon?" Mira glanced down at the whiskey. "Is this
what's going on? Are you drunk, my lord?"

"Far from it," Aidan muttered. Inside he answered her
truthfully. Yes, drunk. Drunk on lust for a strange woman
who smelled of incense, and whose mouth was a wonder-
land of discovery and passion. Aidan picked up the glass
and pressed it gently to Mira's lips, those rosebud lips that
were not Olwyn's. "Taste it. I made it myself."

Mira wrinkled her nose. "It smells medicinal."

"It is. Drink it, 'tis good for you," he said, trying to
smile.

Mira tilted the glass back and took the tiniest sip. It had
barely touched her tongue before she recoiled, gasping. "It
burns."

"Aye, good." Aidan leaned forward and inhaled her
scent, roses and powder and freshly laundered clothes.
"Kiss me, Mira. Let me taste the whiskey on your tongue."

"You are absolutely scandalous," Mira declared. She
cast a glance at the closed door. "Someone could come to
my rooms, and they would form the worst opinions of me."

"No one will come." He leaned in closer, felt her breath
quicken. "Kiss me the way you did that night."

Mira laughed shakily. "I don't want a repeat of the same mistake."

"Nothing more will come of it," he promised. "Just kiss me. I need you to kiss me like you did that night."

"You *need* it?"

"Aye," he answered slowly, and it was the most honest he'd ever been with Mira. He needed to find some passion with the woman who would be his wife. "I do."

Mira rolled her eyes heavenward before she placed a tiny hand on his chest. She held it there, as if keeping him at bay, before she leaned forward and pressed her lips to his.

Her kiss was hesitant, timid, the kiss of a child. It reminded Aidan of his youthful pursuit of pretty girls and stolen moments with the gardener's daughter behind the solarium, when every touch was new, and every sensation was a messy mix of fear and thrills.

Aidan deepened the kiss, moved his mouth over hers, lips opening, tongues touching, and he felt like the worst sort of scoundrel, for he kissed a woman while wanting another.

The little hand on his chest began pushing him back, insistent. He remembered the way Mira had kissed him the night he'd taken her virtue, full of unskilled desire and plenty of enthusiasm. Where was the girl who'd practically attacked him when they'd slipped into a private room for a few kisses?

Mira pulled away, breathing heavily, her cheeks flushed and her eyes snapping with anger. "I said I didn't want a repeat of that night. Why do you press me?"

"The night things went too far, you were different."

"No. I was as I always am. 'Twas you who was drunk, and who would not listen to my pleas for you to stop."

"Aye, I'd drank too much, but I was not so drunk, Mira. I remember more than you might realize, and your pleas were mingled with touches and sighs and passionate kisses."

Mira blushed to the tips of her ears. "I wasn't like that."

"You were."

"I am a lady."

"You are a woman."

Mira got to her feet and glared down on Aidan as if he'd called her a whore. She looked like an angry little girl, all ruffles and lace, pouting lips and rosy cheeks. "I've had enough, my lord. I think 'tis time you left."

Aidan got to his feet and took his whiskey in hand. The night had not gone as he'd hoped. He met Mira's eyes, the color of a clear blue sky, and said simply, "I'm sorry."

He'd been saying that often of late, and always to women, he thought.

"Will you join me for breakfast?" Mira asked, her demeanor once again formal and dignified. Her head was slightly to the side, her face a mask of cool patrician composure. Gone was the upset young girl who'd just ordered him from her room.

How did she dissemble so quickly? he wondered. His life stretched out before him then, and he saw he was destined to forever spend his days with a woman whose heart and mind were a secret from him.

"As you wish," he answered. Aidan bowed slightly before he turned and left. He heard her close the door behind him then, the metallic rasp of the lock being turned. It was the sound of his future, being barred from his own wife by her sense of propriety.

Aidan tucked the whiskey bottle under his arm and headed down to the lower level, in search of drunken solitude. He felt the fool, looking for truth and whiskey-flavored kisses from a woman of high birth, a woman who'd spent her entire life until that moment being schooled on what not to say and how not to behave.

Aidan made his way to the library, his favorite room in the manse. It had floor-to-ceiling bookcases, two-storied with an upper loft that housed a reading nook. The walls were paneled in dark walnut, and the floors were thick with wool rugs. It had been designed for quiet thought, and Aidan couldn't think of anything he needed more.

As he entered, he saw his grandfather seated in one of the leather chairs by the fire, a book on his lap and a whiskey by his side. And Aidan amended his former notion—what he most needed was sound advice.

"Grandda, am I disturbing you?"

Patrick raised his head from the book and eyed his grandson with a slow, careful perusal, from his face to his posture to the bottle tucked in the crook of his arm. "The hour is still fairly early, lad, but you've the look of a man beset with late thoughts."

Aidan lowered himself into the chair opposite Patrick and stretched out his legs in front of the fire. "Late thoughts," he said with a little laugh. "Aye, they're that. And dark, too."

"What's troubling you, lad?"

Aidan sighed heavily, poured his whiskey, and settled back into the comfort of the deep chair. Here, with his grandfather, he could set down his burden. Patrick was a dependable source of strong, solid wisdom, and Aidan relied on him, respected him, and loved him deeply.

"I'm in trouble, Grandda," he said simply. "I'm not in love with Mira, and in truth, I don't think I even like her very much."

"Oh, aye?" Patrick responded in his typical way, patient, listening. He let Aidan take his time, sip his whiskey, and gather his thoughts.

"I went to visit with her tonight, alone in her rooms. I thought maybe I could look for something more, find a deeper bond or connection between us. I never thought I'd

have with her what you've got with Grandmum, or what
my da has with my mum, but I'd hoped we could find a
spark."

"And you didn't find what you went looking for."

"No. I didn't."

Patrick sipped his own whiskey and regarded his grandson over the rim of the glass. "There's no vows spoken,
yet, lad."

"'Tis complicated."

"What's the trouble? Are you afraid of breaking her
heart, or your word?"

Aidan sipped deeply, felt the familiar burn make its way
down to his belly. He'd not told anyone why he was marrying Mira, letting them think as they wished. Aidan did
not answer to anyone, nor would he dishonor Mira further,
by revealing what had happened.

Still, he knew Patrick was a man of honor, and also a
man who'd made his share of mistakes. There would be
no judgment between them, but plenty of understanding
and discretion.

"August twelfth of last year I attended the annual lawn
party that the Gilberts throw. You know the one, where
they roast an entire pig and everyone is supposed to wear
a pair of pig's ears?" Aidan rolled his eyes and Patrick
laughed. Such were the bizarre ideas some people thought
festive.

"Mira was there, of course, and we had a nice time together, laughing and generally enjoying the day. By the
time we'd changed for the ball that evening, I admit, I was
rather smitten with her. So we went off to the ball together,
with her father, and things were quite fine until her father
took sick. Something about pork not agreeing with his
constitution. He went upstairs and found a guest bed."

Patrick seemed to know where the story was headed,

because he grunted his understanding, and then sighed, long and deep.

"Aye," Aidan said slowly. "The night wore on, the champagne flowed freely. We found a private place, ostensibly to talk, but things progressed beyond that. Well beyond that. In what amounts to a moment of incredibly bad judgment, I became obligated to marry Lady Mira Kimball or else be a cad."

"You were raised to do the right thing," Patrick said simply. "Of course you proposed marriage."

Aidan shrugged and downed the rest of his whiskey in a big gulp, barely tasting it. "You know, Grandda, 'tis my own fault, and I take all the blame for that night. She was innocent, and I was"—he met his grandfather's eyes and let out a mirthless laugh before saying—"not so very innocent."

"I know how 'tis, lad. I was young once, and a sailor, aye?"

"Right." Aidan poured himself another generous draught, and offered Patrick the same. Patrick declined with a wave of his hand, and Aidan continued talking. "As I said, 'tis all my fault. But I must say, I think she had it in mind. Maybe not for things to go that far, but she'd had her eyes on Padraig and me, and the moment I showed any interest, she pounced. You may have noticed that the pickings at court are slim, and Mira is accustomed to wealth and prestige. I don't think she's looking to be a baron's wife, nor the wife of a man twice her age."

"You don't think her interest in you is genuine, then?"

"She's got a half shot at being duchess, aye?"

Aidan spoke those words deliberately, watching Patrick's every detail, hoping that his grandfather would make some sort of gesture or expression that might offer Aidan a clue as to who was the firstborn son.

"And a half shot at not," Patrick answered genially,

without so much as a flicker of recognition. "You're a fine man, Aidan, with a big heart and a face as handsome as *Cú Chulainn*. You've too much to offer to be thinking a woman's after only the possibility of a title."

Leaning forward in his chair, Aidan dangled his whiskey glass between his knees and met Patrick's eyes full-on. He dared to ask what he'd spent a lifetime wanting to know. "Do you know, Grandda? Do you know who was born first, and who will be duke?"

"Your parents decided to keep that to themselves, lad. I'm not a man to undermine such a decision, whether I knew or not. 'Tis not my place to interfere."

"I hate it," Aidan whispered, his frustration seething in his blood. He wished suddenly that his father were there, so he could face him full-on, man-to-man, and demand the truth.

"I know you do, lad, but no matter what, it makes no difference. Be you marquis or earl or duke, you are Aidan Patrick Mullen, and none of those titles begins to define you."

Aidan knew Patrick was right, and he understood that that was precisely how his grandfather had raised his son, Rogan. With honor and dignity that did not come from a title, but from the blood, the heart.

Rogan wanted his sons to find the same strength within themselves, where lordly titles were meaningless.

"I envy you, Grandda." Aidan drank deeply again, feeling the loose warmth of the whiskey wending its way through his blood. "You're free of all of it. You've never been a slave to man or king or country."

"No man, no king, no country, 'tis true. But I am slave to a woman. My Camille is my queen, lad, and I'm merely her vassal. She commands my heart and soul since the day I met her."

Patrick's declaration was not sappy romanticism, but spoken as plain fact. It inspired in Aidan such a pang of envy that it became an ache in his chest. He would never feel that way about Mira. Such love could not be manufactured by want, it was just a gift, and Aidan's mistake with Mira would condemn him to never receive it.

"What will I do?" he wondered aloud. "I am bound by honor to make right what I've done, but I tell you now, I do not wish to take that woman to wife."

A long silence fell between them, and Aidan stared into the fire, watching as the feasting flames consumed what was once living. A log broke and fell into two, shooting a shower of molten sparks up the draft.

After a time Patrick spoke, his words weighed and chosen with the care of a man who knew the full meaning of them. "I've seen marriages made for love, my own included, and I've seen them made for every other reason under the sun. Barring none, the ones made for love have been better."

"What are you suggesting, Grandda?"

"You're a grown man, lad, and as I've said, you've a good heart. You'll do the right thing."

"How will I? I don't even know what that is any more."

They fell to silence once more, and Aidan had finished his drink before Patrick answered, his deep voice low and thickly Irish. "Well, lad, maybe that's true right now. But I do think that your dallying with the *spéirbhean* you've ensconced in the cottage isn't helping the issue, is it?"

Spéirbhean, he'd called her. It tugged a grin from his lips as nothing else could have at that moment. "Aye, Grandda. She is a beautiful dream of a woman. And aye, she does complicate matters."

Chapter Sixteen

The ring of woods surrounding the small cottage came alive with the first touches of dawn. Deer moved through the bare underbrush, squirrels raced, and birds darted from limb to limb. Olwyn emerged from the privy, and though it was cold, the crisp morning air invigorated her, and the beauty of the place inspired joy unlike anything she'd ever felt. She laughed at nothing in particular, just purely happy, her sound adding to the peace of the ancient place.

The laugh froze in her throat as she saw the dog moving through the trees. His tan fur gleamed sleek against his giant, muscular body, his jowls and markings around his eyes black.

He stepped out of the woods and into the meadow, his dark eyes on her, carrying a huge stick in his mouth. His tail was down, not wagging, his ears laid back against his head.

"Go away, Chase," Olwyn whispered.

She glanced to the cottage door; it was at least fifty paces away.

The dog moved toward her, his massive jowls spread out over the stick in a macabre smile.

It trotted nearer still, and Olwyn couldn't move. The dog could easily overcome her if she ran. She remembered Aidan's promise that the dog would not hurt her.

Chase slowed and stood before her, and Olwyn met his eyes. She relaxed marginally, for his eyes were mellow, and nothing like the white-rimmed manic eyes of her father's dogs. Indeed, she thought, Aidan's dog rather reminded her of a horse, for all his size, he had a gentle presence.

Chase cocked his head to the side, and let out a little *woof* from behind his big stick, as if saying hello.

And so it seemed only polite to greet him in return. "Good morning," Olwyn said. "You are a big dog, aren't you?"

The dog took two steps toward her and dropped the stick at her feet. He wagged his tail and appeared rather expectant, as if he urged her to do something. She looked at the stick, thicker than her arm and slimy and wet with drool, and then back to Chase. "Is that for me?"

Chase barked, once, but it was not an angry sound.

And so Olwyn, unsure of what else to do, picked up the stick and offered a nervous smile to the huge animal. "Thank you."

Chase seemed satisfied, for he lumbered around the perimeter of the meadow, sniffed a tree, urinated on it, and then left, crashing through the woods without a look back at Olwyn.

Somewhat bemused, Olwyn took the stick with her as she went back inside, leaned it against the wall near the door, and realized that she'd just communicated with a dog easier than she did with most humans.

By dinnertime Aidan's parents, Rogan and Emeline, had arrived at the manse, and the staff readied rooms to accommodate them and their servants. No sooner had Aidan finished telling his parents what had become of him on his voyage did they hear Chase barking, alerting them that others were arriving.

Rogan's sister, Kieran, and her husband, Matteo, approached as their retinue of carriages rumbled up the drive. They came with their three grown children following them, and all the trunks and maids and manservants that came with such a large group. The entire family gathered to welcome Aidan home, and much to Aidan's dismay, the story of his bout with death had to be told and retold a few more times.

It was, he decided, a story that needed to be permanently buried.

"Where is this amazing Miss Gawain?" Portia de Gama asked. She was the youngest of Matteo and Kieran's children, a stunning beauty with her mother's fine features and her father's sensuality. She wore her glossy dark hair coiled high on her head, and her clear blue eyes were thickly lashed. Every time Aidan looked at her he saw trouble, for Portia had the flash of the devil in her eyes.

"She is staying in the cottage," Aidan answered. "Miss Gawain found herself uncomfortable staying amongst strangers, I think."

"You should see her," Mira said, with laughter in her voice. "She is very unusual."

"How so?" Portia asked, and her face took on an expression of annoyance. She did not like Mira Kimball, and she made no pretense of hiding it.

"She wears a *dagger* in her *belt*," Mira answered with a fair bit of arch glee. "And that is not the oddest thing about her."

"My lady," Aidan snarled. He saw Lord Falconbergh look at him sharply, clearly not approving of the tone Aidan took with his daughter. Aidan ignored him. "That is more than enough."

"I should think that a woman who single-handedly saves a man's life would be unusual, to say the least," Kieran interjected, and she rose from her seat to join Matteo by the fire. Aidan saw Matteo touch Kieran's hand with his, and Kieran nodded in response. They did not even need to speak, Aidan realized, to communicate.

And meanwhile, his betrothed sat near the window, completely unaware that he was ready to drag her from the room and teach her better manners.

"I want to meet her," Emeline announced.

"I think we all do, Auntie," Sophia de Gama agreed. She was the middle child, the very feminine version of her father, with melting brown eyes, and dark wavy hair. Sophia held a glass of red wine in her long, elegant fingers, and her lips were the same shade of burgundy. Aidan looked at his female cousins with a mixture of protectiveness and awe, for they were two of the most beautiful women he'd ever seen.

The third being a Druid with eyes the color of a storm cloud, and hair that was like a midnight sky streaked with lightning. He remembered the feel of her beneath him, the slim, lithe strength of her body, and the smoky, exotic smell of her hair and skin.

Not a moment had gone by since he'd left the cottage that he hadn't longed to go to her, to lie with her in his arms, and feel completely at home. To slumber deeply, the untroubled rest of a man at peace.

That, he realized, was the curse he would have to endure the rest of his life: never feeling totally at ease. It was as if a piece of him was missing, a part he hadn't known existed until for the briefest, best time in his life, Olwyn had filled it.

"Miss Gawain asked to be left alone, and we will all respect that," Aidan stated bluntly. He sent Mira a warning glance, and added, "She is a unique woman, 'tis true, and she deserves far better than to have her clothing poked fun of as if she were a schoolgirl at lessons, yet that is the reception she received upon arrival. If Miss Gawain wants privacy, 'tis a small wonder, and the least we can offer her."

Lord Falconbergh snorted and rose from his seat to look out the window. Mira narrowed her eyes and stared hard at the floor, clearly angered over Aidan's comment.

Good, Aidan thought. Let them both see that he would not tolerate such spiteful, slyly malicious remarks.

Rogan met Aidan's eyes briefly, and in his father's gaze he saw questions and concern. Anger and love were a tangle in his gut, and Aidan made a promise to himself that he would have it out with his father, once and for all. The time for secrets had come to an end.

Aidan went to the liquor stand to pour himself another brandy. As he picked it up, he looked regretfully at the whiskey bottle. In it was scotch he'd distilled himself, a smooth, peaty single malt. He knew it would taste of Olwyn.

He poured the brandy and tried to put her out of his mind. No good could come of his obsession.

A hand came down on Aidan's shoulder, and he cast a glance to his side and grinned. His cousin, Roman, the oldest of his Aunt Kieran's offspring, leaned over and spoke softly for no one else's ears.

"Prey to the cliché, cousin?"

"Aye," Aidan admitted softly. Roman de Gama was like his father in more than just appearance—he read a person well, and was no man's fool. Aidan wasn't sure which cliché Roman spoke of, that of marriage bonds being more a binding than a blessing, or that of falling in love with the person who saved one's life. But either way, Aidan knew both applied. "I am sunk."

"We will have to talk later," Roman said softly, and his hand tightened on Aidan's shoulder in solidarity. Roman's white teeth flashed in a rakish grin. "We'll get you out of it, somehow. If I have to seduce your bride, cousin, I will bear up under the stress and get the task done."

"You may have to stand in queue," Aidan answered, and he inclined his head to where Mira sat. Padraig had taken a seat on the bench beside her and appeared to be engaging a lively conversation, for Mira's face was now bright and gay.

"When it comes to me and women, there's never a line," Roman quipped, and he laughed as he sauntered away.

Aidan shook his head and grinned. Roman's words were far too accurate to be called boasting, for his lean good looks and smooth charm had divested many a young woman of her sense of morality.

Camille came to Aidan's side, and stood on tiptoe to kiss his cheek. "'Twas right of you to speak for Miss Gawain," she murmured softly.

Aidan sighed and shrugged. He hated that his grandmother saw noble motive in his words, when truly, beneath it all, Aidan felt the exact opposite of gallant. Inside he was a writhing mass of unquenched, unstoppable, unfathomable desire for a woman who was not his betrothed.

All he wanted was to go back in time to when he'd lain in a stone hut with that strange, witchy woman, unsure of even the year or the day, but so completely at peace with her that it did not matter. It had been just the two of them, Lóchrann and Olwyn. Simple, unrefined, and more authentic than anything else Aidan had ever felt.

But that was not his reality. In reality he'd promised to stay away from her. And so he would.

Still, there were things he could do for her, without having to burden her with his desire. She deserved far better than stolen embraces.

"Grandmum, I have a favor to ask of you," Aidan said quietly, for Camille's ears alone. He leaned down and whispered his request. "Will you see to Olwyn? She seemed to feel comfortable with you, and I worry that she will be lonely day after day."

Camille smiled and nodded her head. "Of course. And you are kind to think of her needs. I'll see to it she feels welcomed."

Aidan gave his thanks and cast a glance to the corner, where Padraig was seated with Mira, the two of them laughing over something. "Do you think it strange that Pad talks to her so? He is not very fond of Mira."

"Perhaps as your wedding day draws closer, he's growing accustomed to the idea of her being a part of the family." Camille gestured to Kieran and Matteo's offspring, gathered by the fire with their parents, and Rogan and Emeline. They chatted amongst themselves as they drank wine and exchanged stories, hands gesturing, faces animated, their language peppered with Italian words and easy laughter.

"See how they are together, friends now that they are grown?" Camille pointed out softly. "That is the bond our family brings, so tightly knit and aware of the need for such closeness. We are a tough brood to penetrate, Aidan, 'tis difficult to become one of us. Be mindful that Mira very likely feels on the outskirts. I think 'tis very wise of Padraig to see to her this evening."

"Aye. But he sits closer than is proper," Aidan answered.

"You're not jealous of your brother's attention, are you?"

"No," Aidan said flatly, and he wasn't. It bothered him that he could see Mira so close to another man, her bright hair in contrast to Padraig's black, her tiny body dwarfed by Padraig's size and strength, and not care. He should be jealous, protective. But he felt none of that.

Instead, watching as his brother grinned like a wicked Irish bastard and laughed as though he truly enjoyed Mira's company, Aidan only wondered what Padraig was up to.

Camille reached up and cupped his cheek. "You look tired. Are you not sleeping again, love?"

Aidan turned his attention back to his grandmother. "Not so well since I've been home, but I'm sure I'll settle in."

"Have you tried warmed milk? It really does work."

A grin tugged at his lips as he looked down into the caring face of his beloved grandmother. Warmed milk. He nearly laughed.

What he needed was to curl up against Olwyn in smoky,

scented darkness, but he didn't think that those around him would see that as an appropriate aid to a good night's rest.

He gave Camille a quick squeeze. "Aye, Grandmum. I'll be sure to try that."

Early in the morning, Olwyn woke to the sound of scratching at the cottage door. She peeked out the window and saw that Chase had returned. Opening the door a crack, she saw he had a bone in his mouth this time, and he dropped it on the doorstep when he saw her.

"More presents, Chase?" Olwyn asked him with a smile. "You're spoiling me."

The dog wagged his tail and watched her expectantly. She reached down and lifted the slimy bone, and Chase's tail picked up speed. Olwyn smiled, and then unable to contain herself, laughed. "You're a good dog," she told Chase.

Growing bold, she reached out to touch his head, rubbing between his ears as Aidan had done. His fur was sleek and hard, much like a horse's coat: shiny, dense, and thick. Chase held still, his only movement the wagging of his tail, and when Olwyn pulled her hand back, he trotted off into the meadow once more.

She leaned the bone against the wall beside the stick he'd brought her the day before, and wondered if this would become a daily thing. Looking at the scars on her arm, she could only wonder if her father had trained his dogs to hate her somehow, for they'd attacked her without provocation.

Before she had a chance to really think about why her father would have done something so cruel, she heard the approach of horses on the trail and knew that Molly and Alice were coming.

Olwyn rushed back inside and quickly made up the bed

so they would not think her lazy, and hurried to put away
the book she'd been reading the night before. She rinsed
her whiskey glass and turned it over to dry on a towel, and
then ran the comb through her hair.

When she opened the door to let the girls in, Olwyn
was shocked to see that Camille had accompanied them.
She remembered that Patrick had said they'd spent their
wedding night in the cottage, and Olwyn blushed at the
thought.

"My lady," she said, and dipped down into a deep curtsey. "Welcome."

"Good morning, Miss Gawain," Camille said as she
entered. Her bright green eyes swept over the interior, and
she added softly, "Ah, and here 'tis, as perfect as my
memory. Are you comfortable here?"

"I love it, my lady. Thank you for making these arrangements."

Camille turned to Olwyn, and her lips curved in a smile.
"I'm glad to hear it, and now I have a favor to ask of you
in return."

"Of course. Whatever you need."

"Come with me into town, my dear. I have an errand to
see to, and would be grateful for the company."

A slight, troubled frown touched Olwyn's brow as she
envisioned what would likely happen—the stares, the
whispers. Would the people of Southampton think her a
witch?

Camille saw her hesitation and overrode her worries.
"'Twould please me to have you as my guest. Please, Miss
Gawain, let me show you our town and treat you to a
fine meal."

Olwyn let out a little sigh. She couldn't deny Camille
anything. "I would be honored."

Alice and Molly fixed Olwyn's hair, brushing it into
long, silky waves before pulling it back from her face.

They secured it with a ribbon and left it to hang to her waist before setting to the task of helping her to dress, her gown now cleaned and brushed and pressed. Though it was shabby, Olwyn was grateful that it was neat and tidy so at least she would not embarrass Camille too much. As she buckled her belt and slid her dagger into place, she saw Camille looking at her weapon with an expression of amused tolerance.

"Wearing it has become a habit," Olwyn explained, her cheeks flushing. "Does it offend you, my lady?"

"Not in the slightest," Camille replied easily. "There was a time when I wore a dagger myself."

A well-bred lady born to privilege who'd felt the need to arm herself? Curiosity and surprise made for a pleasant departure from Olwyn's insecurity about her dress and appearance. "Oh? Will you tell me about it?"

Camille smiled and opened the door. As they stepped out into the chilly morning air, she said, "Yes, I think I will."

The ride into Southampton wasn't too long, and as they rode Camille told Olwyn of when she was a young girl, living at Beauport with her family. She told a story of abuse and manipulation, of degradation, beatings, and a man who overstepped his boundaries in the most heinous way. And by the time they'd arrived in town, Olwyn understood a small portion of why Camille had chosen to arm herself with a dagger hidden beneath her skirts.

Olwyn felt a kinship with Camille, for they were both women who spent their youth longing for a mother's kind touch, and they both knew more than their share about being born to a parent who would go to great lengths to control them.

Snippets of her life in her father's keep flashed in Olwyn's mind, and she was more and more certain in the time she spent away from Rhys that he had used his words against her.

Olwyn could only wonder how much of what Rhys had told her was true.

The town of Southampton bustled, even first thing in the morning, the cobbled streets alive with vendors selling textiles and fabrics, meats and fish. Sailors, fresh in from the morning tides, wandered the streets, easily identifiable by their thick sweaters and rolling gaits. Alehouses were open, and as they went by Olwyn saw that a few men were already at the bar, leaning over full mugs of ale and plates of eggs.

The air reeked of food and fire smoke, horse dung and tanned skins. When their carriage came to a stop, Olwyn alighted, full of excitement. The noise of the calling vendors clashed with horses' hooves and wagon wheels ringing on the cobblestones. Whitewashed buildings lined the street, the windows lined with empty window boxes that would spill bright flowers come spring. Women moved briskly up and down the streets, most with children in tow, going about their business in a way that suggested they'd heard the cries of the vendors too many times to take notice.

The town was at least ten times larger and more crowded than *Penarlâg,* and Olwyn was struck by the fact that no one seemed to take notice of her. Relief washed over Olwyn, for there in Southampton she was not an object of ridicule; no garlic bulbs pelted her, no insults were hurled at her. She walked down the street beside Camille, and was able to enjoy the sights in peace.

They dined in an inn's front room, and Olwyn felt like a lady as the staff brought them tea and scones, fruit and honey, tasty pastries and coddled eggs. As they ate, Camille told her stories of when Aidan and Padraig had been babies, and what a delight they'd been.

And when they'd finished eating, Camille dabbed her lips with her napkin and said, "And now, my dear, I have another favor to ask of you."

"My lady?"

"We are having a dinner tonight to properly welcome Aidan home, and I was hoping that you could join us. The entire family wants to meet the woman who saved Aidan's life, and it would please us all greatly if you would let us honor you this night."

Olwyn opened her mouth to demur, but could not form the words. For all she could think of was Aidan, and her heart raced and her palms sweated.

Lóchrann.

She wanted to see him again, to be close enough to smell his skin and breathe his essence. She wanted his regard on her, those dark blue eyes to travel over her, to feel the vibration of his desire in the air.

He would be with Mira, she knew. He would be reserved and stiffly proper with Olwyn, would be polite and dignified. She knew he'd be wearing elegant clothes, as would everyone else, and he would smell of soap and cologne and not her exotic incense and his whiskey.

But he would not be able to deny his darker longings, and she knew that, too. Her Lóchrann of the darkness desired her in ways that were visceral and elemental. And if she went to the dinner, perhaps she would see glimpses of that need, that aching, urgent pull that tethered her to him as nothing else.

Just one of those moments would be worth whatever else the evening would bring.

"Yes, my lady," Olwyn said softly, her voice low and husky despite her effort to sound normal. "I will come."

If Camille noticed, she gave no sign. She paid for the meal and rose, leading the way to the shop next door. Olwyn followed without paying attention, her only thoughts for

Lóchrann, and the minutes that spanned the time until she would see him again.

She barely noticed that Camille had led the way to a dressmaker's shop, and when Olwyn took note of the walls of fabrics, the bundles of laces and bags of buttons, the racks of partially sewn gowns and drawers spilling undergarments, she began to realize what Camille had in mind.

She turned a surprised look to Camille, who only smiled. "Will it offend you overmuch if I purchase you a gown or two?"

"That's not necessary," Olwyn answered quickly, her face flushing with deep embarrassment. She'd thought Camille had turned a blind eye to her appearance, but apparently, she hadn't. "I am quite comfortable as I am."

Still, her eyes moved longingly over the pretty gowns, feasting on the fabrics that were a delight to behold: silks, brocades, velvets, and lace of every color.

For a woman like Olwyn, whose entire wardrobe was fashioned ancient garments found in closets, and pieced together from bolts of fabrics traded for foodstuffs, it was a veritable assault of beauty on her eyes.

And then she saw it—a huge mirror mounted against the far wall.

Fabrics and gowns forgotten, she murmured to Camille, "My lady, do you mind?"

Camille followed her gaze and looked puzzled for a moment. It dawned on her then, for she said, "You've not seen yourself?"

"Not that I can recall," Olwyn confessed quietly. She raised her hands to her face and touched the planes of her cheeks, the shape of her nose, and met Camille's eyes. "Am I so ugly, my lady?"

"Go see for yourself," Camille answered gently, and with a raise of her hands she gestured for the shop staff to give them privacy.

Olwyn walked toward it with the pace of one moving toward the gallows. She heard her father's voice, calling her hideous, saw Mira's face, etched with revulsion, and recalled Padraig looking at her curiously, asking why Aidan came to her.

A young woman came into view in the mirror, and Olwyn held her breath as she looked at herself.

The first thing she noticed was her eyes, and in that instant, meeting her own bold stare in the looking glass, Olwyn understood why people stared at her. They were gray and clear, but also arresting, otherworldly, primal, and fierce, something like an animal's gaze. Thickly fringed with black lashes, they were beneath thin, slashing black brows, and her skin, so fair and white, was stark against her black hair.

She was a study in neutral contrasts, shades of black and white and gray, save for the seashell pink of her lips. And they were soft looking, feminine and plump, feline in their shape. She licked her lips, saw her small tongue dart out, and she laughed at the sight of her mirror image doing as she did, like magic. As she laughed she saw her teeth where small and white and straight, no half-rotted witch's fangs.

She was slim, the bones in her face and hands and neck delineated, and her body was nicely made, with a tight, tiny waist and breasts that were full and round and in proportion to her shape.

She reached up and untied the ribbon that held her hair back. Waves of shiny black tresses cascaded around her face and shoulders, and there it was, a narrow streak of pure white running down her left side like lightning slicing through darkness. With the odd streak and her piercing eyes, she understood why they called her a witch, for she was most certainly striking, and with her outmoded garments, and a dagger in her scarred, thick belt, she looked unusual and a little dangerous.

But there was one fact that was irrefutable.

"I am beautiful," she whispered.

"You did not know?" Camille asked her, standing behind her in the mirror. "Surely you must have noticed the way men respond to you."

"Only one," Olwyn murmured, and she saw her own blush in the mirror turn her cheeks pink.

"You are a rare beauty, Miss Gawain. That's a fact."

A swell of pure anger that was so violent as to be hatred welled in her chest, a squeezing hot fist of razors around her heart.

Her father had lied to her all those years.

Olwyn saw the rage rise in her face, for her eyes became flinty and cold, and her brow raised to form a peak above one eye.

"All my life he told me I was hideous," Olwyn said, choking the words out. "He told me that no man would want me, that I was a piebald beast of a woman."

Camille moved closer, and she put her hand on Olwyn's back, a comforting pressure. "He lied to control you," she said simply. "'Tis cruel, but effective."

"How could he? My own father." Olwyn wanted to weep, but not because she was sad. She wanted to cry because she was so angry that Rhys was not there, that there was nothing she could do with the rage except feel it for all its impotence. "I stayed with him. Was loyal, and for it he lied to me."

"Sometimes you do the right things for the wrong people," Camille said gently. "And when enough time has passed, you can take comfort in that."

Olwyn nodded, knowing that Camille was right. She had done the right thing for the wrong man, and in that wisdom came another insight. Doing the right thing said more about Olwyn than it did about Rhys. He was still a liar, but she was no longer his victim.

Like her mother before her, Olwyn had escaped.

She took a breath, and then another, and finally another. The anger dissipated slowly, and finally she let it go. Rhys could not control her any longer.

Meeting Camille's gaze in the mirror, she told her, "Thank you for bringing me here. I will never hear his voice in my head again."

Camille gave Olwyn a squeeze before wandering the shop. She picked up a gown of shimmering silver silk and brought it to Olwyn. "You would be stunning in this. 'Twould please me greatly if you would try it on."

Olwyn twisted her hands in her scratchy woolen skirt and eyed the dress with trepidation. It was the gown of a lady, the fabric so fine it could have been spun by a fairy, shining with a mystical, metallic gleam that shifted in the light. "I dare not."

"'Tis a gown, nothing more. Pieces of cloth sewn together," Camille urged her softly. "Do not be afraid of it."

"Such a thing must cost," Olwyn's voice faltered, and she cleared her throat and forced out, "a fortune."

Camille approached Olwyn and laid the gown in her arms. "All of my life I have never wanted for anything material. But as I told you on our ride here, I never had much kindness shown to me until I met my husband. Since then I've learned the value of such blessings, but I've also learned that gifts are sometimes harder to receive than they are to give."

Camille reached out and touched Olwyn's cheek with the backs of her fingers, a maternal gesture that went straight to Olwyn's heart, where the little girl who'd cried for her mother still lived on. "Please, let me give you this gift. I would be grateful if you would allow me to be kind to you."

Chapter Seventeen

After having managed only a few fitful hours of sleep, Aidan spent the day with Padraig and Rogan discussing business. They reviewed documents and plans, looked at proposals, and projected risk-to-gain ventures.

Shipyards full of frigates meant hour after hour of maps and charts, trade routes and bids. The family's land holdings meant attention had to be paid to the many acres of land, houses, tenants, crops, and rents, that all needed to be duly given their attention.

All the while, though, as Aidan spoke with his father, his mind raced with other thoughts. *When will you set me free of the worry? Tell me it isn't me. Tell me I won't have to follow in your footsteps. Tell me I am free to be my own man.*

And by the time they had wrapped up everything, Aidan's restlessness raced like a fire through his blood.

Ready to escape his own reality for a while, Aidan went for a thundering ride. He rode his stallion to the ocean, pushing the horse to his limits as they raced across the shoreline. The horse kicked up huge clumps of watery sand, and Aidan leaned into the frigid wind, so cold it burned his lungs.

When his steed had had enough, he eased up and headed back to the manse. Night drew in, and Aidan deliberately skirted the woods, avoiding any sight of the trail that led to the cottage.

He could not get Olwyn out of his mind, but at least he could stay away from her.

He'd failed miserably in his effort to find something with Mira that even vaguely resembled what he felt for

Olwyn. There was no replicating something so visceral, and he had been a fool to even try.

His thoughts were consumed with Olwyn, an attraction that came from a place Aidan didn't fully understand. He knew not why or how it came to inhabit his soul, yet it was there, an inexorable possession of his desire.

That was hard enough to reconcile, but there was a deeper truth that was even worse.

Roman de Gama had unknowingly made him see what he'd been trying to avoid, had asked a question that had only one answer, and Aidan was forced to surrender to the truth of it. He loved her.

It was not just mindless attraction, or lust, or infatuation, although he felt those, too. It ran deeper, was more meaningful, and yes, he admitted to himself, it was love.

He loved her the way he loved his cottage and Chase, his whiskey and the sea, the quiet company of horses and the untamed cry of a soaring hawk. He loved her the way he loved simple pleasures, an unmitigated, straightforward love that lacked complexity or reason. He loved her the way he loved life.

She was distinctive and different, honest and sincere, earthy and elemental. She was unlike any other woman he'd ever known. The truths of who she really was and what she saw in him had spoken to Aidan's heart, opened it, and now existed there like a hidden treasure he could show to no one.

The fact that Olwyn wanted him in return made it even harder to stay away from her. She was so close by in the cottage; she slept in his bed, read his books, and felt the magic of the place the way he did. And she desired him, of that he was certain, could feel it in her body, see it in her eyes, and taste it on her tongue. He dared to wonder if she loved him, too, a dangerous thing to contemplate.

He entered the manse, fatigued and irritable, ready for

a drink to numb his thoughts and feelings. He glanced at the timepiece on the mantle, saw that he was late for dinner.

Dreading the evening ahead with Mira and his family, Aidan took his time and went the long way to the dining room, wending through the east wing. The halls were quiet, the servants finished with their above-stairs duties. He passed by the suite of rooms his grandparents used, and stopped. He heard a small noise come from inside, and saw the flickering of a single candle beneath the door.

Patrick and Camille were never late for dinner, and would not keep the entire family waiting on them.

Wondering if all was well, he knocked softly. When no one answered, he pushed the door open and was greeted by complete darkness. The scent of an extinguished candle hung on the air, along with the faintest scent of roses.

"Mira?" he called softly. "Are you in here?"

Silence hung thickly, and no answer came. Aidan strode over to the mantel, fumbled for the tinder, and lit a candle. The room was neat, nothing seemed disturbed. In the bed-chamber he saw that the bed had not yet been turned down, and the fire had been laid but was not lit. Nothing seemed out of the ordinary, and yet a prickling on the back of his neck prompted Aidan to look around a bit more. The bathing alcove yielded no discovery, nor did the balcony.

"Aidan?" His grandmother said from the doorway. "Is something wrong?"

"No, I think not. I thought I heard something, but nothing seems amiss."

"Come and join us," Camille said with a smile. "We are all waiting on you."

"Is Mira there?"

"She was, before she went off to fetch the drawings of

her wedding gown in order to show Portia and Sophia. Why do you ask?"

"No reason." Aidan waved his hand to dismiss the notion that Mira had been snooping in his grandparents' room as absurd. He took Camille's elbow and escorted her to dinner.

As they walked he said, "Did you happen to find a chance to drop in on Miss Gawain today?"

"I did, in fact. We had a lovely visit."

"How is she?"

"She seems very well."

Aidan wanted to ask if Olwyn had inquired about him, did the cottage smell of incense, did she seem as if she missed him? But instead he said, "Good, good. Thank you."

"She is an interesting girl. She reminds me a bit of myself when I was young."

"How so?"

Camille glanced up at her grandson as they approached the parlor where the family gathered, their conversation and laughter spilling from the room. She smiled as she entered, turned to Aidan, and said, "She is not afraid of who she is."

Aidan didn't reply, for his throat had gone suddenly dry. There, amidst his grandparents, cousins, aunt, uncle, parents, and brother, stood Olwyn Gawain.

She wore a glistening silver gown, stunning in its simplicity. It hugged her breasts and then cascaded the floor, skimming her curves along the way in a fashion that was nothing less than mesmerizing. Her black hair was glossy and piled high on her head, twisted with a strand of jets that winked and glittered in the light of the many candles and fire.

She wore no jewelry or other adornments, and in Aidan's mind, needed none. No necklace or earrings or ribbons or lace could further enhance the exquisite loveliness of her face, and the pure Druid magic of her beautiful, luminous, uncanny gray eyes.

Spéirbhean, his mind whispered.

He watched as Padraig poured her wine and handed it to her, and as her slim fingers embraced the goblet, he felt a pang of jealousy for the glass, that it felt her touch and would be raised to her mouth. Another punch of envy followed, stronger than the first, as Padraig stayed in her presence and engaged her in conversation.

And damn his cousin, Roman, too, for like a moth to flame he wended his way over to her, bringing her a small plate of cheese and figs.

So they would vie for her, would they? Bastards, he named them both silently.

They would never know her the way he did, never appreciate her earthy appeal, never feel for her what he felt.

Rogan approached Aidan and pressed a glass of whiskey in his hand, then drew near enough to speak for his ears alone. "Mind your stare, son."

Aidan looked away and drank deeply, just as Mira entered the room. He didn't glance her way, didn't trust his face to not betray his feelings.

Mira crossed the room and took her place at Aidan's side, and as her rose perfume touched him, he wondered if his first instinct had been correct. Had Mira been snooping in Patrick and Camille's rooms, and if so, what could she possibly be looking for?

"I secreted the drawings back into their hiding spot," she chirped to Portia, and with the tip of her fan she playfully tapped Aidan's arm. "No trying to find them, my lord. You will have to wait and be surprised."

"You will be a lovely bride," Sophia said, and she took a seat beside her father, Matteo, on the sofa. "Someday I want a wedding gown as fine."

Kieran smiled teasingly at her daughter. "You could wear my dress, Sophie. Wouldn't that show how much you love me, if you'd wear it?"

"That thing? Mama, you must jest. 'Tis terribly out of fashion."

"Your mother was a vision in it," Matteo interjected softly.

Kieran tilted her face up to his and smiled, "'Twas when I was young and beautiful, signore, a long time ago."

"It was yesterday," Matteo corrected her.

Aidan scarcely heard them. He surreptitiously watched as Olwyn sipped her wine, saw the shine of it on her lips, and he licked his own. From the corner of his eye he saw Mira take notice of the way he looked at Olwyn. He knew his gaze was covetous and inappropriate, insulting to his betrothed, and offensive to everyone else present. And still, he couldn't stop himself.

"You look amazingly well this evening, Miss Gawain," Mira said with a sweet smile. "'Tis just incredible what a difference a bath and a new frock can make in a woman's appearance."

"Thank you," Olwyn said simply, and if she took offense at the untoward jab at her earlier appearance, she showed no sign.

"Whoever fixed your hair is a miracle worker," Mira continued on. "All those tangles have been combed out, and I can't even see your odd stripe of white."

"Yes, Molly and Alice are both very patient and kind," Olwyn said easily, and again to her credit, her face betrayed no affront.

Aidan reached his arm around Mira and rested his hand on her shoulder. He gripped it hard enough to send a warning.

Mira looked up at him briefly, a smile on her lips and spite in her eyes.

She turned back to Olwyn. "I say, I scarcely recognized you when you arrived this evening. You look fair civilized." She laughed, and added, "Where is your dagger, Miss Gawain?"

Before Aidan could take Mira to task, he saw Olwyn's left brow form that witchy peak he had come to know so well, and knew she needed no defense from him.

"Come outside with me, my lady, and I will show you," Olwyn invited coolly.

Mira gasped, scarcely audible beneath the choked laughter that went around the room as each person struggled to hide their mirth behind their hand, a sip of wine, or a sudden interest in a piece of art.

Aidan noticed, however, the nasty look Mira's father sent his family, stern disapproval followed by a disdainful glance at Olwyn. The earl then faced Aidan full-on, a challenging gaze meant to prompt him to rise to his betrothed's defense.

Meeting his future father-in-law's stare, Aidan did nothing.

Camille rose from her chair and raised her glass. "I'd like to be the first member of our family to offer a toast to Miss Gawain, for her intrepid heroism, and above all, for returning our Aidan home to us, alive and well."

Aidan raised his glass, noticing the rise of color in Olwyn's cheeks, and the rapid throbbing of her pulse in her neck.

She was a vision, unequivocally, uncommonly lovely, he thought, and his gaze swept once more over her long, slim figure. He had known the shape and texture and feel of her body against his, the smell of her hair, the taste of her skin and mouth.

He would never know any of it again, and the bitter truth of that became a nasty taste on his tongue.

Olwyn offered a nervous smile as everyone called out

"here, here," and she blushed deeper still as the glasses clinked in musical tribute to her.

"Thank you," she said, as they all drank to her. She met Aidan's eyes across the room, and his pulse picked up its pace. She spoke as if to him alone. "It was well worth the risk."

A servant appeared in the doorway and announced dinner, and the group moved toward the dining room. Aidan had Mira's fingers on his arm, and he watched as Roman escorted Olwyn. His cousin had the lean good looks of his father, narrow and tall, sensual and rakish. Certainly Olwyn was not immune to his charms, Aidan thought.

He recalled how he'd planned on finding Olwyn a man who would appreciate her enough to take her to wife, and the idea now seemed absurd. No man seemed good enough, not Roman who was a romancing knave, nor his brother, Padraig, who had sworn off marriage and seemed content to woo women and race horses when he was not absorbed with business.

In truth, he could not think of any man worthy of her. No matter who came to mind, no matter how likeable or upstanding they might be, their faults became too apparent when he considered pairing them with Olwyn.

As everyone took their seats around the large table, Olwyn sat between Padraig and Roman, and as they dined the two men kept her laughing and chatting.

By the time they retired to the ballroom, Aidan felt as though he'd been tortured on the rack for hours, stretched beyond his limits, his tolerance worn thin.

He noticed Olwyn's face as they entered the ballroom, and was touched by her look of wonder, saw the grandeur through her eyes: crimson velvet furniture and draperies, the towering ceiling painted with murals, shining parquet floors, and mammoth chandeliers lit with candles and dripping with crystal.

The musicians struck up as they entered, a trio that played the harp, guitar, and tin whistle. The moody, ancient music was of the Celts who'd once roamed the land, evocative of misty moors, standing stones, and star-crossed loves that could never be.

Roman immediately asked Olwyn to dance, and Aidan heard her politely demur. "I do not know how to dance."

"I will teach you," Roman promised her with a rakish grin. "You are already very graceful in your movements. One dance with me, and you will be sweeping across the floor like a swan."

"I doubt that," Olwyn said, but she put her slim white hand in Roman's and let him pull her into his embrace.

Aidan watched them glide across the floor, and yes, she was graceful. In his arms she looked nubile and ethereal, a slender, shimmering dream of a woman.

Rogan asked Portia to dance, and Patrick invited Kieran to join him, and so Aidan, feeling like a knave, swept Mira into a dance with him.

Her gown brushed his legs and her waist felt pleasingly narrow against his hand. He looked down into her face and tried to see the sweetness that had once attracted him, but all he saw was the petty, insulting remarks she'd lain against Olwyn in an effort to diminish her.

How had he once felt passion for Mira, a consuming wanting to possess her that he'd never felt before, and hadn't felt since that one night? It didn't make sense, for he didn't even want to kiss Mira, let alone take her to bed.

"You must stop staring at that woman. 'Tis most untoward," Mira scolded.

Aidan knew Mira had every right to be upset, and did

not offer a defense. "Aye, you're right, and I'm sorry. I will strive to comport myself better."

"Is she so attractive to you?" Mira cast a glance Olwyn's way. "I find her appearance odd to the point of being disturbing."

"She is different," Aidan said neutrally, and finished the statement in his mind—*from any other woman.*

"Well, I don't care for her, and I most especially didn't care for the way she practically threatened me with violence." Mira pursed her lips in a pout. "You should have defended me."

Aidan resisted the urge to thrust her away from him, for she had the look of a simpering, spoilt child. He spoke distinctly, lest she misunderstand a word. "Make no mistake, I do not condone your behavior this night, and I will never rise to defend it."

"You'll allow her to speak to me in such a way?"

"When you've invited it? Aye. I will."

"A husband is supposed to honor his wife, and hold her dear above all others."

Aidan blew out his breath and without thinking first, blurted, "We shouldn't get married, and we both know it. I don't love you, you don't love me, and that one night should not consign us both to wedded misery."

Mira's mouth dropped open, becoming a rictus, really, gaping open as if she lacked the sense to shut it. And then she drew in a deep gasp, her eyes wide. Recovering somewhat, she said in a hissing whisper, "You are a cad, a rogue, a scoundrel. How dare you? You drunkenly forced yourself on me, and now, mere weeks from our wedding, you try to jilt me? I will not stand for it."

Aidan remembered the night well, and it had not been force. However, it seemed clear that that was how Mira chose to remember it. He tried to reason with her. "Is this what you want? A loveless marriage full of sniping at each other because we made one mistake? Wouldn't it be better to go our separate ways and see if we can each still find happiness?"

"I will not have this discussion here," Mira bit out, "with all of your family and my father watching on, as you insult me and try to worm out of your manly obligation."

"I'm asking a simple question: is a lifetime together worth one night's mistake?"

"Well, when you're pleasant, I quite like you," she answered, as if their attraction were something he could control. "That alone is more than many marriages can boast. And, as we are on the subject, do not forget that I accepted your offer of marriage and did not tell my father you got drunk and practically raped me. I should hate to have to do so now, but as I was divested of my virtue, I hardly have any choice. For that matter, a law-suit would be in order as well. Breach of promise is the least of the charges I could lay against you."

He looked down on her and wondered what he'd ever seen as pretty, for she had a spitefully superior expression on her face, and her mouth was twisted in a smug smile.

Aidan bit his tongue and abandoned the subject. She was correct about one thing—it was neither the time nor place to have such a discussion.

But Mira had to add one more dig. "You'd better ask yourself, my lord, if you want a wife of good breeding or a woman scorned. Because frankly, I have the capacity for being both."

Aidan gripped her harder than necessary, and she gasped, her eyes reflecting anger and fear at the same time.

"Don't threaten me, my lady. You'll get more than you've bargained for."

"Making threats is far beneath me," she said haughtily. "I am, however, not above reminding you that you have not yet paid for what you've taken. If you think I will let you walk away unscathed, you sorely mistake how greatly I value myself."

Before Aidan could reply, Padraig approached them, bowed, and extended his hand to Mira. "May I cut in?"

"You can, brother." Aidan handed over Mira to him, and walked away without looking back.

He'd moved to the edge of the floor, and saw his mother looking at him. Aidan smiled for her benefit, but Emeline wasn't taken in by it. She rose from her chair and came toward him, looking divine in her creamy, velvet gown. Her gold hair was coiled and sleek, and her face was timelessly beautiful. She took up her place beside him.

"I have not interfered with you overmuch, Aidan. You are a man, and as such, you do not need the meddling of your mother in your affairs," Emeline said without preamble.

"However?"

Emeline's expression changed, and as her sapphire eyes narrowed a bit, Aidan realized she was quite angry.

"However, indeed. Tonight I have watched you disgrace your betrothed and yourself, and completely overstep the boundaries of propriety where Miss Gawain is concerned. I did not raise you to behave so indecently to any woman, let alone the one you will take to wife. So I ask plainly, my son, as 'tis so obvious that you do not love Mira Kimball enough to esteem her, why do you marry her?"

Aidan felt anger bubbling in his chest, a stew of frustration, weary self-possession, and age-old resentments. "I am not going to explain myself. You hold your secrets dear enough, so forgive me if I don't feel obliged to bare my soul in return."

Emeline pulled back as if he'd struck her. "How dare you liken the two? Your birth order affects you not at all, and *will* not until the unhappy day that your father dies. You have been denied nothing but a tiny scrap of information, withheld to protect you and Padraig from being treated in any way differently as you grew, and now from young women questing prestige over true love. You may not agree with our method, Aidan, but do not ever doubt our motive."

"Has it ever occurred to either of you that you might be going about it wrong? Have you ever thought of how it feels for Padraig and me, to look to the future and not know our place in it?"

"Of course," Emeline answered simply. "Parenting is fraught with doubt and worry, and I was always afraid of making mistakes with you and your brother. But your father was certain this was best, and I agreed with him. He'd been raised without the foolishness and decadence of court life, without the nonsensical labels by which people seek to define themselves and others. Such things are meaningless, and though we raised you for the most part in England, we wanted to spare you the characterization that certain titles would bring. We wanted you to be able to be just yourself, Aidan Mullen, and let that be enough."

Aidan turned away from his mother's angry eyes, hating himself for being unpleasant when the evening had been intended to welcome him home. "I'm sorry, Mum. I should not have spoiled the night," he said, and he meant it. It seemed all he did of late was apologize to women. "'Tis a discussion for another time and place, one we should have with Padraig and Da as well."

Emeline laid her hand on Aidan's arm. "Let me speak to your father. Perhaps you've the right of it. You're both nearly thirty years old, and it could be that your father and I have clung too long to our ideals."

Aidan didn't respond, for his eyes were drawn to Olwyn in Roman's arms. She giggled as he twirled her and pulled her close again. Aidan feasted on the sight of her, an earthy girl in a heavenly gown. He couldn't control himself—he gazed on her with all the love and lust he felt, an open, unguarded, seething expression of pure passion.

"You watch her with far too much ardor," Emeline observed quietly.

"I know," he said softly.

The last strains of the song faded, and the musicians struck up a new song, this one a slow, aching melody.

Roman walked Olwyn toward Aidan, and with a guileless expression in his dark eyes he presented Olwyn to him. "Cousin, the lady saved your life. Will you not even offer her a single dance?"

Padraig had whirled Mira across the floor, and she and he were engaged in a discussion as they glided around the floor. Aidan glanced once to his mother, saw her look of disapproval, and then met Olwyn's crystal gray eyes.

And in that moment, nothing else mattered. Not Mira, or his parents, or even his own honor. He wanted Olwyn Gawain any way he could have her, no matter how briefly, and so he bowed before her, took her hand in his, and pulled her into his arms.

Before Camille had invited Olwyn to join the Mullen family for dinner, Olwyn's experience with opulent ballrooms and dancing had been limited to fairy tales and her imagination.

Yet here she was, beautifully gowned and in Aidan's strong arms, feeling the heat of his body and the current of his desire as he swept her across the floor.

She tilted her head back so she could watch his every nuanced expression. She remembered how she'd once thought him a prince, his handsomeness both intimidating and fascinating.

But now she knew the taste of his mouth and his skin, the secret thoughts of his mind, and the warm shelter of his body over hers. And she wanted more, wanted all of him, and scarcely noticed how handsome he was any more, for it was not his appearance that drew her. What she felt for him was blind, the other senses in full command, obsessed with touch and taste and smell and sound.

He looked deeply into her eyes, and did not hide his yearning for her. It was there, burning, for anyone to see.

"My lord," she whispered. "Your family watches."

"You know me by another name."

"Lóchrann." The word on her tongue made her crave smoky darkness, the hard throbbing of his body against hers, and the complete surrender to her desire for him. "They watch."

"Tell me the truth, Olwyn," he urged her, his deep voice thick with feeling.

"I have only ever been honest with you."

"I know 'tis true. A lie would burn in your mouth." His eyes traced her lips so intently she could nearly feel the touch of his regard. "Tell me how you feel about me."

"You consume me."

He lowered his eyes and swallowed heavily, looked away and then brought his gaze back to meet hers. In his sapphire depths she saw a war being waged. "You do not hesitate."

Olwyn smiled up at him. The strains of the music were haunting, a melody that suited her yearning. "My lord, I have spent a great deal of time alone. It allows for plenty of introspection."

"I, too, have been doing a great deal of thinking."

"Have you found any answers?"

"I've had a few revelations, aye."

He looked troubled, his lips flat, eyes haunted, and a tiny jumping muscle flexed just below the hollow of his cheek.

And Olwyn wanted to comfort him, to have him tell her

his troubles, to press her lips against all his tetchy nerves. Oh, yes, she wanted his worries and his concerns, and she wanted them whispered to her in the dark.

But she'd have to let the space of one dance suffice. "What's wrong, Lóchrann?"

"'Tis not curiosity."

His words brought a bittersweet smile to her lips, for she knew he spoke of the wanting between them. The sort that kills cats, he'd called it.

No, it was far more dangerous than that, she reflected, more the variety that ruined lives. "I never thought it was."

"Staying away didn't make it easier," he said.

"We didn't give it long enough."

"I think it would take a lifetime."

Olwyn's eyes traveled across the planes of his face, his neck, his wide shoulders. She envisioned the skin beneath his formal black jacket and crisp white shirt. That skin was soft and golden and taut, stretched over hard muscle and bone. Her gaze dipped lower, to the place on his chest where her father's scalpel had nearly taken his life.

She remembered holding Aidan's hand when she thought him dead, how easily she'd fallen in love with him even then, a headlong dip into danger, the love of a man denied his life and the lust for the man reborn, all combined into a muddled mix of emotions that Olwyn didn't dare try to deny.

"Come to me tonight, in the cottage," she invited him in a hushed whisper. "No one need ever know."

Surprise lit his eyes first, and then heat, as the idea took root. He smoldered with her invitation, and his refusal was half-hearted. "You deserve better than that."

"Maybe I want whatever part of you I can get," she breathed. Her eyes were on his mouth and then his hair, and she remembered the feel of it, the silky soft warmth. "It isn't uncommon for men to keep mistresses."

"If I allowed you to settle for that, I'd hate myself for the rest of my life."

"I admit it isn't the fairy tale I dreamed of when I was a little girl, but I am a woman now, and I am practical. If stolen moments are all we can have, perhaps we should seize them."

He pulled her closer and leaned down to press his cheek against hers. It was a scandalous dance, too close, too intimate.

Olwyn reveled in it.

"You deserve the fairy tale," he said softly.

She could feel the heat of him, pumping as if from a furnace, the faintly gritty roughness of his shaven jaw pressed to hers, and the slight tremble that shook them both.

The music was slowing further, nearing the end.

"Once upon a time," he whispered against her ear, the heat of his breath sending more shivering trembles through her body. "There was a beautiful maiden imprisoned in a crumbling old keep. Some called her a witch, and others thought her an ancient Druid.

"A man was brought to her, so close to death that no signs of life could be felt. The maiden, though, believed in his life, so much so that she risked her own to save his."

He pulled back and looked deep into her eyes, and his were limpid, dark blue pools in which she was willingly drowning.

"She woke him," he breathed. "He returned to life, reborn, awakened in a way he'd never been before. And he saw in her the truth: that she was neither witch nor Druid, but a woman unlike any other. She saw in him deep truths that no one else had ever even thought to look for, and he loved her for it.

"So it came to be that as the stars fell deep into darkness, she lay with him in the smoky, scented air, their bodies curled together so that every move she made was his movement, and every breath she took was his breath.

"And when he slept, it was a deep sleep. And when he

woke, he was fully awake. She did this for him until he came fully alive, more than he ever felt possible."

Aidan paused as he watched her, his gaze traveling over her face as if he was committing to his memory her every detail. His voice grew sad as he said, "Life took them down separate paths, but it never changed the way they communicated. It remained that way forever, the two of them joined in a way that was more than physical, untouched by time or distance, so much so it became a voiceless song only they could hear."

Olwyn's throat was constricted so tight it prevented breath, and she felt her blood pulsing in her veins, a thick, hot pounding that was life in its most primal form.

She knew that in his own way, he was telling her that he loved her.

Olwyn blinked a few times, hard, determined not to weep. This was the way she'd always known it would be. She had understood from the beginning that he was a man of the aristocracy. A man with obligations and an intended bride. A man not for her.

The music faded and he let her go. His face was drawn tight, and his eyes shimmered as if he, too, fought tears. He lifted her hand, pressed a kiss to it, and then turned on his heel and left the ballroom without another word.

Chapter Eighteen

Morning dawned. The sky slowly turned from indigo to the palest lavender before turning into a pink-tinged blue that gave way to a beautiful, clear sky.

Olwyn watched the sunrise at the cottage door, leaning against the frame as she cupped her hot tea, the warmth of the pottery permeating her hands. She wore a thick warm wrapper that Camille had insisted on purchasing for her, along with slippers and new stockings. Behind her sat a trunk full of new gowns, and the underpinnings needed to wear them.

It was an embarrassment of riches, but Olwyn had been unable to refuse them, for she'd sensed the great joy that her acceptance of the gifts had given Camille, had seen it in the sparkle of the older woman's green eyes and the beauty of her smile.

Shortly after sunrise, Molly and Alice arrived, having learned that Olwyn was an early riser. So the hour had scarcely reached eight by the time they'd finished helping her dress.

Alone once more, Olwyn faced an entire day to fill.

She smoothed her hands over her new gown, a creation of dark purple that Camille had said turned her skin to cream. She felt the shape of her body beneath the fabric, and remembered Aidan's hands on her, holding her as they danced.

Olwyn took a deep, trembling breath, thinking of how he'd looked in her eyes as he told her their fairy tale. She'd seen in him such turmoil, such conflicted emotions.

And she would never, ever be the same.

She tried to take her mind off him by reading, but Shakespeare's Romeo had Aidan's face, and the words he spoke came from Aidan's lips.

No good could come of it, she counseled herself sternly. Aidan would marry Mira.

Tossing the book aside, Olwyn made a snap decision to abandon the cottage and her thoughts. After readying herself, she pulled on her new warm cloak, and went outdoors into the brisk, clear morning. She spied the trail beside the run-in barn, and recalled that Aidan said it led to his distillery. Curious, she took to the path, and soon enough she heard the familiar noise of Chase bounding through the woods.

She turned to see the dog coming toward her, this time with a wet sandy piece of driftwood in his mouth.

"Hello, Chase," she said with a smile as she accepted his latest gift. She no longer felt fear of the massive dog, for though he was the size of a horse, he had the gentleness of one, too. "I'm going for a walk. Will you come?"

The dog settled in beside her, and grateful for the company, Olwyn followed the trail. Chase sniffed a few trees as if greeting old friends, urinating on them as he saw fit.

The woods were peaceful, the chilly air redolent of pine and the salty tang of the sea, quiet but for the sound of crunching leaves beneath their feet and the occasional rustle of chipmunks in the underbrush.

She noticed the tree line gradually thinned again, and spotted another meadow, this one larger than where the cottage was located. Two buildings inhabited the space, one tall and large, made of wood and stone, the other a low narrow wooden structure with long windows spanning all sides.

Curious, she approached the tall one first, and peeking

in the windows, she saw it was the distillery. She tested the door and found it unlocked.

Pushing it open, she was assaulted by strong smells: grain and malt and yeasty fermentation. The air reeked of alcohol, so much so that she nearly felt dizzy from the scent.

Chase had entered with her, and he sniffed with interest at the stairs that led up to a narrow loft that spanned one side of the structure.

Several huge copper vats and tanks took up most of the floor space, and a squat cast-iron mill dominated a far corner. Sacks of grain were piled up in another corner, one of which had a hole, leaking barley onto the hewn floor. Oak and cherry casks dominated one entire wall, stacked all the way to the ceiling, each one neatly labeled and dated, some going back more than ten years.

And she surrendered to the inevitable occupation of her thoughts. Aidan possessed her mind and heart, consuming her once more with longing for him.

This was another of Lóchrann's places, she thought. His domain. This was where he made the whiskey that tasted of darkness and kisses, heat and desire.

With her knees weak and her head spinning from the fumes, she explored the place, touching the things Lóchrann had touched, being a part of the things he held dear.

Aidan watched her from the shadows, high up in the loft. Behind him on his desk his record book was all but forgotten, his quill bleeding where he'd dropped it.

She moved in and around the tanks, her slim fingers trailing over the gauges, knobs, and the proof safe as if she were caressing flesh.

He took in her every detail, feasting on her appearance. She looked beautiful, her hair glossy and her skin luminous.

He wanted her to look up again so he could see her eyes, those disquieting, piercing, fierce eyes of hers.

Quick as a blink he saw Olwyn turn. Her arm lashed out, followed by the flashing blur of her dagger's blade. It made a sibilant sound as it cut through the air, and he instinctively leaned forward. Before Aidan could see Olwyn's quarry, he heard the high-pitched squeal of a scuttling rat, followed by the sick thud of the knife burying itself right behind its head.

And then there was silence.

He watched as Olwyn approached it, her body language hesitant. Laughter nearly escaped his control, for she looked frightened of the dead vermin.

He admired the shot, too, for she'd hit the rat just behind its ears where it would sever the brain stem, a clean puncture that didn't make for too much bloodshed.

Olwyn used the piece of driftwood she carried to poke at the rat and hold it down. She heaved a big sigh, bracing herself, before she leaned forward to retrieve her dagger. And then he heard her gagging.

"I'll do it," Aidan called down to her. "No need to add your breakfast to the mess you've made on my floor."

She gasped and whirled around. "I didn't know you were here, my lord."

"And a good thing you didn't. I see how you react when you've been startled." He descended the stairs and came to stand over her kill before turning his gaze to her. "You did tell me you hated rats, aye?"

"They are disgusting. Vile." She shuddered with revulsion. "Aye, I despise them."

Cocking his head toward the impaled rat, he lifted a brow and grinned. "Well, with that in mind, I'll try to stay on your good side."

He braced his boot against the body of the rat, its belly fat from feasting on grain, and pulled on the hilt. It was wedged in tightly between muscle and bone, and came out with a nasty sucking sound.

"You know, Olwyn," he began nonchalantly as he took the dagger to where he kept clean rags and a bucket of water. "Most women just scream when they see a rat."

He wet a cloth and cleaned the blade before handing it back to her, hilt first. She took it without a word, opened her cloak, and slid it into her belt, which she wore wrapped around one of her new gowns. His grin broadened at the sight of the scarred, ragged leather cinching the fine purple velvet around her tiny waist. "Only one weapon?"

She raised her brow into that witchy peak, reached behind her back and pulled out her pistol.

"Ah, yes, of course," he laughed. "I wouldn't have expected less."

Olwyn's tone was acerbic and the glitter in her crystal gray eyes was purely offended as she said, "Perhaps you prefer a woman who cares more for the fashionable drape of her gown over the foolishness of walking through woods alone, weaponless. I am not cultured, my lord, but neither am I a fool."

Aidan laughed as he looked her over admiringly. "I never said I preferred any such thing, and in truth, there's not a thing about you I would change."

Her expression changed, turned uncertain. His words seemed to discomfit her, for she looked away from him, a blush rising on her cheeks. But a word was drawn from her lips, reluctant, a thin whisper. "Nothing?"

Aidan's gaze swept over her, from her new, fashionably elegant gown, cloak, and shoes, to her tattered belt and serviceable dagger. What he saw was a woman who was fierce and beautiful, practical and enigmatic. "No, Olwyn," he told her softly, meaning the words with every bit of his heart. "Not a damned thing."

A smile broke across her face, a luminous combination

of pink lips, glowing skin, shining teeth, and sparkling eyes. She took his breath away, she did. His *spéirbhean*.

He wanted to pull her into his arms and kiss her, feel his mouth on hers, their essence mingling, tongues mating. He wanted to slide the hem of her gown upward, revealing her long, slender legs, and touch her in the center of her being until she cried his name. His blood became a race in his veins as he envisioned her nude, the riches of her body: ebony hair inlaid with argent, silken skin of alabaster blushed with a pale pink rose, and eyes the color of priceless clear crystals.

She would burn for him, he knew. Olwyn's sensuality was as earthy and real as nature itself.

Because he couldn't say any of that, he held her gaze and told her, "'Tis good to see you, Olwyn."

Olwyn took a step closer to him, as if drawn by his thoughts. She had her head tilted back so she could look into his face. With an expression of pure concern, she reached up and cupped his cheek, her hand cool and full of comfort, a healing touch. "Have you not been sleeping, Lóchrann?"

"No, not too much," he admitted. He tried to make light of it. "And to think I thought I'd slept enough to last a lifetime."

"Is this a trouble you've always had?"

"Aye," he answered a bit too abruptly. For it would do no good to tell her that when he'd lain with her, their bodies fitted together as if they were two pieces of a puzzle, he'd slept a restful, dreamless sleep.

"Would you like some of my incense? It helps me, I think. You might find it works for you, as well."

He imagined the slim curl of exotic smoke slowly filling his sleeping chamber, and lying awake in his wide lonely bed, aching for her. "No, Olwyn. Thank you, but no."

She still had her hand on his face, and her fingertips

brushed over his cheek. "It isn't good for you to go too long without rest," she gently admonished him. "You don't want to take ill."

"I'll be fine. I'm used to it." Even as he spoke, it occurred to him that his sickness aboard the ship and the resulting coma were probably a result of his extended sleeplessness, always pushing himself, never truly rested.

Olwyn reached back to stroke his hair, her soft touch weakening his legs. Her striking gray eyes held his in thrall; he was unable to break free of her gaze, and didn't desire to.

"I didn't much care for the ending of your fairy tale, Lóchrann," she whispered. "It was a good story up until the last bit."

"Aye, you know, 'tis quite a coincidence you would mention that. I was awake a long time last night, and spent a good portion of it thinking about things." He put his hand over hers. "Thinking about you, and how I feel about you."

"And how is that?" she asked, her expression turning wary, her voice the barest sigh.

Staring into her eyes, he told Olwyn the simple, complicated, inexorable truth. "I love you."

Her eyes went wide on his admission, and she pulled her hand away as if she'd been burned. She turned and half-stumbled away before bracing herself on one of the mashing vats. "And now what?"

He saw that her shoulders were heaving, as if she gasped for breath.

He wanted to answer her question, but he didn't quite know how.

Indeed, how could he extricate himself from his predicament with Mira? And what was more, how could he spend the rest of his life without Olwyn by his side?

"I don't know what it means," he admitted. "I only know

how I feel. Let's write a new ending to the fairy tale, Olwyn. Let's figure it out together."

Olwyn clutched the rim of the copper vat. She had her eyes shut tight, drawing inward, trying to come to some semblance of reality.

Love.

Love?

Men like Aidan Mullen didn't love women like Olwyn, her mind insisted.

But a man like Lóchrann might, her heart whispered.

And then Olwyn spun around, facing him, uncertain, afraid. "You can't love me."

"Oh? And how's that?"

"It isn't possible."

"Well, then, you're either a miracle worker or a witch, because, 'tis possible. 'Tis true."

"I am common, strange, and backward. I am not the right woman for you, and am in truth, hardly suited to be your mistress, let alone anything more significant. Fairy tales are fiction." Her heart pounded, but she managed to add, "And no one would write a story about a woman like me."

He laughed, a smooth, deep chuckle that blended well with the scent of the whiskey. Olwyn, as upset as she was, couldn't help but love the wild ease with which he laughed and smiled, an Adonis of a man with a devil's grin and an intoxicating voice.

Aidan moved closer to her, reached out, and twined his hand with hers. He gave her a little tug, and grinned. "You know, Olwyn, that's a debate for another day. Here we are, alone and with time on our hands. What do you say we put aside our worries and enjoy the day?"

Olwyn's head reeled from his words, the fumes, and the rush of blood thrumming through her veins.

"Just like that?" she asked. "You tell me something so deeply meaningful that my heart nearly explodes, and then just like that, you want to go casually on with the day?"

He laughed again. "Aye. 'Tis exactly like that."

She was weak where he was concerned. Weak in her knees, weak in her heart. There was no denying him. "So what do you want to do, Lóchrann?"

Aidan's fingers were tight on hers, his grip an anchor, a lifeline.

"Let's go to the beach."

Memories of the trader's stories wended through her mind, of rolling waves and rocky sand and shells that washed onto the beach like a million little miracles.

"I have always wanted to see the ocean," she said wistfully.

"Let me show it to you. I want to be there when the sea captures your heart. I want to watch your beautiful eyes grow wide with the wonder of it."

For Olwyn, a woman who'd lived a life of solitude, loneliness, and silent misery, such generosity and kindness and genuine interest in her happiness came as a shock to her system. She felt as if she had been an empty glass, and Aidan Mullen had poured into her until she overflowed.

"Lóchrann." The word came out as a sob, and tears filled her eyes, splintering her vision. "You are like a dream, too fantastic to be believed, and yet you make me want to be a part of your life so much it terrifies me. So much so, that only last night I offered myself as your mistress. And now today, you say such things and make me even more confused. I cannot trust this dream, Lóchrann." Her breath came in gasps and she laughed, a bit hysterical. "When will the dream turn to a nightmare? They all do, you know."

"Don't be afraid," he said. "We're in it together, and to hell with what lurks in the shadows."

Aidan pulled her to him, wrapped his arms around her,

and held her close. She clung to him, her mind a tangle of fearful hopes and desperate emotions so raw they burned.

And he was the balm, the healing nostrum. Olwyn pressed her face into the warm folds of his shirt, breathing deeply his scent, clean linen and woods and pine, rather like the way the woods smelled after a cleansing rain.

He kissed the top of her head, the chasteness of which was belied by the strength of his arms around her, and the vibration of his desire in the air. "Come now," he murmured. "No tears."

Olwyn tilted her head back so she could look up at him. He had a faint smile playing around his lips, and concern in his sapphire eyes, as if he was unsure which way her emotions would swing. She managed to smile for him, and she said, "You've the right of it, Lóchrann. Take me to the ocean."

"Aye, I will. Give me just a few minutes here."

While Aidan shooed Chase out of the distillery, disposed of the dead rat by tossing it into the woods, and finished up with his ledgers, Olwyn took a peek inside the mews.

The low building had large, plentiful windows that displayed the vast expanse of sky, but the birds wore leather hoods to prevent them from seeing what they could not have. They heard her, though, for the moment she'd entered they'd begun shifting their weight on their perches, swaying with anticipation that they might soon be riding on a wave of wind, tasting their temporary freedom and screaming with the sheer exhilaration of it.

The fierce birds were magnificent, prized for hundreds of years by nobles and landowners for their hunting skills. Olwyn remembered back to Aidan's casual suggestion that they trap a rabbit, and how she'd been amazed that he'd risk being charged with poaching game.

And now she understood. Aidan was a landowner, and

as such, he had the right to hunt and trap. It struck Olwyn as bitterly unfair, for Aidan and his class were well fed and had more than they needed, while a man who might secretly trap a rabbit to feed his hungry family would be fined or imprisoned if caught.

Aidan lived in a world where he could do as he pleased, where his wealth and titles opened doors for him that were closed to most of the populace. He moved through a society that would overlook nearly anything he did, simply because of his name.

Olwyn looked down on her new gown, ran a hand over the luxury that wealth afforded. It seemed so unfair, and yet, it was the way of things, and she knew that fairness was not a part of life.

"Olwyn?" Aidan said as he entered. He had his voice low and soft so he would not disturb the birds. "Are you ready to go?"

"Aye," she answered, before gesturing to the hawks. They were all in motion of some sort, opening their beaks, spreading their wings, shifting from talon to talon, cocking their heads, and listening with fierce attention. The room was filled with the tinkling of the belled jesses that trailed from each bird's legs, the music of captivity. It made a pain bloom in Olwyn's chest as she felt their restless wanting for what they could not have. "They all want to be free."

"'Tis not their lot in life."

He said it simply, matter-of-fact.

"You are a man who longs for freedom," she said softly. "You ought understand them better than most."

"Aye, and I do. Which is why I see to it that our falconer flies them often."

"But he brings them back."

"They belong here. They belong to me," he said, and for a second his voice revealed his own bitterness. He recovered and said, "I see it as guardianship, Olwyn, not an imprisonment. For as much as they are here in my mews, they are spared winter's harshness, and they are sheltered from storms and starvation. They hunt for me, but I am merely their steward. Just as I belong to my family, and I serve them as they do me, my birds of prey receive more than they sacrifice."

Olwyn watched one of the hawks as it strained at the end of its leash, great wings beating the air the way a drowning man thrashes in water. He opened his beak and screamed, and the primitive sound sent shivers down her spine.

The bird screamed again, and it was as if something were stabbing Olwyn in her heart.

"He so wants to fly freely," she murmured, and a lump formed in her throat as she saw the bird's desperation.

"He is my favorite, and by far the most untamed," Aidan said from behind her. Slipping on a thick leather glove, he trilled a few notes that calmed the bird, and urged him back onto his perch. "He is called Shaughraun, because of his tendency to go astray. It takes a falconer of great experience and patience to get Shaughraun to return once he's flying high."

The bird was striped with brown and cream, his belly nearly white. He had thick, powerful legs ruffled with creamy feathers, and talons that could break a man's arm.

"He is magnificent. Powerful," she said.

"Aye, he is."

"And he is enslaved, despite his strength. He's given what he needs and he's well treated, but it's just a luxurious cage," she said, her throat aching. "Forgive me, Lóchrann, but I need to leave. I know this is just the way of things, but it plagues me nonetheless. I feel their desperation to escape, and it's too much for me, for I felt much the same for far too long."

She turned and rushed from the mews, and when she emerged outside and the sun shone down on her face, she held her head back and breathed deeply.

She was free of the dungeon and her father's keep, she reminded herself. She was not his captive anymore.

So why, then, she couldn't help but wonder, did she feel the strange prickling of her intuition? If she didn't know for certain that her father could have no idea who Aidan was or how to find her, she would have sworn the tingles that raised the hair on the back of her neck were a premonition of danger.

Aidan's hand came to rest on her shoulder as he stood behind her. Slowly, he turned her to face him. He cupped her cheeks in his large hands and tilted her head back so she would look fully into his eyes.

"For today, let's leave it all behind," he said softly.

"Yes," she answered him, as her fears and worries slipped away beneath the warmth of his touch and his regard.

For today, he'd said. The words resonated in Olwyn's heart. Today, the here and now. It was all the time there was.

Let the worries fester and rot, she thought. For today she would see the ocean for the first time, with Aidan by her side.

Riding behind Aidan on his horse, Olwyn had her arms wrapped around his middle, her cheek pressed against his back. With her eyes closed, she listened to the steady thumping of his heart as she felt the heat of him sink into her.

They rode in silence, each of them absorbed in the simple pleasure of being together in the quiet splendor of the woods. Chase ran ahead of them on the trail, leading the way, and above them swallows darted through naked branches and dipped low, skimming the ground.

The soil turned slowly to dark, rocky sand as the knotty, gnarled trees thinned and gave way to the grassy dunes. The horse took the trail with familiar ease, and Olwyn leaned forward. The winds picked up and the salty smell of the sea grew stronger. Olwyn inhaled deeply, breathed it in.

And then she saw it, the dark, bluish gray of the ocean. It rippled and heaved, as mesmerizing as fire, as magnificent as anything she'd ever seen. Her eyes were drawn to the horizon, where the sky merged with the sea, and then to the waves as they rolled and spread onto the shore. Sunlight glittered on the swells, and white-tipped waves curled in the distance.

Olwyn tightened her arms around Aidan and said, "Thank you for bringing me here."

"Hold on, Olwyn," he responded, and he kicked his horse into a run.

They sped along the shoreline, kicking up clumps of sand and water in equal measure. Wind and bits of sand stung her face, and her hair streamed free behind her. Chase raced beside them for a while, barking with excitement, and she heard Aidan laugh freely. He thumped his horse again, let him have his head. Chase gave up the race, his happy barking becoming more distant as they thundered ahead. The ride was fast and fierce, and Olwyn loved every second of it.

When they'd reached an area where piles of enormous rocks jutted into the sea, Aidan slowed the wild pace.

Aidan reined in his stallion and dismounted before reaching up to help Olwyn slide to the sand. "Take off your shoes and stockings."

He saw her expression of shock, and he laughed. "Come on, Olwyn. We're beyond such shyness, aye?"

Aidan bent and shucked his own boots and stockings, set them on a rock, and turned away to give her privacy.

With a blush rising on her cheeks, she did as she was told, and unhooked her stockings from their garters and rolled them off, tucked them inside her new shoes, and set them beside Aidan's. Her dainty velvet shoes and his large black boots looked intimate together, side by side.

The sand beneath her feet was cold and damp and coarse, and she sank into it as she walked toward him, holding up the hem of her new gown. The wind whipped her skirts, her cloak, and her hair, and she laughed with the exhilaration of it, as if freedom itself was contained in the wild wind that blew across the water.

Chase loped around, his nose high in the air, sniffing. He began barking, different than his happy bark, and he took off toward the trees.

Aidan saw the question in Olwyn's eyes. "He probably smells deer."

Olwyn brought her attention back to Aidan, and saw that he, too, was happier just for being near the ocean. His hair had also come undone and it blew free in the wind, tousled streaks of flax and honey and gold. With his bare legs and his shirt billowing with the wind, he looked more relaxed than she'd ever seen him, natural and completely at ease.

"What do you think?" he asked her, raising his voice to be heard over the din of the waves and the whistling of the wind.

"I never want to leave," she answered with another laugh.

His grin grew wider. He swept a hand to encompass it all—the sea, the ocean, the rocks, and the land itself. "Aye, this is why I live at Beauport. Nothing compares."

Olwyn couldn't decide what was more beautiful to her—the wild restlessness of the ocean, or the untamed masculine strength of Aidan standing before her, his feet buried in the sand and sunlight gleaming in his hair.

"Lóchrann of the darkness," she said softly. "Lóchrann

of the sea. Lóchrann of the cottage, the distillery, and the mews. Lóchrann of my heart," she dared to finish, and the words came out as nothing more than a strangled whisper.

Aidan walked toward her, and Olwyn's heart picked up its pace. He reached out, lifted a lock of her windswept hair, and pressed his lips to it, inhaling as if he held a flower. "You unravel me," he said. "Piece by piece, a dissection of my soul. You have never looked more beautiful to me than you do right now. I want to kiss you, Olwyn. Here on the sand, in front of the sea, with the wind in your hair and the sun sparking your eyes to crystal fire."

Her lips parted and shook, but she did not keep from saying what nagged at her. With Aidan, she could be nothing less than boldly honest. "You are engaged to be married, and you said you would not keep me as your mistress. So where does that leave us, my lord? Stealing kisses until we part ways?"

"I have decided to end it with Mira, no matter what the outcome. I do not love her, I never did, and I know that I never could. My heart, you see, has been stolen by a very special Druid witch, and 'tis eyes of gray that I see when I close my own."

Olwyn's heart raced like Aidan's stallion had, kicking up doubts and hopes, fears and dreams.

But she'd promised herself that tomorrow's worries would not spoil the perfection of the day, and so she leaned toward him in silent invitation.

Chapter Nineteen

Aidan wrapped his arms around Olwyn's waist and held her to him. His body was warm, shielding her from the cold air that blew in from the sea. As he looked down at her, the beauty of his sapphire eyes captured her and held her in thrall.

Her feet sank into the sand, the chilly, gritty grains of it a new, wondrous sensation. With the wind in their hair and the din of the ocean beside them, Olwyn felt completely caught in nature's grip, at one with the primitive surroundings. Certainly, she thought, there was nothing civilized about the damp heat between her thighs or the tingling in her groin that made her crave his body in ways she didn't quite understand.

She strained into him, the sheltering sanctuary of his body. When he held her, everything else fell away.

Olwyn closed her eyes, ready for the dizzying crush of his mouth on hers. But what followed shook her, had her trembling.

He brushed his lips over hers, tender, tasting. And she felt the ripple of pleasure pass through his body, too, a simultaneous shiver that took them both.

A sigh slipped from her lips, an involuntary sound of wanting. He heard it and dipped his head so he could kiss the slim column of her throat from where it had come. He traveled up to her ear, and with the tip of his tongue, he traced the shape and delicate curves of it, stopping to whisper her name.

Olwyn held tightly to him, eyes closed, lost in the feeling of his soft hair sliding across her face, the rasping stubble of his cheek on her skin, the warm caress of his mouth, and the beauty of the moment.

Aidan groaned, the sound of a man at odds with his desire and his restraint. He could not have both.

He held his mouth to her ear once more, his voice a harsh whisper. "I will not steal from you, Olwyn. What do you give?"

She wasn't completely certain what he meant, whether he asked for her kisses or her body or her future, but it didn't matter. The answer, it seemed, would be the same. "I give you everything, Lóchrann."

His groan slid into a sigh, the sound of surrender. He had a hand cupping her head and the other splayed across her lower back, easily spanning the narrow nip of her waist. He made her feel fragile and vulnerable, and yet she was aware of the power she had over him. The size and strength of him didn't frighten her. She could deny him with a word, and by his honor alone, he would obey her wishes.

Aidan slid his hands down her body, skimming her curves before they settled on her hips. His fingers tightened around her, her blood, already a hot thrum, began a wild race through her veins. He pulled her closer to him, an intimate press of his bulging manhood against her belly.

She felt a hot spurt of fresh desire for him, knowing that he wanted her just as much as she wanted him. It was a heady, wanton knowledge, lusty and lewd. She knew it was shameful, but she didn't care. She wallowed in it.

His lips took hers again, and this time he did not hold back. Olwyn reached up and slid her fingers through his wealth of dark gold hair, her tongue sliding against his, her body writhing beyond her control. She wanted his skin on her skin, the weight of him on top of her, and to finally know the feeling of him possessing her completely.

As if reading her mind, he let go of her long enough to lift her off her feet and sweep her down to the sand. He laid her atop her cloak, and covered her with the long length of him.

She felt her skirts sliding up her legs as he gathered up the fabric until his fingers stroked the line of her garter, touching her sensitive, naked skin. She shook in his arms, worried he would reach up and touch the center of the wet heat that throbbed between her thighs, and also worried that he wouldn't.

"I can feel the warmth of you," he said, his voice husky and tight. "It beckons me like a drug."

"All I am, I give you," she whispered.

"Aye, you do. But I will only take you when you are mine to have forever."

Aidan held her close, so close that his heartbeat was hers, and her breath was his. He looked down on her, intensity etching his features. His eyes traveled over her face, her hair, her neck. "I cannot imagine my life without you in it."

Olwyn swallowed heavily, for inside raged a desire so strong she could scarcely bear its force, and alongside it a strange and awful terror grew apace. She tried to disregard the fear by focusing on Aidan and the sheer pleasure of feeling his body pressed so close to hers.

But he must have seen something pass through her eyes. "What troubles you?"

"Nothing at all," she murmured, as she reached beneath his cloak so she could stroke his back. She felt the tension and strength in his muscles, and delighted in the feel of them rippling beneath her fingertips.

"Your face hides naught."

There was no use trying to deny it—fear brewed in her belly and prickled her neck. "Lóchrann, I am afraid."

"Don't worry, Olwyn. I just want to hold you, to lie here with you."

"It isn't this," she whispered. "I find no fear in your arms."

She turned her head in the direction Chase had run, and saw nothing but an empty stretch of beach, and the ragged sketch of dark antediluvian boulders against the sky. "I feel something coming."

"What?"

"Something evil."

Aidan followed Olwyn's line of vision. "From where?"

"I know not."

Olwyn's intuition was like a divining rod, leading her away from danger for much of her life, well sharpened by living with a lascivious drunk and a manic madman. She'd learned early and fast to listen to the subtle vibrations of her instincts.

A tremor ran through her, a single violent quake that shook her. "We must go."

Aidan rolled from her with no hesitation, gathered their things, and sat beside her to brush the sand from his feet before pulling on his stockings and shoes. Olwyn did the same, as waves of apprehension crashed over her as surely as the sea pummeled the shore.

He stood and reached a hand down to help her up, and as Olwyn put her narrow, slim hand in his much larger, square, strong palm, a tiny bit of her fears abated. Aidan was powerful, and he would protect her. That much, she knew.

And yet a voice inside her asked a question for which she had no answer. *What if it is Aidan who is at risk, and you are the one who has brought danger to his door?*

Worry gripped her belly. Could it be that her father was near?

She told herself that Rhys could not have found her; it

was impossible. He had no money, no horse, and no way of knowing where she'd gone. Any investigating and searching he might do would have to be conducted on foot, and would certainly tax Rhys's physical limitations.

It had occurred to Olwyn that Rhys might be determined enough to find her by asking around Chester to find out who'd been buried recently, but by doing so he'd most certainly confirm suspicions of his illegal anatomy studies. Olwyn had learned from painful experience just how much more Rhys valued anatomy over his only daughter.

"Olwyn, you are pale."

She offered him a wan smile. "I'm fine."

"You don't look it, aye? Tell me what's going on with you. Tell me what evil you fear. Whatever it is, we'll face it together."

Olwyn noticed how he watched her with concentrated attention. The hand that held hers was hard and tough, a hand for fists, the hilt of a sword, the butt of a pistol. And he waited for her answer, trusting the honesty she always gave him.

Her prince charming he might actually be, prepared to slay a dragon for her.

But what if the dragon was her own father?

"Perhaps it is the unknown I fear," she said, hating herself for denying him the whole truth. But she'd not endanger Aidan by telling him her suspicion, for she knew he would search the recesses of England and Wales to protect her.

She knew her father's ruthlessness. He was a man whose fall from grace had been so long ago that kindness was a long forgotten memory. Insanity and cruelty had conspired to make him nothing more than a shadow of a man, with bitter hate where his heart had once been. If Rhys Gawain saw Aidan as a threat, he would kill him from a distance.

"Olwyn," Aidan prompted her, "tell me."

Olwyn didn't dare give voice to the fear that her father might be coming for her. That was something she would have to deal with on her own.

Instead, she gave him another piece of her truth, the part that sprang from the deep well of her insecurity. The part from which Aidan could offer no protection, because he was the very root of the problem. "Perhaps I don't trust the promise I taste in your kisses."

"Trust is earned," he said mildly, and the attention in his eyes changed, grew warmer. "You'll see soon enough."

"Oh, will I?" She laughed, an inappropriate thing to do, but still it bubbled out, a jittery twitter. He spoke of forever and having her in his life as if it were an accomplished fact, a thing already done.

She remembered being in his home, feeling like an urchin, a beggar.

There Aidan stood, tall and strong, sunlight gleaming in his tawny, streaked hair and on his smooth, golden skin. A dashing Adonis, a knight of the realm. A marquis or an earl, and maybe a duke. He was the hero of every nursery fable and fairy tale she'd ever read.

Too good to be true, her mind jeered. *Too good for you.*

Aidan took a few steps closer to her. She caught his scent, borne on the sea air: expensive linen, crisp and clean, mingled with his soap. She remembered when he'd smelled of her incense and his skin had been bare against hers, his breath a soft tickle through her hair, his heartbeat beneath her cheek. *Lóchrann of the darkness.*

The memory made her tremble.

"Don't worry, Olwyn," he bade her softly. Reaching out, he stroked back a long lock of black hair that the wind had tossed across her face. "I won't let anything bad happen to you. You're with me now. Only good things are in your future." He shrugged and his lips quirked up in the ghost of a smile. "'Tis not just material things I mean, though there's enough of that. But I'm talking about good things between us. Meaningful things. The pieces of ourselves that we'll share with each other and no one else."

Behind him, the ocean surged and heaved, rolled onto the shore and ebbed back again, an endless cycle.

The beach they stood upon was owned by Aidan and his family. The very idea staggered Olwyn's mind. And the woods behind her—they owned them, too. As they did the grand mansion, and the land that it stood upon. How much of England belonged to these people, and how did a poor girl like her fit in to such a picture?

Aidan had said he couldn't imagine his life without her in it.

But Olwyn couldn't envision herself in his life.

And oh, God, he'd said he loved her.

Somewhere along the way he'd turned the tables on her. He was no longer the man whose life she'd saved, for he seemed insistent on rescuing her in equal measure.

It all became a muddied mess, for she could not reconcile Aidan of the manse with Lóchrann of the darkness. She understood all too well the dark, intuitive fear that snaked beneath her skin like a serpent, and most of all, she did not know what to do or where to hide.

She thought of the kindness that Camille had shown her, the warmth of Aidan's family, the ease and welcoming grace they'd shown her.

If Olwyn brought danger to their doorstep, she would never forgive herself.

"I need to go." The admission came of its own volition. And she did, despite the desolation that harrowed her as she thought of leaving and never seeing Aidan again. She needed to go far enough away that Rhys's madness would not touch Aidan or his family.

"Of course," Aidan said, as if he were soothing a small

child. "By God, you've grown even paler still. Are you unwell, Olwyn?"

Concern touched his eyes, making her feel even worse. She'd never met a compassionate man before, and yet, here he stood, full of genuine caring and sympathetic worry for her.

For *her!*

"Olwyn, will you answer me?"

"I'm fine," she managed to say. "Truly."

"The first lie you've told me." Aidan's expression changed, took on the look of a wolf that had caught the scent of blood. "Why?"

"Please, take me back to the cottage."

"Tell me what you're thinking." He didn't bother with more questions. This came as a pure demand.

And suddenly she knew that he could feel her too deeply, that he was connected to her in the way of the ocean to the shore.

Before she could even attempt to think of a lie, Aidan's patience ran out. He whistled for his horse, and within two fluid steps he swung up into the saddle and pulled Olwyn up onto his lap. They were in motion in an instant, racing across the beach, heading directly toward the place where Olwyn's gaze had been drawn.

His arm was a thick steel band around her, his chest a wall of muscle behind her, his thighs hard and firm beneath her bottom.

And his voice was low and angry in her ear. "If you'll not answer me, Olwyn, I'll go and see for myself what's lurking in the shadows. I'm not a man to hide from anything, aye? Accustom yourself to that."

Olwyn couldn't help herself, and she laughed again. More peals of that edgy, nervous laughter. He overwhelmed her with his strength, and more than that, unnerved her with his bold ownership over her person. He was like the prince who'd slain the dragon, climbed the keep's walls, and carried the girl off with no intentions of returning her.

Olwyn was not a princess from a fairy tale. She was about as far from one as a woman could get.

The prince had carried off the wrong girl in his strong arms. The thought made her laugh again, this time a sadder sound that accompanied a blooming ache in her chest.

"Oh, it's funny, is it?" he asked, peering down on her askance. "You infuriate me, and I amuse you. That's perfect."

"Well, Lóchrann, what now? We'll charge off into the forest on the back of your war steed, and what?" She shrugged, trying to ignore the fear that rippled beneath her skin. "Call me a coward, but when I sense danger I run from it."

His body relaxed a bit, the arm that held her became less imprisoning, and he slowed his stallion's pace. "You sense danger in the wood?"

"Aye," she confirmed slowly, unsure of how much to say. She had no intentions of leading Aidan right into danger's path. Far better for her to slip away and lead Rhys away from Aidan and his family.

Aidan met her eyes again. "Fine, we'll do it your way. We'll go back."

He wheeled the stallion around and headed in the opposite direction, and Olwyn relaxed ever so slightly.

"Thank you, my lord. I will feel much better once I'm back in the cottage."

Aidan grinned, and turned in an instant from prince charming to the devil himself. "Oh, well, Olwyn, you're not a fool, aye? Surely you'll think it ludicrous to stay alone in a cottage in the middle of the wood, like some lamb that's been led to the slaughter? We can both agree 'tis best that you come back to the manse with me. This way, you'll have nothing to fear, aye? And I'll be certain you're safe."

And as she opened her mouth to argue, he tightened his hold on her once more and kicked his leggy stallion to a breakneck pace, carrying her off to his lair, just like a wolf with a stolen lamb.

Mira moved across the wide-planked attic floor, as silent as a ghost. Light filtered through windows that were set deep into gables, illuminating motes of disturbed, drifting dust.

She was supposed to be napping, and she glanced at the timepiece she'd pilfered from her father. She had about an hour more to look around before she needed to slip back into her rooms to dress for dinner.

It made for slow going, only being able to sneak away for a few stolen moments at a time, never able to fully devote herself to the monumental task of shifting through generations worth of belongings.

Mira creaked open a chest and riffled through musty, moldering baby clothes, fashioned after designs of a hundred years ago.

"Not it, not it," she muttered, and in her frustration, she closed the lid too loudly.

Catching the tip of her tongue between her teeth, Mira placed her hands on her hips and cast a sweeping glance around the vast attic. It spanned the length and width of the mansion, and was filled nearly to the rafters with old furniture, trunks, toys, books, and the various detritus of an ancestral family home.

It would take forever to open every carton, she despaired. She kicked at the one that had just disappointed her, and blew out her breath.

"Where would you put such a thing?" she whispered to herself as she opened a new trunk.

She thought of Bret Kimball's journal, the passage she'd read so often, and poured over with such attention that she had it memorized.

> *Today I gave it to her, and as I watched it slide onto her perfect finger, I realized she would finally be mine. It fit her, not just in size, but symbolically. A Kimball ring on a Bradburn hand. Soon she will take my name as well, Camille Kimball. 'Tis a fantasy come true, and my hope is that someday she will see things as I do. I just know I can make her forget that Irishman, if she'll only give me a chance to show her who I really am inside.*
>
> *I laugh as I write this, for I hear my own earnestness and know it sounds as if I am a lovesick swain. Were anyone to read my words, they would hardly suspect that 'tis the vilest treachery that has brought me to this day. I can hardly believe it myself, can scarcely comprehend the man I have become.*
>
> *As true as that may be, today I asked that delightful creature to be my wife, and she agreed, however unenthusiastically. I placed the Kimball ring on her finger, and saw hundreds of years of my ancestry glittering with promise. I think she liked it well enough. She should. 'Tis a stunning diamond, the center stone as big as my thumbnail, surrounded by sixteen smaller stones, a ring for a queen. I will spend the rest of my days with her in atonement, as I did today when I brought her candy, flowers, and even the brandy she likes to drink in secret.*

Mira rummaged through another trunk and then sat back on her heels. The ring was not in Camille's jewelry collection in her rooms, and Mira could only wonder what had become of it.

Asking directly what Camille had done with it was out of the question; by doing so she would have to reveal the existence of Bret Kimball's journals. No matter what, Mira would never do that. Her great-uncle had spoken of all sorts of dastardly deeds, and Mira would not see shame brought on her family's name.

But that ring with the diamond as large as a man's thumbnail was a *Kimball* ring. Bret had said it had been in their family for hundreds of years. Camille Bradburn had had no right to keep it after her uncle died. No right at all. The injustice of it galled Mira to no end. Did Camille sell it? Give it away? Or had she packed it away and forgotten about it?

Mira was certain of one thing: the ring couldn't have possessed any sentimental value to Camille. Bret's journals made it clear enough that she'd had no love for him. Indeed, it was clear to Mira that Camille had been in love with Patrick all along.

So the fact that Camille hadn't seen fit to return the *Kimball* ring to the *Kimball* family smacked of thievery of the lowest sort. She'd taken it under false pretenses, after all, accepting Bret's marriage proposal when her heart belonged to another.

Mira checked the time and sighed. Time to return to her rooms and get ready for the evening ahead.

She rolled her eyes and groaned aloud at the prospect. She had a plan to see to it that Aidan's roving eye was brought back in line, but didn't look forward to its execution. After all, it was risky to try the same trick twice, and Mira didn't like risk in general, much less when the stakes were so high.

But Mira Kimball was not about to be made a laughingstock by getting thrown over for a common nobody. She could see the writing on the wall—he was more than halfway to jilting her.

Mira would do what she had to do to keep her grip on Aidan.

After they were married, he could stray as he pleased, discreetly of course, just as all gentlemen did. But by God, she would see to it that he spoke the vows and secured her a proper future.

Mira Kimball was not going to settle for anything less.

And after all, she consoled herself, it had worked once, beautifully. Like a charm, in fact. It would work again.

Chapter Twenty

"What do you think you're doing?" Padraig demanded, his voice full of incredulity, his eyes hot with annoyance. "You can't bring that witch here and ensconce her under Mira's nose. Not after last night."

"I'll do as I please." Aidan brushed past Padraig and went to the drink cart. He poured himself a small splash of whiskey, and sipped without really tasting it.

Aidan couldn't think of much else other than Olwyn, and the look of angry betrayal in her eyes when he'd all but dragged her into the manse. She hated being in his home; that much was clear.

Olwyn had stood with her narrow back to him, silent, her mood impossible to read.

And Aidan had ached to pull her to the bed, to hold her, to curl up with her, and to find sleep.

But he hadn't. Instead he'd asked for her understanding, and when she refused to look at him or respond, he'd locked her doors so she couldn't leave.

As Padraig demanded answers, Aidan considered that his actions were less than gentlemanly. In fact, if he was forced to be honest, they were nothing short of brutish.

He was so tired his eyes burned. Perhaps it was affecting his judgment.

Behind him, Padraig snorted. "This is a fine time to get your head on straight. Had you had your wits about you last August when you'd insisted on asking for Mira's hand, you wouldn't be in this mess."

"I can always count on you to mind my business for me, brother. Many thanks to you, aye?" Aidan said mildly. He swirled his whiskey and glanced to the door. "She didn't feel safe in the woods. Should I have left her there, then?"

"You could have easily posted a guard at the cottage, instead of bringing temptation literally to your door."

"I wanted her here, where I can see to her myself."

"You want to see to her, aye. See her in your bed, for all that."

"Mind your manners, Dorchadas. I'll not have you questioning her virtue."

"My manners," Padraig said mockingly. "My manners would prevent me from bringing another woman to my dinner table, and announcing casually in front of my betrothed that you'll be keeping her as if you'd brought home a puppy."

"I didn't say I was keeping her. I said I'd reconsidered the wisdom of her staying alone."

"Aye, and did you see the look on Mira's face? Could you not have told her first, privately, and spared her the awkwardness of hearing about it in front of the whole family?"

"I wanted to," Aidan said, feeling his annoyance grow.

He didn't like explaining himself any more than he appreciated Padraig jumping to the wrong conclusion. "Mira was gone. She had told everyone she was napping, but she wasn't in her rooms when I sent a girl to wake her. I asked everyone, and no one had seen her all afternoon. It wasn't until she came to dinner that I saw Mira, and by then 'twas too late to give her the news privately."

Aidan narrowed his eyes and cast an appraising look at his twin, who he thought he knew so well. "You're awfully worried for her feelings, brother."

Padraig tossed back his own drink and set his glass down with a thump. He glared at Aidan briefly, a look that clearly said he didn't like his intentions questioned, either. Rising from his chair, he crossed the room and leaned against the window frame, staring outside into the darkness.

Aidan went to the fireplace where it burned merrily, put his whiskey on the mantel, and watched the fire.

They separated like two boxers to their respective corners, each not wanting to fight, but willing to if they deemed it necessary.

"And you look like hell," Padraig said from across the room. "Have you not been sleeping again?"

"I'll do."

"Aye, you'll do. You'll be back on your deathbed before long. Why don't you go into town and get some sleeping tonics?"

"I've tried them all," Aidan muttered, adding, "None work, save one."

If he could call having Olwyn beside him a tonic.

"So whatever works, use it," Padraig snapped. "You're as hollow-eyed as a corpse."

"Aye, brother, don't worry."

"Well, obviously you lack the sense to see to yourself."

"I never saw you as a mother hen, Pad."

"And I never saw you as someone needing tending, but clearly I was wrong."

"Peck, peck, peck."

"Keep it up, and I'll drag your tired arse outdoors, and peck at you until you bleed."

"My lord?"

Aidan turned at the sound of Mira's quiet voice. She stood in the doorway, a small, soft kitten of a woman gowned in pale powdery blue. She smiled at him, and raised a hand in invitation. "I apologize for my intrusion, but I would have a word with you."

"Of course."

Aidan followed her out into the foyer, ready to be treated to a sharp-tongued reprimand. Instead, she leaned into his chest, her head held all the way back so she could look up into his face. She smiled, and as her fingers skimmed the buttons of his waistcoat, said, "I would like very much to speak with you privately. I think there is much we have to discuss, and I would like to do so without listening ears."

"Aye, you've the right of it. I was going to come to see you this evening."

She brightened even further, obviously pleased. "You were?"

"We need to talk about serious matters, my lady," Aidan said gently. And if he could handle the matter properly, perhaps Mira could be spared any hurt or embarrassment.

"Yes, my lord, please do come to my rooms, just as you did before."

"Very well."

She raised herself on tiptoe and pressed a kiss on his jaw, her lips feather-light and warm. "I am excited," she whispered, and then she was off, her slippered feet skimming the marble floor.

Aidan inhaled the barest lingering scent of roses in the air, the delicate, floral notes unique to Mira, and again wondered what Mira had been up to in the afternoon, when not a soul in the household knew her whereabouts.

Aidan waited until midnight before seeking out Mira. He tapped lightly on her door, lest he wake her if she'd already fallen asleep.

The door swung wide in an instant; she'd been waiting for him. She wore a thin filmy nightgown of the palest lavender, and a matching wrapper, both frothy with ruffles, ribbons, and lace.

"Come in, my lord," she invited softly. She backed away so he could enter, closed and locked the door behind them. It was, he noticed, a vast difference from how she'd reacted when he'd come to her door a few nights before.

He saw that she'd lain out a thick, plush blanket in front of the fire, and placed a tray of food to nibble on, along with a bottle of whiskey and a magnum of champagne. Rose petals lay scattered on the blanket, pink and red and white, and pillows were piled up, plump and fat and perfect for reclining, all illuminated by the warm golden light of the fire and candles.

"I made us a tryst."

"I see that." Aidan glanced again at the spread that Mira had obviously gone to quite a bit of trouble to prepare.

He'd come to break off their engagement, and she'd thought it a romantic rendezvous.

"Come, my lord, and sit by me." Mira sank gracefully to the floor and curled her legs behind her. She leaned on a pile of pillows and patted a spot for Aidan.

Feeling like a cad of the highest order, Aidan sat down onto the blanket. "My lady, I should tell you straightaway that I have come for a serious discussion."

"Come now, my lord," Mira interjected, cutting him off before he could say anything more. "We both know that we need to speak of matters that require deep discussion, but I don't see any reason why we cannot be civil about it."

"Civil conversations are generally conducted across a table," he pointed out. "This is rather an intimate setting for what I've come to say."

"Such gammon," she said, picking up a whiskey bottle. "'Twas only a few nights ago you invited me to sit with you in front of the fire. I am trying to please you, my lord."

Aidan accepted the glass after she'd poured him a healthy draught, and he waited until she'd poured herself a flute of champagne before sipping. She pushed the tray of delicacies in front of him. "Oysters with garlic, cheese and figs, and smoked meats on the most delectable bread you've ever tasted."

Insomnia put Aidan in a perpetual state of hunger, for food, for sex, for sleep. At least there was one craving he could satisfy.

"You must have a few oysters," she insisted. "They were gathered just this evening, and the cook worked wonders with them."

Aidan obliged her, unable to refuse when she'd gone to such lengths. He sucked them from the shell, found them heavily seasoned but delicious. He enjoyed them along with the meats, and had to agree with Mira that the bread was excellent. Mira nibbled on the cheese and figs, sipped her champagne, and when they'd each had their fill, Aidan pushed the tray aside.

"As pleasant as this is, we really do need to talk," he said.

"Very well, my lord. Do you want to go first, or shall I begin?"

Aidan wasn't certain how to go about things, and so he simply said, "I fear you may be very upset by what I have to say to you. Perhaps you'll want to keep your own counsel until you've heard me out."

"As you wish." Mira propped herself on an elbow, and Aidan wondered if she purposefully let her dressing gown slide off her shoulder, exposing the delicate line of her collarbone and the upper swell of her breast.

A curious warmth spread through his belly. Aidan ignored it, and took a sip of his whiskey to chase the bitterness that lingered in his mouth.

He dove into the truth of the matter like a cold lake, head first. "I think we should reconsider our engagement."

"No," she said simply. Her expression did not change, and a faint smile played around her lips. "You're marrying me, and I shall not consider anything else."

"I don't love you."

"I don't care."

"Perhaps you are not understanding me fully. I don't love you now, and I feel certain that I never will."

"Love is for commoners."

"You can't mean that. Surely you want more from life, from marriage? I know I do."

The warmth was fast becoming heat, and Aidan felt himself growing hard. His balls were tight and full, a growing arousal that was nearly painful, reminding him that he'd yet to find release from his many months of abstinence.

Mira laughed softly, like music, and by the light of the fire she looked dewy and soft. He wanted to touch her skin, remembered the texture of her, and wondered where his passion for her had been all along, for it was here now, and he could scarcely control it.

Was he such a beast that he could love a woman and still want to bed another? Where was his loyalty to Olwyn?

"How could I want more from life than to be your wife?" she asked. "You are kind and witty, and I know you will be a good father to our children." Her shining blue eyes traveled over his face and form, and a blush touched her cheeks. "And you are very, very handsome, my lord. Dangerously so. Your kisses are scandalously exciting, and the night things went too far, I dare admit, I became very aware that rendering my wifely due will present no hardship."

Aidan's erection throbbed and his blood pounded through his veins. He couldn't help but notice that her nipples were visible through her filmy nightdress, little pink strawberries on skin that was as white and sweet as cream. He licked his lips and took another drink of whiskey, but the acrid taste in his mouth would not be washed away.

Mira took his glass from his hand and sipped it lightly. She wrinkled her pretty nose and laughed. "Did you not want to taste your drink from my lips?"

He noticed that the hem of her nightgown had shifted up, revealing her small, shapely legs up to her smooth knees.

But no, he thought, he did not want Mira. He wanted sex, for certain. Oh yes, he wanted to slide between a woman's thighs like he wanted to breathe. But not a mindless coupling with a woman he did not love. No, he asserted again. No. Never again.

When he did make love to a woman, it would be with Olwyn, and it would be after vows had been spoken. He wouldn't take another woman's virginity again.

"I cannot stay here with you, my lady. But before I leave, I need to tell you—it is over between us. I will take the blame, agree to whatever story you wish to tell, and I will be named a cad to everyone who knows me. I swear I will protect the secret of what happened between us, and you can go to your future husband with your pride and honor intact."

He kept talking, speaking in a rush so he could say what needed to be said before he lost what remained of his restraint. "I cannot consign us both to a lifetime of lovelessness because of one lapse in judgment. 'Twould be a mistake to do so, I feel it in my bones and my blood. And so I am sorry, my lady, truly, and I wish to make whatever recompense I can."

Mira laughed again, that soft, wafting melody, and she leaned forward and kissed him. Her tongue slid inside his mouth and her tiny hands went straight to his crotch, settling on his throbbing, aching penis like a butterfly landing on a hot stone. She stroked him and he groaned, and yes, her mouth tasted of whiskey, but she smelled of sickeningly sweet roses and the faintest tang of sweat, as if she'd applied too much scent to hide a bad odor.

"Now, now, my lord," she whispered against his mouth. "You must not fret overmuch. 'Tis a case of cold feet, and nothing more, a fear of the unknown and premarital jitters. I promise you, all will be well." She pulled back, looked into his eyes, and with her hand rubbing along the thick ridge of his arousal, said, "You do not need to love me to want me."

Her touch was insistent, forceful, and for all her inexperience, awfully eager. His mind buzzed as if he'd drank far too much, and his thoughts were consumed with the need to push her onto her back and penetrate her.

He tried to cling to a semblance of sanity, reminding himself that this same woman would barely kiss him a few nights before, and had been quite insistent about not wanting a repeat of the night he'd taken her virginity.

Aidan pulled away, and pushed her hand from his lap. "Stop touching me," he said roughly. "I can't think."

A wariness came into her expression, and for a split second she seemed off balance, as if she didn't know what to do. She smiled then, uncertain. "I thought you might want to recapture the magic of our first night together, that perhaps then you would remember why you wanted to marry me in the first place."

"I never wanted to marry you." Aidan heard his nasty tone and knew his words to be insensitive, but he couldn't control himself. He felt like an animal that had been let out of a cage, strangely angry and as randy as a young stallion in a field of females in full season.

"You did. You wanted me."

He saw the quiver in her chin, the shine in her eyes, and yet he could not find compassion for her. Something niggled at him, pricking his memory like a fistful of nettles. "No, I didn't. I wanted sex, and you were there."

"How dare you?" she whispered, clearly horrified.

And out of Aidan's muddled desires and conflicted emotions came one memory: Mira, at the ball, offering him little stuffed morsels of food that had been heavily seasoned, and the lingering, bitter aftertaste of them in his mouth.

Aidan closed his eyes briefly, gathering his self-control. He would have the truth. Using every bit of his will, he clamped down on his unruly longings and forced his buzzing mind to focus.

"My lady, forgive my crudity. That's not what I meant. 'Twas only that you were so beautiful that night that I found myself stripped of my civility."

"You hurt me with your words."

"I am so very sorry." Aidan watched her carefully, and saw the wariness return to her eyes. Intuition prompted him to call her bluff. "I should leave. Again, I'm sorry."

"No," she said, a touch too quickly. "Don't go. We've yet to finish our discussion, and you haven't even heard me out yet. Please, my lord, stay a moment more."

Aidan settled back onto his cushion. "Very well. For a few minutes."

Mira smiled prettily at him, and he watched as she leaned back as well, and this time she shifted so that more of her dressing gown gaped open. He could see the valley between the curves of her breasts, the slight rise of bone beneath soft skin.

It had an immediate effect, making him want to suckle on her breast as he thrust his way inside her. Why he'd found her so irresistible the night of the ball would no longer be a mystery.

"Are you still hungry, my lord?"

"I am, a bit." Aidan reached to the tray and took a piece of cheese and a few dates.

"You didn't care for the oysters?"

"I did. They were quite good."

"Have a few more. It would be a shame to see them go to waste."

Aidan shrugged as he chewed the fruit, trying to seem unaffected despite the sexual hunger that raged in his blood. He was as hard and tightly drawn as a sword, and his mind was muddled and humming with a lust so strong he wanted to wrap his fist around his cock and relieve it, right then, right there.

"Father says that certain foods taste better with certain drinks," Mira said, as casual as if she were speaking about the weather. She poured a fresh flute of sparkling wine and extended it to him. "I have heard that oysters taste excellent with champagne. Taste it, and tell me if 'tis true."

"Taste it for yourself," he invited her.

"They make me ill," she said, as if sad about it. "My skin blotches and itches if I eat seafood."

"I have seen you enjoy fish."

"Mollusks," she corrected. "'Tis mollusks that I meant. Mussels make me ill, also."

"Just the other evening you ate soup with shrimp, mussels, and clams, and you were quite fine."

"No, my lord, I was not. I vomited that night." She shivered in revulsion and stuck out her tongue. "'Twas vile."

Aidan shrugged again, and ignored her request. He took a piece of the smoked meat and bread.

"My lord, the cook will surely be put out with me when she sees all her hard work was for naught."

"If that's the case, why don't I take the rest and set them out for others to enjoy?"

Mira hesitated, and then laughed and waved her hand. "Sometimes I worry about the silliest things. Surely I don't answer to your cook, and for that matter, the ocean is chock full of the little creatures."

He raised his eyes to meet hers, and calmly asked, "What did you use to drug me? A cantharid, no doubt, but which one? Spanish fly, perhaps?"

"I don't know what you're talking about." But her cheeks went very pale, save for two red spots that flagged her skin. She tried to wrinkle her brow prettily, but only managed to look wanly disturbed. "I despise insects."

"Where did you get it?"

"Pardon?"

"Enough, Mira. I'm about three seconds from rape or violence, maybe both. Get to the truth quickly."

She drew back, a hand on her throat, the other pressed protectively against her abdomen. Assessing him with wide eyes that had lost their feigned confusion, she seemed to be weighing her choices.

If Aidan hadn't been so incredibly enraged and aroused at once, he might have felt an inkling of respect for Mira at that moment. He was a man who appreciated a person who could think on their feet and keep their wits about them even when threatened.

But he wasn't in a charitable mood.

Aidan grabbed Mira and pulled her to the floor, covering her with his body. She let out a little yelp and began to struggle, but he ignored her. He ground his erection against her pelvis. "You want me?" he asked harshly. "This is what you want?"

He rubbed against her again, and she let out a little whimper as she said, "Stop."

"This is what you wanted, isn't it? To get me back between your thighs so I'd feel further beholden to you. You might have even gotten pregnant this time, and then you'd have me forever."

She flinched. "You're crude."

He laughed, a cynical sound. "Your sensibilities are too fine for words that describe what's natural, but you're not above drugging a man to get what you want."

"Get off me."

Aidan looked down on her face, flushed now with exertion, and then pushed her from him as he rolled away from her. He couldn't find a single real thing about her, other than her spite. Even her perfume was a lie. Mira Kimball was anything but sweet.

He realized that if Mira had taught him anything about himself, it was that he would not live without the truth.

Getting to his feet, he went to her armoire, opened it, and began rummaging through her things.

Mira rushed to his side and began tugging on his arm. "Please, stop. Stop it now, I say!"

"Call for help," he answered her simply. He dug his hands into a deep drawer, feeling around on the bottom beneath layers of soft undergarments. "Let your father come running to your aid, only to find the tryst you've made by the fire and my cock bursting my breeches. Champagne, pillows, rose petals, and your magic oysters. Oh, aye, my lady. Your father will be interested in what you're up to at the midnight hour."

He stopped and reconsidered. Going through her things would be time-consuming, and Aidan wanted to get away from Mira as quickly as possible. "You know, you've the right of it. I'm going to go have a word with your father right now, and see what he makes of the situation. Chances are, by the time I'm through speaking with him, he won't want you marrying me anyway, aye?"

Mira's eyes grew wider still. "You wouldn't."

"You don't know me at all," Aidan said as he strode from her sleeping chamber.

Mira ran after him and grabbed his arm, hanging on it as he drug her across the floor. "No. Don't." Her voice was pure panic before she changed her tactic. Mira blew out her breath before she said, "Please. I beg you. Don't go to him."

He knew he had her. Mira loved her father above all else, and he felt the same way about her. She'd sooner die than tarnish his opinion of her.

Aidan paused and turned to look down on her. "Truth. Last chance."

"I stole the powder from my father," she blurted. "He uses it when he visits . . . female acquaintances." Her cheeks burned bright red, and she added, "He doesn't know that I am aware of it. And I'm not proud of the knowledge, either, but I've heard him boasting of its powers to other men, and I got to thinking . . ."

"That it would work on me," he finished for her.

"Yes," she whispered.

Aidan cast a glance at his breeches, where his erect penis was a barely contained bulge. It took every ounce of his self-control to keep his lust in check; it poured through him like a molten river of pure sexual hunger. It was no wonder he'd not been able to resist Mira that August night. As he was, he could barely resist the lure of his own hand. "Aye, well, it worked."

"Will you tell?"

Aidan had to grin. The girl was truly audacious. She didn't bother with excuses or explanations, or even an apology, but cut right to the heart of the matter. "I'll make you a deal—you release me from my marriage proposal, and I'll keep your dirty secret."

Mira's lower lip came out for a second, before twisting up to one side. "I don't care for your terms."

"And I don't care for being drugged, but you don't hear me crying rape."

"A woman cannot rape a man. Don't be absurd."

"Mira," he said, hoping she would heed his warning. "I'm losing what little patience I had."

She narrowed her eyes as she looked up at him. "And what will I tell everyone?"

"Tell them you hate me."

"But I don't hate you. I want to marry you."

"I don't love you. I won't marry you."

"You're missing the point," she whined. She stamped her foot and spread her hands, quite at her wit's end. "I am your very best option. There are no other ladies of our station who are as pretty as me, nor as wellborn or as well-bred. I am the very best you could ever get, and all the other men want me. You'd be a fool to let me go."

"Mira," Aidan said, trying for gentleness despite the pounding of his heart and the raging in his loins. "I don't care."

"Stop using my given name. 'Tis rude and vulgar."

"It seems odd, calling you 'my lady,' when you are anything but. Ladies don't drug a man and bed him to secure a husband."

"You could never do better than me," she cried.

"As you say."

"Your family is muddied, their history riddled with commoners and criminals. How dare you think you could jilt me? I am far above your station, in blood and in bearing."

"I will not argue the facts. Do we have a deal? My silence for your absence."

"No one would believe you. A man crying rape. 'Tis pitiful. Laughable, even."

"Would your father believe me, do you think? When I tell him you stole his special powders that he uses for his female acquaintances, do you think he might doubt you for even a second?"

Mira drew back like a serpent ready to strike. "You are vile."

"I am," he agreed easily. "So leave me. Please."

"There are things you don't know. You shouldn't be so smug, for you are making me certain that you are in need of a comeuppance."

"So give me one, Mira. But do it from a distance."

Mira squared her shoulders and met his gaze. For all her petite, kittenish, sunny beauty, she managed to look haughty and commanding. "You have no idea with whom you're dealing."

"Do we have an agreement?" he asked abruptly.

She turned away from him, and as he took in her filmy nightdress and the abandoned tryst behind her, Aidan felt a pang of pity for her desperation.

"Mira, I am certain you will have no trouble finding another suitor. I hope you do, however, exercise better judgment."

"You could give me another chance."

"We're not right for each other. There is no shame in admitting that before the vows are spoken." Aidan ran a hand through his hair and promised himself a dip in the frigid ocean to cool his ardor. After he'd dealt with Mira. "Listen to me, aye? I'm not going to say a word about the cantharid. Let's just call it even, and walk away with as little trouble as possible."

Mira turned back to him, and with her hands gripping the folds of her wrapper high against her neck, she pointed at the door. "Very well, leave. Go and be free of me. But make no mistake, my lord, *I* am not finished with *you*."

Chapter Twenty-One

Aidan kept to the abandoned corridors of the upper level of the manse. His blood was a thick thrum in his veins and he was as hard as he'd ever been, a hot, thick arousal that demanded satisfaction with each heavy pulse of his heartbeat.

His desire was a potent, relentless scream in his mind. Find Olwyn, it said, and pull her beneath your body. He wanted to lick her skin from her head to her heels. He wanted to spend an hour between her legs, savoring every bit of her. He wanted to hear her cry out his name in pleasure, to feel her convulse with the intensity of her rapture.

And so he was led to her door like a moth to a flame, pulled by his love and propelled by his lust. After Mira's conniving, rose-scented falsehoods, he'd never wanted Olwyn more. He wanted her to draw him down into her scented darkness and give him the truth of her mouth, the honesty of her body, and the all-consuming sincerity of her mind.

Aidan paused, his hand on her doorknob. He'd locked her door, imprisoning her as if she belonged to him, a thing, a possession, something he could lock away and keep for himself.

Shame rose up in his body. The emotion was far weaker than his lust, but he still managed to attenuate it ever so slightly.

No light shone beneath her door. He leaned his ear against it to listen and heard nothing. She slept.

His heart raced as the cantharid sped through his system. Aidan knew sleep would elude him even more than usual, as the stimulant effect of the drug would take hours to spend itself.

He leaned his forehead on the cool smooth surface of the wooden door, his hands on either side of the doorframe. He pushed against it until his muscles bulged and burned, feeling like a beast in a cage. Inside him a battle raged, his hunger versus his honor, both demanding their due.

Aidan clamped down on his desires. He would not surrender to his base urges, no matter how fueled they were by Mira's powder.

He'd already carried Olwyn off and locked her away. He wouldn't disrespect her further by entering as she slept and using her body for release.

She also deserved better than to be imprisoned.

Aidan reached into his pocket and withdrew the key to her room. He slid it under her door, hoping that when she woke she would see that he'd given her back her freedom. He'd had no right to take it from her in the first place.

Despite the burning in his blood, Aidan turned and walked away from the temptation of her door.

Time had crept into the wee hours, and the house was silent and dark. Aidan sought out the privacy of his rooms to spend his lust alone. It would be bread and water when he craved honeyed cakes and wine, but he would not inflict a passion on Olwyn that she had not fully inspired.

He entered and shut the door behind him, turned the key and began to strip as he made his way through the darkness to his sleeping chamber. Shucking his jacket and his shirt, he dropped them to the floor, kicked off his shoes, and peeled off his breeches and stockings, leaving them behind him in a pile.

Nude, his cock drawn tight and hard, Aidan found himself annoyed, aroused, and to his chagrin, alone.

His bed had been turned down, and his fire burned low, casting reddish flickering light across the floor. He flopped on his bed, and with a sigh of resignation, wrapped his hand around his shaft.

He closed his eyes and conjured up the image of Olwyn as she'd been the first night he'd brought her to the inn. He recalled the scent of her incense in the air, amber and Tamil mint, musky sandalwood, spicy ginger and exotic cardamom, the smoke a thin white curl that cast a genie's spell. She'd moved in front of the fire, illuminating the shadowy shape of her legs and buttocks.

His hand moved rhythmically, stroking, squeezing.

He wished it were Olwyn touching him, her bare skin pressed to his, her silky hair falling over his face as she kissed him. He could almost hear her voice, whispering his name.

"Lóchrann? Are you there?"

Aidan froze for a second before rolling to his side. He grabbed a fistful of his sheet and covered himself. "Olwyn?"

"I'm sorry," she said quietly, as she came from the shadows of his sitting room. "I was waiting for you in the chair by the fireplace, and I think I fell asleep."

She emerged into the reddish light like a vision conjured by the power of his desire. She wore a plain white nightdress, a narrow column that fell from her slim shoulders with no adornment. Her hair hung down her back, the black of it disappearing into the darkness. As she neared him he could make out her expression: worry and caution, and something he didn't dare to contemplate.

Her untamed beauty never failed to stir him, even when he'd nearly been caught in an act that men went to pains to keep hidden. He wondered if she'd seen what he had been doing, and the thought caused a dark desire to bloom in him as he envisioned pleasuring himself as she watched on.

"How did you get out of your rooms?" he asked her, his voice husky and tight. He wished she would either get in his bed or leave, for he could not count on himself for much more restraint.

Olwyn smiled then, a curve of lips that possessed all the mystery of a woman's knowing. "Your mother."

Her meaning filtered slowly through Aidan's embarrassment, surprise, and unspent arousal. His body throbbed, and he couldn't stop staring at the way the fabric of the nightgown clung to the peaks of her breasts. "Pardon?"

"Your mother, the duchess." He could hear the tone of admiration in Olwyn's voice. "She heard from your brother that you'd locked my door, and she came straightaway. She said that no one has the right to lock a woman away. And most especially, not one of her sons. She said you ought to know better, my lord, you of all people."

"Is that so?"

"Aye. And she told me that many years ago, she'd known just how I might be feeling after being bullied by a man. She said that I had far more choices than I might realize, and she told me to make myself comfortable in this home, and to know that as long as she was under this roof, I would have my freedom to come and go as I pleased. She said she'd see to it herself. No woman, Her Grace told me, would ever be imprisoned as long as she had the power to free her."

Despite himself, Aidan grinned. He came from a family rife with headstrong women, and Emeline was no different. She was a force to be reckoned with.

His musing was interrupted as Olwyn moved a step closer to where he lay. Aidan was naked, abed, and his cock was as hard as stone. It wouldn't take much provocation for him to surrender to his urges, but he realized that Olwyn had no idea that she'd crept into the lion's den.

"And your way of exercising the freedom my mother bestowed upon you was to sneak into my rooms?" he asked softly. "What are you here for, Olwyn?"

Standing before him, she met his eyes with all the ease of a woman who did not understand the force of her own beauty. She could not possibly know how desirable she looked, clad in a simple sheath of white fabric, her black hair framing the Druid magic of her face, a medieval priestess prepared to reveal sacred secrets.

"I wanted to talk with you."

"What couldn't wait until morning?"

"I fear I might have brought danger to your doorstep, my lord." She spoke gravely, her voice hushed and serious as if she confessed a terrible sin. "I feel something coming."

"You're safe here."

"You are not listening. I tell you I *feel* the danger."

Aidan realized she hadn't come to him for a stolen moment, but out of great fear. "Tell me what you feel."

She hesitated, and he noticed that her hands, though clasped tightly together, were trembling.

"My father," she finally whispered. "He is near. Perhaps you find it strange that I can be so certain, but years of being on my guard has honed my intuition. It isn't possible for me to ignore it, nor do I dare disbelieve it."

Aidan remained silent, allowing her the time to find words for the emotions she obviously struggled to articulate.

"My father is not altogether well. He's two men in one, the intelligent man I remember from my youth, and also a madman. It's the madman I fear, the part of him that knows nothing except the voices in his head." Olwyn swallowed heavily before adding, "He cannot keep himself from hearing those voices. And he always obeys them."

Olwyn squeezed her hands tighter together, and in the firelight Aidan could see that she was digging her fingernails into her skin. He leaned forward to capture her gaze.

"Olwyn, I know you are afraid, but do you also understand that I will stop at nothing to keep you safe?"

"And he will stop at nothing to get me back. To put me in my place," she answered him softly.

"Your place is with me now."

He saw her lips trembling, and he longed to cover them with his own, to kiss away her fears. He would never let anything happen to her, nor would he allow anything to take her from him.

Aidan had needed to die to find her, had awakened at her touch. He belonged to her, as she did to him.

"No, my lord. You do not see. You still aren't listening." Her voice was now full of frustration, and her gray eyes gleamed like crystals as they reflected the firelight. "I am the last of his family, the only one of his blood. I was never to leave him."

Olwyn released her grip on her hands long enough to push her hair back from her face. And he saw thin, crescent slivers of blood where her fingernails had been.

And he desperately wanted to go to her, to comfort her. But the drug was potent in his blood, and he knew that comforting her would soon turn to much more. That was not what Olwyn had come for, and he would not disrespect her by turning her midnight confession into a stolen tryst.

"I now know why there were no mirrors in our keep," she whispered. She rubbed her hand over her forearm where thin, silvery scars marked her fair skin. "He controlled me in so many ways, convinced me of so many lies. He made me afraid of everything: the outside world, others' opinions, even dogs . . . and most especially my own face."

"And rats?" Aidan asked, hoping humor would reach through her fear where his words of comfort did not.

He saw the ghost of a smile curve her trembling mouth.

"No, my lord. The rats did that on their own."

"You now know that your father was lying. The opinions of those who spurned you were made out of ignorance and deceptions." Aidan watched her, unable to keep from noticing her every detail. "And the beauty of your face, my love, is unrivaled."

"But there were things that were absolutely true," she insisted. "He did not contrive the madness that exists in him, and if anything, the lengths to which he was willing to go to keep me with him should prove just how determined he has been to see that I never leave."

"But you did leave. You are free of him."

Olwyn blew out her breath and spread her hands. "I suppose there is no explaining my father to you. You'll have to see for yourself."

"I do see." He couldn't keep himself from saying the truth. "I see how beautiful you are in the firelight."

"It isn't exactly compassionate to ogle me as I stand here before you, terrified and worried sick."

"Worrying is just praying for what you don't want, Olwyn. Put your energy to better use."

"And if I am correct, and my father is near?"

"We'll deal with it as it comes." Aidan meant the words completely. Since waking from the sickness that nearly killed him, he'd learned that each moment was the only time there was; the past was gone, the future unknowable. "That's life, isn't it? Each problem can only be dealt with in the moment. And right now, my love, we are here, together in my chambers. The fire is low, the hour late, and we are alone. I'm naked and abed, and you're before me, a vision more beautiful than anything I could have dreamt. I wouldn't change this moment in the slightest, except there'd be less space between us."

She sighed again, glanced around the shadowed room, and seemed to take it in for the first time. Her gaze went from the elegant framed art on the walls, to the cases of leather-bound books, and finally to the mantle that encased the creamy, gleaming marble fireplace in front of a thick Persian rug.

"Such riches," she murmured.

"Things," he said flatly. "Possessions, that if set on fire and burned to the ground, the world does not miss."

"But you would miss them."

"I enjoy the luxuries that wealth brings, but I don't need them. I'm as happy in my cottage or my mews or aboard one of my ships."

"More riches," she pointed out.

"Very well. But just the same, I was as content in the stone hut where you tended me. Belongings, Olwyn, are not the measure of me. I'll ask that you not appraise me by them."

Olwyn folded her hands, let go, and wrapped her arms around herself in an embrace that made her look lonely, at loose ends, and incredibly sad. "I'm sorry."

"Why be sorry? I don't expect you to be comfortable here. I don't expect anything from you, save your honesty. If you can give me that, the rest will come in due time."

Olwyn shook inside, her entire being quaking with emotions she could not suppress and could scarcely contain. As he spoke of words of honesty, she trembled further.

She'd come to warn him of the danger. After considering the situation for many hours, Olwyn decided that Aidan deserved to know what was likely heading his way.

If he was going to protect his family and himself, he would need to know who and what he was up against.

She did not, however, come to tell him the entire truth.

Come morning, Olwyn planned to escape.

If her father could not find her at Beauport, he would leave the Mullen family behind and continue his search for his wayward daughter.

She hadn't sought Aidan out lightly.

Olwyn had thought that she'd steeled herself against Aidan's pull. She'd managed to convince herself that she could come to him and offer him a warning, to see him one last time, and to bid him good-bye in her own way.

She'd even gone so far as to believe that she could resist the urge to lie with him for just one more night, a few hours of the heat of his skin seeping into hers. She told herself that the memory of it would have to be enough, for she could not climb into his bed and expect that she would have enough strength to leave the next day.

What she hadn't planned for, counted on, and prepared for was the erotic sight of Aidan lying naked in his bed, his hand moving over his erect flesh, his breathing harsh and rough in the silence of his chambers.

She'd caught only the barest glimpse of what he'd been doing, but the image burned in her brain like a carnal conflagration. It was all Olwyn could do to keep from sliding beside him on the bed, asking him to show her exactly how he liked to be touched.

The thought was enough to have her gripping her hands together again, holding them in place with her fingernails dug into her raw flesh. Perhaps pain would drown out what her willpower would not.

"You fall silent at the mention of honesty. What are you not saying?"

If he only knew, she thought. Olwyn recognized enough of Aidan's desire for her; if she dared tell him the direction of her mind, she would not leave his rooms with her virginity intact.

The thought was enough to weaken her knees and educe a jittery flutter in her belly.

What, she dared to wonder, was a maidenhead good for anyway?

Fear ran in tandem to her lust, as did hopefulness that it might somehow work out, making for a muddied mix of emotions. She dared to desire him, and yet she felt the fearful presence of her father. But above all, she held onto the thinnest thread of hope, her only lifeline in the turbulent sea of sensations assaulting her senses.

"More silence," he observed. "Should I be concerned?"

Nervous, edgy laughter slipped from her lips, and her legs nearly lost the last of their strength. Olwyn could only change the subject, and with it, she hoped desperately, the direction of her thoughts. "You speak with such assurance, my lord, and question me with such authority. It doesn't escape my notice that you include me in your future in the same breath as you ask me to honor you with the truest parts of myself. You are a man bound to another woman. Have you forgotten your betrothed so easily?"

"I spoke with Mira this evening, and we've agreed to dissolve our engagement."

"So you've unfettered yourself," she said softly, and hoped he could not hear the tremble that shook her voice. "What now?"

Aidan shifted his position in his bed, and as he did the sheet that covered him slid down, revealing the lower portion of his flat belly. His movement exposed more of his body to the roaming, flickering firelight, and Olwyn saw that he was still erect. The part of him that he'd pressed hard and hot against her belly remained thick and long and full.

Her mouth grew dry, her womanhood wet.

Aidan must have noticed the line of her vision, for he pulled his covers up and shifted again so that his hips were once again in the shadows.

"We have a new ending to discover," he said in answer to her question, but his voice had changed in a way that sent more dark longings coursing through her blood. "Or should we call it a new beginning?"

Dawn came on swift wings. Olwyn would leave the manse in only a few hours. To think of never seeing him again when he spoke of new beginnings nearly drove her to the end of her resolve.

Her skin ached for the want of his touch.

Her mind whispered seditious suggestions—lie down with him and abandon the plan of slipping away in morning's light; let Aidan deal with the danger that her father presented. Aidan was a man, after all, her selfishness reasoned. Shouldn't she hide in the shelter of his presence and let him handle matters?

"More silence," he observed.

"Lóchrann," she managed to whisper. "I don't know what to do, and your talk of the future frightens me."

At least that was the truth, she thought.

"I'm sure you're tired. Go seek out your bed, and we can continue this conversation in the morning when the wee hour isn't making things seem more urgent than they actually are."

Olwyn thought of the bed and the rooms where Aidan had ensconced her, the size and luxury of which she'd never seen or experienced before. By now her fire would be burned to cinders, the sheets would have grown cold, and without her nightly ritual, the dark corners were certain to contain the worst of her fears.

And if she decided to follow through with her plan, she would leave come morning and would have to spend the rest of her life wishing she'd spent one more night with Aidan, no matter what the cost.

"Might I ask a favor, my lord?" she said shyly. "The chair in the other room was comfortable enough, and if you wouldn't mind overmuch, could I curl up there and pass what remains of the night?"

"What's wrong, Olwyn?" His deep voice resonated in the darkness, as smooth as scotch and just as complex, such a mix of sensuality, compassion, and caring that Olwyn could feel the vibration down to her bones.

"I don't have my incense," she admitted. "When I am this unsettled, the dreams are certain to plague me." And being near him made her feel safer, but she didn't say that.

Being near him also made her contemplate thoughts most unbecoming of a maiden. She didn't say that, either.

"Take my bed," he offered. "I'll take the chair."

"Never mind. I'll not rob you of your comfort. I'll go."

"I won't sleep anyway. And besides, 'tis the least I can do after bringing you here without what you need to pass the night with no fear. Come lie down, my love, and let me chase the rats for tonight."

His bed would be warm from his body and would smell of him. The temptation to do just as he suggested was as potent as his whiskey, and just as intoxicating.

"You keep calling me that," she breathed, and her body swayed as she stood before him, vibrating with desire and fear and fatigue.

"You are my love," he said softly in turn. "I wish I had a better way to describe what I've come to feel for you, for love is a pale word, overused by dreamers and Irishmen."

His words sent an earthquake through her already fragile core, tearing asunder every last bit of her composure. Tears welled up and stung her eyes, and though she blinked them back they had their way with her, spilling over to fall down her cheeks. Olwyn, unaccustomed to weeping in front of another person, turned so he could not know.

But he did, anyway. There wasn't much she seemed to be able to hide from him.

She heard Aidan get out of bed and approach her, felt the warmth of his skin behind her. Was he nude there, in all his male glory, and was his manhood still erect, a bold thrust from his body? The thought had her struggling to breathe.

"I am sorry to speak to you with such brash confidence," he said gently. "I do realize you've never once said you felt similarly toward me, and yet I keep speaking of the future, of the two of us being together, and aye, I speak too freely of love. Call it what you will, but underneath it all, I suppose I've gone just a bit foolish over you, enough that I cannot forget that you once called me Lóchrann of your heart, and I cannot help but read into your meaning."

Olwyn couldn't speak, for her throat was thick with tears. The enormity of all that Aidan had said overwhelmed her, as she believed it too good to be true. Something would spoil it all, and would turn the dream to a nightmare.

"And once again, more silence," he observed. "It speaks volumes, I think."

He turned and went back to the bed, sighed and sat down. He was quiet for a while, and when he spoke his tone was full of frustration. "I have given you my absolute truths, Olwyn. I've told you what's in my heart, and I've opened my soul to you. In return, I get teary silence. I don't know what else to say or do, for I've offered you all I have and all I am, and yet, you don't seem to want to give me the slightest indication that you feel even a bit for me of what I feel for you. And so I'll stop asking you for what's in your heart, and I suppose I'll stop telling you about what's in mine. Go back to your rooms or sleep on my chair or in my bed, whatever pleases you. But make up your mind what you want, for I'm through with your silences for the night."

Olwyn wiped away her tears with a fierce swipe over her cheeks and spun around to face him. She saw that he had nothing but a drape of sheet over his hips, and that his hair hung in loose sun-streaked waves around his face. His skin was burnished by the reddish light of the fire, his expression cast in shadows.

"I have wanted you from the very first time I saw you, naked and nearly dead in my father's dungeon. I drew your form and I wondered about every detail of you. I saw the joy in your face, I saw the sun in your hair, and in my mind's eye, I imagined your life with me in it. I thought you were my prince, and I fancied that I could kiss you awake and make you love me."

Her voice shook and wavered, but she pressed on. "Can you imagine what it feels like to be me? To be a poor urchin of a girl who only a few weeks ago was the slave to a madman who is also her father? To find that the dream that I dared to imagine has all come true, and to be forced to just wait and see what will destroy it all? You and your family are beyond my reality, and I fit here no better than an ugly old mule in your stables full of pedigreed beauties."

"You fit me better than anyone on this earth."

"I don't, and your saying I do does not make it so."

"You fit me."

"I am exactly wrong for you."

"You woke me."

"No, my father's scalpel did that."

"You make me feel alive, Olwyn."

"I'm poor," she finally breathed, unable to keep air in her lungs.

"I'm not exactly looking for a woman with a dowry, aye? I have money. What I don't have is you."

Once again, he wasn't listening. "I'm uncultured."

"You're perfect."

"I'm not certain I could learn even half of what would be expected of me."

His voice came warm and resonant in the shadowed light. "If you change in the slightest, I'll never forgive you."

"I don't know what to say to get through to you."

"Tell me how you feel about me."

"I love you," she managed to say, pushing the words out despite the shame they aroused in her belly. How dare she love a man like him? Did she profess or confess, she wondered. Still, she kept talking, telling him just how she truly felt. "I've loved you from the moment I saw you, and I laughed at myself, for even then I knew the truth. I was a pathetic girl, so lonely she could fall in love with a corpse."

Aidan stood, and holding the sheet swathed around his narrow hips, he came toward her. With his free hand he reached out and lifted hers, held her palm flat against his hard chest, directly over the beating of his heart.

"I'm real and I'm alive," he said. "But I'm not the prince you imagined, and far from it. Do you love the dream of me, or do you love the reality of the man?"

"You," she said softly. Beneath her hand his skin was warm, vital, like life itself. "You, Lóchrann."

"And if I can accept your poverty, can you accept my wealth?"

Olwyn didn't respond, all too aware that it seemed foolish to have difficulty accepting that she loved a man who had riches. Still, the idea didn't sit well at all, to imagine presiding over a mansion complete with a staff of servants, and in possession of all the accoutrements of affluence.

"Once again, you fall quiet." He didn't sound angry this time. Instead, he grinned. She could hear it in his voice, wicked, untamed. "Perhaps I'll answer for you. It seems you'll correct me easily enough, so I'll give it a go. I take your silence to mean: Yes, Lóchrann, I can accept that you are wealthy, and I shall let you shower me with gowns and jewels as it pleases you."

"I don't want gowns or jewels."

"See? 'Tis easy enough to say what you're thinking, aye? So you'll love me as you like, and we'll keep your belongings as simple as your comfort dictates."

In that instant Olwyn realized that he had her thinking of the future and negotiating her place in his life. He'd somehow managed to turn the tables again. She'd come to warn him of danger before slipping away, and now they were settling the terms of their relationship.

Olwyn also realized that any notion she'd had of leaving was now foiled by her own admission. Now that he knew she loved him, he would stop at nothing to find her. Just like the night that he'd ensconced her in the inn on their way to Beauport, she was outmatched and outmanned. No woman on foot was a match for a man with a fleet of men on horseback at his disposal.

Surrender was her only option.

And with Aidan standing before her, tall and broad of shoulder, with a sheet covering only the part of him that she couldn't manage to stop thinking about, giving in to her love and desire for him didn't seem too bad an option, as options went.

Olwyn admitted defeat by closing the gap between them. She stood close enough that she could smell his skin, clean and warm and completely male. Reaching up, she slid her fingers into his hair, as soft as the first rays of summer sunlight. The fire behind them burned low, illuminating him in shades of red amber, and she saw how beautifully he was made, tight muscles beneath taut skin, his body large but also graceful. His breath came out in a rush, as if he'd been holding it, warm and whiskey-scented.

She felt a shudder ripple through him, and she knew it for his restraint.

"What are you doing?" he whispered.

"I am yielding, Lóchrann."

Chapter Twenty-Two

"There is something you should know," Aidan told Olwyn, his voice suddenly tight. He took her hand from his hair and held her away from him, his grip on her wrist hard. "There is a drug in me, a cantharid. It is a drug for sex, Olwyn, and because of it I'm nearly unable to control my lust. I warn you—touching me will make it impossible."

Olwyn frowned. This admission from him struck her as completely at odds with the man she thought she knew. "Why did you take this drug?"

He sighed, and again she smelled whiskey on his breath. It made her long to kiss him and taste his tongue, to mingle her essence with his, to be one with him.

"Mira mixed a powder into my food to attempt to secure my . . . affection for her."

"A drug can do that?"

"Aye, and 'tis not uncommon. There are many who use cantharides as an"—he cleared his throat, as if resigned to the explanation—"enhancement for their sensual escapades."

"I've never heard of such a thing."

"Aye, well, 'tis true, and it is in me, blazing in my blood. The drug will spend itself in time, but for now, you'd best keep yourself at a distance."

"Did it work?"

"I told you, Olwyn, that it burns in me like a fire eating its way through tinder. Aye, it worked. I can scarcely keep myself in check." Aidan sounded angry, frustrated, and at the end of his tether.

The rise of Olwyn's female jealousy cared nothing for his mood. In her mind's eye, she could only see the silhouette of his erection beneath the thin sheet and the way his hand had moved over it. No, her jealousy didn't care how annoyed Aidan might be. It sought only the answer to one question: "I mean, did the drug secure your *affection* for her, my lord, and enhance your time with her?"

He laughed, harsh and bitter and full of self-mockery. "Aye, once, and 'twas a mistake I sought to make right with wedding vows."

"She drugged you before." It wasn't a question.

His mouth turned hard in response.

A long pause filled the air as Aidan seemed to weigh how much to reveal. He let out another long sigh, and said, "Tonight, I remembered the feeling and the metallic taste on my tongue, and was finally able to figure out just why I'd made that mistake with her in the first place. Lord help me, I did not make it again."

His lips softened, and even in the dim reddish light she could see the defined line of his upper lip, and the slightly fuller bottom curve. His eyes were cast in shadow, but she knew the dark blue of them so well that she saw them in her dreams.

"Put your suspicions to rest, my love. There is only one woman for whom I burn, and she doesn't need to drug me to light the fire in my blood."

He said he burned for her.

"She is me," Olwyn said softly, unable to keep from saying such an improbable and yet audaciously wonderful truth. "You burn for me."

"I do," he said softly. "Only you."

"And you love me," she added shyly.

"I do," he repeated. He smiled, his eyes on hers. "Only you."

"Oh my," she whispered. The enormity of it all came upon her at once.

He wasn't letting her go, and she didn't want to leave.

Her knees grew weak and she took a few steps back, stumbling into the darkness. A memory flashed through her mind, stunning in its clarity, of the time she'd tried to escape her father and had been attacked by the dogs. Their teeth had torn her skin, their foaming saliva mixing with her blood, their barking growls mingling with her crying screams.

"What's wrong, Olwyn? Every time we talk about how we feel about one another, you grow pale and quiet."

"My father will stop at nothing to get me back. I had come tonight to warn you of the danger, and afterward I planned to run away, to never come back, and to never see you again, because I hoped to keep you and your family safe from the danger." She saw him open his mouth to speak, and she quickly said, "I know, Lóchrann. I know, I know. You keep telling me, and I hear you. You will keep me safe, you will protect me, you want me here with you, and if I would have left you would have found me."

"All of that is true."

"But you are the one who is not listening. My father is

coming, and when he arrives you may find I am not worth the trouble."

"Let me be concerned about that, Olwyn. For now, tell me this—will you stay? Of your own volition, will you stay with me?"

It was her turn to sigh, her final surrender. "I will."

"Your word."

"I give you my word. I am now your problem, my lord, as will my father be. I hope you don't regret it."

"Let me worry about me, Olwyn. And let me worry about you, too, aye? If you'll let me look after you, I think you might find I'm rather good at it."

She closed her eyes, unable to keep looking at him. He clouded her mind, broke her rhythm, invaded her soul, and then consumed it, piece by piece until she belonged to him rather than to herself.

She must have read too many fairy tales and fables while ensconced in the rooms of her youth, high up in the crumbling turret. Page after page of princes rescuing maidens, with right and wrong clearly delineated, and good always triumphing over evil. If only real life were that simple.

"The hour grows so late 'tis now early. Is it night or is it morning?" Aidan asked quietly.

"The hour is darkest before dawn, my lord. Perhaps 'tis both."

"Come to bed. You're tired."

She was tired. Tired of worrying, of being afraid, and most of all, of being alone. "Come with me, Lóchrann. Shelter me from the world."

His breath was a hiss between his teeth. "I can't touch you tonight. I can scarcely withstand looking at you, Olwyn. The scent of your incense is on your hair. I can smell it on you, and it makes my blood boil in my veins. You say you love me, and my heart nearly collapses. You

promise to stay, and my knees grow weak with the desire
I feel for you. I tell you this: 'tis not a wise thing to lie with
me this night. My control has never been less controlled."

"To hell with wisdom," she said succinctly. "Hold me,
Lóchrann of the darkness, and soothe this yearning of my
spirit that you have gone to such pains to awaken. As my
worries are now yours, so is my heart, and so I am sorry,
my lord, but you have decided to make it your own. Now
you must tend to it."

"Olwyn," he said on a breath. "I am not a cad to take
you before vows are spoken."

Tension radiated from him, taut with restraint, hot with
desire, so potent it made Olwyn feel at once powerful
and shy.

But shyness had little influence over her yearning to be
with him. Once she'd surrendered, details such as before
or after the vows made little difference to a woman of
Olwyn's practicality. "Take me to bed, Lóchrann, and let
me fret about my own virtue. I think you'll find I'm quite
good at it."

He laughed. It came out as a low, wolfish sound, but it
was a laugh nonetheless. "Is that so?"

"Quite," she said, moving toward the bed. "Now, which
side do you prefer?"

"Whichever side you're on."

"Well, rather than choose poorly, I think I'll place
myself directly in the middle," she said, and heard the
shaking of her shyness in her own voice. She climbed onto
the softness of the mattress, and lay down before she could
change her mind. She'd been right—the sheets and pillows
smelled of Aidan's skin.

Her skin slid against the fabric, silky and smooth, cool
from the air, and smelling of spice and musk, a man's
scent. Aidan's scent.

Her Lóchrann of the darkness loomed above her, his

sheet still twisted around his hips. He faced the low burn of the fire, the mattress against his thighs. The reddish light bathed him and cast shadows in the hollows of his eyes and cheeks, the square line of his collarbones, the defined strength of his chest, the narrow plane of his belly and navel. He looked like a man of legend and lore, tall and brawny and fair, bathed in firelight, drenched in desire.

She could feel his conflict, his tautness. He held himself from her because of his honor, he lusted her because of his love, and he warred with both because of the drug.

Inside the privacy of Olwyn's mind she'd always enjoyed the freedom of her thoughts. They were brashly daring, boldly fearless. She'd learned to keep them to herself, had been taught that such talk was not appreciated.

Aidan, however, seemed to like knowing what she thought, what she wanted, and what truths existed in her mind and heart. And so, lying in Aidan's bed, Olwyn boldly gave her truest self its voice. "Show me what you were doing when I interrupted you."

She saw his belly flex, his fist that held the sheet grow tighter.

"How long?" His voice was deeper and darker than a moonless night.

And she knew exactly what he meant.

"Not long enough," she admitted in a husky whisper. "Had I thought about it, I would have kept to the shadows and watched for a bit."

She heard him suck his breath through his teeth, a harsh sound of need and control that was rapidly crumbling.

"Witch," he said thickly.

It was the very first time she'd been called that word without a stinging in her heart. He said it like a caress, like a compliment. He said it like a man thoroughly enthralled, ensnared, and enraptured by love's spell.

Aidan Mullen, it seemed, could take her all hurts and heal them.

Olwyn smiled and raised her brow. "Aye, I'm a witch. Come set me afire and make me burn."

Aidan dropped the sheet.

And Olwyn's eyes widened at the sight. She'd thought him an Adonis of a man, and she now knew why sculptors paid homage to the male form. He was strength and virile power, all male flesh and muscle and masculine power. His manhood thrust away from his body like a sword, long and straight and thick, and far too large for the place Olwyn knew he longed to put it.

She reflexively held her thighs together. As beautiful as he was to look upon, she couldn't quite reconcile herself to the act she'd initiated. Indeed, she'd invited it. And though no touch of Aidan's had ever been anything but pleasurable, Olwyn could not discount the disparity of their size.

"My Lord," she breathed, and she watched with hypnotic attention as his penis moved with a slow, muscular flex as if it had a pulse all its own. "My Lord."

He wrapped his hand around his shaft once more, moving it slowly as he did, back and forth the way the ocean rolled and receded across the shore. "This is what you saw."

She managed to strangle out, "Aye."

"What you saw, Olwyn, was a man drawn on the rack of need and desire, lying in his bed, alone, lonely, with his heart aching for you, his mind consumed with your beauty, and only his hand to sate the hunger he could not control."

Olwyn's breath went short.

"Do you want to know what I was thinking about?" he asked softly, his hand still moving in that same rhythm.

Olwyn nodded, once.

"You in the inn, with the firelight silhouetting the shape

of you through your thin gown. Your skin on mine, your hair falling over my face, your lips. You, Olwyn, you. Only you, always you. Your honest tongue, your earthy fire. From the moment I woke, I've wanted you."

Olwyn couldn't speak, couldn't move. She lay before him like a sacrificial virgin, clothed in white, trembling with apprehension, mesmerized by his masculinity.

She watched as he stroked himself in long, slow, sure caresses, from tip to base and back again.

Looking up to his face, she saw the shimmer of his eyes as they caught the firelight, and the lines of his face, harsh and drawn as if with pain.

Their eyes locked.

"Lóchrann," she whispered.

"I won't take you tonight, no matter how much I want you. I won't take you until you're mine forever, and I most certainly won't take you when there's a drug in my body."

Aidan climbed onto the bed and stretched out beside her. Olwyn could feel the heat from his body, hotter than fire. He pulled her to him, and she felt his hard erection against her belly as his arms went tight around her. He buried his face in her hair, and she heard him breathe deeply.

"There is a war in me, Olwyn."

His body was once again her shelter, big and thick with muscle and heat and strength. She curled around him, put her face in the hollow of where his arm met his shoulder, inhaled his scent. He smelled of darkness and passion, unequivocally male.

How could she ever have thought of leaving him?

Olwyn reached down and touched the center of his heat. All that hardness leapt in her hand, the skin so hot and velvety, the length and strength of him so hard. He groaned at her touch, his body jerking as if a lash had been lain against his skin, and Olwyn felt a surge of feminine power so great her lips curved in a smile.

She stroked him as he'd stroked himself. "Let me ease your pain," she whispered. "Let me discover you. Let me heal you."

He shuddered, and as she felt the lust and pleasure rip through him, another rush of her own desire sent shivers of heat through her blood.

"You are magnificent, my lord. You are as potent in me as any drug."

"Olwyn. You are killing me."

"Shall I stop?"

He made a sound that was a throttled noise of pure sensual need and his nearly surrendered restraint. He would not ask her to continue, but could not tell her to stop.

"I'll answer for you, Lóchrann, as you did for me. No, Olwyn. Don't stop."

Aidan's body jolted again, and another low sound was dragged from his throat. Olwyn moved her hand faster, learning how to please him, gripping tighter, then looser, moving slower before increasing her tempo. His body was her guide, his noises the siren sound leading her.

Aidan's body tightened like a bow, his muscles bunched and flexed, and he groaned low and deep as his penis throbbed his release. She felt the warm wet spurts of his seed spill over her hand and onto his belly, the earthy, clean scent of it like nothing else.

Olwyn leaned down, inhaled the complexity of his essence, and licked a drop of it from his skin. The flavor was just as the scent, sensual and mysterious and dangerously addictive.

She looked up to his face. He watched her with eyes that glittered in the firelight.

"You taste like midnight, Lóchrann," she whispered.

Aidan pulled her up into a fiercely passionate kiss. He

breathed her breath. He licked and nibbled her lips. He sucked her tongue.

And then he rolled over so that he was above her.

"Let's see what you taste like," he said softly.

And as his head dipped down over her belly, Olwyn understood his meaning.

She could not move, was galvanized by the thought of what he was doing. Her nightdress slid up her thighs, and her breath got lost in her throat. His fingers stroked the soft skin of her legs, and she felt her knees falling apart beyond her control. He touched her at the center, where no one else ever had, and she heard a sound echo in her mind, like a moan, and she realized she'd made it aloud.

Aidan stroked her gently, and shivers coursed through her as heat gathered at her center. He touched her where she was incredibly sensitive, and her body jerked as his had, sensual lashes of pure pleasure ravishing her as if with a velvet feather-tipped whip.

His fingertip moved in circles, and Olwyn became dizzy.

And then he blew gently on her, a steady stream of warm, humid air, and Olwyn whimpered, "Please." But it was a nonsensical request; she did not know what she asked for.

Inside her was a burgeoning, a blossoming. She opened, she grew ripe.

"You are magic," Aidan murmured.

His tongue flicked over her, a soft, wet flame, and she cried out.

"You are beauty," he said, and he did it again. Olwyn opened her mouth, but no sound came out.

"You are fire." This time, he found a rhythm that made Olwyn lose her mind.

Stars burst behind her eyes, and her body became

something new, something different. She clutched at Aidan, unable to do anything but cry as pleasure took her up and over, and cast her adrift on waves of pure release.

When it was over, he held her in his arms as she wept against his shoulder. He kissed her forehead, her nose, her eyelids. He stole each tear with the tip of his tongue, that magical tongue, and in a hushed whisper against her ear said, "Like paradise. You taste exactly like paradise."

Then he wrapped her in the safety of his arms and petted her as little aftershocks from the earthquake shook her. Olwyn held her eyes tightly shut, savoring the miracle of the moment, better than any fable she'd ever wished to disappear into.

She couldn't help but remember the long, lonely nights in her father's house, dreaming of fairy tales and happy endings that could never happen. She'd been so certain of her ugliness, so convinced no man would ever want her. The village pariah, a piebald beast, an obedient servant to her father, and a daughter abandoned by her mother.

She'd been nothing more than a shadow moving through the darkness of her existence.

And it had all been worth it. Every last miserable moment had been worth it, for in its own way, it had put her in Aidan Mullen's arms.

They lay curled together once again, two pieces of the same puzzle completing the other, all soft curves and hard edges fused and fitted just so.

Olwyn lay still and listened to his slow, even breathing with a sense of happiness so deep it was as fathomless as the sea.

She was careful not to move or make a sound, for Aidan Patrick Mullen, her Lóchrann of the darkness, finally slept.

* * *

Thunder woke Olwyn. She came to slowly, aware of Aidan's skin against hers, his arms around her, his breath stirring her hair. The thunder rumbled again, and she realized it for what it was—the harsh knocking on the doors to Aidan's sitting area.

She sat up abruptly, her hand on her throat.

Soft laughter came from behind her, and strong, warm hands ran down the length of her spine. "'Tis not the English army coming for you, Olwyn."

"I shouldn't be in your bed."

"I'll go see who it is. Stay here. No one will see you."

She watched as he slid his breeches over his rounded, muscular bottom, and as he fastened them she whispered, "You are quite the specimen of your species."

He laughed again, and bent down to give her a quick kiss while stealing a caress over her shoulder and down her back. "So are you. I wonder what our children will look like."

The thought tied her tongue. He spoke so easily of the future, a man who'd never had cause to doubt that only good things lay in store for him.

She shimmied back into her borrowed nightdress as the pounding on the door came again, and this time whoever it was came bursting inside, the doors opening with a violent crash of splintering wood and groaning metal.

Padraig rushed into the sleeping chamber, nearly colliding with Aidan, who'd gone running toward the noise.

"What in the hell, Pad! Have you lost your mind?"

Olwyn wanted to die as Padraig's bright green eyes took in the scene: she, sleep-rumpled in Aidan's bed, and Aidan with scarcely a stitch on. His face, so like Aidan's and yet so different, displayed no surprise as he looked from her to his twin. And Olwyn saw something pass between them that she knew she could not define, and would never understand.

"What's happened?" Aidan demanded, and his voice had taken on a terrible tone that Olwyn had never heard before. She desperately hoped to never hear it again.

"'Tis terrible news, Aidan," Padraig said gravely. "You have to come with me."

Aidan dressed swiftly, and as he did, Padraig once again turned his attention to Olwyn. His eyes were hard, his mouth was grim, and Olwyn felt waves of terror gripping her before he even spoke.

"I think you should come, too," Padraig said. "I've a suspicion this is something to do with you."

Olwyn scrambled from the bed. Padraig grabbed his brother's dressing gown and thrust it at her. She slid the thick cashmere garment on in a hurry, wrapped it around her, and belted it tightly. Aidan's robe hung to her feet, the arms trailing well past her fingertips. She didn't enjoy the feel of his garment around her, however, for she knew it branded her as his lover, a woman who'd lain with a man who had, until the night before, been betrothed to another.

Aidan jammed his shirttail into his breeches and pulled on his shoes. "Tell me, Pad."

Padraig didn't respond. He turned and strode from the room, clearly expecting them to follow. Olwyn and Aidan rushed behind him, and Aidan snarled, "Damn it, Padraig. Tell me what's happened!"

Padraig didn't look at either of them, but kept walking down the long corridor. His long legs carried him quickly to the stairs, and he descended them at a pace so fast Olwyn had to run to keep up.

Selfishly she wished she could hide, or at the very least, dress herself. For a reason she couldn't quite name, she longed for the security of her old, ragged gowns, her tattered belt, her dagger, and her pistol.

Aidan clapped Padraig on the shoulder as they reached the landing, spun him around to face him. "Padraig," he said, and Olwyn's heart hurt for him, for his voice was full of worry. "Is it Grandmum or Grandda?"

"No," Padraig answered. His face betrayed his own pain, and a shadow passed through his eyes that chilled Olwyn's heart. He opened his mouth to speak, but a woman's scream filled the air.

Padraig simply said, "Prepare yourself, brother."

And they all took off at a dead run, heading toward the screaming.

Chapter Twenty-Three

Another scream tore through the air, raising the hair on the back of Olwyn's neck. Terror stabbed her with icy daggers, and though her skin felt very cold, her face burned.

I've a suspicion this is something to do with you.

Olwyn could do nothing but follow the men, hurrying through the elegant mansion with the feeling that she was somehow rushing toward her own demise.

A cluster of servants clogged the corridor near one of the rear exits. Their whispers buzzed in the air like the humming of a beehive. One of the younger women cried into a handkerchief, and Olwyn saw that an older woman, pale and visibly upset, patted the weeping girl's back as she spoke softly with one of the stable hands. When they spied Padraig, Aidan, and Olwyn coming, they fell silent and parted, moving well out of their way.

Olwyn walked past the servants of the manse to whom she was a stranger and a person of common birth, an equal to whom they must show deference as she was a guest of the family. She was all those things, and was also wearing the master of the house's robe. She clutched the sagging fabric closed with her fist, lowered her head so that her hair fell forward in a curtain, and did not make eye contact with any of them.

They passed through a large area that Olwyn took to be the servants' hall where they would eat together. It held a long trestle table surrounded by benches and chairs, a few round tables tucked in the corners, and long windows that faced the rear of the property. A fireplace burned merrily at one end, chasing a bit of the chill, and breakfast plates lined the tabletop. They hadn't eaten yet, for she saw that all the plates were still clean, the napkins folded and untouched.

One of the women stepped forward and approached Aidan. She had her hands twisted in her apron, and the cap she wore was different from all the others, a bright red when the other housemaids wore gray or black.

"One o' me girls was headin' to the laundry when she found it, my lord," the housekeeper said, and her soft brown eyes were full of worry.

"What did she find?" Aidan asked. His pace didn't slow as he approached the rear door. It hung open, spilling cold morning air into the galley. Beyond the landing, there were more servants gathered outdoors, and Olwyn saw that Rogan Mullen was outside as well, his black hair gleaming in the early light.

"Ye don't know?"

Aidan flashed a quick, hard glance to Padraig, and then back to his housekeeper. "Never mind it."

He brushed past her and strode through the open door. Olwyn heard Aidan gasp as he saw what caused the stir, and he stumbled slightly before his father reached out and gripped his arm. A low groan came from Aidan's throat, a raw sound full of pain.

To her right she saw a young boy stumble past them, a stable lad by the look of his dress. He was gagging as he made his way to a bush, his arms clutched to his gut. He leaned over the shrub and quietly vomited.

A hand settled on her shoulder, and Olwyn glanced up and saw Padraig towering over her. Grim lines drew his face into a mask of hardness, and his eyes looked like emeralds, bright green and solid as stone. He gave her a slight push forward. "Go have a look, Miss Gawain."

Cold seeped into her bare feet from the frigid ground, making her bones ache, and it took all her strength to move through the knot of people. She did a gallows walk, one foot in front of the other, her movements jerky and wooden.

She reached Aidan's side, and then horror rose in her throat, along with bile. Beside her Aidan dropped to his knees as if all the strength had left his legs, and another of those horrible groans came from him before it dissolved into a harsh sob.

She forced herself to look at the carnage before her, even though it made her stomach churn and her soul sick. It would be the least of her penances, to see what her presence had cost Aidan.

There, lying on the frozen earth, was Chase.

He'd been done like one of her father's corpses, slit down the middle, his entrails and organs removed and arranged neatly beside the hollowed cavity of the dog's body. Chase's eyes had been left untouched, and they stared murkily at the sky.

Blood bathed the ground in a halo of crimson. Chase must have been eviscerated where he lay, her mind noted in an almost detached manner. It had been a bloodbath of a dissection.

Olwyn noticed the slit across Chase's throat, no doubt how he'd been dispatched. It was jagged and gaped open, a macabre second smile that exposed the innards of his thick neck. She also noticed that one of his rear legs had been badly torn and broken. It hung crookedly, shards of bone piercing the skin.

She could picture with deadly accuracy how Rhys had managed to slay the enormous dog. It was painfully apparent to her that he'd trapped him and approached him from the rear, had probably slammed the back of his skull with a cudgel. He must have dragged the unconscious dog to the place where he'd planned to do his work, as no trail of blood ran out of the woods. He'd then grabbed that giant head, pulled it up, and sawn his knife through the arteries of the throat.

Olwyn raised her eyes to the line of the woods in the distance. Rhys was out there, somewhere, watching.

Did he see her? she wondered. Was he looking at his wayward daughter, and smiling with delight as he saw her view the futility of her own escape? Did he see what she wore? The man's robe that marked her as a slut. Her father would not take that matter lightly.

Off to her left another servant came out to see what the fuss was about. She took one look, and promptly stumbled away as she vomited, spewing a hot rush of disgust to the ground.

But Olwyn didn't feel revulsion as the stench of the vomit mingled with the reek of innards, blood, and the unmistakable odor of death. She didn't feel anything.

It was the worst nightmare come to life, and like a person caught in the throes of a terrifying, outlandish dream, Olwyn could not move her legs, could not scream, could not weep, and could not feel.

Deep inside her, something died.

Olwyn recognized the loss like a distant observer,

watching with unearthly calm as the tiniest flame of her newly sparked hope was snuffed out, smothered, and went cold.

She would not mourn the death of her hope. She'd had no right to it in the first place.

Olwyn Gawain turned to Aidan, and he looked up to her, his eyes full of the pain that she'd brought to his door, just as she feared. Tears slid down his handsome face, falling like a clear, cold rain. He opened his hands, those lovely, wide, square-palmed hands that brought her nothing but pleasure, and spread them as if to show her they were completely empty.

Yes, she answered him silently. *I am so sorry. So very, very sorry.*

His eyes, full of grief and hurt and confusion, ravaged her. She ached as if she'd been whipped, but did not look away. Instead, she met his gaze full-on and let it punish her.

"I take it this isn't a mystery to you," Padraig said from behind her. His voice was heavy with emotions he kept tightly contained. "You know who did this."

"I do," Olwyn whispered, finding her voice along with what remained of her former resolve to leave, and take her troubles away from the Mullen family. "It was me."

She brought her eyes back to Chase. His coat gleamed in the sunlight where it wasn't covered in blood, and she remembered his gifts to her, not just sticks and bones, but his gift of making her not afraid of him.

And for it, he'd been brutally killed and gutted, left as a warning and a calling card combined.

"I'm so terribly sorry." What a pitiful word, she thought. Sorry. As if it meant anything, or undid any damage, or even mended a single mistake.

Olwyn glanced once to Aidan's father, Rogan Mullen, the formidable Duke of Eton. Rogan stood tall and stoic beside his son, his face hard and handsome and completely unreadable. He was a powerful man, not just in title and riches, but in his presence. Looking at him made Olwyn feel very small.

"I am sorry, Your Grace," she managed to whisper.

"What do you mean, 'twas you who did this?" Padraig demanded. "'Tis not possible. The damned dog outweighs you by at least six stone."

Olwyn felt all eyes on her—the staffs', the family's, and her father's as he watched from the woods. Her face, as cold as it was, burned. She opened her mouth to speak, but no sound would come forth.

From the door of the manse she heard Camille's voice. "What's happened, Rogan?" she asked of her son.

"Don't come out here, Mum. This isn't a sight for your eyes," Rogan answered, his tone deceptively calm. "I'll come inside in a bit and explain."

Olwyn turned and looked at Camille, whose face showed concerned worry. She was a petite woman, still beautiful in her advanced age, full of grace and dignity. She'd been nothing but kind to Olwyn.

Amidst the Mullen family and their staff, Olwyn felt every bit as much the outsider as when she'd been reviled in *Penarlâg*. Except these people hadn't shunned her. They'd brought her into their lives, welcomed her into their home, clothed, fed, and accepted her. One of them even loved her.

Men from the stables arrived on a wagon. They hopped down and began unloading tarps, shovels, and buckets of water.

"All right, then," Rogan said, gesturing for the staff to disperse. "Let's all return indoors so they can get the poor animal buried and the mess cleaned up."

The servants did as they were told. After they were all indoors, Olwyn remained outside with the Mullen men. She stayed, unable to leave because Aidan was still kneeling by his dog's side, his head bowed and his eyes closed. As long as Aidan suffered his loss, Olwyn felt it her responsibility to bear witness to his pain. The men who'd come with their shovels and tarps hung back a bit, clearly unsure of what to do.

Padraig went to Aidan's side and dropped his hand onto his twin's shoulder. "Come, brother," Padraig said quietly. "Let them do their work."

Rogan turned his bright green gaze to Olwyn once again. "Miss Gawain, if you'll come indoors with me, I'd be most interested in hearing your explanation."

"No," Aidan said. He got to his feet and positioned himself between his father, brother, and Olwyn. "I need to speak with her alone, first."

"We all want to know what's happened here," Padraig said.

"I've a right to hear it first, aye?" Aidan responded harshly. "I watched Chase be born, and I raised him myself." His voice broke, but he bit out, "Leave us."

Padraig made a noise in his throat that sounded like a growl, just as Rogan placed a hand on his back. "He's right, Pad. Let's give him a minute."

Padraig glared briefly at Olwyn, and she felt his disapproval and suspicion. He turned his attention back to Aidan. "I'll go for now, but I'll be just inside, waiting for you. This matter will need to be avenged, brother, and as always, I'll be at your side."

Olwyn held the robe she wore tighter around her body, unable to stop shivering. Her father was out there, somewhere, she knew. Rhys would not have gone to such lengths to inspire horror without finding a spot from which to watch the outcome of his handiwork.

Together, Padraig and Rogan went into the house, leaving Aidan and Olwyn alone, save for the men who'd come to deal with Chase's remains. Aidan made a small gesture and they departed, allowing them to talk in relative privacy.

Standing in front of his murdered dog, he faced Olwyn. He studied her for a long moment before he said, "This is your father's work, aye?"

Olwyn could only manage a small nod.

"And this is what would have become of me."

It wasn't a question.

Olwyn nodded again.

"This is the danger you spoke of. This is what he's capable of."

"And worse," she whispered. Olwyn bowed her head, unable to keep looking at Aidan's face, ravaged as it was with sadness and an emotion she could not name. He looked aloof, distant, and a hardness had taken over his features, making him appear ruthless and cold.

"Look at me."

"No," she managed to choke out. "I cannot bear seeing your pain, and knowing it was I who brought it here."

Aidan cupped her chin and forced her head back. There was no violence in his touch, but neither was their any gentleness. His eyes shone as hard and blue as sapphires beneath the scowl of his dark gold brows, and he appeared like an archangel bent on destruction. His chiseled features were fierce, the line of his lips flat, and his tall, broad body radiated danger.

"Let's be clear on one thing, Olwyn. You came to me and gave me a warning, and I did not heed it well enough. 'Tis a mistake I'll not make again."

Olwyn didn't respond. What, she wondered, was there left to say?

Somewhere out there, Rhys watched on, seeing his daughter in a man's robe, being touched with the familiarity of a lover. She knew there would be no end to Rhys's determination to get her back with him. Rhys saw such matters in very basic terms—she was born a Gawain, and therefore belonged to him.

"More of your silences," he said roughly. "Tell me what's in your pretty head, Olwyn. Tell me now, before I lose what little remains of my temper."

Olwyn realized his grief had turned into anger, and she was glad. Rage would serve him far better than sorrow in the days to come.

Not too far off, one of the men who'd come to bury Chase's remains coughed, and the sound carried to them on air that stank of death, innards, and thawing earth that had been soiled with blood and vomit.

If there would be any blessing to be found in what the poor dog had suffered, it was only that from now on, Olwyn could be certain that Aidan would take her warnings to heart.

"You have two choices, my lord. Your first is to release me, and let me go back to *Penarlâg* with my father."

Before she could finish, Aidan interrupted. "Never."

"He will not stop until it is so."

"Is that what you want, Olwyn? Do you want to go back with him?"

"No," she said with fierce conviction. The memories of the crumbling keep where her father had made her his assistant in the dungeon assaulted her in graphic detail, as did the loneliness that had been like a living death. "No, I don't, but I would rather go back with him than bring more troubles to your doorstep." Tears threatened her thinly held composure as she said, "Your dog, Aidan. Your poor dog."

"This was not your fault," he said distinctly, his tone as firm and bitingly cold as the earth beneath them. And she knew he held to his fury so he would not succumb to his heartache.

"Not your doing," he repeated. "I want you here, no matter what. Do you hear me? I want you, Olwyn."

His words shook her, but Olwyn swallowed down the emotions they stirred. She needed to be certain Aidan understood the stakes. "You must know that by choosing me, you choose to make war with him."

"Then 'tis settled, and war it will be."

"If that's the case, my lord, and your choice is made, there is only more thing to be said—guard your mews, your stables, and your home well, for unless my father gets me back, there will be more blood."

Aidan watched Olwyn carefully. She was paler than usual, and beneath the narrow slash of her black brows, her striking gray eyes were flinty. She met his gaze for the most part, but every so often her eyes flickered to the line of tangle of trees in the distance.

"He's there in the woods, watching, aye?" Aidan asked softly.

He saw the recognition take her face, first the realization that he'd seen into her thoughts, followed by the fear that he'd act on the knowledge.

"Your silences are beginning to be quite eloquent, Olwyn. By the time we've been married a few years, you won't need to ever speak a word."

She blanched whiter still, and if Aidan hadn't been holding in such a mix of potent, penned-up emotions, he might have been amused. Each time he spoke of the future she got that same look on her face: poleaxed, Patrick would call it.

"So he's the sort who'll want to see his creation," Aidan said. "Well, let's give him something to think about."

He pulled her to him and kissed her possessively, his hands wandering down the elegant length of her spine in the manner of a man laying his claim to ownership. She tasted of tears, his and hers combined, and Aidan wanted to weep again. Instead he kissed her deeper, taking the comfort of her body and her mouth and offering his own.

Let her father see that she is mine, he thought.

She pulled back, shaking, and cast a glance to the men who loitered in the distance, waiting to deal with the carnage her father had left. Another quick peek toward the woods, one more look at Chase.

Chase. Aidan's heart broke again, and in the center of that heartbreak was anger so pure and unadulterated that its name was retribution.

"Let's go," he said, and taking a grip on her arm, he towed her into the house.

Padraig waited for them just inside. He leaned against the far wall with his arms folded across his wide chest, a casual pose belied by the intensity of his scowl. "What now?"

"Set up guards at the mews, stables, and around the perimeter of the manse. Give them three-hour shifts, and put Edward from the stables in charge. He'll keep their eyes open."

"Done," Padraig said. "Anything else?"

"Aye. Saddle the horses, ready the weapons, get the hounds, and tell Da, Matteo, and Roman that they're needed. We're going hunting, brother."

Padraig gave a short nod and headed off.

"You won't find him," Olwyn said softly.

Aidan heard the certainty in her tone. "My hounds will sniff him out."

"He'll have thought of that." Olwyn let out a little laugh that possessed no humor. "He'll have thought of everything."

Aidan studied Olwyn for a long moment. There was no way to reassure her that he knew of, no words that would set her mind at ease. She'd come to him in the night to warn him of the possibility of danger, and had awoken to the reality of her father's madness on Aidan's doorstep. All her life, Rhys Gawain had manipulated her with lies and cruelty, imprisoned her, and made her feel completely bereft of hope. To Olwyn, Rhys Gawain was omnipotent, a fearsome ghoul without a conscience.

"We'll find him, Olwyn," Aidan promised her gravely.

"You think he's not much of a threat because he's old and mad."

"He is those things, aye? You told me yourself he's lost his mind."

"He has," she affirmed quietly. Her clear gray eyes took on the look of the hunted, warily alert and weary of running, giving her the appearance of a woman who'd seen far too much at far too young an age. "But there is more to him than that."

"That may be true." Aidan held her arm tightly, and thinking of Chase, he said, "However, the same can be said of me."

As Aidan led Olwyn through the manse, he noticed that the activity had returned to normal somewhat as the staff prepared and served the morning meal. The halls smelled of ham and warm bread, and as they approached the dining room, Aidan could hear the musical sounds of porcelain and crystal being placed on the table.

Olwyn pulled back with a slight struggle. "I'm not dressed properly, my lord."

"Aye, we'll see to that."

He ducked his head into the dining room and spotted his mother, who was seated at the table with Mira and her father. His Aunt Kieran was there as well, along with Portia and Sophia, whose pretty eyes were full of upset and concern. Mira looked up and met Aidan's gaze briefly before seeing that Olwyn was behind him. She took in Olwyn's garb and quickly turned her face toward her breakfast. A blush rose on Mira's cheeks, and Aidan wondered briefly if it was embarrassment or anger. He dismissed the thought just as quickly and addressed Emeline. "Mum, a word?"

Emeline stood and hurried across the room, wrapped her arms around him and hugged him like she'd done when he'd been a boy. She smoothed his hair back from his face and made small shushing sounds before murmuring, "Your father told me what happened. Oh, Aidan. Poor lad, are you handling the shock?"

To Aidan's surprise, as his mother comforted him, he felt a pang of sadness so great it nearly brought him to his knees again. It seemed absurd that her gentle hands and compassionate eyes could affect him so. He towered over her, a grown man outweighing her by almost double, and yet her sympathy and caring had fresh tears nipping at his eyes. "I'll do," he managed to say.

"What a horrid thing, and how devastated you must be," Emeline said as she stroked his cheek. Her hands were soft and loving and smelled like his childhood. "Is there anything I can do for you?"

He tamped down his emotions and forced his mind to the matter at hand. Taking his mother's hand away from his cheek, he gave it a squeeze and dropped it before it shattered what remained of his control. "Aye, Mum, there's something." Pulling Olwyn in front of him, he thrust her toward Emeline. "You won't let me lock her up, so you're going to have to watch her. See to it she doesn't try to leave."

Olwyn gasped and swiveled in his grip. Stormy gray eyes met his, lit with outrage. She raised her left brow into a witchy peak, and he knew he was in for a fight. "I'm not in need of supervision."

"Sure you are," he said easily. "We've got a lunatic running around our property who's murdered my dog, and left him as some sort of sick warning that he's out there. He's after you, and will stop at nothing to get you back. So don't stand before me and say you're not in need of minding, because if I know you half as well as I'm certain I do, you're likely to try to settle the matter on your own with nothing more than a dagger and a pistol in your belt."

"And apparently, to hear you tell it, without my wits," Olwyn said acerbically.

"Get her back?" Emeline interjected. With sapphire eyes that glinted with a sudden sharpness, she cast her gaze upon Olwyn and asked, "How are you acquainted with the person who slaughtered that poor animal?"

Aidan inwardly groaned; his mother missed nothing.

"He is my father, Your Grace." Olwyn spoke the words without equivocation.

"I see." To his mother's credit, any shock Emeline might have felt did not show on her face. "Well then, 'tis no wonder why you left his home and have no desire to return."

"Aye," Aidan said, grateful to his mother for her incredible capacity for compassion. "And so you'll understand that we're needing to keep tabs on Miss Gawain, for she might begin to feel 'tis her responsibility to lead him away from here."

Aidan noticed that Olwyn had grown stiffer still, her spine rigid, her hands fists. He didn't have time to indulge her mood. "Mum, will you watch her?"

Emeline cut to the heart of the matter with her usual gracious forthrightness, and she addressed Olwyn without answering him. "While my son's discourtesy is inexcusable, I suppose we'll attribute it to the shock he's suffered and forgive him. Please, Miss Gawain, take a seat at the table and see if you have any appetite. After all you've been through this morning, perhaps a bite to eat would make you feel better."

"Why don't you come sit by me, Miss Gawain?" Mira's voice fell as sweetly pretty as a rainbow across a sunny sky, and just as unexpected.

Everyone in the room turned their attention to Mira, who laughed softly and gestured to the chair beside her, indicating that Olwyn could take the seat.

"My lady?" Aidan said, wondering at her mood. In the morning light Mira looked delicately regal in an ecru gown trimmed with matching lace, her golden hair elegantly swept away from her face. She most definitely did not have the appearance of a woman who'd drugged a man in an effort to seduce him.

Mira breezily waved her hand in the air. "Let's not make more of our personal matters than need be, my lord. We are all adults here, and if this morning's unfortunate discovery has shown us anything, it's that we're all in this together. Clearly, with a madman roaming the property—no offense meant to you, Miss Gawain—my father and I are not safe to take to the roads just yet. As we'll be staying on until the matter is settled, we might as well make the most of the situation, and at the very least, we should all be pleasant with one another."

Mira's father smiled at her indulgently from across the table as he buttered a scone. "Good show, my pet. Trust you to have a level head and wisdom in the face of something so troublesome."

"I can't see the benefit to going about it any other way, Papa."

Olwyn stood in front of Aidan, her shoulders back and unyielding, her head held at a proud angle. She turned briefly, long enough to send him a glare that spoke volumes—she was not happy about being ordered about, having motives assigned to her, or with Mira in general.

"I suppose you've taken my choice," she said to him stiffly.

"Your protection is more important than your pride."
More important than anything, he thought. Aidan couldn't
imagine what he'd do if something happened to Olwyn,
and he wasn't going to take the smallest gamble with her
safety.

"I know I've already warned you, my lord. But I hope
this time you will understand that I don't say the words
lightly. He's more dangerous than you know. His life is a
misery, and he has nothing to lose."

"I have everything to lose," Aidan said softly, and not
caring who saw, he lifted a shiny black tress from her
shoulder and brought it to his lips. "I'll be careful."

She softened a bit, and in her eyes he saw frustration
and mounting fear. "What will you do with him?" she
whispered. "Will you kill him?"

"He's trespassing on my property with intent to cause
harm, and he's killed one of my livestock. 'Tis my right."

"Will you?"

"Do you wish him spared?"

Olwyn bowed her head. And did not say anything.

"Enough of these silences. Trust me enough to tell me
what you want."

"I don't know," she admitted on a breath. "He is my
father."

Aidan tried to imagine what she must be feeling, how
torn and confused she had to be. And despite what had
been done to Chase, Aidan let his compassion for Olwyn
move him. "If at all possible, I will show mercy."

She nodded. A tear wobbled on the thick, black fringe
of her lashes and fell. "He wasn't always this way," she
said softly.

He knew what she was telling him—that the father of
her childhood had become a monster, but that she could
also remember better times.

Aidan heard riding boots ringing on the marble floors

as the men in his family strode toward the dining room. They were ready.

Aidan spoke to Olwyn quietly, his voice for her ears alone. "As much as it isn't your fault, it must be dealt with."

She nodded again. "I know."

"Mum, will you take Olwyn above stairs so she can get dressed for breakfast?"

"Of course," Emeline answered.

Aidan touched Olwyn's chin and tilted her face so she would meet his eyes. Something in her expression made him uneasy. Knowing that Olwyn thought the entire matter was her fault, and also that she was not a woman to be underestimated, he said, "You behave."

"You be careful," she answered.

Without another word, Aidan left Olwyn in his mother's care, and with Padraig, Rogan, Matteo, and Roman flanking him, the Mullen men went hunting.

Chapter Twenty-Four

The day passed with excruciating slowness. Olwyn followed the example set by the other women, and went along with their routine. By late afternoon her nerves felt as stretched as a harp string, and by the time the ladies sat around the fireplace to attend to their needlework, Olwyn felt sick from swallowing her apprehension.

Other than the occasional glance to the doorway, no one else showed any signs of worry. They chatted about everyday things, gowns and shoes, memories of gatherings they'd all attended, and the recent birth of a foal in the stables.

Inside Olwyn's body she boiled like a kettle of water, her mind warning that if she didn't do something soon, she would explode in a torrent of steam and screams.

She stood in a flurry of skirts, and Emeline raised her eyes from the tapestry that was stretched on a rack before her. "Are you well, Miss Gawain?"

"Aye . . . I mean, yes, Your Grace," Olwyn stammered. "But if you wouldn't mind, I'd like to lie down for a bit."

"Poor dear, you must not have gotten much sleep last night," Mira said in a tone so sweet it seemed impossible that she was so tactlessly referring to the fact that Olwyn had arrived at the breakfast table in Aidan's robe.

"Of course," Emeline said, ignoring the gilded barb. "I'll see to it you're settled."

The two women left the drawing room behind.

"I am very sorry, Your Grace," Olwyn said softly, grateful to have a moment alone with Emeline so she could say what had been eating at her all day.

"Whatever for?"

"Your husband, your sons, and the rest of your menfolk are in danger, and it is because of my presence here."

"Nonsense. You cannot control your father's actions. He put my family in danger. Not you."

"If not for me, none of this would have happened."

"If not for you, my son would not be alive," Emeline countered succinctly.

"If something happens to one of them . . ."

Emeline cut her off with a delicate interruption. "I learned long ago not to entertain such thoughts. Whatever happens will be dealt with as it comes. Until then, we carry on as best we can. 'What if' is an endless cycle."

Olwyn remembered Aidan's words: *Worrying is just praying for what you don't want.*

And so she fell silent and promised herself that she would only pray for good things, such as wisdom and strength and courage, for she felt in desperate need of all three.

As they walked through the corridors of the manse, Olwyn snuck a glance at Emeline's bearing, noticing how regally she carried herself, like a queen. She wore a gown of pale bronze velvet and a simple necklace that suspended an enormous sapphire pendant. Her golden hair was sleekly coiled and had been secured with carved ivory combs.

Emeline must have caught a few of Olwyn's furtive sidelong glances, for she said, "It may take some time before you feel more settled here. I speak from experience, you see. Years passed before I grew accustomed to my husband's way of life."

Olwyn managed a small nod, unable to reply. Emeline spoke as Aidan did, of a future that included Olwyn.

They continued on for a while, their heels tapping on the marble floors. They took to the wide curving staircase, and as they mounted the steps, Emeline added thoughtfully, "My son is a good man, and stubborn when he wants something. I ought to know, as we've butted heads in the past. He is much like me, for better and worse." Emeline laughed. "Isn't that the way? We cannot help but pass along our faults with our finer traits."

Olwyn nodded shyly, wishing that she could feel more comfortable with Aidan's mother. But Emeline had a smoothly confident and self-possessed air about her that awed Olwyn.

"I am much like my mother was, I think," Olwyn told her softly. "She was terrible with a needle and thread, but could grow a flourishing garden in even the rockiest soil."

"That's the good."

It was Olwyn's turn to laugh. "She was also stubborn and full of grand dreams and notions of splendor."

"I don't think it so terrible, to want to find splendor amongst the shadows," Emeline said. Emeline had stopped in the long corridor. Her sapphire eyes, so like Aidan's, were full of compassion. "Did you lose your mother when you were young?"

"She left me." The blunt admission startled Olwyn; she hadn't meant to say that. She quickly corrected the statement. "I mean, she left us. My father and I. The splendor of her dreams must have seemed real enough to her after all, and I suppose the shadows felt more like gloom."

"I'm sorry," Emeline said, her tone rich with empathy. "It must have hurt you deeply to be abandoned by her."

"Aye," Olwyn breathed, remembering the nights she'd lain in bed, wondering what she had done that had been so bad that her mother hadn't wanted her anymore.

She could recall Talfryn's soft voice telling her their story, the one she and Olwyn made up as they went along. Each time they told their tale, it grew and became a bit grander, but also stayed essentially the same. It was the story of the sad little girl who sought out the English king and asked him for shelter from the dragon of Cymru.

"I got through it," Olwyn added, hoping to not sound morose.

"We all do." Emeline smiled, and laid a gentle hand on Olwyn's shoulder. Something about the expression in her eyes made Olwyn think that perhaps the Duchess of Eton knew something about enduring hard times. "My son is a good man," Emeline repeated. "He'll be the dream come true for the right woman."

"I do not dare to dream for much," Olwyn confessed. "Some things seem dangerous to want."

"I know of what you speak." Emeline's smile grew mysterious, and her expression became faraway. "But there is a certain magic that makes such dreams possible."

There was no fighting or hiding Olwyn's earnest desire to know the secret to such happiness. "What is the magic, Your Grace?"

"Love is most of it," Emeline said simply. "But that's the easy part, for it usually happens beyond our control."

Olwyn said nothing, relying once again on the silence that Aidan despised. In the face of Emeline's gentle words, Olwyn had none of her own.

"The difficult part is the believing," Emeline added. "Do you believe in fairy tales, Miss Gawain?"

"Some of them." Olwyn heard her own faltering tone, but she was unable to keep her voice strong when inside she felt as fragile as the last leaf in autumn, ready to disintegrate at the slightest touch.

Emeline resumed walking toward Olwyn's rooms, and as she did she said, "Believe in the ones that make you happy, Miss Gawain, and then dare to dream and dare to love. Most of all, dare to believe that the very best things are not only possible, but that you are worthy of them. If you can manage all three, magic happens. Trust me. I know."

Olwyn had been wrong. Lying in bed alone in the encroaching darkness did not make waiting less arduous, but in fact, had her nearly coming out of her skin. Only one solution made any sense at all, and so when Molly and Alice came to dress her for dinner, she asked them to send her regrets.

Aidan had seen fit to provide her with a full bottle of his whiskey. Mentally thanking him, she poured herself a drink and went out to the balcony.

She shivered as she looked to the woods, for no moon shone through the complete darkness.

How long would they search for her father, she wondered. And to what lengths would Rhys go to see that he wasn't caught?

Olwyn's imagination had become sharply honed after years of solitude; in many ways it had become her refuge, for she could disappear into a dream and forget her reality.

Now, her ability to produce vast, detailed scenarios became torture, as her mind provided her with rich tapestries of evils that could have befallen Aidan. She saw him strung up in a trap, or garroted as he rode beneath a taut rope.

The whiskey slid down her throat and burned in her belly. Olwyn sipped again, deeply.

Courage, wisdom, and strength, she thought, repeating them in her mind. Belief, dreams, and love.

Why, she wondered, were positive thoughts so much more difficult to attain?

From the interior of her rooms she heard a noise that sounded like a tap on her door, and Olwyn rushed inside, hoping it was either news of Aidan or even better, him in the flesh, coming to tell her that all was well.

She flung open the door and her heart sank.

"May I come in?" Mira asked as she crossed the threshold.

"No."

"Too late." Mira leaned toward Olwyn, sniffed the air, and then tittered with laughter. "Drinking spirits, Miss Gawain? Do you also smoke cigars?"

"I would, if I wanted to. Unlike you, I don't pretend to be someone I'm not."

"You don't know anything about me."

Olwyn raised her brow and looked Mira up and down, taking in her sumptuous evening gown, the sparkling jewels she wore around her neck and on her earlobes, and the tiny, glittering tiara perched atop her golden head. "I know enough. Truth be told, I know more than I care to."

Mira swept across the room in the manner of someone on a mission. She turned when she reached the fireplace, and posed herself as if she were a princess addressing a sea of commoners. She pursed her pretty lips, and though she stood several inches shorter than Olwyn, held her head in a way that had her looking down her nose. "Your accent is coarsely vulgar, isn't it? You really ought to seek elocution lessons, if you don't mind my saying so."

"You could guard your ears by leaving."

"I came for a purpose. Despite how your appearance, and dare I say, *existence,* offends my sensibilities, I'll see it through."

"How brave of you."

Mira smiled, but it had more to do with the baring of teeth than actual joy. "Yes, I do have business here," she murmured.

"Get on with it, then."

The clock on the mantel behind Mira chimed, signaling the hour had reached eight. Where, Olwyn wondered, was Aidan?

"I want you gone," Mira said simply, and then she continued with the demeanor of an impatient parent lecturing a wayward child. "You will leave here, and you will never come back. I will give you funds with which to support yourself, as it is quite obvious you cannot return to your vile, awful father. I have made arrangements for you to be transported to an inn for the night and for your transportation to the Americas, departing tomorrow on the morning tide."

Olwyn couldn't help it. She laughed. All her fear and upset and anxiousness of the day melted into hysteria, and her giggles became howls until she was doubled over, wiping her eyes with her sleeve and gasping for air.

Mira's cheeks grew red. "I assure you, I am quite serious. You will do as I say."

"You're absurd," Olwyn said, still laughing. "A comical farce."

"You will do as I command you!" Mira drew herself up stiffly.

"Get out," Olwyn said, wiping her eyes again as she suppressed further giggles. "I've no time for your silliness."

"You underestimate me." With her hands balled into tiny fists and the skirts of her gown shaking, Mira looked like a petulant brat who didn't want to share her favorite doll. She stamped her foot. "I want you gone."

Olwyn walked to the door, prepared to open it and bodily escort Mira out if she didn't leave willingly.

"Don't you turn your back on me, peasant," Mira decreed in a voice that shook with anger. "I will not tolerate your insolence."

Olwyn slowly turned and faced the other woman, her mirth completely gone. She raised her brow and said, "Aye, I'm a peasant, and aye, I'm insolent, as well. But you are not my mistress or my queen, and I don't take orders from spoilt little girls who've worked themselves into a fit of pique. My advice to you is to leave, for I'm feeling my own temper rise."

"Are you threatening me?" Mira hissed.

Olwyn followed Mira's line of vision, glanced down and saw that her hand rested on the hilt of her dagger. She smiled. "It's a fact that I *could* cut your heart out, but not necessarily a fact that I will."

"Oh, you are far too full of yourself."

"Is that so? I would make the exact same observation

about you. It seems we've found some common ground, after all."

"Everything about you is common." Mira said the word like it was a curse.

"Not so," Olwyn corrected. "I am uncommonly good at many things."

Mira narrowed her eyes. "Such as bedroom skills, apparently."

Olwyn felt herself blush, but she didn't otherwise allow embarrassment to show. "I'm capable of gaining a man's attention without resorting to deception and deceit, if that's what you mean."

"I don't know to what you could possibly be referring," Mira said coolly. "I am, have always been, and shall forever be the very best match for any man of quality. I've never deceived a man, because there is simply no need."

"What's with all of this, then? If you're so desirable and in demand, why are you trying to get rid of me?"

Mira pursed her lips to the side, the patrician line of her brows furrowed. She seemed to decide on honesty, for she blurted, "I will not be made a laughingstock, do you hear me? I will not have it be known that my betrothed jilted me in favor of you, a common Welsh peasant with the face of a hobgoblin and the fashion sensibilities of a fishwife."

Olwyn laughed at Mira's description of her, and was amazed that she could hear such words and not feel any pain from them. "Don't forget to add that I'm a piebald beast of a woman. It makes for better storytelling."

"'Tis a tale that will never be told. You are leaving tonight, escorted by my father's manservants. Through them I've made all the arrangements." Mira placed a hand on her chest and leaned forward, her expression purely sincere. "Please know, Miss Gawain, that I don't have a grudge against you, personally, though I do think you represent a severe lapse in judgment on my former betrothed's behalf, but I suppose there's no accounting for what will turn a man's head. In any event, I do hope you will understand that I simply cannot allow you to continue on here, for I will absolutely not be reduced to playing second to your fiddle. You see, in the upper classes of society, a woman's reputation is all she has."

"I suppose it would be naïve of me to think you might worry less about what people thought of you in favor of being a person you could be proud of."

"Such gammon," Mira said dismissively. "You wouldn't have the faintest idea of what I'll endure if Aidan Mullen takes you to wife on the heels of jilting me. You cannot possibly imagine how I'll be laughed at and whispered about. 'Tis impossible for you to know the embarrassment I'll feel. Where you come from, such things don't matter a whit, but in my life, 'twill become all-consuming. It won't matter what reason I give as to why the betrothal was dissolved; if he is with you, they will draw their own conclusions, and I will not suffer their disdain. Do you hear me? I will not."

As Olwyn listened to Mira, it struck her that Mira cared so much about the judgment of others that opinions had become her reality. It made Olwyn's experience in *Penarlâg* worth the pain, for it had forced Olwyn to define herself by her own standards, and to find her own worth in ways that had nothing to do with what she looked like or what she wore. How odd, she thought, that she would come to view being reviled as a blessing.

That realization sparked a tiny flare of pity for Mira, that her self-worth was tied up in the gossipy, and by the sounds of it, disapproving people in her acquaintance. It seemed the villagers of *Penarlâg* had something in common with the wealthy English aristocracy after all.

"I'm sorry," Olwyn said, meaning the words. "None of this was intended to cause you any upset."

"And so it won't." Mira took in a deep breath, and let it out slowly. She met Olwyn's gaze boldly, and squared her shoulders. "I'm unaccustomed to coercion, but like all challenges presented to me, I am prepared to do whatever it takes to get what I want. And with that said, let me lay out for you exactly why you will do as I say—I am in possession of journals written by my great-uncle Bret Kimball, the heir to our family's dukedom. He was engaged to be married to Camille Mullen, long ago. I will summarize the worst of it—Camille's father was a bastard, and whilst 'tis likely too late to prove that, 'twill most definitely cause a stir in the House of Lords. Add to that, Amelia Bradburn used to beat Camille with a strap. According to Bret's accounts, Camille's back is webbed with scars because she would not stop whoring herself to Patrick Mullen."

Olwyn gasped, appalled that Mira could speak of Camille being scarred with what sounded like glee, and that she would refer to such a gracious woman as a whore. "You have no right to speak of such things."

"Oh, it gets worse," Mira said with long, drawn out pleasure. "Camille was made pregnant by Patrick, before they were married, and suffered a miscarriage some months later. Bret indicates that he was *still* willing to wed her, and in fact gave her a Kimball family heirloom ring—that she never saw fit to return—and yet, not more than a few days later, Patrick Mullen was discovered in her sleeping chamber, and Camille was so very drunk, on spirits—which should elicit a bit of sympathy from you Miss Gawain—that Camille could not even walk! Camille, it seems, was not above taking a man's ring, accepting his offer of marriage, and still continuing to drunkenly whore herself to a common Irishman like some sort of fishmonger's daughter."

"You are a guest in their home," Olwyn said, truly

aghast. "How can you speak so disrespectfully of people who've been nothing but good to you?"

"I'll do more than speak of it, Miss Gawain. These journals are lewd, and full of details that would completely humiliate the Mullen family. I assure you, I have only given you a sampling of what's actually in them." Mira crossed her arms over her chest and lifted her chin, clearly smug in the role she'd chosen for herself. "If you do not do as I say and vacate these premises tonight, those journals, every last tawdry, implicating page of them, will be published by my father's newspaper in weekly columns that will be certain to keep the aristocracy riveted. There will not be a single person of the Mullens' acquaintance who will not know their family's most shameful, mortifying secrets, and the Mullen family will be the ones who are made the laughingstock. Not I."

"You are truly disgusting."

"Call me what you will. I care nothing for your opinion."

"Whatever happened to you, to render you so completely without compunction?"

"Your answer," Mira said with false patience. In truth, her eyes glittered with delight, and Olwyn couldn't help but wonder which Mira would prefer: Olwyn to leave England forever, or to have Bret Kimball's journals published. Both options seemed to delight Mira. "What say you, Miss Gawain? Will you force my hand and cause the Mullen family public ignominy? Or will you allow me to see to your passage to the Americas, and accept my offer of compensation for your absence?"

Olwyn fell silent, unable to totally comprehend what Mira had planned for the Mullen family if she did not comply. She imagined leaving and never seeing Aidan again, and pain stabbed her chest. And then she imagined

Camille's humiliation if Mira went through with her threats, and the pain grew.

"Haven't you caused this family enough trouble?" Mira asked. "That poor dog, and now the men are forced to find its killer. If one of those men are hurt or killed in the process of catching your insane father, 'twill be completely your fault, Miss Gawain. I hope you know that the Duchess will not be so kind to you if her beloved husband dies at your father's hand, nor will Camille think you are her darling project if her treasured son or grandsons are murdered because you lured your father here."

Olwyn's blood grew cold, sending chills down her spine. She couldn't help but picture Mira's words coming to fruition, and it made her feel sick to her stomach.

"If your silence indicates you're thinking about the outcome of the lurid journals being published, I hope you are also wise enough to consider that unless one of the Mullen men kills your father, your presence here will consistently bring danger to their doorstep. For that matter, if they do kill him, you will have forced a man to kill another, and he will have murder on his conscience. All for *you*." Mira tilted her head to the side and swept her gaze up and down Olwyn's form. "Are you worth all this trouble, Miss Gawain? Are you worth murder?"

Olwyn's mind answered the question for her. *No. She wasn't.* No matter what Aidan might say to the contrary, Olwyn knew in her heart that she wasn't worth the humiliation of an entire family. And to think of the murder, the blood of her father on someone else's hands . . . it made Olwyn's sick feeling turn to churning nausea.

"You really are quiet, aren't you? Not laughing any more, I see." Mira walked across the room and stood in front of Olwyn, close enough that she could smell her powdery rose perfume. "Where are the threats to cut out my heart now?"

"You don't have one."

"Oh, such melodrama. Of course I do, and I truly regret having to go to such extremes, but you can't honestly expect to come into this household and rob me of my future husband without a single consequence. If anything demonstrates your naiveté, 'twould be that. Really, Miss Gawain, 'tis quite childish for you to not expect retaliation of some sort, and after all, 'tis *me* you're dealing in this matter. I may be young, and am most certainly well-bred, but make no mistake, I am a force of nature."

Olwyn's mind spun and her heart thudded hard and fast. She felt as if she stood on a precipice, where jumping meant certain demise, but remaining assured the same.

She envisioned leaving, and knew that in time Aidan would find a new woman to love. It pained her to think of him with someone new, to imagine her curled against his strong body, her cheek on his chest. It became a physical pain as she could practically hear the new woman calling him Lóchrann, knowing that she would grow old with him and would be privy to the secrets of his heart.

But Olwyn had no right to cause more suffering. She'd done enough when she'd led her father to the Mullen home. To know that by remaining she would cause humiliation of the highest order to people who'd been nothing but kind to her was more than Olwyn could bear.

With all those thoughts came another, and as Olwyn considered just how deceitful Mira was capable of being, she said, "Let me see these journals."

"You doubt me," Mira said with a tinkling laugh. "How charming. Come with me, Miss Gawain, and I will happily show you."

Mira swept past Olwyn and led the way to the double doors. When she opened them, Olwyn saw that just outside stood two of her father's manservants, waiting in the corridor. Acknowledging their presence, she said to Olwyn over her shoulder, "You'll understand I don't trust you, either. If you want to see them, you'll have to leave your pistol and your dagger behind. No offense, Miss Gawain, but I cannot have your fiercer nature taking over. Mind you, both my men are armed. They will not allow you to assault me."

Olwyn reluctantly removed them, and followed Mira and her men out of the rooms. She couldn't make a decision without being certain the journals existed.

With the entire family downstairs dining, the house was silent but for their footfalls on the thick carpet. The halls were inviting, the walls covered in creamy peach silk and the dark hardwood floors cushioned with Persian runners. Art was in tasteful abundance, with paintings on the walls and sculptures set on elegant tables. Olwyn walked by it all without seeing.

Just as she'd feared, her dream had turned into a nightmare. There was no incense to burn to chase the bad dream away, no clever ploy to fix the problem.

If she stayed, she would cause more suffering.

Mira's rose perfume filled her chambers as they entered her sitting room. The servants rushed to light the lamps and candles as Mira swept across the room to a locked chest. Using a small key she'd taken from her reticule, she opened the trunk. Out wafted the smells of cedar and old leather. She lifted one of the books and carried it to the writing desk, set it down, opened to a random page, and began to read aloud.

> *25 May, 1741*
> *I shall consider today a success. I met her, the beautiful Camille. She is everything the duchess has promised, lovely beyond my imagining. Though she is not without flaw. It seems there is an Irish sea captain who has caught her fancy. The duchess tells me they were*

riding alone in the wood, and when they emerged,
Camille's hair was mussed and her eyes were bright.
Needless to say, this shocking behavior—

Mira glanced up to Olwyn and raised her brows. "You do realize she's ruined at this point? I don't know how it works in the Welsh mountains, but in London society this sort of thing is simply not done." She turned to the back of the book and leafed through the pages, found one that struck her fancy and continued reading.

> *13 January, 1742*
> *I visited with Camille this afternoon, and smelt the brandy on her yet again. I know she imbibes in an effort to forget the Irishman, but the unseemliness of the drink on her breath nearly overwhelms my desire for her. It seems enough that I should have to overlook her lack of virtue, but I am also forced to overcome the fact that she'd carried his child. The drink seems a final straw, as I envision her years on, a drunken beauty staggering as she flees my presence.*

"Shall I go on? I assure you, 'tis more shocking than anything I could fabricate. Trust me when I tell you, Lady Camille Bradburn Mullen would not enjoy seeing my uncle's words printed for all of England to read. And read it they would, I assure you, with the great delight of people titillated by the downfall of one who once had everything." Mira flipped through more pages and stopped at another. "Here's the part where Bret speaks of how Amelia had too much port one night and let it slip that her husband, Kenley Bradburn, was nothing more than a bastard, the get of an Irish horse trainer who'd charmed his way into the mistress's bed."

"Stop," Olwyn said harshly. It felt voyeuristic to be listening to details of Camille's private life, no matter how long ago the events took place. "You have no right to read such things, let alone publish them."

"I have every right. I *own* these journals, and will do as I see fit with them. They are part of Kimball history, and if I choose to make that history public, 'tis my affair." Mira spread her hand over the pages possessively, and added, "Of course, I'll edit out any of the passages where my uncle paints himself as less than innocent. There's no need to speak ill of the dead, is there?"

"There's no need to speak ill of anyone," Olwyn replied acerbically. Never when she'd been living with her father, alone and longing for love, had she imagined that it would come at such a price. The injustice of it made her angry, and her inability to stay with Aidan without causing further harm had her more frustrated than she'd ever been in her life. "All you'll get from this is my absence. I don't see how that seems worth such an extreme measure. Were you to follow through on your threat, an entire family and all of their friends would despise you."

"Such fire you have. Look at yourself, Miss Gawain. You're all in a lather, aren't you? And though you have no lack of passion on the matter, you seem to forget with whom you're dealing. Do you honestly think I'd care that the Mullen family would be angry with me?" Mira answered her own question with a flat declaration. "Hardly. As for the Mullen family and their feelings, why, I have my own hurts to nurse. Life is full of injuries, disappointments, embarrassments, and upsets, but 'tis the responsibility of the press to print the truth wherever they find it. Why should the Mullens be protected? For that matter, if Camille Mullen had spent half a second considering the consequences to her actions, she wouldn't have anything to hide. Therefore, I refuse any accountability anyone might wish to place upon me. I am merely making fact a matter of public record, and there is no crime in that."

Mira glanced at the timepiece on the mantel and let out a little sigh of impatience. "'Tis getting very late, Miss Gawain. You've had enough explanation, and I assume you're reasonably intelligent. By now you should have had enough information and proof to have made your decision. Tell me now, for my offer to help you leave England expires after I leave this room."

Mira set herself to the task of closing the journals, placing them back into the trunk, and turning the lock with an authoritative click. Keeping the key in her possession, she snapped her fingers and pointed to the leather-bound chest. "Harry, carry this out of here when we're finished, and I want it borne away from this manor to the place we discussed. You'll consider this as valuable as your position with my family."

"Yes, my lady," Harry said quickly.

The room fell quiet as Mira turned her complete attention to Olwyn. The smaller woman folded her hands together and held them just beneath her breastbone. She gazed upon Olwyn, her blue eyes assessing and watchful.

In Olwyn's heart she knew what she had to do. It galled her to capitulate, but stubbornness wasn't worth causing pain to people for whom she cared so very deeply.

"I'll go," she whispered.

Mira smiled brightly. "Excellent choice, Miss Gawain. Brilliant." She took another look at the time and her voice became efficiently businesslike. "Let's get started. We've plenty to do for the final preparations."

Chapter Twenty-Five

As Olwyn walked the corridors back to her rooms, she heard noise from the lower level, loud, deep male voices, the soft murmurs of females speaking, and the rushing footsteps of servants as they attended to their tasks. She heard the baying howls of hounds, and smelled melting beeswax and a freshly extinguished candle.

The men had finished their search for the night. That meant they'd either captured or killed Rhys Gawain, or would resume their search in the morning.

Olwyn didn't know which to hope for.

Turning around, she gave a final glance back to Mira, who stood at her open door. Mira held up her hand with three fingers raised, and a victorious smile curved her lips.

Olwyn quickly turned, and rushed away. Mira's gesture indicated three o'clock in the morning, the time Olwyn was to slip out the eastern door of the manse, through the servants' exit. There, Harry, Mira's manservant, would be waiting. Harry had volunteered to be part of the night watch that would patrol the manor. He would take Olwyn to a waiting carriage, and would escort her to the docks.

Olwyn wiped her damp palms on the skirt of her gown as she approached the top of the large curving staircase. Down below she caught sight of Aidan as he stood speaking with Padraig and Rogan. His hair shone darkly gold in comparison to the other two men, his posture relaxed, and his expression composed.

He didn't have the look of a man who'd just taken another's life, she thought with a sense of relief.

Aidan stopped talking and turned as if he could feel her gaze upon him. His sapphire eyes traveled up the stairs until he spied her. He grinned at her, and she felt it down to her toes and up to the tips of her ears.

No murder, his smile said. No worries.

Olwyn felt ill. Her leaving would hurt him, her staying would hurt him.

Aidan said a few more words to his father and brother before taking the steps two at a time, his cloak flaring out behind him, exposing his pistol belt and sword. He looked like a black-winged Adonis, his body armed for war, his face as handsome as an angel.

On the landing, he grabbed both her hands in his. His brow crinkled, and his eyes grew concerned. He brought her hands to his lips, held them palm up, and kissed them both, one at a time. "Cold and damp. Have you been afraid all day?"

"Aye," she whispered.

"All is well, my love." His deep voice was soft and reassuring, and full of such caring it broke her heart. "We had the hounds sniff the ground where Chase was to gain your father's scent, and we ran them all over the property. We went through all the fields, the entirety of the woods, and along the shore. If your father were still on the premises, the dogs would have scented him. So rest easy tonight, Olwyn love. You're safe here, and even though 'tis not likely Rhys is near, we'll secure the property and will have watchmen and the dogs on patrol."

Three a.m., her mind whispered.

"There wasn't a trail of his scent in the wood?" Olwyn asked.

"A bit. The dogs followed it out to the road that leads back to town for a while before they lost it."

Uneasiness settled in Olwyn's belly, cold and fluttering

with tetchy nerves. "How could he have disappeared so quickly, and on foot?"

"We think he isn't," Aidan replied simply.

"He has no money for a horse."

"He could have stolen one."

"I suppose."

He assessed her carefully. "Still afraid."

"Aye," she said shakily. Afraid of leaving, afraid of staying, afraid of never seeing his face again.

Those sapphire eyes didn't leave hers. A long moment passed and he said, "I'm sad for Chase, and I'll miss him forever, but what happened . . . Olwyn, I don't blame you in the slightest, and I don't want you to blame yourself. You suffered at your father's hands for far too long, and I don't want you to suffer another day, do you hear me? Not another day, my love. You suffered enough, aye? You've suffered enough."

"I can't bear it." Tears threatened to consume her. "I keep seeing him in my mind, again and again."

"I know," he said gently. "But I rode long and hard today, and I had plenty of time alone with my thoughts."

"What did you think of?"

"You. Me. My life here, my family. Chase. And then I thought of you some more," he said with a smile. "Chase was a good dog, and he died doing what he was born to do—guarding us all. He died in service like a soldier, in a war he didn't declare, and in a fight that wasn't fair. But he was out there in the woods because it was his duty, and while he was with me, I treated him well, I loved him, and that's all I could have done.

"At the core of myself, I'm just a man, Olwyn. A Mullen, aye, and possibly a duke someday, but all that doesn't matter in the end. I'll live my life as it is, and I'll do what I was born to do: be a good man, love my family, make a life, take a wife, and love her well. I'll do those things, and if I live my life that way, I'll die happy. With you at my side. All those things, with you at my side."

How much pain could a heart take and keep on beating? she wondered. He spoke of his future and the happiness she brought him, and pieces of her died, bit by bit, until she was certain she would disintegrate into a pile of dust.

"Aidan," she whispered. "Lóchrann." Knowing how he hated her silences, it was all she could say.

"Did you eat anything all day?" he asked with concern. She shook her head to the negative and he laughed softly. "'Tis no wonder you look beside yourself. Let me call up a tray for you."

"I'm not hungry."

"I'll feed you," he said, and he pulled her close to the shelter of his body. He felt warm and hard, and he smelled like spice and musk, horses and leather. "I'll sit you on my lap and give you tiny morsels."

"No, truly. I have no appetite." *Except for you,* she added silently. *For you I have insatiable hunger.*

"Olwyn," he said gently. One word. Her name. And he filled it with so much emotion that her knees grew weak.

She knew he wanted to take care of her, to ease her in any way he could, and she didn't have the strength to deny him anything. It would be their last night together, she realized with another sharp pang of pain. "All right, Lóchrann. Perhaps a bite or two would do me good."

He gave her hands a squeeze. "Good. Now let's get you settled."

As he led her toward the direction of his chambers, she resisted. "Your brother already thinks I'm . . ."

"The rest of the world be damned. This is my home, and I want you with me." Aidan sent her a sidelong glance and added, "We've both had a hell of a day."

That, Olwyn decided, was as true a statement as had ever been uttered.

She went willingly.

After all, she thought, the hour had scarcely passed ten. She had only five hours left with him. She wouldn't waste a second of them.

By the time Aidan finished building the fire, a knock at the door heralded a large tray brought up from the kitchens. Cheeses, breads, sweets, and sliced meats had been artfully arranged alongside dried fruit and seasoned oysters, the latter of which made Aidan laugh.

He pushed the oysters aside, and with a grin he said, "I don't think I'll ever eat these again."

"Did they make you ill?"

"Aye, very," he replied.

Aidan lit candles, poured them each a small glass of whiskey, and withdrew a blanket from his bed. Taking her hand, he led her over to the fire where he'd placed the tray on a low table. He took a seat in a comfortable armchair, took Olwyn onto his lap, and pulled the warm blanket over her.

He cradled her like a child, his strong arms around her, his hard thighs surprisingly comfortable. "No one has held me like this since I was a girl," Olwyn said shyly.

"Who held you? Your mother?"

"Aye. Just like this, by the fire, beneath a blanket. Me on one knee, my brother on the other, curled against her in the big rocker. She'd tell us stories." Olwyn leaned against his wide chest and lay her head in the hollow just below his collarbone. She fit against him as if his body had been made for hers.

"You've missed her deeply."

"I have. I do, still. When I'm ill or afraid, I miss her." Like now, Olwyn thought, when faced with a horrible decision and feeling completely alone. "I wasn't so bad a child, I don't think."

"Of course you weren't."

"But she left me behind, just the same. One evening she kissed me goodnight, and in the morning she was gone. Just like that."

"No note?"

"Nothing. But I remember that when she came to my bed to say goodnight, she'd looked sad and tired. She spent a lot of time sitting on the side of my bed, smoothing my hair, touching my face. 'Always know you're a special girl,' she'd said."

"I have to agree with her there." Choosing a small piece of cheese from the selection, he held it to her lips. "As promised."

Olwyn ate from his fingertips, a strange and wonderful sensation. The subtle flavor had heavy notes of cream and the essence of apricot and salt, and it made her realize that she was, in fact, quite hungry.

"You're beautiful," Aidan said, watching her. "I've never seen a woman who could make eating look like an art form. I could get addicted to feeding you."

"I'd grow fat."

He picked up a fig and fed it to her, and the flavor melted on her tongue, chewy, sticky, sweet.

"Fat with child, someday," he said softly. "Would you like that, Olwyn?"

"I don't know, actually. I've never held a baby, much less cared for one." She recalled the red-faced, squalling babies riding their mothers' hips in her village, eyes squeezed shut as they gave loud voice to their displeasure. "They cry a lot, no?"

"They do, a bit. But they laugh a lot, too. Have you heard a baby laugh, Olwyn?" She shook her head, no, and Aidan chuckled low and deep. "That alone is worth the trouble."

Aidan fed her more, bites of cheese and fruit, bread and morsels of meat. When she was finished he handed her the glass of whiskey he'd poured for her, and took up his own. They drank in companionable silence, wrapped in the blanket before the flickering fire, and Olwyn knew that for the rest of her life she would recall that particular moment as truly, completely perfect.

The whiskey was like Aidan himself, balanced, mellow, complex, and strong. The amber fluid slid down her throat and heated her body and her blood.

In a few hours she would leave this beautiful man behind, and would never see his face, hear his voice, or feel his warmth again. The injustice of having to give up Aidan so soon after finding him struck Olwyn as fundamentally unfair, for she'd had just enough of a taste of happiness to know she'd crave him for the rest of her life.

So she'd seize what little she had left of him.

"Lóchrann," she whispered. "I am ready to go to bed with you."

She heard his breathing stop, felt his muscles tense.

He'd told her before he would not take her unless they were wed, so she added, "Handfast with me. For a year and a day, in the ancient tradition."

She shifted in his lap so she could look up into his eyes. They reflected the firelight, the way they had when they'd been alone in the stone hut. Reaching up, she slid a finger along his jaw, feeling the bristle of his incipient beard. "You are now, and shall always be, the only man I will love. That is my vow, as sacred as any ever made, though it be unsanctified."

He regarded her with a strange expression, one she'd never seen before. He looked emotional, caught off guard, and yes, he looked hurt, and deeply. His words betrayed the latter. "A year and a day, Olwyn? Are you looking for something temporary?"

"It's the traditional vow," she said weakly, knowing that he could likely feel and hear the brewing tears in her voice. "I want you," she continued in a broken voice. She swallowed and added, "Tonight."

"Not forever?"

"I do want you forever," she said, and the truth of those words, combined with the dishonesty contained within them, made her heart break and her soul sick. But she didn't stop there. Hating herself for using his words against him, she said, "Did you not tell me that the only time we have is now. The past is gone. The future is unknowable. We have tonight, Lóchrann. It's the only time there is."

He studied her for a long while, his face inscrutable. Olwyn wondered what he thought of her bold proposal and her bawdy admissions, but she didn't dare ask. Instead, she held silent, mentally cursing Mira Kimball, her petty insecurities, and her cold, calculating heart that had brought Olwyn to this place.

"The very first day I woke and met you," Aidan began, "I thought I'd gone through time somehow, and I mistook you for an ancient Celt of some sort, one of the auld folk." He laughed a bit, a rueful, embarrassed sound. "And there you were, more unearthly beautiful than any woman I'd ever lain eyes upon. I wanted you then, wanted my imagining to be true. I wanted to disappear into that new life with you, handfast with you, and make you mine."

"Were you disappointed to find out who I really was?"

"No," he said with a mix of tenderness and exasperation. "Olwyn, you've been more real to me than anyone I've ever met. I had to die to become alive, to come fully awake and see my life for what it was. Most of all, to see myself for what I could be."

Her heart was full, and yet it was broken. This was the best part of his loving her, she thought, when he gave her pieces of himself he didn't show anyone else, little gifts more valuable than gold. "What could you be?"

"Happy," he whispered, and his arms grew tighter around her, like a wordless promise that he would keep her in his arms forever.

She cupped his cheeks in her palms, and spoke her truest feelings. "*Cariad, dw iń dy garu di,*" she told him softly. Darling, I love you. She knew he wouldn't understand the words, but needed her own tongue to give her heart its proper voice. "*Mi caraf chwi a`m boll galon.*" I love you with all my heart.

Aidan seemed to know what she meant, for he answered her in Gaelic. "*A chuisle, tá mé chomh mór sin I ngrá leat.*"

"Take me, Lóchrann. Take me to wife, and then take me to bed."

Aidan rose with her still in his arms, carrying her as if she were weightless. His easy strength never failed to amaze her, for it was not so long ago that his strong body succumbed to an illness so great it rendered him nearly lifeless.

He set her down near the fire's hearth, and bade her to wait. Crossing the room quickly, he opened his armoire and rummaged for a minute before returning to her side. In his hand he carried a small pouch, a gold chain, a silk cravat, and the cashmere tie from his robe.

"Give me your left hand," he said.

Olwyn lifted her trembling hand and put it in his wide palm. His skin was warm and calloused, and his hand enveloped hers.

He took the tie of the robe and began winding it around their clasped hands and wrists, binding them together. His eyes held hers as he said, "This is made of wool, so we will always be warm. 'Tis also elemental, of the earth and the land we live on. Let this be symbolic of our need for each other."

He did the same with the silk cravat. "Silk is soft but is quite strong, is difficult to tear but is easily cut. Let us always remember that as strong as our love is, we must be careful with it, and also with each other."

He finished with the chain, wrapping it around them in a shimmering bond of gold. "It is rare, this metal, like our love. 'Tis purified and worked and wrought through fire, made into a thing of beauty that is unique. Gold is valuable, but only to those who desire to own it, and the truest measure of its value is assigned by the people who have it, and the people who want it. Let's forever know that our love has only the value that we assign it, and let us always make certain we count it as the most precious thing between us, something that cannot be bought or traded or sold. Also, we'll let this gold that binds us symbolize the riches we bring each other, for wealth cannot protect us from loneliness, or bring us love. What we have between us makes us rich, Olwyn."

Olwyn studied their clasped, bound hands, and a scalding tear escaped her control, for in a few hours she would rip their vows apart.

"You look awfully sad for a happy bride."

"I love you, Lóchrann. Beyond my own life, I love you."

Something flickered in his eyes, like the flame of a lantern's wick being turned up. "I vow I will love you, Olwyn Gawain, cherish you, hold you, and keep you safe, until death parts us."

"A year and a day," Olwyn breathed. "The handfast vow is a year and a day."

If he did not promise forever, she thought, perhaps he would not hate her for the rest of his life.

"In the ancient custom, I take you as my wife for a year and a day," he conceded, but his expression changed.

Olwyn hurried to make her vow, grateful he couldn't see into her soul, and read her treachery. "I, too, take you, Aidan Mullen, my Lóchrann of the darkness, as my husband. I vow I will love you and hold you dear, forsaking all others, for a year and day." *Forever,* her heart screamed. *I will love you forever.*

"Now we kiss," he whispered.

Over their clasped, bound hands, Aidan leaned forward and took her lips beneath his. His skin smelled faintly of fresh sea air and fire smoke, and his mouth tasted of whiskey and passion. She leaned into him, and as he pulled her lower lip between his, her legs grew weak. He traced the outline of her mouth with the tip of his tongue, and her breath caught in her throat. And then he deepened the kiss until she became dizzy and hot, damp with desire, overwhelmed with love.

She clung to him as he pulled back, not wanting the kiss that sealed their vows to end.

When Olwyn had been alone and lonesome, she'd dreamed of a wedding day she'd been certain she would never have. Imagining the gown, the flowers, the harp music, and her prince had been a fanciful distraction, a fantasy that Olwyn had perfected over years of meticulous, fruitless planning.

And now, in the candlelit darkness with the fire warming them, their hands bound together with wool and silk and gold, she could not think of a single thing that would make the moment more perfect. She didn't want a fancy gown, or a castle, or a prince. What she wanted was precisely what she had—a man who loved her for the person of her heart. On this, their wedding night, the music they moved to was their pulse, and the flowers that bloomed were hidden, a fragrant, secret garden that lived in the darkness of their souls.

Aidan slowly unwound their binds and set them aside. "We're supposed to exchange gifts, aye?"

"I have nothing to give you."

He grinned and inclined his head toward the bed. "That's generally what a bride brings, and as gifts go, I'll admit 'tis my favorite."

"And along with that, brides bring a dowry," she pointed out.

"I've always thought dowries outmoded and a bit ridiculous, to be honest," Aidan said. "I don't need to be compensated for taking the woman I love to wife. I'm glad you come with nothing. It allows me to give you all I have."

"I don't want anything but you. All the riches of the world are right here, before me."

"That may be so, but would you humor me, Olwyn?" Aidan opened the little pouch he'd taken from his armoire and upended it into his palm. Out slid a ring that caught the light of the candles and turned to sparkling fire.

In his large, square-tipped fingers, he held the ring up for her inspection. It bore three diamonds in a row, each the size of a large pea. The setting itself was simple platinum with a touch of filigree.

Olwyn eyed the ring as if it were about to explode. "I don't have that much humor."

He laughed. "Aye, well, they're maybe a bit on the large side, the diamonds."

"If by 'large,' you mean the size of hailstones."

"Very well, think of them like that. Like bits of ice that won't melt."

Olwyn could scarcely breathe. "Lóchrann, I am a simple girl."

"Pardon me the observation, love, but there's not a simple thing about you." He held up the ring so it would catch more of the light, and it sparked in sharp flashes of blue and white.

"These diamonds belonged to my great-great-grandmother, Elizabeth. Tomorrow I'll take you to see her portrait; it hangs in the gallery. If you look, you'll see she is wearing a bracelet set with six of these stones. Years ago, my grandmother, Camille, had the bracelet taken apart and the stones put into two rings, one for my future wife, and one for Padraig's.

"The day Grandmum gave these to us, I remember she smiled as she touched the stones. She told us that Elizabeth had been a woman of many secrets, and had a great passion for life. She also told us that we were to find a woman whose secrets were like a vault that only required the proper key to open, and who could teach us a few things about how to live life with great passion and no regrets."

Aidan lifted Olwyn's hand, and as if he didn't notice that she trembled like a child, he slid the ring onto her finger and grinned when he saw it was a perfect fit. "I think Grandmum will agree that I've done as she instructed."

The gems blazed with fire on her finger, and Olwyn couldn't help but notice how beautiful her hand looked adorned with the jewels. It could have been the hand of a princess or a lady, and it boggled her mind that such a thing was happening to her at all.

The clock on the mantel chimed eleven, marking the passage of another hour.

Unable to keep her composure for another second, Olwyn threw her arms around Aidan's neck, and buried her face into the hollow where his chest met his shoulder. She breathed deeply his scent, wishing she could pull his essence inside her and keep a part of him forever.

Tears fell like rain, unbidden and unstoppable. Aidan smoothed her hair and shushed her in her ear, soft, meaningless sounds. When she continued to weep, he held her back a bit so he could see into her eyes.

"'Tis just a ring. You don't have to wear it if you don't want."

"Lóchrann . . ."

He cupped her face in his hands, making her feel so small and delicate against his larger size and greater strength. Kissing her cheeks, he stole her tears, one by one, until she had none left. "I'll drink your tears and take your pain. You make me happy, Olwyn. I want to do the same for you."

She reached up and took his cheeks in her hands and kissed him deeply, tasting her tears in his mouth, along with the traces of his whiskey.

He pulled her against him and deepened the kiss. She felt his body grow hotter, harder, and felt the urgent press of him against her. She strained into the shelter of him, wanting him on top of her, inside of her.

"Right here, Lóchrann, by the fire," Olwyn whispered against his mouth.

"The bed would be more comfortable for you. 'Tis sometimes painful for a woman, the first time."

Olwyn recalled the size of him, and knew it would probably hurt when he entered her. But her desire for him was burning and strong. "I don't care about pain. I want you inside me, and I want you by the fire, just the way we were in the hut those nights when you held me close. I want to see you like that, my Lóchrann of the darkness, bathed in light."

"Very well," he said softly. "But wait a moment and let me see to your comfort."

He went into his sleeping chambers for a bit and soon returned, his arms laden with pillows and thick fluffy quilts. He made a nest by the fire, poured them each a bit more whiskey, then returned to his rooms. When he came back, he wore a sheepish expression on his face as he held out his hand, palm up.

She saw the small black lump, and laughed. "Stealing from me?"

"I had Alice and Molly bring me a bit of your incense when they brought up your things from the cottage. But 'twas not *stealing,* exactly. I thought I'd keep it on hand in case you spent the night with me again."

"And here I am."

"Aye," he said with a slow grin. "I'll light it."

Olwyn sank down onto the cushioned floor and watched him. He moved with grace for such a large man, she thought as he found a small dish in which to set the incense. Using a thin piece of burning kindling, he lit the small fragrant lump until it burned. Aidan sat down before her, held up the tiny flame to her, and said, "Make a wish."

Olwyn smiled, closed her eyes, and wished fervently to never leave him. Opening her eyes, she blew on the incense softly, coaxing it to a red-tipped smolder. Thin, curling white smoke rose between them like a genie escaping from a bottle, and the room filled with the scents of amber and Tamil mint, sage and sandalwood, cardamom and ginger. It was the smell of shadows and surrender, of lust and Lóchrann.

His face was wreathed in smoke, his dark sapphire eyes lit with firelight and desire. He was, quite simply, the most beautiful thing she'd ever seen.

"Don't tell me what you wished for," he said, "or else it won't come true."

"I wouldn't risk it."

Aidan set the incense on the table and retrieved their whiskey. He held it up and made a toast. "To beautiful brides, handfasting, and wedding nights."

Olwyn held up her glass, clinked it to his, and made her own. "To princes who really do come for the girls who dare to dream."

They sipped until the last of it was gone, and dizzy from scotch and smoke, Olwyn leaned into him. "Now, Lóchrann. I don't want to wait another second."

He pulled her to him, his skin scented with incense and fire smoke, with whiskey on his tongue and passion in his embrace. The fire cast light and heat in equal measure, the flickering flames bathing them in a glow of gold. His kiss was demanding, his body hard and hot, and Olwyn surrendered completely to him, melting against him like fire-warmed honey.

Aidan's clever fingers worked open her lacings, and soon he was pulling the garment from her shoulders. He slid her gown from her, and she laughed as she shimmied from its confines. Displaying a fair amount of knowledge in female garments and underpinnings, he soon had her completely nude and stretched out before him. He made fast work of his own clothes before sinking down to her side.

His eyes swept over her, taking in her every detail, but she felt no shame. Instead it felt perfectly appropriate, intimate and elemental. She was woman and he was man, naked before the fire.

"You are art," he said reverently. "Were I an artist, I would paint you just so." He ran a hand over her body and shrugged in a way that did not convey indifference. "Alas, I am without a brush. I'll have to improvise."

He leaned over her feet, and starting at her toes, licked her skin lightly. She gasped and laughed a little, nervous laughter that was tight and charged with eroticism all at the same time.

"Flesh the color of the inside of a seashell, pearly, creamy white, tinted with a kiss of pink," he said. "Were I an artist, I would gratefully spend hours getting the shade of your skin just right."

His tongue slid up to her ankle, then her calf, and up to her knee, just in the crook.

Olwyn's breath went shallow, and there was no more laughing, for he licked up higher, mid-thigh, and she well recalled the feel of his tongue between her legs, like liquid flames that burned her to ashes.

"Were I an artist," he whispered, his breath hot on her skin, "I would spend an eternity trying for the shade of sable between your legs, the silky black softness of it, the pink of you there. I would spend a lifetime, and not a second would be wasted."

His tongue passed over her center, as he'd done before, and she cried out as her blood turned to fire and lightning filled her vision. He moved higher, to her navel, and then further up, stroking her ribcage, and then her breasts. He licked the tips of her nipples, and beyond her control her body arched into him.

"Pink the color of strawberries submerged in champagne," he murmured. "Were I able to capture such beauty, I would be immortalized as one of the masters. But I am just a regular man, and despite the beauty of my muse, I have no talent with brushes and oils."

His tongue moved to her neck, and he kissed the soft nape behind her hair until her toes curled and her body grew limp. Kissing his way back down the length of her, he stopped at the apex of her thighs. He glanced up to her, grinned in a way that was wicked and darkly male, and said, "I suppose I'll just have to work with what I have."

"To hell with brushes," Olwyn said softly. Her blood was on fire for his touch and her fingers itched for the feel of his body beneath her hands. She returned his grin with a raise of her brow. "But beware, Lóchrann, for I'm also possessed of artistic mediocrity. I, too, shall have to make due."

"That's a promise," he said, before dipping his head lower.

That magical tongue moved over her once more, and with her head full of incense and her body strung like a musical instrument, he made her as weightless as smoke, and her cries were his melody.

Just before she burst into flame, he lowered himself over her. His blunt flesh probed her, and she opened to him, welcoming him into her body. He felt so heavy and strong, and she clung to him as he slid inside her, fitting deeper and tighter and fuller than she could have ever imagined.

"You're inside me," she breathed.

"A bit." His breathing had gone shallow and she felt the tension in his muscles as if he held himself back at great cost.

"There's more?"

"Aye." Aidan chuckled a little, a deep, breathy sound. "Am I hurting you?"

Olwyn held him tighter. "I want all of you."

Aidan made a throttled noise, and he pushed inside her until she cried out.

He froze.

"Is there more?"

"Sorry, love."

She laughed, out of pain and pure happiness combined. "Just finish it."

With another thrust he was buried inside her, and Olwyn squeezed her eyes shut against the pain. She'd wanted it to be a beautiful memory she could take with her, but instead it felt as if he were ripping her in half.

With a muscular flex of his body, he withdrew himself and reached down between her legs, his finger once again finding the spot that felt like fire and lightning. And when she was once again squirming for something she couldn't name, he moved between her legs again.

She tensed.

"This time it'll be better," he promised, and he kissed

her lips and eyelids and nose and chin as he slid back inside.

It hurt less than before, and he found a rhythm that made strange licks of heat curl in her body, making her think of incense smoke rising. He moved slowly at first, and soon she began to feel the build of something deeper in her body. Once again it was quickening, a burgeoning and blossoming.

She cried out again, but not in pain. She moved, not knowing what to do but trying to match his pace. He groaned, and female power surged in her veins. Growing braver, she slid her hands down his back and cupped his round bottom, feeling the flex and strain of him as he rode her.

And she was like Salome, risen from the smoke to gyrate and entice a man with her hips. Olwyn moved and he groaned again, even as pleasure, deep and visceral, speared her. She clenched her hands, gripping him, and he made another sound of pleasure.

It was magic, this giving and taking of pleasure while being joined with the man she loved.

"You feel like heaven must," he murmured. "So good, love. So, so good."

Pressure and pleasure built inside her until she felt as if she would laugh and cry all at once. It became a driving force, swirling like an eddy in which she felt she might drown. "Lóchrann?"

"Aye, love. Aye."

And he moved again, a hard thrust that sent her into the darkness where there was no light or air or sound that was anything more coherent than a cry of complete abandon.

She felt his muscles bunch, and he groaned and gave way to his own release with a few heavy pulses deep within her.

He leaned his forehead on hers, filmed with sweat, and his breathing was heavy and harsh. It slowly returned to normal, and with him still inside her, he pressed soft kisses on her face.

Aidan cuddled her close, put his mouth to her ear, and whispered, "And so for the beautiful, witchy Druid and her Lóchrann of the darkness, love had finally triumphed."

Chapter Twenty-Six

The clock on the mantel chimed, signaling the time—half-past two. Reddish light spilled from the glowing cinders on the hearth, all that remained of the blazing fire.

And as Olwyn looked to Aidan beside her, she knew the time had come to say good-bye.

She curled close to his body, let his heat seep into her one last time. He slept, his breath rising and falling, deep and even. Studying his features, she memorized them as they were, a mental picture she would carry for the rest of her life. Lóchrann of the darkness, the strong bones in his face, his square jaw, and the way his eyelashes lay on his cheek, boyishly long, lighter at the root and darkly fringed at the tips.

She slid like a wraith from the nest he'd made, pulled her shift over her head, and gathered the rest of her garments in a bundle. Stopping at the table, she reluctantly removed the ring he'd given her. It had been a pleasure to wear it, even temporarily, and for a few hours be marked as Aidan's wife. Olwyn pressed a kiss to the diamonds, and laid the ring down beside the empty whiskey glasses.

Aidan's door opened without a sound, and as she closed it, she listened for one final moment to his breathing. Tears burned at her eyes, but she did not indulge them.

She hurried through the dark corridors, her bare feet noiselessly skimming along the thick runners. When she reached her rooms, she was breathless. A glance at her timepiece—a quarter 'til three. Rushing, she pulled on her old garments, the long woolen gown with the belled sleeves, topped with a sleeveless outer mantle of smoky plum. She buckled her belt, slid in her dagger and her pistol, and braided her hair so it would keep from her face.

Olwyn stuffed her meager belongings into a duffel bag, and left the garments Camille had purchased for her. Like the diamond ring, they were not hers.

She caught a glimpse of herself in the looking glass as she left, the silvery moonlight illuminating her in shades of gray, and saw herself as she used to be—a poor girl in a handsewn gown, moving through the shadows.

The hour chimed three as she left the rooms behind, and once more she was soundlessly moving through the corridors, this time in the direction of the servants' stairs. And when she emerged from the manse into the darkness, Harry was there. He took her arm and her satchel without a word, and rushed her away from the safety of the house.

Olwyn had never in her life felt more afraid or more exposed. Somewhere out there, her father lay in wait, and despite Aidan's hounds losing the scent, Olwyn didn't doubt for a moment that Rhys was nearby. Her intuition prickled like sensitive skin rubbed with the grittiest sand, and as she hurried across the property her heart pounded a wild tattoo.

Her heart. It had been ripped apart, and now was ragged and tattered. She wondered if Rhys cracked opened the cavity of her chest, would the pumping organ look different? Would it be battered and bruised, as it felt, or thickly engorged with shame and sorrow?

Olwyn heard the whinny of a horse, the answering stamp of another, and soon the carriage came into view. Its black veneer shone in the moonlight, and when the driver opened the door, she saw it was lit within by a hanging lantern. Olwyn climbed inside as Harry stowed her bag.

He ducked in his head, and spoke with the hurriedness of a man who knew a killer could be near. "There's a lap robe if you need it, and the warming pan should be stocked with coals. If you require anything further, rap smartly on the roof."

Before Olwyn could reply, he was gone. He closed the door, and the carriage dipped and bounced as the men took their positions. Olwyn grabbed hold of the armrest as the conveyance lurched into motion.

But she pushed down her feelings, as no good could come of wishing for things to be different.

The carriage jounced along at a teeth-rattling pace. She heard the driver spurring on the horses with sharp calls. The wheels squeaked and the floorboards groaned as they rolled on, faster and faster.

Fear built in Olwyn, real terror that was an internal scream. She rapped on the roof as Harry had said to do, but the sound was lost in the noise.

"Stop," she cried out.

She heard the driver yell 'yah!' and the rattling grew louder still as they hurtled through the night. Olwyn fastened her hands on the bench seat, gripping the velvet as she tried to hold herself somewhat steady. The lantern swung wildly on its hook, the oil sloshing over the base until it suffocated the flame, and the interior went dark.

And then she heard a thud, and a man's scream.

The carriage careened wildly, rocking side to side. Olwyn imagined the crash that would soon come, and wondered what would kill her—the impact, a shard of glass from the window, or perhaps a jagged-tipped spear of wood torn from the wreckage.

A high-pitched whistle pierced the air, and the horses slowed their pace. Olwyn leaned back into the cushion as the carriage slowed. She pulled her dagger and waited, and when the conveyance came to a stop, she crept to the door.

She turned the handle and pushed the narrow door open. Silence greeted her as she emerged; the night air was a chilly slap on her face. Olwyn coughed and gagged, all at once beset by the overwhelming stench of excrement.

Turning, she screamed. There on top of the carriage was her father. Rhys had a slim rope wrapped around his wrists and hands, and he quickly garroted Harry before letting him drop lifeless to the ground.

The other driver's body was slumped to the side, and in the moonlight Olwyn could see his head was missing.

She gasped and began to sway on her feet, feeling as if she were trapped in a nightmare.

"I stretched a few lines across the road, from tree to tree," Rhys said gruffly, seeing his daughter's line of vision. "Took off this one's head, but only sliced the other through the chest. Too tall for my trap. Had to finish him, else he would have just bled for hours."

"Murderer," she managed to choke out.

"Bah! I meant for the lines to knock them off horseback or carriage seat, only so I could take them hostage and ransom them for you, girl. The crazy bastards were going so fast is why this happened. Not my fault."

Rhys pushed the headless body over the other side, and when the dead man hit the ground, the sound distinctly like a sack of potatoes being dropped, Olwyn bent at the waist and vomited.

"Gone soft, I see," Rhys said with derision.

Olwyn spat the final, bitter dregs of her sickness onto the ground, and began to slowly back away.

"Get back here, girl. Get back inside the carriage. We're going home, you and I. We've some matters to discuss."

She didn't respond, but kept moving back, one step at a time. Her every footfall was an effort, as if she waded through thick sand. *Nightmare,* her mind whispered.

Rhys hopped down from the bench atop the carriage and began advancing on her. "You know what you are? You're a treacherous traitor to your own blood, and that makes you not worth a sheep's fart, if you ask me."

He drew closer and she saw he was coated in dark smears of what reeked like horse dung. The blood on his hands was black in the moonlight, and a manic smile twisted his face. "Oh, Olwyn, my girl, you should have seen your man looking for me today. They ran all around, their dogs barking and their horses blowing hard." Rhys laughed and ran a filthy, bloody hand through his wild hair. "A little horse shit was all it took to keep them off my scent."

The night spread out around Olwyn, dark pockets of moonless shadows that were just out of reach. She couldn't run to them, for her legs were gravid and thick with fear, rooting her so that just moving became an enormous effort.

"So like your mother. Piebald and strange, ready to run off the first chance you get. Well, didn't I always tell you that you are a Gawain? Your mother didn't share my blood, girl, but you do, and you can't run from who you are."

Run.

And in that moment she moved like the wind, set free of her nightmarish tether, spurred on by pure fear.

Olwyn ran as fast as she could, legs pumping, heart racing. Each breath became a searing heat in her lungs, and she heard the ragged sound of it in her ears.

Rhys was on her tail. He wasn't as young or strong, but he was propelled by insanity. He yelled out, "Don't run into my lines, Olwyn. You'll only get hurt."

She kept going, desperate to get out of her father's reach. She ran and ran. Rhys called out, his voice faltering and broken; she couldn't hear what he'd said. The gap between them widened, and she was too young and strong to be caught by him.

Olwyn hit something hard and warm, and felt arms go around her. She screamed again, and was once more overtaken by the stench of horse manure.

Drystan laughed. "I've wanted you like this for years," he said. "Hot and breathless and in my arms."

Olwyn still had her dagger in her hand, but he held her around her upper arms. She slashed at him and managed to slice his thigh. He yipped in pain and she snarled, "Back off."

She could smell Drystan's blood mingling with the excrement, and the stench of his sweat beneath both. She gagged as they struggled, and he gripped her harder, trying to subdue her and prevent her from nicking him again with her blade.

Rhys came upon them, his breath like great dragon bursts. "Turn her," he commanded, and Drystan, like an obedient minion, spun Olwyn around.

Rhys limped along, and when he drew close enough to where Olwyn struggled with Drystan, he pulled his hand back and slapped her across the face.

Pain exploded behind her eyes in blinding starbursts. She cried out and squeezed her eyes shut. She didn't see the next hit coming, but felt it blast through her cranium. Blood filled her mouth and when he hit her again, it sprayed onto the ground as her head fell to her chest.

He rained blows on her arms and shoulders and belly, screaming all the while, venting his rage, repeating the same four words again and again, "Traitorous whore, mutinous cunt."

And then he stopped, and went completely still and silent. Cocking his head to the side, he whispered, "Do you hear?"

Her body and head throbbed with pain, and Olwyn raised her face to his. Well aware of how real the voices were to Rhys, she'd learned the long and hard way not to try to convince him that they spoke for him alone.

"Aye, I do," Olwyn said softly. "I hear them."

In the moonlight, his obsidian eyes glittered. And then he sighed, as if he were suddenly sad and broken. His shoulders sagged. "I don't want to hurt you, Olwyn. You're my girl."

She knew what to say when this version of Rhys manifested itself. "Pappy," she murmured in a small voice, using the sobriquet she'd given him when she'd been a tiny girl. "I'm sorry you had to hit me."

"I never liked disciplining you."

"It's not your fault. You just want me to be a good daughter, loyal and true."

"Aye," Rhys said, but there was a subtle shift in his demeanor that sent a warning through Olwyn's battered body.

Her mouth was full of blood and bile, but she managed to say, "I'll be much better now that you've taught me this lesson."

Drystan had her by the upper arms and held her, facing her father. Olwyn tightened her hand on her dagger's hilt. If Rhys had a weapon, she hadn't seen evidence of it, unless he still had his length of rope. She shivered inside, imagining the garrote snapping her neck.

Olwyn held the dagger's point down, hoping that Rhys wouldn't be coherent enough to realize she had her knife. He might succeed in killing her, she thought, but it would not go easy for him. And at the very least, if he managed to take her back to Wales with him, she wouldn't have to worry that Rhys would do any more harm to the Mullen family.

"You held a pistol in my face," Rhys growled as his mood shifted once more to rage. "You locked me in a cell."

He hit her again, square across the face, this time with a closed fist. The intensity of the blow forced Olwyn's head back into Drystan's and the back of her skull crashed into his nose.

Drystan cried out and let go of Olwyn's arms, cupping his nose to stem the bleeding.

And she was free.

Olwyn took off, racing across the dark, barren fields in the direction of the manor house. She tripped over a log, righted herself, and kept going, ignoring the blood that filled her mouth and the pain throbbing behind her eyes. The cold air tore her throat and burned her lungs. A shout came from behind her but she didn't dare look back. Her heartbeat became thunder in her ears.

Her foot caught in a trip line, another trap set by her father. She went flying through the darkness and when she hit the ground hard, her breath left her in a whoosh. Shaking off the stun of the impact, Olwyn tried to stem her heavy breathing long enough to listen for footsteps. They were coming, her father and Drystan, grunting as they slowly made their way to her, two older men out of shape and aware that traps lined the grounds.

Scrambling to regain her feet, she gasped. "My dagger," she whispered. She'd lost her grip on the hilt when she'd fallen.

Feeling around on the frigid ground, she crawled on hands and knees, her fingers brushing desperately over the dormant grass.

Rhys and Drystan grew closer.

Fear stabbed icy spears into her bowels. Visions of

Chase passed through her mind, and she pulled her pistol from her belt, where she'd jammed it at the small of her back. One shot. Two men. And murder forever on her conscience.

So be it.

Off to Olwyn's left she saw a cluster of bushes and trees that led toward the untamed woods, dark clumps of blackness in the moonlight. She swiftly began to crawl toward them, keeping her belly low on the ground. As she moved she heard the distant rumble of horses, felt the vibration in the earth beneath her chest.

Aidan.

She envisioned the decapitated driver who'd had the misfortune of moving swiftly beneath one of her father's lines, and she couldn't help but see Aidan murdered in the same way. Her blood, cold with fear, began to heat with anger that her father could be so cruelly calculating, so heartlessly heinous. The fury fueled her, and so she fed it until it became rage.

And then she saw the distant glitter of her knife's blade, winking coolly silver as it caught a shaft of moonlight. Olwyn scrambled across the ground like a scuttling crab, her breath coming in short bursts as blood leaked from her mouth and nose.

The hoofbeats grew closer, and Olwyn reached her dagger with relief, grabbing the familiar hilt into her fist before crawling further into the shadows. Crouching, she wiped her face with her sleeve and waited, watching.

Three men on horseback rode into Olwyn's view, and though they were garbed in black and cloaked in night, she knew Aidan was one of them. They moved with caution, their heads down and close to their horse's neck, keeping to the wide-open spaces where the traps were not so easily set. Olwyn felt a tiny bit of relief when she saw their posture. They must have seen her father's traps and were taking heed.

Olwyn's eyes, well accustomed to the darkness, saw the shape of rifle's muzzles protruding forward, and she knew they'd come prepared for violence.

A shot rang out, and Olwyn strained to hear something, anything. Another rifle barked, and the reek of cordite reached her, a hot, angry scent that hung in the air.

The men on horseback drew closer, close enough that Olwyn could have called out, but she held silent, knowing that distractions could kill.

And then she saw him come from behind the mounted men. Rhys emerged from a shadow with two pistols in his hands. He paused and took aim, and Olwyn reacted.

She stood, and cried out, "No!" Her dagger left her hand, turning over and over again in a winking arc. Rhys turned at the sound of her voice, and the knife missed its aimed target, his chest, and instead took Rhys in his left arm, high and near the shoulder.

He screamed out an obscenity, dropped one of his pistols, and tried to pull out the knife.

The riders wheeled their horses around, and one broke free and came thundering toward her. Olwyn waited, and when Aidan drew near, she didn't need to look into his face to see his anger.

She took his proffered hand and let him swing her up into his lap, his hard, hot body like an unwelcoming wall that she slammed against as she settled into the saddle.

"So much for your vows," Aidan snarled. "You didn't last the night."

"You don't understand."

"Aye. I don't, and I never will."

Rhys had given up trying to pull the dagger out as the riders approached him. He took off at a run, heading toward the woods, clutching his wounded arm to his side. Olwyn glanced all around, searching for Drystan but not seeing him. Coward, she named him, fleeing the moment he was outnumbered.

Momentarily sheltered in a tangle of trees and bushes, Rhys turned and raised his pistol. Olwyn could see that his hand shook, and knew he was badly injured. Not a moment's pity moved her.

"It's me you want," Olwyn cried out, and she raised her own pistol and took aim. "You've killed enough innocents."

She heard Rhys's growl, coming deep and low and in their native tongue, "*Cer I grafu.*" Go to hell.

Olwyn answered him likewise in Cymraeg, their language that the English called Welsh. "Aye," Olwyn said. "In due time, you and I both."

Aidan spurred the horse on beneath them, faster, taking her away from her father. Olwyn swatted at his hands as they held the reins. "Slow down. I cannot aim."

"Get back here, Olwyn!" Rhys screamed out.

"I must be the one who does it," Olwyn told Aidan, her voice breaking with emotion she could no longer control. "He is my problem. I won't have anyone else bear the burden."

"Quiet," Aidan commanded her. And his voice was different, cold, harsh, and humming with fury.

"Take me back." Olwyn swung around, holding her pistol up in a hand that quaked as she tried once again to take aim at her father. The tremble became a wobbling shake that she couldn't steady. "It must be me who does it."

A bark of a rifle became her answer, and Olwyn watched as Rhys crumpled to the ground. Aidan spurred his stallion on toward the manor.

"I brought ten men with me in total," Aidan said, his voice still hard and remote. "You'll never know which one took his life, and that's as it should be."

Another shot rang out in the night.

A sob welled up from within her chest, a great, heaving cry of anguish.

Aidan's arm tightened around her waist. "I'm sorry, Olwyn."

Between sobs she managed to say, "It had to happen this way. He was mad. Completely mad."

"Aye, but no daughter should have to see such a thing."

"He was once a good man. I remember."

"Hold those memories and let them see you through." Aidan's tone didn't change, and it hurt her heart to hear him speak to her in that horrible voice, impersonal, polite, saying all the right things but without the warmth she'd come to know.

Aidan continued, "We'll have a memorial for him if it'll please you."

"No," Olwyn whispered. She'd be gone by the time dawn lit the sky. No matter that the threat of her father no longer existed for the Mullen family, there was still the matter of Bret Kimball's journals.

Sobs wracked her chest, pulled from a place she could not name and by a tide she could not stem. She was the last of the Gawains—her mother long gone, her brother dead of disease, and now her father, murdered for his madness. She put her hands over her face, wanting to weep bitter, useless tears, but they would not come.

They approached the manse. In the rear of the house, guards were assembled on the terrace. Golden light from lanterns lit the area in a yellow halo, and men's deep voices filled the air. Olwyn tried to compose herself, gulping in air in big, trembling breaths. The night and its trials were not over. She needed to find strength from somewhere to do as she must.

The stallion beneath them slowed in response to Aidan's strong hands tugging on the reins. He helped her to dismount, and as the light touched her skin, she heard his breath intake sharply. His voice came low and deep and full of dismay, "Oh, Olwyn."

Aidan cupped her chin and gently raised it up, his eyes traveling over her every detail. Once again, Olwyn could only wonder what he saw when he looked at her. Had she been deformed? she wondered. The ugly girl revealed to be beautiful after all, only to have her newfound beauty stripped away?

"That," he said softly, "is going to hurt precisely like hell in the morning."

He folded her into his embrace. Olwyn melted against him, her arms sliding around his narrow waist. She held him close, so close that his breath became her breath, and the rising of his chest against her cheek became her only world.

And just as quickly, Aidan let her go.

He looked down on her, his face etched in light and shadow. She thought she saw sadness in his expression, and worse, disappointment.

"I'm sorry," she said.

"Sorry for what? For running away? For putting yourself in danger? For not telling me what you'd had planned?" His voice became hard and cold once more. "Or is it because you lied to me and took vows of marriage that you had no intention to honor?"

"For everything."

His lips flattened. She could feel the emotion pumping from him, words he didn't say, anger he wouldn't express.

"Aye, well," Aidan said finally. "Everything's maybe a bit more than one word can smooth out."

He looked down on her, his hand tight around her arm as if he knew she only planned to run again. The silence that fell between them became unaccountably complex, fraught with things they didn't speak of, and knotted with problems not easily solved.

Olwyn could only speak the truth, as plain and simple as it was. "I never wanted to hurt you," she whispered. "Never."

"You had your reasons, I assume."

"I did."

"And will you tell me?"

She hesitated, and then spoke the truth again. "No."

"Well, then. You can save your apologies. I'll have all of you, Olwyn, or none at all." Aidan's lips tightened as if he held back his thoughts at great cost. "Let's get you indoors," he said at last, steering her toward the door. "And into a bath, aye? Olwyn, pardon me for saying so, but you stink."

Aidan took Olwyn to the suite of rooms where he'd once locked her away. In short order he had the servants filling the bath, lighting the candles, and laying a fire.

Olwyn stood in the center of the room, waiting. When the preparations were made, Aidan turned to her.

"I'm sorry about your father."

Sadness filled her chest and throat again. She nodded her acceptance, unable to speak.

Aidan opened the armoire and riffled through the garments that Camille had purchased for Olwyn. "When you leave again, make sure you take the cloak and the gowns. They were a gift, and they belong to you," he said, pulling them out and laying them over a chair. "The maids will help you dress after your bath."

Olwyn said nothing again, unwilling to lie and too afraid to tell the truth.

Aidan reached up to the top shelf and pulled down a thick, tapestry traveling bag. "You can keep this, as well, and I'll have someone come and drop off a pouch of money. And you'll take it, aye? No wife of mine will go traveling without a cent to her name."

Her heart was breaking. "You're letting me go?" she managed to choke out.

"Aye," Aidan answered curtly. "Stay or go, 'tis up to you. I'm through with proving you can trust me, and I'm tired of trying to convince you to make a life with me."

He turned and went to the door, opened it, and looked back on her for a long moment. The dark gold slash of his brows were drawn in a frown, and his full lips were flat. A muscle in his lean cheek flexed again and again. "I'll send word to the stable hands. A carriage will be brought around to take you wherever you want to go. You won't need go into hiding or throw me off the trail, so you can go on ahead and have them take you to where you're really going. I won't come for you."

A soft sob escaped her throat, but she didn't otherwise make a sound.

It seemed to reach his heart, for his expression softened somewhat. "Why don't you spend a few nights in an inn before you make any decisions. You could likely use the rest, and also the time to heal and mourn. You have plenty of time to decide what to do with yourself once you're gone from here. No one's chasing you any more. Not even me."

Chapter Twenty-Seven

There would be no sleep for Aidan. Prowling through the corridors of his home, he wanted nothing more than to hit someone, and to have them hit him back. Something to cause pain and to receive it, as well.

In the absence of someone to fight, he went to the parlor in search of his whiskey.

The candles were lit, a fire burned, and Padraig was in front of the fireplace, his long legs stretched out before him. He had a glass of scotch in his hand, and the cloak he'd worn when he'd ridden out with Aidan was tossed over a chair.

"Is it taken care of, then?" Aidan asked as he entered.

"Aye. They're seeing to the bodies, and I've got a few men busy searching out the traps he'd laid. When dawn comes, I'm sure we'll find them all."

"Good."

"And the witch?"

"Taking a bath before bed. Or maybe she's leaving. I don't know what she'll do, and I'm through trying to figure it out."

"Are you past your infatuation with her, then?"

Aidan shot Padraig a hard look. It wasn't so much what Padraig said, as the tone he used when he spoke of Olwyn. "What's your problem with Miss Gawain?"

Padraig didn't hesitate in his answer. "I don't like the way you are when she's around."

"How so?"

Padraig didn't answer, but knocked back the last of his whiskey and stared into the fire for a bit.

Though the greedy flames burned bright and fast, it had only been recently lit and the room still held the chill of nighttime. Aidan sought out a glass, poured a healthy draught of his whiskey, and took the chair opposite his brother. He drank deeply. The amber fluid burned in his belly and warmed him.

Olwyn would leave, Aidan knew. As much as that hurt him, he'd let her. He'd meant what he'd said. He was finished with trying to convince her of the life they could make together. If she didn't want him, or didn't think herself worthy of the things he could offer her, there was nothing more he could do.

Aidan hoped she found happiness elsewhere. He loved her enough to want the very best for her, always. Even if he weren't the man to give it to her.

A burning started behind his eyes and spread to his chest.

Yes, Aidan admitted to himself, he wanted to weep. But because his brother sat across from him, he held the emotion at bay.

"She takes you from me," Padraig said quietly, his green eyes still on the flames.

Aidan glanced sharply to his brother. Rarely did Padraig say anything about the connection they felt for one another. It was an unspoken thing that existed between them, silent, continuous, and unbreakable. And more often than not, unmentioned.

"No other woman's ever done that," Padraig continued, his words carefully spoken as if he'd given them great thought but was reluctant to reveal his truest feelings. "When she's about, I don't *feel* you. 'Tis like you're just a brother, or maybe a friend, and nothing more." Padraig turned his gaze toward Aidan and met his eyes. "I suppose that means you're in love with her, aye?"

"Aye," Aidan answered slowly. "I am."

"But you say you'll let her go?"

"Aye." The word came out as flat and hard as an anvil's surface.

Padraig's eyes gleamed green and bright in the firelight, eyes just like Rogan's and Camille's. Bradburn eyes. They'd turned mocking in a way that suggested their moment of honesty had passed. That's brilliant."

Aidan shrugged with an indifference he didn't feel and knocked back a searing swallow of whiskey. "'Tis complicated."

"It seems simple as hell to me." Padraig got up and crossed the room to pour himself another splash. "But what would I know? I've never been in love."

"You were," Aidan contradicted softly. "You forget who you speak to, brother. I remember her."

Padraig didn't argue; they both knew of whom he spoke.

Before Aidan could say anything further on the subject, Rogan and Emeline entered the parlor, wearing their bedclothes and wrappers.

"Your mother couldn't go back to sleep until she was certain you were both sound and well," Rogan said.

"We are." Aidan went to his mother and embraced her. "Go back to bed, Mum," he said gently. He glanced at the mantel clock and saw it was the earliest hour of morning. "'Tis a horrid hour in which to greet the day."

"I might as well stay up," Emeline said with a sigh. She laid her hand on Aidan's cheek, a gentle touch that belied her toughness. "There's something we were going to speak with you about, anyway. 'Tis best you're both here."

Emeline took a seat on the sofa, and Rogan dropped down beside her. He ran a hand through his black hair and regarded his wife with a gimlet eye. "'Tis early enough for this sort of talk, *anamchara*."

"I think 'tis long overdue, actually." Emeline faced her two sons and folded her hands in her lap. "The day you were born, I turned to your father and told him that I wanted you raised with fairness and equality. I couldn't bear the thought of one of you being touted as the heir, while the other was considered lesser, for you are both equally precious to us. Your father's solution was plain enough—we kept it secret between the two of us who was the firstborn."

A servant, obviously aware that much of the household had risen, brought in a tray bearing tea service. She set it down without a rattle, and Rogan thanked her and instructed her to close the doors on the way out.

"To be honest, I'm glad we did as such," Rogan said easily after the doors were firmly closed and the family had their privacy. "But I agree with your mum. The time for secrets is long past, and we've been remiss in keeping the truth from you both."

Aidan had had enough. He stood abruptly. "I don't want to know."

Emeline's surprise shone plainly on her face. "Oh? You've been the one most annoyed with us for not telling you."

"Not any more," he said bluntly. He cast a glance to Padraig, who seemed indifferent to the knowledge now, as he always had been. "Do you care to hear this, brother?"

"Not really," Padraig answered. "I don't care about titles and inheritances. If it comes to pass that I need to follow in Da's footsteps, I will, and with pride. But I don't need it for my happiness. I never did, and if the knowing will change my life now, I'd rather live without it."

Aidan felt a strong wave of love and admiration for his brother, who'd always understood that basic truth. It had taken Aidan years to figure it out, and without Olwyn, he doubted he ever would have learned what Padraig had already known.

"Mum and Da," Aidan began, aware he needed to explain his reasons when he'd pressed so hard for answers over the years. "I needed to make peace with who I was, and it took me a long while to figure out that the peace I was looking for wasn't going to be found. I'd had to earn it, you see."

"And did you, son?" Rogan asked.

"Aye. I'm not a man to be measured by my titles, I know that now. I'm not a twin to be compared to his brother, either. I'm just myself, Aidan Mullen, and for what it's worth or what that means to anyone else, it's enough for me."

Aidan's gaze met his mother's, and he saw in her sapphire eyes, so like his own, pride and love that ran deeper than the sea. "I'm sorry, Mum," he told her softly, "for every last bit of trouble I've given you about this subject. You had the right of it all along."

Dawn was lighting the sky, casting pale pinkish shadows through the open drapes. Aidan saw that the morning sky was clear and bright, and he had a sudden need to see to a task that was long overdue.

He strode across the room, kissed his mother on the cheek, and grabbed Padraig's cloak. His brother regarded him curiously, and Aidan grinned at him and said, "*A dearthair, a leathchúpla, a anam.*" My brother, my twin, my soul. He clapped down a hand on his shoulder, and gripped him hard. "Never anything less, brother."

Padraig stood, hugged him, and slapped him on the back soundly before letting go. Aidan went to the door, opened it, and turned back to look at his family. They were his heart and soul, the people of his blood. His beautiful mother, with her compassionate nature and gentle wisdom; his darkly handsome father, who was the strongest man he'd ever known; and his brother, his childhood friend, his biggest rival, his most trusted confidant.

"See you at dinner," Aidan said simply. And it felt good to know they'd be there, even if Olwyn was not.

He left the manse and jogged lightly to the stables, his breath a frosty cloud in the morning light. After ordering his favored stallion to be saddled, Aidan leaned against the doorpost and looked out over the rolling hills of Beauport. The air smelled strongly of the sea, the salty tang luring him to the ocean's edge. The mansion stood high and proud in the distance, the early rays of sunlight glinting on the many windowpanes. He saw the beauty of the land, the majesty of the manor home.

It would forever feel empty without Olwyn.

He'd need to change rooms, for he'd see her before the fire, would feel her in his bed. He wouldn't be able to spend time in the cottage, as she would haunt the very air there. The beach, the distillery, the mews, and the very woods themselves. She had turned them all into something different, made them more meaningful with her presence.

Olwyn had also summarily rejected everything Aidan had ever offered her. He would need to remember that when the pain overwhelmed his heart.

Aidan turned back to the stable hand as his horse was led to him. He took the reins and said, "Tell my manservant to pack my belongings. I'll be moving to the London home for a bit."

He swung up into the saddle and urged the stallion out into the morning. The air was crisp and clear and fresh. It gave no hint that the night before had been one of hand-fasting rituals and lovemaking, rejection, violence, and murder.

It was a new day.

He would not beg the woman he loved to stay. If she wanted her freedom, he wouldn't stand in her way of pursuing the life she truly desired. Too many people stagnated in their lives, going through motions meant to make others happy. Aidan knew, for he had once been one of them. He wouldn't dream of asking someone else to sacrifice their happiness for his. If Olwyn wanted to go, Aidan loved her enough to step aside.

He looked up to the sky where thin white clouds blew in from the sea. It was indeed a new day, he thought. A day of life, each one a gift not to be squandered. He'd died and been reborn. No more of his days would be wasted.

Aidan rode to the mews.

When he arrived, he dismissed the falconer and entered the low building. The birds swayed on their perches, setting their jesses to jingling as they moved from talon to talon, each hoping to be flown into the wide open sky. Their hooded heads turned and cocked, the great birds listening with the fierceness of blindfolded captives.

Aidan went to Shaughraun, his favorite of all the raptors. He stroked him over his brown and white striped body, his finger trailing along his white belly and lower, over his thick legs ruffled with creamy feathers. He blew gently across the hawk's hooded face and trilled a few familiar notes.

Shaughraun trembled with urgency. The bird opened his beak and screamed, a wild, primitive sound that cried for freedom.

Aidan slipped on his thick leather glove and nudged the bird onto his wrist. Shaughraun's talons clamped down, biting into the thick scarred glove, and Aidan carried him outside.

The fresh air filled Shaughraun with wanting, and he beat his wings and strained at the leash Aidan held so tightly. With deft motions, Aidan removed the bird's jesses and hood and dropped them to the ground. Shaughraun's sharp eyes took in the surroundings, and his head cocked upward to the sky.

"Aye, Shaughraun," Aidan whispered. "Today is your

day, and your future now belongs to you. Go, fly, and be free."

With a quick motion, he removed the leash and tossed the bird into the air. Shaughraun opened his wings and took to the wind, spiraling upward and flying high until Aidan could no longer see him. A wild scream sounded in the distance, and Aidan grinned.

"Farewell," he said as he looked upward. He bent and picked up Shaughraun's jesses, slipped them into his pocket, and then wiped his hand over his face. The tear that fell was bittersweet.

As Aidan prepared to mount his stallion, he heard the crunching of footsteps coming from the path that ran from the distillery to the mews. Thinking it the falconer, Aidan called out, "No needs to bring back Shaughraun, Clive. I've set him free."

"It's you I'm here for," came a rough deep voice from around the corner.

His accent was Welsh.

Aidan pulled his pistol and moved to the safety of the mews. The man that came into view wore tattered clothes in desperate need of washing, smeared as they were with thick, brown streaks of horse dung. His long, lank hair hung in greasy waves, and his thick nose and watery eyes told the tale of a penchant for drunkenness.

He had no weapon in his hands, and Aidan highly doubted he would have any skill at marksmanship in any event, given how the man's hands trembled for want of the drink.

The man reeked so badly that Aidan's throat smarted.

"Who are you?" Aidan demanded as he lowered his pistol.

"Drystan," he replied, as if it were an explanation. He glanced back to the distillery. "You're a blender?"

"Would you fancy a nip?"

Drystan licked his lips. "Aye, if you're pouring."

Aidan went to the door of the distillery, unlocked it, and entered after biding Drystan to wait outdoors, not wanting his stench to foul the brew. He found an opened bottle and poured a generous draught into a glass. Returning outside, he held it out of the odorous man's reach, and said, "First, you'll tell me a bit more of who you are, and what you want."

Drystan's mouth was salivating such that he swallowed heavily a few times before he could speak. "I worked for Rhys Gawain, up until the wee hours of this morning."

Aidan grew tense, wondering if this man posed a threat to Olwyn. "With your trespassing here, I hope you realize you're risking the same fate as your employer."

"I mean no harm," Drystan said, his eyes on the drink. "I'm coming to you now to make you an offer, is all."

"An offer."

"Right." Drystan reached into his grubby coat jacket and withdrew a ratty paper that was faded and browned with age, and was crisp and blackened on the edges as if it had been burned. Drystan swallowed heavily again, his gaze following the sloshing of the whiskey as Aidan held it. "Thought you might be interested in buying a bit of information about the girl. I'll sell it to you, if you'll help me get back home. And if you throw in a few bottles of that whiskey, I'll tell you about the truth of what went on in that keep."

Olwyn woke slowly, reluctant to leave the dream that had wrapped around her as warm and safe as a blanket. In her dream her mother had been telling her their story, and Olwyn could hear Talfryn's voice clearly, a sound she'd longed for since the day her mother left.

A soft sobbing sigh came from her throat as reality

crashed into her dreamscape. She rolled to her side, her beaten body achy and sore despite the salts the servants had added to her bathwater, her face tender in spite of the cool compresses they'd pressed to her bruises. But none of that compared to the hurting in her heart.

She'd lain on the bed after her bath and wept, too heart-sick and beaten to do anything else. Sleep must have come to her, for as she looked at the clock she saw morning had arrived.

Olwyn forced herself to her feet and caught a glimpse of herself in the cheval mirror. Her cheeks were bruised, her lips split and swollen. Aidan had been correct—she did feel precisely like hell.

She wondered briefly if Rhys had been buried, and then dismissed that thought from her mind. There would be no further mourning for him. The father she remembered had died years ago, and the man who'd taken his place had been a murderer and a madman.

Olwyn hefted her bag and tossed her cloak over her arm. No one would stop her from leaving, and so she had no need to sneak away.

Aidan had given her freedom to make decisions. She hoped she had chosen wisely.

Olwyn left the room and walked through the corridor. Though she noticed the opulence of the manse, it no longer made her feel completely uncomfortable.

She heard Emeline's voice in her memory—*Do you believe in fairy tales, Miss Gawain?*

Olwyn mentally answered the question: she didn't believe in magic, but she did think there was a certain enchanting charm in choosing to imbue happenings with as much meaning as one might desire.

As for fairy tales, Olwyn believed in them as much as she did the dark, evil goblins that crawled from the shadows of a gibbous moon to steal away what little magic one allowed for themselves.

She heard Emeline's words again—*I don't think it so terrible, to want to find splendor amongst the shadows.*

Could there be splendor there, hidden in the darkness where Olwyn had only known dragons and goblins to reside? If Olwyn opened the doors wide and exposed everything to the light, would the evil shrivel, die, and blow away like dust caught in a cool, pleasant breeze?

Olwyn found herself standing outside Camille's door.

There was, she decided, only one way to find out.

Olwyn knew what leaving would mean for her. She knew she'd never see Aidan again, never hold him close and be joined with him, never again know the bliss of lying with him in the darkness where she alone was privy to his truest self.

But what of staying?

Mira and her bloody journals, she sneered inwardly. Mira and her selfishness.

Olwyn could only wonder what Camille would think of Mira's threats. She'd sensed in Camille great strength, determination, and wisdom.

Believe in the fairy tales that make you happy, Miss Gawain, and then dare to dream and dare to love. Most of all, dare to believe that the very best things are not only possible, but that you are worthy of them. If you can manage all three, magic happens. Trust me. I know.

Olwyn suspected that the Duchess of Eton knew far more about the power of dreams than most people.

Raising her hand, she knocked sharply on Camille's door.

And Olwyn Gawain let her dreams, her trust, and her belief have their way with her until they became stronger than her fears.

Camille's voice came from behind the door. "Who calls?"

"Olwyn Gawain, my lady. Might I have a brief word with you?"

"Of course. Give me a moment."

The time she stood in the corridor spanned an eternity. Her heart became a thunder in chest and her hands shook and grew damp. She wiped them on her skirts and patted her hair, wishing she'd taken more time with her appearance.

Trust, she told herself. Believe.

She didn't need to tell herself to love. She did that already, completely and with such passion that it forced her to surrender to the power of hope.

Camille opened the door. Her lovely face betrayed her curiosity, and though she wore her bedclothes, her hair was immaculately brushed and pinned. Camille's vivid green eyes assessed her from her head to her heels, taking in the bruises, no doubt, and the cloak and traveling bag as well. She stood back and beckoned Olwyn with a graceful wave of her hand. "Come in, Miss Gawain. You've the look of a woman with much to say."

Olwyn stepped into the luxurious suite, entering the sitting room where a fire burned merrily and the drapes were wide open to the morning light. The room smelled of lavender and lemon oil, and the plump chairs by the fire looked inviting as they were, draped with warm lap robes, the table between them laden with books of poetry.

Camille gestured to the closed doors that led further into the suite. "My husband is still abed," she said in a quiet voice. "But he sleeps soundly. We won't disturb him if we chat by the fire. Take a seat, please."

Olwyn obediently sat. Camille came around and took her own chair, pulled a throw over her lap, and tilted her head to the side as she settled into the cushions, one arm trailing casually over the back of the chair.

Olwyn didn't know quite where to begin.

"My lady, I want you to know that I hold you in the very highest esteem."

Camille raised a brow as if amused. "Thank you, though if you want the truth, I'd rather hear about what happened to your beautiful face."

"Well . . ." Olwyn hesitated. The truth, ugly and shameful, had tied her tongue.

"Did I ever mention to you that my back is striped with scars? My mother did not believe in sparing the rod, lest she spoil the child." Camille leaned forward, and took Olwyn's hand and lightly squeezed. "I promise you I'll understand."

Trust. Believe. Above all, love.

Olwyn began with Mira and the journals, of Mira's plans to humiliate Camille and expose her father as a bastard. Olwyn told Camille of her love for Aidan, and their private handfast. She admitted her selfishness, in that she'd taken Aidan's vows and given her own, knowing she'd leave. And then she recounted the rest, telling the truth as it was, plain, raw, and without even the thinnest veneer of civility.

Olwyn's fingers drifted upward to her cheek, pressed lightly against the soreness there. "My father is dead, my lady. And I am at a loss as to what I should do. I love your grandson more than I love my own life. And I hope you don't mind my saying so, but I've grown to love you, too. I cannot bear knowing that my staying here with Aidan would cause such harm to you and your family, and yet, I cannot bear to leave him."

"Full circle, indeed," Camille murmured.

"My lady?"

Camille sighed and smiled gently. "That girl had the

look of Bret Kimball, and I could only hope that she didn't also inherit her great-uncle's selfish, narcissistic heart."

"So it's true?"

"Every word," Camille said simply and without shame. "I was a headstrong girl, and though my mother's methods were harsh, she rarely beat me without provocation. All the things I did in my youth were in the pursuit of freedom and happiness. I loved a man who was completely unsuitable for me, and I would have crawled on my belly through a desert to be with him. For him, I would have done anything."

Camille smiled at Olwyn with all the secrets and mystery of a woman's heart. "We handfasted in private, before God and under the light of the moon, a secret love and a marriage that was not only unsanctified, but was also dangerous and forbidden. And as a result, my heart is free and happy, and my true love lies in my bed even until this very day, and so I consider the scars on my back to be battle scars from a war well worth fighting."

Camille rose from her chair, her strength a palpable thing. "Come, Miss Gawain," she said to Olwyn. "There are people in this world who can't abide seeing other's happiness. They cannot be permitted to win the wars they wage."

"But my lady, if she has the journals printed, your entire family, and you most of all, will be shamed."

Camille laughed, a melodic, free, easy sound, like water rippling over a rocky stream. "For the man I loved, I defied my family and the entire English aristocracy. Do you truly think I care a whit what they might say about me now?"

Crossing the room, Camille pulled on the silken rope that hung beside her door to call for her maid. She then returned to Olwyn, and took both her hands. "I'm glad you came to me, and that you, too, found a love worth fighting for."

Camille's smile widened, and her green eyes shone brighter and more beautiful than emeralds. "I admit to a bit of bias, but I do believe my grandson's rather worthy of the battle."

"He is, my lady," Olwyn said, her voice choked with emotion. "Quite."

In the face of Camille's certainty and bravery, Olwyn felt her spirits rise. Before her was a woman of indomitable strength and courage, and it inspired Olwyn and touched her deeply.

Olwyn squared her shoulders and raised her head high, ready for war.

Chapter Twenty-Eight

Camille saw to her toilette with the serenity of a woman unconcerned by trivial matters. She emerged from her dressing room perfectly gowned in a fashionable shade of pale green, her hair smooth and immaculately coiffed. She offered an assessing glance at Olwyn. "Much better."

Camille's maids had assisted Olwyn with changing into one of the finer gowns Camille had purchased for her. The pearly pink fabric clung to her breasts and then fell in a long column to the floor, the bodice trimmed in black grosgrain. They'd fixed her hair, arranging it in a high sweep off her face, with trailing curls cascading down her back, the black of her hair striking against the pink gown. Her face, bruised as it was, benefitted from a touch of powder, and her lips were glossed with a soothing balm.

Holding up one finger, Camille bade Olwyn to wait. She fetched a necklace of black jet and fiery iridescent opals. "This will look perfect."

Olwyn allowed Camille to fasten the piece of jewelry around her slim neck, and then turned to face herself in the mirror. The girl that looked back at her from the silvery looking glass was slim and lovely despite being battered. Her eyes had a wary, cautious expression, as they always did when she approached her own reflection.

Olwyn suspected it would take her years to get accustomed to seeing beauty in the mirror.

Her hand involuntarily went to her waist. No belt cinched her middle, and her dagger had been lost in the battle with her father. She felt naked without it, a girl without defenses.

"There are better ways," Camille said.

Olwyn turned to face her, and saw that Camille had gone to the tall armoire that sat opposite the fireplace, opened it, and was rummaging in a deep drawer. She returned with a large velvet pouch, and handed it to Olwyn with a strange smile.

Before Olwyn could open it, Patrick emerged from their sleeping chamber. He was fully dressed, still handsome for his age, and as he bent to kiss his wife, Olwyn felt a sharp pang of longing. Someday, she hoped, Aidan would be Patrick's age, and he would greet her in the morning with a kiss and a softly spoken word.

Camille said a few words to Patrick, asking for his assistance in preparation for the battle to come, and when Patrick left to do her bidding, she turned back to Olwyn. "Go on. Open it."

Plucking open the ribbons, Olwyn reached inside and withdrew a dagger sheathed in black leather. Its pommel was plain and sat within an odd metal catch, and buckled straps hung from the sheath. It appeared to be old, but was also well-maintained, the leather scarred and split in places, but still supple and smooth.

"'Tis meant to be worn beneath your skirts," Camille said, and a fond look came over her countenance as she saw Olwyn with the dagger. "I think I mentioned to you that once upon a time, I felt the need to arm myself with a dagger as well. And I'll have you know, that weapon has served to comfort a few other women in our family. 'Tis fitting, I think, that Aidan's wife should wear it.

"Put it on, Miss Gawain, if it makes you feel better prepared to deal with life's unexpected contingencies. And should the time come that you're ready to set it aside, keep it in mind for another woman who might be in need of a bit of extra confidence. After all, we do let our men look after us, but there often comes a time when we need to see to ourselves."

Olwyn pressed the catch open and slid the knife from the sheath. It was balanced and feather-light in her hand. She smiled with delight, and instantly longed to practice throwing it as she had her old dagger, again and again into a hay bale until she could hit with absolute precision. It felt wrong to take more, and yet the power of the weapon inflamed her, and she didn't want to refuse it, either. "You're certain, my lady?"

"Quite," Camille answered definitively. She laughed again, girlish, easy music. "And see? No need to ruin the line of your gown."

And she couldn't resist any longer. Olwyn latched the dagger securely within the sheath, raised her skirts, and strapped it to her upper thigh, high above her garter. It shone like black death against her white skin before she dropped her skirts back down to the floor.

Camille raised her brow and smiled knowingly. "Do you mind the feel of it?"

"On the contrary. I rather fancy having a secret weapon, rather than wearing one in my belt for all to see."

And she did. The leather sheath warmed against her skin, molded to her thigh in a way that was purely scandalous for how it made Olwyn feel. A woman shouldn't become aroused by wearing a weapon, Olwyn chastised herself.

"Yes," Camille said softly. She lifted another packet, tucked it under her arm, and said, "I've a secret weapon of my own, my dear. Let's go launch it, shall we?"

Mira woke late, and lay in the warm soft comfort of her bed for a time, enjoying the morning. The fire was out, and so she snuggled in the thick blankets until the urge to urinate forced her from the bed.

Once on the hard, cold floor, Mira did a little jig of

happiness, for by now Olwyn Gawain would be aboard a ship, bound for the Americas.

She called for her maid, who was sleeping in the small alcove off her bed chamber, and began to dress to greet the day. She took special care with her appearance, for she'd noticed Padraig's attentions had been rather pleasant toward her. The scamp, Roman de Gama, had shown her interest as well, but no matter how devilishly handsome he might be, Mira did not forget that he was common. Roman was fun to toy with, but Padraig Mullen still provided the best option for her next suitor.

While her maid coiffed her hair into a charming array of ringlets, Mira daydreamed about her wedding to Padraig. He'd be tall and dark and dangerously handsome in an expertly cut jacket and breeches. She would be as beautiful as any bride has ever been, and her gown would spark envy in every woman's breast. Most definitely, Mira thought with delicious vindictiveness, those unmarried tarts, Portia and Sophia de Gama, whose beauty annoyed Mira to no end. Portia and Sophia might be incredibly beautiful, Mira consoled herself, but they would never be well-bred, and Mira was both.

She pressed her rose water behind her ears and along her inner wrist, as a lady does, and when her maid wasn't looking, she trailed some between her breasts, as she'd heard the scandalous woman did. That Padraig Mullen was a roguish male animal, and would have to be baited with a sensual hook.

Delighting herself, Mira imagined the surprised and envious faces of the other girls at court when they heard that Mira had called off her engagement to Aidan, and had instead decided to marry Padraig.

After all, Aidan had assured Mira that he would not contradict her story of why they ended their betrothal. And when the announcement would be made that Mira had chosen Padraig, she was certain to make them all positively green.

Mira Kimball, after all, was the only woman desirable enough and of such impeccable heritage, that both men would vie for her hand.

Not just brothers, but twins! She laughed with delight at the thought. And not just twins, but the most eligible and handsome of all the men in England.

A smug smile curved her lips, for all would know that Mira had had her choice of both of them.

She eyed herself critically in the mirror and found herself without flaw. Her cheeks glowed with health, and her hair was the perfect combination of girlish bounce and womanly sophistication. The gown she'd chosen for her celebratory day of Olwyn's passage to America was an elegant creation of buttery yellow silk and white lace. Mira noted that her eyes had never looked so blue, her face so pretty, and her smile so radiant.

Mira Kimball left her room and descended the stairs to take her breakfast. As she passed through the corridors, she noticed a few young serving girls with their heads together, gossiping furiously.

"Back to work," she shooed them, and they scattered with satisfying swiftness. When Mira was mistress of her own household, she would not tolerate such indolence, but even as a guest in someone's home, she felt it her duty to intervene.

Sweeping into the dining room, she saw her father was already there, dapper in his riding clothes and taking his tea, toast, and eggs as he did each and every morning. Mira smiled at him, and went to peck him on his cheek with great affection. "Papa, you should eat some fruit," she scolded lightly.

"Fie on that. I'll eat what I like." Andrew dabbed at the

corners of his mouth as his gaze traveled over Mira. "You are ravishing, my pet. Simply stunning."

"You do go on." Mira took her seat across from her father and eyed him with all the love and devotion in her heart. There was no other man who could ever compare to the perfection of Andrew Kimball in Mira's heart.

The dining room smelled divine, and though Mira thought the table and chairs quite nice, she would, were it her home, do something about the silk moiré on the walls. Its subtlety lacked substance, in her opinion. She mentally redecorated the room in toile, what with all things French being the rage.

"Good morning," Camille said as she entered the dining room.

Mira spared the older woman only a passing glance. Hussy, she mentally named her. Tramp. Whore to a commoner. "Good day, my lady. Have you taken note of the weather? I think I smell spring in the air."

"Yes. 'Tis a beautiful morning. Magnificent."

Mira nearly swallowed her tongue, for entering the dining room behind Camille was Olwyn Gawain.

That striped hag had the audacity to look directly into her eyes and smile. Mira's surprise quickly turned to indignation and fury. Olwyn had pointedly ignored her directive! And her face, though powdered, was definitely bruised.

"I thought you'd spoken of traveling, Miss Gawain," Mira said sweetly, and she congratulated herself on her calm demeanor. Surely no one could guess that inside she was positively murderous.

She could nearly hear the gossiping cackles of the other girls who would know that Aidan had jilted Mira for that strange and disturbing woman.

"I had a change of plan," Olwyn replied, and she took a seat at the table beside Camille.

Perfect, Mira thought. Two trollops who lacked any respectability, side-by-side and as chummy as childhood friends. Just perfect.

And then it dawned on Mira that Olwyn might have revealed the existence of the journals and Mira's threat to make them public.

The whore. She wouldn't dare. But Mira's belly began to flip over, again and again.

"I'd love to hear about your new plans for adventure," Mira said. "Why don't you come with me to the parlor, and you can tell me all about it?"

"Actually, I'm quite hungry." Olwyn sat back as a servant set a steaming plate of porridge, eggs, and fruit on the table. She smoothed her napkin across her lap, lifted her fork, and began to eat as if she hadn't a care in the world.

Camille did the same, sipping her tea and chatting with Olwyn about the horses and her hopes for certain foals that would most certainly become beauties. Patrick Mullen had come into the room as well, and he joined them in their conversation and the breakfast, as if they had no more concerns other than the weather.

Mira looked across the table to her father, who ate without concern. She wished the table were not so wide so she could kick him to alertness.

And then Patrick, Camille, and Olwyn stopped talking and the silence in the room became deafening. It expanded, hummed, and became a living thing that began to smother Mira until she could take it no longer. She quickly stood and splayed her hands on the tabletop. "Miss Gawain, we really must speak at length."

"I suppose we should," Olwyn replied coolly. She fixed her predatory, animalistic gaze on Mira and raised a brow until it formed a tiny peak. "Your man, Harry, is dead, as is your driver. Your efforts to rid yourself of my presence landed them in my father's trap. I am very sorry for their loss, and for the sadness it will surely cause their families."

Mira held her hand to her throat and gasped.

"Harry?" Andrew said, clearly confused as to whether or not Olwyn was speaking of his manservant.

"As for me," Olwyn continued, "I shall be staying on here, at Lady Mullen's invitation."

Mira narrowed her eyes. "I don't think that's a viable plan, Miss Gawain. There are those who will have an opinion of your staying on here as a guest without any chaperone."

"I don't give a rat's arse to what anyone thinks," Olwyn said.

Olwyn's crudity shouldn't have surprised Mira, given the source and her vulgar commonality. But a blush burned Mira's cheeks. "I hardly think that appropriate talk for the breakfast table."

"Yes, you're correct. Perhaps we should, instead, speak about the journals you've threatened to publish."

The flipping nerves in Mira's belly became full on churning.

"Yes, let's," Camille agreed happily. She gave her attention to Andrew Kimball, who now listened with rapt attention. "The journals Miss Gawain refers to were the work of your uncle, Bret Kimball. In them, he documents various happenings from our shared past, in which he has chronicled his betrothal to me, my travails with my mother, Amelia, and most of all, of my love affair with the man who is now my husband, and the pregnancy that resulted." Camille cast a hard look to Mira, a shimmer in her verdant eyes that suggested she wasn't the least bit pleased. "Did I cover all the basics, dear?"

"Yes," Mira said faintly, her mind spinning.

Never had she thought Olwyn would go to Camille. And when Mira dared to glance at her father, she saw that he, too, was surprised and dismayed. Whatever happened, he must not think her less than perfect, Mira thought suddenly. Her father's opinion of her superseded anyone else's.

She rushed to speak, desperately trying to take control of the situation. "As you know, Papa, I'm the keeper of our family's history. I may have mentioned the content of the journals to Miss Gawain, which as I reflect on it now, was rather indiscreet of me."

"You're straying from the point," Camille said pleasantly. "You told Miss Gawain that she was to leave England, or you would publish the journals, page by page, in your father's newspaper."

Andrew's face grew dark. "Mira?"

Not my pet, or darling, or even my child. Mira clutched the tabletop to keep her balance.

And then, to make matters worse, Aidan strode into the room. He was wind-tousled and handsome, roguishly dressed all in black. Mira's heart pounded a little harder, and for an instant she could recall the precise feel of his hands on her body, and his tongue on her neck.

Aidan stopped when he saw Olwyn, and Mira watched them appraise one another. Olwyn's expression softened, became nakedly intimate, and Aidan's eyes did not move from hers. The look of him was such that Mira's heart became a bitter ache in her chest. No one, and most especially not Aidan Mullen, *her former betrothed,* had ever looked at her that way. Yet there he stood, staring at that awful Welsh peasant with love burning in his eyes.

"Mira," Andrew's voice snapped her back to attention. "What's this about printing private family journals in my newspaper?"

Mira's bluffing had backfired in the worst way, and she had no idea how to bring it all around and get her own way. She could just see all the girls laughing behind her back, and could virtually hear their sharp jabs pointed at Mira's inability to keep Aidan Mullen's attention.

Why couldn't Olwyn just have gotten on the ship? she mentally whined.

Camille interjected, "Before we go further, my lord, indulge me a moment."

Reaching into a pouch, Camille withdrew folded letters and laid them on the table. Facing Mira, she said, "These are letters written from your great-uncle Bret to my mother. Herein, he speaks rather openly about many things, including having committed murder to escape paying a gambling debt." Camille's voice grew quiet and very serious. "He also speaks of raping me."

Mira gasped, certain she hadn't heard Camille correctly.

"He raped me," Camille said softly. "As a result, the child inside me died. Your uncle was not a good man, Mira. He was my mother's pawn in a game he never had a chance of winning."

Bret Kimball, a murderer and a rapist? Mira shuddered to think that someone of her ancestry could be so repugnant. Surely the letters were forged.

"Why did you never tell me, Grandmum?" Aidan asked gently. "It must have stirred old feelings to have me betrothed to a Kimball. A word from you, and I would have called it off that instant."

Mira had never wanted to hurt someone physically in her entire life as she did in that moment. How dare Aidan Mullen speak so casually of tossing her aside?

"I didn't think it appropriate that Mira should bear Bret's stigma," Camille said. She looked pointedly at Mira. "People's truest colors always show themselves eventually." Camille pushed the papers in Mira's direction. "Go on ahead, and publish Bret's journals. You can publish these side by side, for all I care. I am no more afraid of the truth now than I was when I was a young woman. I made my choices, some good, some bad, and I lived with all the consequences. But I never forgot that my greatest sin in other's eyes was loving the man who they deemed wrong for me." Camille reached to her side and covered Patrick's hand with her own, adding, "When in fact, he was more the right man than anyone else ever could have dreamed."

With all eyes on her, Mira had never felt so small nor so angry. How dare Olwyn go to Camille, and how dare Camille draft fake letters in an effort to sully her uncle's name?

"He gave you a ring, a Kimball family heirloom, and you had no right to keep it!" she blurted, unable to keep silent any longer. "You stole it! Nine generations passed that ring along, and it ended with you, a Bradburn who married a commoner. What did you do with it? Did you sell it to finance your common husband's shipping business? Or did you toss it in a drawer to be kept as some sort of memento?"

Camille laughed at her accusations. "Hardly. I sent it back to your grandfather. According to your family's tradition, your father should have been given that ring for his wife, and it should have then passed to you, when you became betrothed." Camille turned to Andrew, who'd grown redder still. "My lord? Do you recall the ring?"

Andrew stammered something, cleared his throat, and then shrugged as he met Mira's eyes. "I lost it in a card game, shortly after your mother died," he confessed lamely.

"*What?!*" Mira shrieked. "You gambled away a piece of our history? That was *my* ring! Intended for *me,* and then my sons! How dare you lose it as if it meant nothing?!"

"'Twas a piece a jewelry. A bauble. If you're that upset about it, I'll have another made for you just like it."

"*You cannot replace such a thing,*" Mira gritted out distinctly. "'Tis an heirloom."

"Then I'll see if I can buy it back for you," Andrew said, obviously growing annoyed.

"Is that what you were looking for when you were snooping in my grandmother's rooms?" Aidan asked.

Mira felt her face, already red and hot, reach scalding proportions. "I'm certain I don't know what you're talking about."

She stared at Aidan across the room. He raised a brow and her belly churned even as her heart ached. She didn't know what she was more upset about—his rejection, or the possibility that he would reveal her secret about the Spanish fly.

To her relief, he remained silent.

Drawing herself up to her fullest height, Mira looked down her nose at all of them, her jilted fiancé, his tramp, her own father. And Camille Bradburn, the slattern who'd started all the trouble. "I shan't discuss this matter further."

Mira turned on her heel and left the room stiffly, but stopped at the sound of Camille's voice.

"The journals."

"I'll give them to you. You can burn them for all I care."

"Get them now."

"Fine," Mira said, and she picked up her gown and prepared to flounce away.

"And then leave Beauport," Camille said flatly. "You're no longer welcome here."

"As you wish." Mira tried to hold back the tears. She'd never been thrown out of anyone's home before, and though she despised the Mullens', it still stung.

"I am sorry for my daughter's actions," Andrew said, and Mira found that her tears were gone.

She whirled around, confronting her father. "How dare

you apologize to these people when you've not even bothered to do so to me?"

"Mira," he said, a warning heavy in his tone.

"I thought you were different," she said frigidly. "I see now you're just like any other man, tossing away what a woman values without a care, or even the decency to consider how she might feel about it. And when she dares to confront you? 'Oh, well, 'tis just jewelry,'" she mocked. "'A bauble. I'll buy you a new one.'"

She narrowed her eyes, more deeply betrayed than she'd ever felt in her life. "I thought you were better than any other man. I thought you were perfect."

"We can have this discussion privately," Andrew said, but his tone revealed his own hurt at his daughter's disappointment. He glanced over at the others, and his face reddened once again. "No one is perfect."

"I'll not ride with you," Mira pouted.

Andrew crossed the room, turned to Camille, and bowed. "So sorry," he said again. And then he took his daughter by the arm, and steered her from the rooms.

As Mira tried to pull from his grasp, her father's grip tightened. "I have spoiled you, pampered and petted you, and this is how you repay me? All this fuss over a ring you've never even seen."

And Mira smiled inwardly even as she pouted and pulled her arm away, knowing that soon enough she'd have her father begging to take her shopping for rings that very afternoon.

He'd all but forgotten about the journals and her threats to publish them. He'd not even mentioned her efforts to coerce Olwyn into leaving England, she thought victoriously.

The rooms she'd devoted to showcasing her family's venerable history were better off without Bret Kimball's vile journals, she decided as she made faux struggles against her father's discipline.

And Mira decided that she would buy a ring with a diamond the size of her father's thumbnail, and would have it surrounded by yet more fiery gems. If her father were to disappoint her as any other man would, then let him make it up to her as a man should, with presents and apologies.

Surely with a ring such as that on her finger, no one would be gossiping about Mira's dissolved engagement.

Chapter Twenty-Nine

Camille tapped her papers together and slid them back into their pouch. "Poor Bret," she murmured. She sighed, long and deep, and added, "His life was never his own."

"He hurt you, my lady, and took the life of your child. Forgive me if I do not pity his lack of choices," Olwyn said, her own heart aching for Camille and all she'd endured for the love of her husband.

"He did those things, 'tis true." Camille glanced beside her to where Patrick sat, silent and still, willing to allow his wife to handle the matter as she'd seen fit. But he'd been there, Olwyn thought, ready to fight for her, if she needed him.

Camille smiled wistfully, her eyes on her husband, and added, "But here I am, and he is long dead."

Patrick stood and extended his hand to Camille. He inclined his head toward Olwyn and Aidan. "Come, love. I think these two have much to discuss, aye?"

Camille rose from her chair. With her eyes on Olwyn, she said, "I'm grateful."

"For what, my lady?"

"For everything," Camille answered simply.

She patted Olwyn's hand before leaving the room with Patrick. They closed the French doors behind them, leaving Olwyn and Aidan alone in the dining room.

Olwyn lifted her eyes to meet his. His expression had become inscrutable.

"It wasn't so many hours ago that you said you loved me," she said, feigning a boldness she didn't at all feel.

"Aye, and a few hours ago you said the same. And then you left." His eyes were as hard as his voice. "You could have told me what Mira had threatened. I would've seen to it."

She wanted to say something, anything. No, she corrected herself. She wanted to say the right thing, the words that would make Aidan understand the truths of her heart the way only he could. She longed to speak the words that would have him forgiving her, pulling her into the shelter of his body, and speaking words of love in her ear.

But she stood before him, mute. If there were words that could make all those things come true, she did not know them.

She could fake boldness, but she couldn't seem to manage the trick of pretending to know the answers.

Aidan frowned and glanced away from her. "I let you go, Olwyn. If it isn't the threat of your father, or a person like Mira, it'll be something else. Nothing can make you leave if you truly want to be with me, so go. Be free."

The morning light streamed in through the windows and cast Aidan in its radiance, but despite it, he looked cold and remote, a wealthy, well-dressed lord who appeared to be angry, annoyed, and impatient to be on his way.

He brought his hard sapphire eyes back to hers. "Do you hear me? I think 'tis best if you leave."

The floor felt as if it were made of sand, and she was sinking, sinking.

"My affection can only be pushed so far, Olwyn. I can't spend the rest of my life trying to convince you of what exists between us, and most of all, I can't make you feel worthy. If I thought it would have any value, I'd say let's move into the cottage and live simply, but there's the matter of my wealth, my heritage, and aye, my future. I may be duke one day. Could you be my duchess, Olwyn? And barring that, at the very least, you're looking at being my lady, bearing titles of your own, and becoming part of my life as 'tis. Do you want that?"

The insecurity his words caused must have shown on her face, for Aidan said, "Aye, I thought not."

Silence fell between them, not a single noise to break the deafening dearth of words. Olwyn tried to see her life without him, and it was an empty place, devoid of meaning. And then she attempted to envision herself as Aidan's lady, and failed miserably.

"I cannot change who I am to suit you better," he continued, his voice hard and matter-of-fact. "And I cannot forget that the only time you'd ever seemed completely comfortable with me was when you'd been secretly planning to leave."

He looked her over from forehead to feet, his deep blue eyes brooding and sad. "I've loved you more than any woman. I wanted to marry you, to make a family with you. I saw my whole life before us, and every moment had you in it. But when you left, Olwyn, I knew that I was all alone in that life I was building for us."

Loved. He spoke of his feelings as if they were gone.

"More of your silences," he observed softly, and his eyes grew sadder still. "Once again, I open my heart and show you what's inside, and 'tis greeted with nothingness."

Olwyn clung to what Emeline had said, her words all but a promise. She forced herself to speak. "I stayed," Olwyn whispered. "I believed, I trusted." She swallowed hard against the lump in her throat. "I loved."

"This isn't make-believe, Olwyn, or some story I'm whispering in your ear," he said impatiently. "I thought we'd made that sort of thing come true, but then reality had its way with us, aye? The reality is that we're two real people who are well suited in some ways but not well matched where it really matters, and we both need to just accept that. We can't, much as it seems so very, very seductive, spend our entire lives wrapped up alone in the darkness."

No more silence.

"I want you, Lóchrann," she choked out. "I love you, with all my heart, and I never would have left if I hadn't thought it absolutely necessary. As to our future, I can only promise that it's what I want. I want you. I know I want you, and if I can have you, I'm certain I can learn the rest."

He arched a brow. "Can you?"

Olwyn floundered. She really didn't know what was involved with the promise she was making. And she didn't care for his tone, either, rich as it was with doubt.

"I'm bright," she said stiffly. Her pride had been stung, and it chased down the worst of her fears and filled her with a bit of indignation. "I'm also rather resourceful and quite strong and clever. I'm certain I could learn whatever I needed to know, if someone were to teach me." She raised her brow, matching his doubtful expression with challenge in her own. "I'm at *least* as intelligent as Mira Kimball. Whatever she knows, I can learn."

"Is that so?"

She thought she saw a glimmer of humor return to those deep sapphire eyes that she loved so well, and a drop of hope returned, as welcomed as water in her desert of doubt. Perhaps all was not lost.

"Aye," Olwyn said, and then thinking of how Emeline and Camille spoke, corrected herself. "I mean, yes. Yes, my lord. Most definitely."

"Will you fight for me, Olwyn? Will you fight for us?"

"I will."

"Start now."

Her feelings were clear enough, but her words were trapped in a jumble in her throat, indefinable emotions she wasn't sure she could properly express.

She had to try.

"I love you," she professed softly. "I love you in ways I don't understand, with feelings that make no sense, and with a force I cannot control. It's bigger than me, this love. Bolder than me, better than me." A tear wobbled in the corner of her eye, and finally fell. Her words were a pale description of the way she felt. Her hands became fists of frustration, and Olwyn whispered, "I love you as I breathe, as I sleep, as I live. I love you because I don't know how else to go through this life. And whether you'll have me again or you'll let me go, I'll love you until the day I die."

Aidan sighed, pulled out a chair, and fell into it. His long legs sprawled out before him, and he leaned his head in his hand. "I'm tired, Olwyn. Do you know I don't sleep well at all without you in my bed?"

The dam broke and hope flowed into her heart. Olwyn unclenched her fists and gave him a little smile. "No?"

"No. I just lie there, staring at the ceiling, wondering what's wrong with me."

"Have you tried warm milk, Lóchrann?"

The corners of his mouth twitched. "Aye."

"No good?"

"No. Not good at all."

Olwyn made a sympathetic noise in her throat. "I've heard of herbal tonics. Perhaps you could try some of those?"

"I've had them all. Nothing. I stay awake until my eyes feel like they're going to bleed."

"Bleeding eyes. How awful."

"Aye. Not for the faint of heart, I assure you."

"I should say not." Olwyn tilted her head and lifted her shoulders. "So it appears I'm your only solution."

"Aye." Aidan brought his eyes up to meet hers, and in them she saw her future. "Only you. I suppose I'll have to keep you here with me, if I'm to get any rest at all." He beckoned her over. "Come here, witch."

Olwyn crossed the room quickly and he pulled her onto his lap. Aidan's arms wrapped around her, his embrace hard and strong, safe and warm. She leaned against his chest and heard his heartbeat. It was, she decided, the sound of her own pulse. Without him, there was no life for her.

Beneath her, he shifted, reached into his pocket, and withdrew the ring she'd left on his table. It caught the sunlight and turned to silver fire. "This time, you'll leave it on, aye?"

Olwyn held out her hand and he slid the ring onto her finger. "I will."

"'Tis perfect on you. A perfect fit, just like you for me." His hand smoothed her hair and then traveled down her back, stroking her beneath the fine fabric. "You look beautiful, Olwyn. You look like a lady."

Olwyn sighed and closed her eyes. "It's just as well I look the part, if I'm to spend a lifetime learning it."

"Aye, and I'm certain it'll take you bit to learn what's expected of you." Aidan's hands were now on her hips. "I'll begin with your first lesson: a lady always takes her husband to bed after breakfast."

"Does she?" Olwyn smiled as she nuzzled his neck. He smelled of fresh air, clean laundry, and the faintest hint of fire smoke and incense. "That doesn't seem very ladylike to me."

"'Tis, I assure you." Aidan's hands began easing her gown upward, stroking along the insides of her legs as he raised her hem. "Your second lesson: a lady always disrobes in broad daylight, as a lady understands her lord's need to see her beauty on full display."

Heat curled through her blood, and desire dampened her loins at the prospect. "You're certain that's not indecent?"

"Quite."

Aidan paused.

"My lord?" Olwyn breathed, pressing kisses along the curve of his ear.

"Guarding paradise with a sword?"

Olwyn glanced down and saw he referred to the dagger.

"Yes." She laughed then, and resumed kissing his earlobe. She could feel him beneath her bottom, hard and throbbing with wanting. "There are large snakes seeking entrance."

His laughter rumbled in his chest, low and deep and as smooth as his whiskey. His hands were well above the dagger now, and doing most interesting things right at the hottest, wettest part of her. "Indeed, Eve. There most certainly are."

Aidan's gaze swept over Olwyn as she lay before him, completely nude, her skin still flushed with pleasure. "You are, without a doubt, the world's most beautiful, blushing bride."

She smiled with contentment and stretched like a cat, her lithe body gleaming in the afternoon light. Their clothes were strewn from the door to the bed, and his body hummed with drowsy, sated post-coital bliss.

A long time ago when he'd been young and had his heart broken over his first flame, his mother had given wise advice: never, she'd told him, did he want someone who didn't want him back.

He held his warm and willing wife in his arms, and thought that truer words had never been spoken. Olwyn was with him because she wanted to be, and the rest would sort itself out.

Aidan's thoughts returned to the odd man who'd sought him out by the mews. He kissed Olwyn on top of her head and held her close. There was no room for anything but truth between them, and he didn't want to start their life together with a secret lurking in his pocket. "Olwyn?"

"Hmm?" She tilted her head back so she could look up into his face. Those arresting gray eyes were uncanny and incredibly beautiful. He wondered briefly how she could stir him so, for even with the trouble on his mind and his body aching for sleep, he felt himself growing hard and hot for her again.

Aidan forcibly turned his mind to more pressing matters. "I have something I need to tell you about, but I'm not sure this is the time."

"Is it bad news?"

"I don't think so, but are you tired, love? Would you rather I wait until after you've slept?"

"You have to tell me. Now that you've said as much, I'll not be able to think about anything else."

"Right." Aidan kissed her forehead and then the tip of her nose. "Just a minute." He got out of bed, found his coat tossed over a chair, and rummaged through the pockets. He found the paper and returned to the bed, only to find Olwyn sitting up with the blankets clutched to her chest. She looked poleaxed again, her eyes wide and scared. "Don't worry. It's nothing horrid."

"Just tell me what it is."

"Early this morning, your father's assistant, Drystan, sought me out whilst I was at the mews."

"He did?" Olwyn's lips curled in disgust. "What did he want?"

"To sell me information."

"About what?" Her brow furrowed. "Drystan never did much in our household besides assist my father and try to drink himself to death. What sort of information could he possibly think was valuable?"

"Well, there's this." Aidan held out his hand and showed her his medallion. It was scratched and the gems had been pried from it, but Aidan knew that much could be repaired. "He was afraid that I'd figure out that he had this, so he sold it to me. Wasn't that kind of him?"

"He's a prince, that Drystan," Olwyn said dryly.

"Aye." Aidan's belly did a little flip, and he hoped he was doing the right thing. "And then he wanted to talk about your mother."

Her face drained, and became very, very white. "What did he say about her?"

"She didn't leave you, Olwyn," he said as gently as he could manage. She deserved to know that she'd been loved and wanted. She deserved the very best.

He reached out and touched the streak of white that ran through her hair like lightning tearing through a midnight sky. Her mother's legacy, and the perfect summation of Olwyn herself, darkness streaked with light, a mark that identified her as different, unusual, and striking.

"She did leave. I woke one morning and she was gone."

"Aye, because your father made her go. He'd found out that she'd been planning to run off with you, and in turn, he'd had Drystan drive her off in the night and leave her. Apparently, your father threatened to hurt you if she tried to come back for you." He didn't tell her that Rhys had sworn he would murder Olwyn in her sleep. According to Drystan, Rhys had put the fear of her daughter's life in Talfryn.

Aidan handed Olwyn the paper that he'd purchased with a few cases of whiskey, a wagon and horse, and a sack of coins. A fortune for a piece of paper, but what Drystan hadn't known was Aidan would have paid anything for the letter he held. "Your mother wrote this to you, and begged Drystan to give it to you in secret."

Olwyn stared at the paper, her eyes wide. She was so still and quiet that Aidan began to fear he'd gone about telling her in the wrong way.

"Olwyn? Are you all right?"

"Bastard," she breathed.

"Aye," Aidan answered her grimly. "The both of them."

"I shall never mourn him," she said with a quiet fierceness. "Burn his unshriven corpse if it isn't already buried, and if it is, take me to his grave so I can spit on it."

"Olwyn."

"I hate him. I'm glad he's dead, because if he were not, I'd be a murderer within the space of time it would take me to find him. I'd bury my dagger in the cavity of his chest, precisely where his heart was missing."

"Olwyn."

"And Drystan. I'll hunt him down, slice his testicles off, and feed them to him. That rat. He knew all those years what had become of my mother, and he kept it from me. I'll kill him. I'll cut his throat and spit in his neck."

"*Olwyn.*"

She brought her eyes up to his, the clear gray of them piercing and primordial. And Aidan decided then and there that his wife was most definitely not a woman to cross lightly.

"Olwyn," he said again, this time with a nudge at her slim hand as it clutched the paper he'd purchased for a small ransom. "Hate them as you like, and you'll get no argument from me, aye? But don't you think the marauding bloodshed and violence can wait long enough for you to read the letter?"

She looked down on the paper as if she were terrified of what it could contain. His chest ached as he took in her expression, hope and fear combined. He prayed the letter eased her heartache. The girl who'd spent her life feeling abandoned deserved to know the truth.

"Have you read it?" she asked in a hushed voice.

"It's written in Welsh."

She brought her eyes back up to his, and he watched them fill with tears.

"I thought she didn't want me any more." Olwyn tried to take a deep breath, but it caught in her chest and became a sob.

He prayed that the words Talfryn had written ten years before brought Olwyn some comfort, a soothing nostrum to her feelings of rejection.

Olwyn held the folded paper so tightly her fingertips were white.

Aidan cupped Olwyn's face in his hands, smoothing away her tears with his thumbs. He leaned forward and kissed her until she stopped weeping. He would drink her tears, kiss her wounds, and protect her forever. Pulling back, he looked into her beautiful eyes, magnified with tears and fringed with long, spiky wet black lashes.

Only moments before she'd been thirsty for blood, and now she wept the fearful tears of a deserted young girl who had desperately missed her mother. It was like Olwyn herself, he realized, very, very complicated, and yet also really quite simple.

The woman, such a strange, uniquely fierce and tender creature, had completely bewitched him.

He put his hand on hers. "Do you trust me?"

"Absolutely," she whispered.

"Then read it, love. Whatever it says, and whatever comes, we'll face the truth together." He loved her so much it almost hurt, his heart full and tight as a drum. "That's marriage, aye?"

Olwyn took a deep breath, steadied by his words and his love. His hands on her were big and wide and strong. He made her feel treasured and protected. He made her feel safe.

Safe enough to face whatever came, just as he said.

Olwyn looked at the paper that ten years ago, had been held by her mother. It was thin and torn, stained and burned on the edge, a scrap of a page that looked as though it'd been ripped from the back of a book.

She glanced up quickly to Aidan, who waited patiently, and then took another deep, steadying breath and carefully unfolded the letter.

My darling daughter,

it began, and Olwyn began to cry, reading through the magnified, fractured vision caused by her tears.

> *I pray you get this letter. Know this—there's not a thing of this earth I want more than to take you with me. I think of you waking and finding me gone, and my heart breaks. I love you, Olwyn. Nothing can change that, not your father, or this hated distance he'll put between us. I will ache for you for the rest of my life.*
>
> *You're old enough to remember our stories. Think on them, Olwyn. They were never just fairy tales.*
>
> *My precious daughter. I love you forever.*
>
> *—Mama*

Olwyn rocked to and fro, her arms wrapped around her middle. Aidan held her as she wept, great wracking sobs and heaving gasps for air.

Olwyn remembered Talfryn's hands stroking her face as she fell asleep, the fables whispered in the darkness, and her mother's warm weight on the side of her bed. Those moments had been the happiest, safest times of Olwyn's childhood.

When she finally calmed, she looked up in to Aidan's

face, saw his concern. And even as tears still fell freely, she smiled for him, wide and happy.

"She wanted me," Olwyn said simply. It meant the world.

"Of course she did," he answered her. The look in his eyes shifted from concern to curiosity. "You said she left when you were only three and ten?"

"Yes. It was winter, just after my birthday."

"That was only ten years ago, Olwyn."

She glanced from the letter to her husband, understanding his meaning.

He grinned. "You know, love, this will be one of those times when you'll see that wealth isn't just for buying gowns and grand homes. I'll put every last resource I've got into finding your mother. I promise you this—wherever she is, we'll find her."

Olwyn recalled the winter that her mother had been taken away, realizing then and there that no matter what came to pass, the history of that event had been rewritten. No longer would she think of it as the winter that Talfryn left her, but the awful time that her mother was taken away.

That winter had been bitterly cold, and if Drystan was telling the truth, he'd driven her far enough away that Talfryn could not easily return. He'd left her alone and penniless.

"What if she didn't survive?" Olwyn asked softly.

"If she's even half as resourceful as her daughter, I'm certain she did."

A small smile curved Olwyn's lips. Talfryn had indeed been a formidable woman. "It was she who taught me how to handle a pistol and a dagger."

"We'll find her," Aidan said firmly.

And in that moment, Olwyn felt the thrill of possibility all around her, and pure happiness filled her in a way that it never had before. Daylight poured in through windows, and her Lóchrann of the darkness was with her.

No more nightmares. No more fears.

His broad chest was bare, the scar from her father's scalpel faded to a pale pink, a thin line that told the tale of the day she'd watched him bleed, and knew he lived.

She'd saved his life, and in return it seemed, he'd saved hers right back. He gave to her until she was full, and the only thing left to do was to simply be grateful.

"Thank you, Lóchrann."

He grinned. "You're so *serious.*"

She had to smile back. If this was marriage, the laughing, the sharing, the honesty, and the sensual delights found in bed, Olwyn understood why people vowed to do it until death. "Seriously in love."

"And seriously beautiful."

Olwyn reached for him, and he readily took her in his arms, wrapping her once again in the safety and shelter of his embrace.

The thing about fairy tales, she thought with an inward sigh of joy, was that happily-ever-after was how they ended. The story was the part written for anyone to read.

His naked body was warm and hard against hers, his skin soft and scented with incense. Her hands stroked over his back, and she felt the play of his muscles as he stroked her in turn.

She was wise enough now to know that the endings of the stories were just the beginning of the very best part, and the reason the rest wasn't told was simple. It was private.

Epilogue

Beauport, England, 1807

Bees droned and cicadas sang during the hottest part of the day, and Olwyn fanned herself as she sat in the shade just outside the cottage, waiting for Aidan to return from the distillery. The sun streamed through the overhead canopy of leaves, casting the meadow in gilded greenish light. The roses were in full bloom, climbing over the cottage in thick, heavy abundance.

The babe kicked hard, stealing Olwyn's breath with its force, and she pressed against the dome of her belly. Lad or lass, she had no way of knowing, but the doctor assured her the child would be born in the fall.

Rising from her chair, she made her way into the cool interior of the cottage and returned to work. The quill lay bleeding beside the papers that had consumed her attention the past six months. Her fable, *The Dragon of Cymru,* was complete, and she was putting the final touches on the illustrations.

She never would have guessed that the time she'd spent drawing her father's corpses would have served her well. Her pictures vibrated with life, rich with detail and symmetrical musculature.

Lifting her quill, she immersed herself in the fictional world of angry dragons, misunderstood witches, and lost, trapped princesses who kissed their princes awake.

Her child stirred in her belly, her mind whirled with fresh ideas, and the afternoon droned by outside the cottage, warm and sundrenched and lazy until Aidan appeared in the doorway.

"A moment more, Lóchrann," she bade, holding a hand in the air. She put the final touches on the dragon's wings, and then set the quill aside. "I'm ready."

Olwyn slid from her stool as Aidan came to look at her work. His hand smoothed across her belly as she showed him her latest drawing.

She suddenly swiveled in his arms and kissed him deeply. He pulled back, laughing.

"I know what you're up to."

"Mmm, whiskey," Olwyn murmured. "Kiss me again."

He obliged her, kissing her until her head spun in a way that had nothing to do with the spirits that pleasantly flavored his tongue. Her head fell back. "I'm drunk on love and fumes."

"That's all the whiskey you'll get until the babe comes. As to the kisses, you can have as many as you want."

"'Tis the worst part of pregnancy." Olwyn pouted a little bit, feeling quite in the mood for a drink, a book, and an ottoman on which to rest her feet.

"Worse than the vomiting?"

Olwyn wrinkled her nose. The early stage of her pregnancy had been a rough few months she'd not yet forgotten. "No. Not worse than that."

"Right, so stop complaining. I've a great bottle saved, and when the laddie comes we'll crack it open to celebrate."

With her arm in his, they strolled from the cottage and climbed into the sporty little curricle. Aidan chirped to the horses, and the conveyance bounced into motion as they rode along the newly cut path Aidan had had made so that Olwyn could get to the cottage without trouble.

"Can we go by the gardens?"

Aidan glanced over to her and smiled. He drove to the gardens without a word, and as they approached, Olwyn's heart swelled with happiness. There in the enormous field were two huge gardens that ran side by side, one brilliant and heavy with roses, the other burgeoning with vegetables. The air was ripe with scents of fecund earth, sun-ripened tomatoes, and sweet, seductive blooms.

Talfryn worked side by side with the other gardeners, chatting as they pruned.

"Mama," Olwyn cried out.

Talfryn turned to greet them. She wore a floppy hat and a cotton gown, making for a pretty, slim figure in the field of multicolored blooms, and her smile brightened the very sunlight itself. "Olwyn, I've fresh flowers for you," she called.

They'd found Talfryn in London. She'd found work for a wealthy family who owned a large solarium, and had spent the years tending to their gardens.

Just as Talfryn's letter had admonished Olwyn to find the clues in the stories she'd told her long ago, Olwyn had followed the trail of flowers and growing things to find her mother.

Now, reunited with her daughter and getting ready to welcome her first grandchild, not a day went by that Talfryn couldn't be heard laughing.

It was, quite simply, music to Olwyn's ears.

Olwyn held her hands on her belly. The kicking had stopped with the motion of the curricle.

Aidan put his arm around her and pulled her closer to him. She looked up to him, her Adonis by sunlight, her Lóchrann of the darkness.

"I've been thinking," Aidan said.

"About?"

"The child."

"What of him?"

"I was thinking he'll need a dog of his own."

Olwyn laughed. "So you want a dog, Lóchrann?"

"Aye, well, I suppose it's not just for the child." Aidan

leaned back against the seat, and looked around the property as if he were seeing it for the first time. His demeanor grew solemn. "I've been thinking quite a bit about becoming a father. It's not all giving the babe a dog and riding lessons. I'll have to instill values and morals, and see to it he grows up to be a man of honor. And Lord help me if the babe's born a lass; I'll have to lock her in a tower to keep the boys away." A slight frown troubled his brow. "It's a lot consider, this becoming a da. I'd never really thought about it until the seed was planted, aye?"

"I'm scared, too," Olwyn admitted. "And I'm terrified at the thought of the birth."

"Ah, love, I wish I could do it for you."

"No, you don't."

He laughed. "Aye, well, maybe not as much, but if I could, I would." Aidan touched her face, a quick, gentle stroke of his hard fingers over her soft skin. "I hate the idea of you being in pain."

Reaching up, she caught his fingers in her own and held them tight. "You'll be a great da."

His eyes crinkled at the corners. "Do you think?"

"I know."

Aidan sighed and leaned his forehead against hers. "Well, I guess we're in too deep to back out now, aye?"

"It seems so." Olwyn breathed in his scent, his skin warm from the sun. He was her heart, her soul, her world.

"Well, there's one thing for certain," he said softly, his deep voice as smooth as the mellow whiskey that scented his breath. "We're in it together."

Author's Note

While doing research for this novel, I encountered two true stories that galvanized my imagination, so much so that I was compelled to use the information in the writing of this novel. I share them with you in an effort to show that fact is, indeed, stranger than fiction.

Before the stories, some facts:

The study of anatomy on human corpses was only legal if performed on the bodies of executed criminals. However, England only executed about fifty to sixty persons a year, making the picking very slim. Hence, the body snatchers, also known as the resurrection men.

A fresh corpse was valued at about six month's wages, and therefore, worth the risk of being caught stealing one. The penalty for stealing a corpse was rather light, a slap on the wrist you might say, by English court standards. The reason for this was simple: the courts in England knew the anatomists were doing important work, and therefore didn't inflict harsh punishments for the crime. However, the English courts did NOT take the same stance on the matter of theft. Theft was a crime punishable by death, and so the resurrection men were sure to strip the bodies of their garments before taking them, leaving the pile of discarded clothes behind in the crypt or the grave. Moral: in possession of Uncle Joe's body = not that big a deal. In possession of Uncle Joe's shirt = the triple tree at Tyburn, and a chance to make your own contribution to science.

It's estimated that about eight percent of England's population was buried alive. This alarming discovery was made when old bodies were exhumed to make room for the freshly dead, and upon opening caskets, scratch marks were found on the insides of the coffins. This fact was so widely known that many people went to the trouble of telling their loved ones that they wished to be buried with poison or a pistol when they died, so that in the event of being buried alive they could dispatch themselves. It's also why wakes were held. Quite literally, the practice was to lay the body out and see if the dearly departed was dead, or if they would wake. Remember, this was before stethoscopes and brain scans. The absence of a discernable pulse or breath usually meant the person had perished, but not always.

On to my stories: the first was of an anatomist who got the locally executed criminals delivered to his doorstep, like a newspaper or the milk. And so, each morning, he'd check out back on the stoop and see what the day held in store. One early morning, however, he found a naked man holding a burlap sack. The man had obviously been tried, convicted, and executed for a crime, but the noose hadn't quite finished the job.

The anatomist took pity on him and thought that maybe, for some reason, God had spared this man. He helped him escape, and sent him into a new life with clothes on his back and a few coins in his pocket. Many years later, the anatomist ran into the man on a busy London street. The man had a wife, a few children, and had become a prosperous merchant.

The second story was of a family that journeyed from England to Virginia to visit relatives. The ship they traveled on was struck by an outbreak of smallpox, and many dead (or were they?) were thrown into the seas to prevent the spread of contagion. By the time the ship arrived in America, the family's youngest daughter was gravely ill, and when they reached their plantation, she was dead. They immediately buried her in the family's crypt so as to avoid further contamination.

About seven years later, a young soldier of the same family was killed in the Civil War. They brought his body home for burial, and when they opened the crypt they found the tiny skeleton of the little girl by the door.

Dear Readers, if you bothered to read all of this, I hope you enjoyed this glimpse into this author's brain, for the question I'm most often asked is, "Where do you get your ideas?" I found myself absolutely riveted by the idea of a person being so far gone as to be thought dead, buried alive in a way that would absolutely guarantee death, and then finding their life had been saved by the most improbable of all means: resurrection men.

I also hope you took pleasure in the novel itself, for while the collision of facts and imagination breeds works of fiction, it's always the stories of people, and those who read them, that make them real.

My very best regards,
Tracy MacNish

GREAT BOOKS, GREAT SAVINGS!

When You Visit Our Website:
www.kensingtonbooks.com
You Can Save Money Off The Retail Price
Of Any Book You Purchase!

- **All Your Favorite Kensington Authors**
- **New Releases & Timeless Classics**
- **Overnight Shipping Available**
- **eBooks Available For Many Titles**
- **All Major Credit Cards Accepted**

Visit Us Today To Start Saving!
www.kensingtonbooks.com

More by Bestselling Author

Janet Dailey

Bring the Ring	0-8217-8016-6	$4.99US/$6.99CAN
Calder Promise	0-8217-7541-3	$7.99US/$10.99CAN
Calder Storm	0-8217-7543-X	$7.99US/$10.99CAN
A Capital Holiday	0-8217-7224-4	$6.99US/$8.99CAN
Crazy in Love	1-4201-0303-2	$4.99US/$5.99CAN
Eve's Christmas	0-8217-8017-4	$6.99US/$9.99CAN
Green Calder Grass	0-8217-7222-8	$7.99US/$10.99CAN
Happy Holidays	0-8217-7749-1	$6.99US/$9.99CAN
Let's Be Jolly	0-8217-7919-2	$6.99US/$9.99CAN
Lone Calder Star	0-8217-7542-1	$7.99US/$10.99CAN
Man of Mine	1-4201-0009-2	$4.99US/$6.99CAN
Mistletoe and Molly	1-4201-0041-6	$6.99US/$9.99CAN
Ranch Dressing	0-8217-8014-X	$4.99US/$6.99CAN
Scrooge Wore Spurs	0-8217-7225-2	$6.99US/$9.99CAN
Searching for Santa	1-4201-0306-7	$6.99US/$9.99CAN
Shifting Calder Wind	0-8217-7223-6	$7.99US/$10.99CAN
Something More	0-8217-7544-8	$7.99US/$9.99CAN
Stealing Kisses	1-4201-0304-0	$4.99US/$5.99CAN
Try to Resist Me	0-8217-8015-8	$4.99US/$6.99CAN
Wearing White	1-4201-0011-4	$4.99US/$6.99CAN
With This Kiss	1-4201-0010-6	$4.99US/$6.99CAN
Yes, I Do	1-4201-0305-9	$4.99US/$5.99CAN

Available Wherever Books Are Sold!

More by Bestselling Author
Fern Michaels

__About Face	0-8217-7020-9	$7.99US/$10.99CAN
__Wish List	0-8217-7363-1	$7.50US/$10.50CAN
__Picture Perfect	0-8217-7588-X	$7.99US/$10.99CAN
__Vegas Heat	0-8217-7668-1	$7.99US/$10.99CAN
__Finders Keepers	0-8217-7669-X	$7.99US/$10.99CAN
__Dear Emily	0-8217-7670-3	$7.99US/$10.99CAN
__Sara's Song	0-8217-7671-1	$7.99US/$10.99CAN
__Vegas Sunrise	0-8217-7672-X	$7.99US/$10.99CAN
__Yesterday	0-8217-7678-9	$7.99US/$10.99CAN
__Celebration	0-8217-7679-7	$7.99US/$10.99CAN
__Payback	0-8217-7876-5	$6.99US/$9.99CAN
__Vendetta	0-8217-7877-3	$6.99US/$9.99CAN
__The Jury	0-8217-7878-1	$6.99US/$9.99CAN
__Sweet Revenge	0-8217-7879-X	$6.99US/$9.99CAN,
__Lethal Justice	0-8217-7880-3	$6.99US/$9.99CAN
__Free Fall	0-8217-7881-1	$6.99US/$9.99CAN
__Fool Me Once	0-8217-8071-9	$7.99US/$10.99CAN
__Vegas Rich	0-8217-8112-X	$7.99US/$10.99CAN
__Hide and Seek	1-4201-0184-6	$6.99US/$9.99CAN
__Hokus Pokus	1-4201-0185-4	$6.99US/$9.99CAN
__Fast Track	1-4201-0186-2	$6.99US/$9.99CAN
__Collateral Damage	1-4201-0187-0	$6.99US/$9.99CAN
__Final Justice	1-4201-0188-9	$6.99US/$9.99CAN

Available Wherever Books Are Sold!
Check out our website at **www.kensingtonbooks.com**

Romantic Suspense from
Lisa Jackson

See How She Dies	0-8217-7605-3	$6.99US/$9.99CAN
Final Scream	0-8217-7712-2	$7.99US/$10.99CAN
Wishes	0-8217-6309-1	$5.99US/$7.99CAN
Whispers	0-8217-7603-7	$6.99US/$9.99CAN
Twice Kissed	0-8217-6038-6	$5.99US/$7.99CAN
Unspoken	0-8217-6402-0	$6.50US/$8.50CAN
If She Only Knew	0-8217-6708-9	$6.50US/$8.50CAN
Hot Blooded	0-8217-6841-7	$6.99US/$9.99CAN
Cold Blooded	0-8217-6934-0	$6.99US/$9.99CAN
The Night Before	0-8217-6936-7	$6.99US/$9.99CAN
The Morning After	0-8217-7295-3	$6.99US/$9.99CAN
Deep Freeze	0-8217-7296-1	$7.99US/$10.99CAN
Fatal Burn	0-8217-7577-4	$7.99US/$10.99CAN
Shiver	0-8217-7578-2	$7.99US/$10.99CAN
Most Likely to Die	0-8217-7576-6	$7.99US/$10.99CAN
Absolute Fear	0-8217-7936-2	$7.99US/$9.49CAN
Almost Dead	0-8217-7579-0	$7.99US/$10.99CAN
Lost Souls	0-8217-7938-9	$7.99US/$10.99CAN
Left to Die	1-4201-0276-1	$7.99US/$10.99CAN
Wicked Game	1-4201-0338-5	$7.99US/$9.99CAN
Malice	0-8217-7940-0	$7.99US/$9.49CAN